FAST EDDIE

FAST EDDIE

a novel in many voices

Robert L. O'Connell

William Morrow and Company, Inc.

New York

Library of Congress Cataloging-in-Publication Data
O'Connell, Robert L.
Fast Eddie : a novel in many voices / by Robert L. O'Connell.
p.   cm.
ISBN 0-688-16690-3
1. Rickenbacker, Eddie, 1890–1973—Fiction.   2. World War,
1914–1918—Aerial operations, American—Fiction.   3. World War,
1939–1945—Aerial operations, American—Fiction.   I. Title.
PS3565.C542F37   1999
813'.54—dc21   99-11687
CIP

Printed in the United States of America

First Edition

1   2   3   4   5   6   7   8   9   10

BOOK DESIGN BY OKSANA KUSHNIR

www.williammorrow.com

To Boo Herndon,
Ghostwriter in the Sky

Author's Note

I would like to thank all those who took time out from being dead to answer my questions and provide valuable background. Now, I suppose there are those of a more suspicious turn of mind who would stoutly maintain that I have mangled the events of the Great Man's life to fit my own twisted agenda, and that this book is, in fact, fiction. I can't disagree with them. I must admit that with few exceptions the words attributed to Rickenbacker and all other characters are really my own, as are what cynics might label certain flights of fancy with regard to key conversations, personal relationships, shady transactions, and other occurrences previously untold. How could it be otherwise? I have it on good authority that the Real Eddie was a far more tiresome individual than my Eddie—the Mythic Eddie, the Eddie of the Collective Consciousness, Eddie the Blunt Instrument of the Lord Himself.

Ever conscious of his image, Fast Eddie changed the spelling of his last name from Rickenbacher to Rickenbacker during World War I to make it appear less Germanic.

I'll say one thing for Rickenbacker:
the son of a bitch was hard to kill.

—Yahweh, Lord of Hosts

FAST EDDIE

Chapter One

About a mile out from where the Olentangy River snakes through downtown Columbus, there stands a barn. Outlined against the grizzled Midwestern sky, it is big and red and festooned with a fading Bull Durham sign. On the peak of the roof you can make out the figures of three boys, two clinging to the weather vane in the middle, and a third on a bicycle unfurling an umbrella. After checking to make sure it is properly fastened, he begins pedaling furiously down the incline, clutching the handlebars with one hand and the umbrella with the other. When he passes over the eaves, the umbrella collapses upward with a sharp pop, and the boy heads straight for the ground, hitting a pile of sand with a bicycle-wrenching thud. After a while the boy gets up and staggers away from the wreck. It was the first flight of Eddie Rickenbacher . . . his first crash also. There would be others.

ELIZABETH   He vas not what you vould call a good boy. Always racing around, you had to vatch him all za time. Once, over on Grant Boulevard, he ran out in front of a horsecar and bounced against the curb zo hard I thought he vas dead. But he got right up. Another time I was digging in za garden, and Eddie was on his knees helping me plant potatoes. Vell, he got too close, and I whacked him with za hoe. Made a dent in his skull. But by za night he vas okay. He ate a good zupper.

   We vas real poor when we moved out on East Livingston Avenue. The lot took us a whole two years to save up for. . . . A hundred and forty-five dollars it cost. William—God protect his soul—

built the house without help from nobody. It had two rooms downstairs and two in the attic—za children slept zere. Ven we moved we had only Mary, little William, Edward, and Emma, za baby. But they kept coming—Louise, Louis, Dewey, and Albert before we vas finished.

The reason they kept coming must be attributed to the randy presence of William Rickenbacher, the elder. Seldom did a night pass that he failed to join his wife in the conjugal act. Without warning he would roll on top, pounding away like a jackhammer. Elizabeth's feelings on the subject have gone unrecorded.

ELIZABETH He vas a strong man and a gut provider. Never once did he hit none of us, except when we deserved it.

On these grounds we can assume there was considerable malfeasance in the Rickenbacher household. But there is another perspective . . . Eddie's.

EDWARD V. RICKENBACKER, *Rickenbacker*
"What a wonderful childhood we had! Of far greater value than mere riches was the opportunity to work together, play together, learn together and produce together, all under the loving yet strict Old World guidance of our parents."

BOO HERNDON, THE GHOSTWRITER He was always putting crap like that in the autobiography. He had an interesting life, but he could never stop moralizing. I probably shouldn't have written the damn thing, but I needed the money and I knew he would never give me any credit—which he didn't.

The sole surviving photo of William Rickenbacher reveals a stolid visage replete with thick eyebrows and a low-slung jaw; if he did not exactly look like a Neanderthal in a suit, neither did he much resemble Thomas Jefferson or other thoughtful types. The repudiation of physiognomists notwithstanding, it is easy to imagine such a countenance holding a rather clear-cut sense of crime and punishment.

MEMORABLE BEATINGS

In Pursuit of Drug Enforcement: Bill, my older brother, was as big as I was little, and wasn't afraid of throwing his weight around. It forced me to plan ahead. One day I got wind that he and some of the older boys were sneaking smokes in an old shack after school. The next afternoon I got there first and climbed up on the roof next to a hole, so I could look down inside. After a while the boys arrived, and soon I could see them lighting up in the dark. "Gimme one a' them, or I'm tellin'." They laughed, but when I mentioned Papa, Bill gave me one fast. All went well for a while, and Bill and I were even selling the other boys tobacco in little bags for a penny apiece. But then Mama caught us with the goods and told Papa. He took us out to the shed and without another word began whaling away. He didn't use a switch or a stick, just his big flat hand. Later we both had to eat standing up, and that night I slept on my stomach. Just thinking about it makes my rear end throb.

For the Sake of the Public Order: As our street filled up with new families, I was joined by more and more kids with big brothers who also pushed them around. Always an organizer and realizing even then that there is strength in numbers, I decided to start the Horsehead Gang, the inspiration for the name coming from a poster advertising the local racetrack. Gradually we fell into a pattern of misdeeds that today would be called juvenile delinquency. Our path of destruction eventually led us to knock down all the public mailboxes on Miller Avenue. The police knew exactly who did it, and soon enough a representative of the law paid Papa a visit to chat about what he called the "Horse's Ass Gang." This time it was just me getting pounded, so I got Papa's full attention. It was what I would call a Sunday whipping—top-to-bottom. I was stiff for a week, but you can bet your britches I never disturbed any more mailboxes.

With Psychotherapeutic Intent: When I heard that President McKinley had been shot, it didn't bother me at first. But then it dawned on me that I too was mortal. I felt more than simple fear, it was more like a bolt of despair from an uncaring cosmos. In my imagination I saw time as a highway running on as far as the eye could see. As I moved along, a succession of amazing events and scientific miracles came into view. But at some point not too far down the road I would be pushed off to the side and my life's journey would end. Nothing could be more painful to the mind of a nine-year-old, and I would creep off by myself and hang my head in desolation. One day Papa discovered me. "Vat's zis, Edward?" Impulsively, I croaked out the thoughts behind my misery. Papa's reaction was swift and appropriate. "Vat's a young fellow thinking crazy stuff like zat?" (Whack!) "Life and death is God's business, not yours." (Whack!) "I'll teach you to vaste time ven you could be doing something useful." (Whack!) The licking did not exactly cure my drooping spirits, but it did convince me of the dangers of negative thinking.

As effective as Père Rickenbacher's parenting skills were, he was not the only authority figure in young Eddie's life.

My faith in God never dimmed. For Mama introduced us to Him early and well. Each night she made sure every little Rickenbacher knelt next to their beds and recited the Lord's Prayer. But prayer was simply a way of getting the Lord's attention. Mama made sure we understood that God above was our friend, as concerned with our problems and anxious to help us as she was. I have always dealt with God as I would with a highly placed friend, certainly with respect, but also with complete assurance that He has my best interests at heart. When I pray, He answers. It has happened all my life.

GOD   Cheeky little bastard, afraid of nothing, including Me. I first noticed him in Sunday school sniffing around Blanche Calhoun—sweet kid, I took her in '19 with the Spanish Flu. Anyway, young Eddie did nothing but cause trouble, trying to kiss Blanche, shooting marbles in the vestry, smoking out back—absolutely no respect. It annoyed Me, so I thought I'd arrange a few more brushes with death to see if I could get his attention. The usual stuff—falling out of trees, sand tunnels collapsing on top of him, once I had a train almost run him over, before I made Bill pull him clear. Nothing worked; the kid was incredibly tough. More than once they brought him home in a wheelbarrow unconscious. But in a few hours he was up and around, no worse for wear. It got frustrating and I thought about something more serious, maybe paralyzing him; but that seemed kind of harsh considering what was about to happen to the family.

That afternoon remains as clear in my mind as if it were yesterday. On his way to the job—he worked the night shift running a pile driver—Papa stopped by the little workshop we had added to the shed. I was in the midst of constructing an antigravity machine. The key was magnetic attraction. I was going to suspend a BB between four strong magnets—two set on a horizontal plane and two along a vertical axis. I wasn't having much luck. But I was sure, once I had everything lined up just right, that it would work well enough to make me famous.

Papa saw right through the whole thing. "Sure za BB vill float; but vat good is zat? Vat does it do? Zat is no machine! Machines are useful!" Then he began telling me about his pile driver. "Simple, it lifts a veight and drops it down on ze end of a pole, und drives it into the riverbank." Wham! Wham! Wham!—illustrating by slamming his fist into the palm of his other hand. "When the pole is stuck in ze mud good and solid, it becomes a piling. You can build a building on a piling—now zat's something useful."

"Zos boys over in Dayton, the Wrights, had a good bicycle shop before they started fooling around with flying. Flying's for za birds! So vat they got that contraption to take off. Vat good is it? Now maybe zis horseless carriage has a future—runs on the ground, carries people. That's smart.

"Zis is za time to be a young fellow, Edward. Lots of new things are in za vorld. If you vork hard you can be a part of them. But remember, only useful things!" That was the last advice Papa ever gave me.

ELIZABETH   When we first heard, we thought maybe it vasn't zo bad. Like alvays, William had gone to work. There vas hanging around the schwartza, Billy Gaines. William had fired him the day before. Now he told him to get out—get off the property. When he wouldn't, William pushed him down in the mud. Zat was all, nothing else. But when William turned his back, the schwartza cracked him over the head with a carpenter's level. Zey took William to ze hospital, and after a while he came to. He recognized me and vun of the nurses who lives in the neighborhood. He held my hand even. But then he went into a deep sleep, and in the middle of the night he just stopped breathing. That was it, dead at forty-five. It vas August 26, 1904.

Ve brought him home, and had the viewing in ze sitting room. Zey all come, friends, neighbors, everybody who knew him. After Pastor Pister conducted the services and everybody left, I got the children to stand around Papa's casket. I told them to take vun last look, because in za morning he would be gone. I told them that things vould be hard from now on, and made them promise that those that vas fortunate would share vith those that vasn't. That vay nobody would be in need or vant for nothing.

BOO HERNDON, THE GHOSTWRITER   He told me his father's skull was fractured on the job by a swinging piling. That's the way I wrote it up. But then Finis Farr, his biographer, found the court records. William Gaines was tried and convicted of manslaughter and served ten years in the Ohio penitentiary. The whole thing must have been pretty painful for Rickenbacker, even sixty years after the fact. But that's the way he was. Truth was what he made of it.

ELIZABETH   Scared? You can bet I vas scared. Me with seven kids and no insurance, no vork, nothing. The papers made a big thing of the picnic they had for us out at the racetrack. It didn't amount to much, a lot of food zat went bad in a couple /of days and $73.24—not even enough to cover za bill the bastard Irish undertakers handed me at ze grave site. When ve came home that night, ve vas broke. I put the children to bed, and just sat downstairs like I vas in a trance. "They're going to take my children to ze orphanage and me to ze poorhouse." The family, I had to keep it together, but couldn't think of no way. I just kept thinking of them taking us away. Then I looked up and it vas Edward.

It was a fateful night. After I tossed about sleepless, something powerful drew me downstairs. I tiptoed down the steps and saw Mother with her head bowed, sitting at the kitchen table. I searched my soul for some words of comfort. Finally, I blurted out the thing I know now she most wanted to hear. "Whatever happens, Mama, I promise to make you proud of me." She reached out and touched me softly on the cheek as though I was the one who required consolation. Dumbstruck, I could do nothing but slump down in a chair and stare blankly.

I sat there for a long time before I grasped that I was at the head of the table . . . Papa's place. Mama knew, but she said nothing. It was years before I really understood what had taken place in those few minutes.

ELIZABETH   Maybe he vasn't quite the hero he made himself out to be. But he vas the first to pull his own weight, zat I can tell you. Sure ze others contributed. But Edward vas the first one to understand what was at stake. It made a difference. He vorked hard and brought in real money—at least until he hooked up vith zat Lee Frayer and za racing cars.

OPPORTUNITIES TO EXCEL

Eddie arose the next morning, at age thirteen and a half, poised to enter the world of adulthood. Casting aside the frivolous trappings of youth, he stuffed his school bag under his bed—he would have thrown it in the garbage had he not known Elizabeth was fanatical about wasting anything, no matter how useless. After a light breakfast—there wasn't much to eat—he set out to find gainful employment. He didn't have to worry. Business was good. But it could have been lousy. The fact was that unlike our own unrelentingly automated, worker-hostile environment, the big machine that drove America in the early twentieth century was as hungry for humans as it was for coal and iron ore. Indeed, the briskly polluted atmosphere of Columbus was fecund with opportunities for wage slavery.

Eddie had walked barely two miles before he came upon the Federal Glass Factory on South Parsons Avenue. After a few moments' hesitation, he entered the shack marked "Employment Office," and asked for a job. The balding factotum behind the desk looked at him dubiously.

"How old are you, kid?" The child labor laws stipulated that the factory could not hire a boy unless he was fourteen and had completed the eighth grade.

"I'm old enough, and I've had enough school."

I was skinny and undersized. He probably didn't believe me. Maybe the firm wasn't worried about exploiting minors. At any rate, I was told to report back at 6:00 that evening.

"You'll be here from six at night till six in the morning, six days a week. Six, six, and six, you got that? Your salary is three-fifty a week. If you're afraid you don't have it in you, then don't come back."

"I'll be back . . . don't worry."

In a flash Eddie had it all—miserable wages, indescribable working conditions, and every little boy's dream, the opportunity to stay up as late as he wanted. It was the same basic package that was being crammed down adolescent throats all over the country. Some literally died from it. Most persevered. A few even thrived.

SAM CRAWFORD, NIGHT FOREMAN   He wasn't exactly the pick of the litter, and it was rough work. I never thought he'd last. You see, we made tumblers by hand in those days. First, the blowers would shape 'em up, and set 'em down on steel platters. Then it was Eddie's job to carry 'em over to the tempering oven. But these platters was heavy and attached to long poles; so you couldn't get no leverage. Also you had to hold on tight, or they'd twist in your hand and dump on the floor. You'd see the kid staggering around like a drunk, back and forth, back and forth. But he had damned little breakage, and he kept showin' up. Sometimes, when it got slow I'd turn my back and let him sneak behind the ovens and catch a nap. When the work began to stack up, I'd go back there and kick him in the ass and threaten to fire him. But I always let him sleep a while first.

ELIZABETH   Edward he stopped going to school. I vorried that there vould be trouble, and, sure enough, the truant officer came to ze house. I didn't know vat to say; so I thought I vould take him upstairs. There was Edward, curled up on the bed, dead to ze vorld. "He's been vorking all night, every night but Sunday." The truant officer looked at me, shook his head, and tiptoed back down the stairs. This vas the last ve saw of him.

It was no picnic. I was constantly tired, and glassblowing was a dead end if you were lucky and an early grave if you weren't. Near the end of one bleak night, I came to the conclusion that I was finished with the Federal Glass Factory. I walked up to Mr. Crawford and quit.

"What's the problem, kid?"

"I hate it here."

"Okay, have it your own way. But look, if you can't find an opening, this one will still be waiting."

"Like a rattlesnake," I thought as I walked out of there at 3:00 A.M. Just fourteen and out of a job. But three hundred yards further down Parsons Avenue stood the Buckeye Steel Casting Company. At 6:00 when the employment office opened its doors, I was there first. I laid it on thick for the fellow interviewing me, telling him I had plenty of experience with castings.

"Awright, kid," he rasped through clenched teeth and an unlit cigar. "You start in an hour. Seven in the morning to six at night— a buck a day." I quickly learned that the only difference between casting glass and casting steel was that the new job was even more dangerous. There were compensations—day work, one hour less on the job, and all of six bucks a week! Money like that meant that poverty and the Rickenbacher family would soon be strangers.

ELIZABETH   He only lasted maybe three months at za foundry. Then he jumped to a beer factory, capping bottles. "Mama, it's cleaner, it's closer, and it's safer. You can't be afraid to quit." After vork sometimes you could smell za beer on his breath, but ze money vas ze same. And he brought home every penny. He vas a good boy that way. So every Sunday, his day off, I give him a quarter to do vhatever he vants. He was vorking hard, time to relax vas vat he needed.

Having pretty much lost track of his school chums and the kids in the neighborhood, the temporarily liberated Rickenbacher would head off on his own after Sunday school, flush with his mother's generosity. During the summer months this invariably meant a trip to Olentangy Park. Arriving in style on the trolley for a nickel—a rare luxury to an inveterate pedestrian—Eddie stretched the day by swimming in the river, hanging out, and judiciously choosing the four rides his remaining twenty cents afforded him. Surfeited with honky-tonk bliss, he would then head home, sauntering along dreamily.

One day something new and different happened. A good ways past the park entrance, standing near a patch of woods in the gathering darkness, was a girl about sixteen with frizzy hair in a tight dress.

"Hey! Com'ere," she said in a half-whisper, stopping Eddie in his tracks.

"Who, me?" he replied, having trouble making sense of the situation.

"You wanna have some fun? You got any money?"

"Uhh, I don' know. I mean sure I got money."

"Well, I'll let you do anything you want for a buck."

Not exactly sure what "anything" might encompass, Eddie was instantly certain he wanted to enter into this financial transaction. But as he attempted to negotiate further, his throat tightened.

"Uhh, I don't have it now . . . but I can get it. . . . Tomorrow . . . after work. . . . I'll meet you here."

"Whaddaya think, I'm gunna stand here all night?" She looked nervous, but she didn't try to walk away.

"I promise . . . I'll have the money. . . . if you'll just *be here!*"

"Well, I'd have to make a special trip. On a Monday there ain't gunna be any other business. . . . Okay, but I guess it's gunna cost you a buck-and-a-half an' you better have it all."

"I will . . . I will . . . I promise."

Thus assured, she moved one step closer and slid her hand down to Eddie's crotch. Without thinking he reached around and placed his own hand on her buttock. She let him keep it there for maybe three seconds.

"Okay, sport, enough free samples."

GOD   Absolutely outrageous. Barely pubescent and already consorting with harlots on the Sabbath. Sally Zarnetski—the clap-ridden little chippy. It was all I could do not to flatten the both of them with a bolt of lightning. But it was a nice evening, and I was in a pretty good mood. Young Rickenbacher, though, had another thing coming if he thought he was going to lose his innocence with her. So the next afternoon, as Sally walked toward the agreed-upon spot, she would encounter a glut of customers the likes of which she would not soon see again. In short order she met, satisfied, and infected a banker, two firemen, a randy cop on the beat, and, I regret to say, an Episcopalian minister. The experience left her five greenbacks richer, somewhat shaky on her feet, and with absolutely no intention of keeping her appointment. Meanwhile, Eddie waited and waited . . . and waited. It was half past nine and pitch black before he retreated homeward utterly dejected. Given My plans I knew I couldn't keep him frustrated forever. But for the moment his right hand would remain his only solace.

BOO HERNDON, THE GHOSTWRITER Everybody in New York knew he chased skirts. But he had to maintain this smarmy facade—a veritable soul of chastity. I don't know who he thought he was fooling.

Back in Ohio, Eddie's immediate future would continue to unfold in fits and starts as he hopped from miserable job to miserable job, a cavalcade of drudgery that found him setting up pins in a bowling alley, making heels in a shoe factory, cleaning out passenger cars for the Pennsylvania Railroad, loading fifty-pound blocks on an ice wagon, and in general lifting, hauling, sweeping, picking up, putting down, and persistently busting his chops.

This numbing sequence relented slightly when Eddie found himself polishing headstones for Abraham Zenker's monument works over on Grant Boulevard. Old Man Zenker was a friend of the family, and encouraged his young charge to move into the more creative end of the business. Eddie's first shot at metamorphic immortality was a marble marker for the departed senior Rickenbacher. "FATHER," it said with enviable brevity. There followed from the pious hand of young Rickenbacher a representation of the Bible and an angel, both of which he presented to Elizabeth, who accepted them with scarcely concealed glee at her boy's emerging passion for aesthetic endeavor. But she was less bullish on the health benefits of work whose main by-product was lung-clogging dust.

One Sunday I was upstairs taking a nap when something woke me, and I heard Mama talking with Mr. Zenker.

"Edward looks like a scarecrow, and zere is tuberculosis in za family. Vorking vith you in such a place is maybe not za best thing for him."

I already had a sore throat, and a more-or-less steady cough. As the day wore on it grew gradually worse. By morning the stone-cutting profession and I were finished.

A NEW BEGINNING

Art's loss soon proved technology's gain. On the very next day Eddie was wandering around downtown contemplating his boundless future, when he spotted a small crowd bunched around something truly monumental. Quoth the raven, " 'Twas a Ford"—a brand-shiny-new turtleback runabout, the first in Columbus. The hawker who had brought this mechanical marvel to the fair but skeptical Buckeye city was just meeting a bit of sales resistance, when he heard a nervous adolescent voice from the back of the pack.

"Hey, Mister . . . You ever give rides in that thing?" Sensing an opportunity to instill some badly needed consumer confidence in the reluctant Columbians, he was not about to refuse.

"Okay, kid, climb aboard."

PHIL PARTAIN, FORD SALES REP FOR CENTRAL OHIO   I never seen a kid like him. We're toolin' around, and he's actually bouncin' up and down on the seat, crazy with questions: "How fast will it go? What kind of engine? Where's it made? How much does it cost? What kind of grade can it handle?" But mostly he kept asking, "How fast?" That was basically what he wanted to know.

We must have been going 15 miles per hour. In those days not one kid in a hundred got to ride in a real automobile. I got off that Ford certain of what I wanted to do with the rest of my life. I could feel it, the boundless potential of internal combustion pulling me irresistibly towards the future.

GOD   Like a fly drawn to shit. I finally had young Edward where I wanted him, or at least moving in the right direction. You see, it was a time of stampeding egos; this progress thing had captured the imagination of practically all of them. The arms and legs I gave them weren't good enough anymore. They all basically wanted to speed things up, to drive and fly even further from Eden. Well, I wasn't going to stop them, just give them enough rope. But most were timid. It's the same with any flock. You need a few Judas sheep—basically crazy, desperate, or stupid enough to take the first couple of ill-conceived steps so the rest will follow. Leadership . . . the necessary ingredient in any social disaster. That's where Rickenbacher came in. That's why I bothered with him.

Eddie may have found his niche, but it was a state-of-the-art, high-tech, utterly romantic niche already crowded with aspiring visionaries intent on getting rich and breaking a few limbs in the process. Penniless, sixteen years old, with only a seventh-grade education, he had few obvious qualifications for admission. Yet below these superficial handicaps lurked a flinty shrewdness, an intuitive understanding of internal combustion—anything involving cylindrical objects moving back and forth in a tight sleeve was bound to appeal to the Rickenbacher psyche—and a considerable facility for breaking bones, mostly other people's.

Still, it wasn't easy getting in. After a month's searching, Eddie found his initial position in the automotive industry sweeping up in a large warehouse on Chestnut Street known as Evans' Garage. It was exactly that, a place to store vehicles and perform minor service—adjusting carburetors on gasoline models, recharging electrics, and fixing flats. But for Eddie it was heaven. A building full of cars, and basically nobody watching. In short order Eddie managed to seize the engine of a one-cylinder Packard which he inadvisedly started without checking the oil; marooned himself and a Waverly electric three miles outside of town after failing to top off the batteries, and badly bent the front axle of a Franklin in the process of attempting a corner at an unreasonably high rate of speed. In all of these mishaps the mechanically inclined Rickenbacher managed some form of repair sufficient to elude the negligent eye of the peripatetic Mr. Evans.

GEORGE EVANS, AUTOMOTIVE ENTREPRENEUR I don't know what ever possessed me to trust that kid with other people's property. He seemed all right at first, always busy, got to work early and left late. Then customers started complaining about their cars running weird or not running at all. One day Dr. Selzer fired up his Franklin and the damned thing just drove itself into a wall before he even got out of the garage. Finally, I come home early from a trip to Toledo, and I find him underneath a little Cadillac with the whole goddamn engine spread out in pieces on the floor. Now the Lelands made these buggies to very precise tolerances, so there was no way of getting the motor back together short of sending it to the factory in Detroit—which we did. But that was it for Rickenbacher.

ELIZABETH Disappointed, but not surprised . . . zat's how I felt when Edward told me that he vas fired by zat Evans. You should have seen his face. He vas a sorry sight. And I was already vorried over him. It vasn't so much za money—Bill, and Mary, and even little Emma had jobs. It vas this business with ze cars. It was all he could talk about . . . cars, cars, cars. He didn't seem to care no more about a job, only ze cars. Then he starts taking this correspondence course from Pennsylvania; mechanical engineering he calls it. A waste of time I called it; sitting around the house all day, reading books. He hardly even went out, except to hang around Frayer-Miller—even sneaking over there ven he should have been in Sunday school. I really thought Edward vas going off his rocker.

It was destiny, I was sure of it. Right in my home town the Frayer-Miller Company was already building automobiles—just a single model, a touring car with a gasoline motor. But it was a real factory, making everything needed in a real car except the tires. And there was more. They were in the midst of developing three racing cars for the famous Vanderbilt Cup Race on Long Island. The very idea got my heart pumping. Racing! It was the most exciting thing I could think of . . . the only thing I could think of.

Soon enough I got in the habit of wandering over to the plant a little past quitting time, and pressing my face against the windows, hoping to catch a glimpse of those race cars. Instead, I was the one that got caught.

"Lookin' to break in; is that what you're doin', kid?"

"No sir, Mr. Frayer. I just wanted to see what you're working on inside."

"Who are you, kid? And how do you know my name?"

"I'm Eddie Rickenbacher . . . and . . . uhh, everybody knows you. You're Lee Frayer, the designer and chief engineer. And I want to help you build these cars."

"Well, that's flattering, kid, but we've got enough help. I can't think of anything you could do."

He just hadn't looked around. Even through the windows, I had never seen a filthier shop.

"Mr. Frayer, there's plenty of work to do in there. I'll be back first thing tomorrow."

And I was, at 6 A.M. I located a broom stashed and forgotten in the corner and got busy. By the time Mr. Frayer got there at 8:30, I had finished about half of the main shop including the lathes and drill presses. One side was clean as a whistle, the other still looked like a tornado had run through it.

"You sure made a difference. I'll give you that. Okay, you're hired. When you're finished, report to Millbank upstairs and help him with the carburetors."

LEE FRAYER   He was a go-getter, that kid. It was as if he had jumped out of a Horatio Alger novel, Ragged Dick or Tattered Tom come to life. Moving all the time, into everything, trying to absorb all of it at once. To talk to him, he didn't seem that bright. But one day I found him buried in one of those ICS mechanical engineering texts. I kept an eye on him for the next several days, and it seemed that every spare minute found him with his nose in that book. Plainly, this was somebody with potential. So I set about training him more formally, rotating him around the entire shop until he mastered each task—engine assembly, wheel fabrication, transmissions, chassis, brakes, the whole nine yards. He soaked it up like a sponge; cycled through the entire operation in less than two months. Then I sent him over to engineering, not to work on the touring car, but to become familiar with every damned part in the Cup racers.

These low-slung gems represented the best of Frayer-Miller, not a thing on them wasn't devoted to speed and durability. As the race approached, excitement in the shop grew to a fevered pitch. In 1904, William K. Vanderbilt, of the famous New York Vanderbilts, had bankrolled the first race as a way of promoting advanced designs in the American automotive industry. Yet so far European marques had dominated the series, even though the winner took home the famed Vanderbilt Cup, along with $10,000 in prize money. But just about every U.S. auto company was betting that 1906 would be different. There was a lot at stake, especially for the smaller builders. And not just a matter of prize money. If one of Lee Frayer's cars won, he could sell Frayer-Millers as fast as he could build them. And better yet, his name would become a part of automotive history.

Mr. Frayer intended to ship the cars down to Long Island three weeks ahead of time for testing on the actual course. He was slated to drive the number-one racer himself, and Frank Lawell and Cy Belden would drive two and three. Ike Howard was chief of the crew, including the riding mechanics.

When it came time, I walked over to the rail yard to give them a hand loading. Just as the last racer was being tied down on the flatcar, Mr. Frayer came up to me. "Get home and pack a bag. You're coming."

LEE FRAYER It was kind of a spur-of-the-moment decision, although I must have had it in the back of my mind all the time. And the more I thought about it, the more sense it made. You see, the fellows Ike chose for riding mechanics were all big men, fat really, not one of them probably under 200 pounds. Now Eddie couldn't have weighed more than 135 dripping wet. Sixty or seventy pounds either way is no small matter in a race car. So he got the nod. Started his career. Kind of ironic actually, since he eventually grew into a rather large man himself.

New York World, September 16, 1906
 . . . The recently arrived Frayer-Miller racer is an unusual and highly advanced design. It has wheels fabricated of tough steel wire rather than the usual wooden spokes. The chassis rails between the front and rear axles are radically stepped downward, creating a ground-hugging profile and significantly lowering the center of gravity. But most notably, the engine is cooled by air rather than water, a departure which eliminates the heavy jacketing around the cylinders and the leak-prone radiator, substituting instead a massive blower in the tapered nose of the vehicle. To look at, the Frayer-Miller is small, almost jewel-like, exuding speed. But as with so many brilliantly conceived racing machines, it is untried and loaded down with question marks. . . .

That first morning on Long Island I was so excited I thought I might jump out of my skin. The cars were unloaded and Ike Howard had number one set up for a run. Handing me a pair of goggles and a linen helmet, Mr. Frayer went over my instructions. "Look, Eddie, it's important to keep an eye on the oil pressure gauge. If it drops into the red, you've got to pump it back up fast. Understand?" I nodded my head. "Next is the tires. Watch them as if your life depended on it—because it does. And let me know absolutely as soon as the rubber wears enough to show fabric. Now, I'll be focused on what's going on in front of us. So you've got to look back, and let me know if anybody's trying to pass. The engine is going to be too loud to talk, so tap my knee once for tires and twice if somebody's on our tail. You got all that?" he finished, smiling. "Yes sir!" and the next thing I knew we were careening down the straight on Jericho Turnpike at 70 miles per hour, the wind pressing me so hard I had to lean forward. The car skidded around every corner and took the course in a series of leaps and lunges. But the danger never even crossed my mind.

The next day was different. As we roared into a sharp curve I sensed we were going way too fast. I saw immediately the brake pedal was pressed flat to the floor. A cable must have snapped and there was no way we were going to make the corner. We zoomed off the course, flew over a ditch, and landed in a sand dune. The wheels caught and we rolled. The impact shot me out of the car and threw me about twenty feet. I had the wind knocked out of me, and I was afraid for a few minutes that I was badly hurt. But after a while I got up and limped over to where Mr. Frayer was sitting. "Sorry, kid. Brakes failed. But that's racing." It sure was. That's how it went for most of the next two weeks. Up and down. Break the car, fix the car, lumps and bruises.

IKE HOWARD   That Eddie was an eager beaver. After a run, he'd be back in the garage with the crew tryin' t' make himself useful. He weren't much good as a mechanic, but he was always there ready to fetch somethin' if you needed it—a spanner, a lug nut, whatever. Johnny-on-the-spot, that one. And boy did we need help. It seemed like the goddamn cars was fallin' apart faster than we could put 'em back together . . . overheatin', crackin' pistons, you name it. And then those fool drivers kept runnin' 'em off the road. We had our hands full, I can tell ya, and Eddie pulled his weight, that's for sure. I don' know when he slept exactly. There was a lot goin' on, and he seemed to want to do it all."

He certainly did. During the weeks leading up to the race Eddie was being exposed to levels of wealth and sophistication he never dreamed existed. Auto racing had already cast its spell over the postadolescent segment of the plutocracy. Scarcely anything, except perhaps flying, attracted young males with money more than the opportunity to squander their lives in pursuit of manifest reassurance that they were cagier, braver, or more opportunistic than the other fellows, and therefore deserved to be rich. And with the boys came their wives and sweethearts, decked out with all the genetic advertising and pheromone stimulants that money could buy. Eddie no sooner caught a whiff of this heady potion than his limbic brain told him exactly where he wanted to spend the rest of his life. Now, on the basis of breeding and education, he had absolutely no claim to consort with these ethereal beings, except on the most demeaning terms. But his position as one of those who climbed aboard a race car and raised his middle digit in the general direction of Fate did accord him a certain entrée. And Eddie Rickenbacher was nobody to turn his back on opportunity.

ALICE WHITNEY PAYSON   Remember him? Unfortunately yes. It was the year of my eldest sister's debut, and we had come in from Quogue to attend a reception my uncle Jack was holding for the Vanderbilt drivers. I was just fifteen and feeling none too comfortable, when this fellow dressed like a gardener walked up as if he had known me all his life. He had this odd vulpine smile on his face, and stuck out a greasy paw for me to shake. "I'm Eddie Rickenbacher, one of the racers." That was bad enough. But then he had absolutely nothing to say. Just continued staring and smiling. It was excruciating. I didn't know what to say or do. We just stood there. It would have been droll had it not been so painful and pathetic. If someone had told me then that this creature would one day be lionized, I would have lost all faith in humanity.

As the days passed the pressure built. Each morning the course was crowded with cars struggling to squeeze the last ounce of performance from their straining engines and chassis. I watched the grease–spitting chain-drive Locomobile, the massive Pope-Toledo, and the badly outclassed modified production Oldsmobile, all practicing lap after lap. Numbering among the foreign models were the French Panhard, Darracq, and the huge de Dietrich, the English Bentley, as well as the famous German Mercedes and Italian FIAT. But the pre-race competition was greatest among the Americans, since there were twelve of us and each country was allowed only five contestants. The U.S. entries would be decided in a six-lap elimination scheduled for September 22nd.

It turned out to be pretty much a wash for Frayer-Miller. Frank Lawell was going great guns when his crankshaft broke on the third lap, ending his chances. Belden went off the track on the same lap, crashing badly. Only Mr. Frayer and myself survived, limping home in fifth with a misfiring motor. We were in the big race, but just barely.

LEE FRAYER   The morning of the Cup race I was tight as a drum. As Ike and the boys rolled out number one, my mouth was so dry

I could barely speak. Then I noticed something on the car that broke all the tension. There on the cowl, neatly painted below my name, was "Edward Rickenbacher, Riding Mechanic." I started to get mad, but then I began laughing. The kid had nerve, you had to hand him that.

The race began well enough for us. Fred Wagner, the starter, flagged the cars onto the course every half-minute. Just ahead was Hugo de Naranja in a FIAT; then it was our turn. The flag dropped and Mr. Frayer floored it. The needle on the oil pressure gauge was right where it should be. I looked ahead on the course, and Naranja was already slowing with engine trouble. An omen, I thought. We're going to win! And so it seemed for a while. In the first four laps we passed six cars. The tires were wearing well, the engine was running strong.

Then, as we crested a hill, a misguided rooster chose that instant to cross the course. There was no way we could avoid him. Feathers exploded, and there was a loud thump as the unfortunate animal was drawn into the cooling fan in the nose and dispatched. But in the process the blower was ripped apart. We kept going, but soon enough the car started to overheat. At first I heard only a slight rapping. Then it grew into a pounding. Something important had come loose in the engine. A car in back was gaining fast. I signaled Mr. Frayer. He nodded and the big de Dietrich roared past. Mr. Frayer continued on. The pounding was deafening. The pistons were ready to seize. At last he cut the ignition and rolled slowly off the track. A year of work and an investment of $50,000 had come to nothing. For a long moment he simply sat there. Finally he sighed and turned to me.

"It's over."

That was true, but only temporarily.

Chapter Two

Abilene, Texas
December 1, 1909

Dear Mother,

Today was a proud day in the history of the Rickenbacher family. Your son Edward took a big step up the latter of sucksess. I personly drove William Jenings Brian the famous presidential candidate and champien of the little man to his lecture and the parade in his honor with thousands waching. My picture was on the front page of the Abilene Bee, and maybe all over Texas.

You see Mother part of my job here is to keep my eyes open for good oportunities for good publisity. When I heard Mr. Brian was here, I drove right over to his hotel in a shiny new Firestone-Columbus and went into see him. "Mr Brian," I told him; "I have a brand-new Firestone-Columbus, one of the best automobiles made in America, and I would be proud to drive you while you are here." Well Mother he said it would be a plesure and before I new it there I was with the great William Jenings Briant, him in the back seat and me in the drivers seat and every body else waching. It was a fether in my cap and good for business. The very next day a crowd of folks who saw me in the paper showed up in the showroom ready for a demunstrashun ride. And they liked the car to.

Mother I sincerely hope you are as proud of me as I am. I think about you all the time and I realize without your inspurashun I would not be making $125 a month and have friends all over this state. I miss you more than I can say. You will always be my best gal. And here is a surprize for you, I think I will be back in Columbus for Christmas.

Your loving and obedient son,
Edward

P.S. They grow them big down here in Texas. When I left Columbus in June I stood 5 feet 9. Now I am 6 feet 2 and I weigh 165. Tell Bill and the rest to wach out!

LEE FRAYER Around six months after the Vanderbilt race, Clinton D. Firestone invited me to come over to the Columbus Buggy Company and design them a superior automobile. "Carte blanche, you provide us the prototype and we'll build it." It was too big a challenge to turn down, and the first person I thought to bring with me was Eddie. He wasn't much of a draftsman, but he was skillful and crazy enough to test the car to its absolute limits. No doubt about it, Eddie was a comer. If anything though, I underestimated him. Maybe everyone did.

It was the chance of a lifetime . . . and more. I had been without a father for too long. Now Mr. Frayer, a man I respected more than any single individual, demonstrated that he truly cared about my future. How could I do anything but try, with everything that was in me, to prove his faith was justified?

BILL RICKENBACHER At the time Eddie moved over to CBC I was working as a clerk in a dry-goods store. It kind of stuck in my craw . . . my little brother being made head of the experimental department of a respected firm. I grew up with him, and I knew he wasn't *that* smart. But now it wasn't just Mother, everybody was saying that Eddie was the success of the family. It was hard to take. Yet I had to admit he did have moxie. And after a while I just kinda got used to it.

Much remained to be done before the new touring car was ready for testing. So while they finished development, I was put in charge of working the bugs out of the motorized version of the famous Columbus high-wheeled buggy. These tests were critical in our understanding of the vehicle's stability. The process was thoroughly scientific. I took the car into the same curve a little faster each time, until I reached a speed sufficient to drive it into a skid. There were other adventures. Once, when I was testing a new brake design on a steep hill, the whole thing gave way and the buggy just took off. The next thing I knew I was hitting the ground as the 800-pound buggy flew over me. Torn pants and a few cuts and bruises . . . all in a day's work.

But you can bet that kind of testing gave me special insights into the vehicle's weaknesses. With the engine it was the intake and exhaust valves. The little clamps that held the valve springs in place often shook free. So I made it my business to carry a few extras in my pocket whenever I went out. That little bit of information would do me a lot of good as it turned out.

HORACE TILDEN, TOOL AND DIE MAKER   One day we got word that Old Man Firestone had taken out one of the buggies, an' broke down up by the Scioto River storage dam. Me and the boys was just hitchin' up a wagon to go out an' fetch him when up comes young Rickenbacher with a full head of steam. "I'm goin', not you, and not with any horse." With that he jumps in a buggy and takes off.

CLINTON D. FIRESTONE   It was hot as hell that day, and I wasn't exactly thrilled when help arrived in the form of a scrawny seventeen-year-old. I remember saying something like, "I wanted a man, not some squirt kid." Well, that didn't seem to faze him. Instead, he very calmly explained that Lee Frayer had sent him to diagnose and fix whatever trouble had developed. I didn't have much choice, so I let him loose on the thing. First thing he does is crank it, which I could have told him wouldn't do any good, since the thing had lost all compression. But then he takes something out of his pocket and starts fiddling with the valves. Well, as God is my witness, he had that engine purrin' like a kitten in less than five minutes. Right then and there I knew this was a young man headed for better things.

FINIS FARR, *Rickenbacher's Luck*
"It was a scene of American folklore—the industrialist in a pickle helped by a poor but modest and efficient lad who is cheerfully

working his way up. Somewhere ahead lies Easy Street, with or without the boss's daughter."

Later that day Mr. Frayer called me in. "What in hell did you do for Firestone? He thinks you walk on water." After that hardly a day passed that Mr. Firestone didn't stop by to check up on me. He had gotten my name from Frayer, and always used it. "How's things, Eddie?" "You got those buggies in tip-top shape, Eddie?" "Anything else you need here, Eddie?"

CLINTON D. FIRESTONE A couple of weeks after the incident at the dam, our distributors in New Jersey contacted us. They were about to hold a demonstration at the Million Dollar Pier in Atlantic City, and the buggies kept getting stuck in the sandy roads around the beach. They wanted somebody to come out pronto, and deal with the problem. Well, I thought about it for a while, and then it occurred to me. Why not send the kid? Frayer and some of the others didn't seem very happy; but something told me I had made the right choice.

Despite my obvious youth, the local dealers welcomed me as a bona fide representative of the company. And they didn't waste any time, taking me right down to the beach to show me exactly what the problem was. The buggy's thin tires dug down deep enough into the soft sand so that the resultant drag caused the clutch to slip, and the vehicle to bog down hopelessly. I tinkered with that clutch until I was at my wits' end, but no amount of adjusting seemed to help. Then I thought, "Why don't the brakes slip? What's the difference?" Right away I fitted a brake band to the clutch. It worked like a charm. That little buggy just ripped through the sand.

The dealers were encouraged but still skeptical. Then one of them suggested bringing the buggy out to the sand dunes behind the beach. No motor vehicle had ever climbed the dunes, but our little gem, with its new clutch band, skedaddled right up and over. With that they rejoiced and the agent from Atlantic City even hustled over to the local paper, which dispatched a photographer. The next day there I was, as big as life, in the morning edition. I made sure I bought at least twenty copies for the folks at home. Mr. Firestone was so impressed that he had several thousand brake belts made up, and sent a couple out to each buggy owner across the country.

Columbus Buggy Company Service Advisory, June 25, 1910

This is to inform you that use of the heavy-duty clutch band recently supplied to you free of charge should be undertaken with caution and for very limited use only. These bands place extreme stress on the clutch bearings, which then become subject to catastrophic failure. Henceforth, the Columbus Buggy Company can no longer be responsible for clutches broken in this manner, and repairs must be undertaken at the owner's expense.

At last the touring car, the five-place Firestone-Columbus, was finished and ready for me to test. It looked like a world-beater. Lee Frayer had put his heart and soul into that car, but before I took it out for the first time, he took me aside. "Give it hell, Eddie— the only way we'll know when and if it will break is if you break it." I wasn't about to let them down. By the time the tests were over I had flipped it twice, got hung up on a stump, and hit a cow. I did so much repair work that in the end I could have taken that car apart and put it back together in my sleep. The motor, built by Northway based on Frayer's design, became as much a part of me as the little buggy's already was. During this period I learned that engines have a language of their own. From that time on, when a power plant was not running up to specs, I had only to listen and I knew exactly what it was saying.

LEE FRAYER The touring car was going great guns. It was smooth and reliable and sold for less than $2,000. In January 1909, one of the worst months on record, we took it from Columbus to Chicago, for the automobile show. Through 250 miles of mud, snow, and nonexistent roads it ran like a charm. We arrived in time to wash and polish it up, and folks practically overran our stand for demonstration rides. I had Eddie driving prospects all over Chicago. He must have done a pretty good job sweet-talking them, since we took orders for eleven cars in just three days. After we got back to Columbus the orders kept streaming in, and we found ourselves working night and day to satisfy what would become a long line of happy customers. Then out of nowhere came trouble.

WESTERN UNION

6/10/09

COLUMBUS BUGGY COMPANY
FIFE AND MILLER VEHICULAR AGENTS, DALLAS

RECEIVED NEW TOURING CARS. ALL THREE FAILED TESTS AF-
TER TEN MILES. SEND PLANS TO FIX IMMEDIATELY, OR WILL
SHIP BACK TO COLUMBUS ON 1 JULY.

FIFE

BARNEY FIFE (SENIOR)   I swear my jaw dropped when I saw
him. First they send us three piles of junk, and next they send a
scrawny kid to fix them. I had about had it with CBC. "I'll give
you one week," I told him. "If by then those three cars aren't
working to our satisfaction, you and them are finished." He didn't
say a word, just nodded and headed down to the shop.

I fired up one of the cars, and it told me right away that it was
healthy enough. But the midafternoon sun was blazing when I
pulled out of Fife and Miller, and sure enough, after about five
miles the engine started to get hot. I kept going. Soon the radiator
boiled over, and finally the motor quit, the pistons having seized
in their cylinders. The problem was obvious; fixing it was another
thing entirely. Rather than a water pump the motor employed a
thermosiphon. It had performed adequately up North in the winter, but not in Texas in the summer. And nothing I tried did the
slightest good.

By Saturday my time was running out and so was my patience.
In a weak moment I had invited an attractive young woman I met
in Dallas for a ride in the country, taking care to bring along two
extra containers of water. It was a bad mistake. The Frayer-Miller
guzzled both in short order, and left us stranded in the middle of
nowhere. My companion was growing more distraught by the minute, and I was on the edge of panic. Then I noticed a few mean-
looking longhorns gathered around a water hole. Before I knew it
I was pouring cold water into a sizzling hot engine, one of the
stupidest things you can do. The water jacket creaked and groaned,
but didn't crack. After a while I started it up and headed back,
much to my date's relief.

The following morning I took the same car out and it ran perfectly no matter how far I drove it. What could possibly have hap-

pened to keep it from overheating? I paid a chemist to analyze the water in the radiator. It was simple rainwater. Then it hit me. Northway had matched the pistons to the cylinders with extremely small tolerances, so when they got really hot they expanded and seized. By adding cold water I had contracted the pistons slightly and then frozen them to those smaller dimensions. I tried it with the other cars, and by midafternoon they were all running fine. Satisfied at last, the two partners now felt free to offer the cars to the buying public. With my help all three went quickly, and Mr. Fife hurried off to the telegraph office to order more, so long as I would stay on for a while. It was the beginning of my career in sales. I figured that when Mr. Frayer found out what I had done, he would be pretty mad. So postponing my return made sense. Meanwhile, the cars may have lost a little compression, but we had gained a stateful of potential customers.

GOD What a combination, infernal machines, half-witted Texans with too much lucre, and young Edward, four-flusher in training. They couldn't buy his preshrunk chariots fast enough—this, decades before Spindletop oil, anything resembling a road system, and only cows to visit. I'll tell you, in a universe full of black holes, quarks, and pretzel logic you can't say they didn't provide Me some comic relief.

ED HUTCHINSON, RANCHER I seen his picture in the paper with that asshole Bryan. Didn't have anything else to do, so me an' a couple of the boys went over to Fife and Miller to see the car. Well, he comes on with this line of bull so's you couldn't shut him up. Finally, I says: "Young man, I'll make you a proposition. If you can drive me and my friends out to my ranch with no trouble, each of us will buy one of these things." He gets all buggy-eyed and excited, runnin' around gettin' the car ready. 'Course, I neglected to tell him my spread was around a quarter-million acres an' about a hundred-mile trip. Firestone-Columbus didn't do bad, neither. We was about a mile from the ranch house when Anna Lee, my daughter, comes ridin' up on a Pinto pony. Now Anna Lee was a looker, an' she sure turned this young man's head. Drove that thing right off the path and into a big rock. Bent up the axle something terrible. He looked kinda green. But we all had a good laugh an' told him we'd buy the cars anyway, since there weren't many girls as pretty as Anna Lee to distract us.

ANNA LEE HUTCHINSON Later when I read about his exploits in the Great War, I wasn't surprised at all. Even back then he was real self-confident. You could tell right away he was goin' places. But he was also impertinent. That first night, as soon as we got out of my parents' sight, he tried to kiss me. Finally I said, "Mr. Rickenbacher, this is not my idea of fun. If that's what you want, there are other places you can go." He really did seem sorry. But he just couldn't keep his hands to himself. I liked him though, an' I was glad to see him when he came to call again.

CARMELITA, EMPLOYEE OF THE CRUZ DE LUZ Like all the tall thin gringos he was hung like a caballo. But this was not the problem. When he first arrived and asked my price, I told him two dollars for the hour, four dollars for the whole night. Right away he gives me four silver dollars. For me, I am thinking, this is good. Like all of them—two, perhaps three times—then off to sleep. Not him. The first time he spent he didn't even lose the erection. He must have been on top of me for an hour. After that he would rest for a few minutes, then back on top. Again and again, it went on all night. When he left at last I was sore as a bride and too tired to work the next day. I warned the other girls. But when he returned, Lourdes happily took his four dollars. She was such a slut.

ELIZABETH True to his vord, Edward returned home ze night before Christmas. Tall, handsome, in every vay a young man, he brought presents for everybody. In za morning ve all vent to hear Pastor Pister preach the Gospel, knowing Edward's gifts and a fat Christmas goose vere waiting for us. It vas the most joyful Christmas I can remember. Zat night, after the others had gone to bed, Edward came down and looked at me real serious. "Mother, I paid off the mortgage. You own this house now." I couldn't think vat I had done to raise such a vunderful child.

But alvays there are those who don't understand generosity. You see, Edward brought back a ring with a tiny diamond and gave it to that Blanche Calhoun he used to know at church. He was real innocent then, and didn't understand zat others might try to turn this around. Next thing ve hear the family is spreading rumors they are engaged. Vat lies!! Edward swore to me he never said a vord about marriage. And them saying he ruined their daughter!! Vell my boy vas headed for bigger things, and no little gold digger vas going to stand in his vay!

Mr. Firestone took him aside at the plant and told him he vas too valuable to go back to Texas. Instead, he vas going to Omaha, sales manager for ze whole north-central territory, $150 a month and six men vorking for him. Zat vas no rumor. And he vas gone before those Calhouns could spread much more of their filth!!

Omaha marked a turning point in Eddie's hegira. Hawking rattle-traps to ranchers at the beck and call of Fife and Miller was one thing, running an entire district office with its own advertising budget was another. A man could make decisions about how best to stick the good name of Firestone-Columbus into the public's eye—especially if that man had a little castor oil in his veins and wasn't afraid to take a few chances. Soon enough Eddie was ripping the bodies off touring saloons, juicing up Lee Frayer's new four-cylinder engines, and going out to do battle with the local champions of Stutz, Marmon, and Cadillac on the dirt tracks that sprang up like anthills on his parched territory. He won more than he lost, and by the end of the season most drivers learned to stay out of his way. In Nebraska City he ran the local Chalmers Detroit dealer off the side of a dam and into the lake. Nothing personal, but there was $200 riding on the outcome. One weekend at Aksarben—Nebraska spelled backward—he cleared 1,500 greenbacks. Now all of this was certainly good for business; but it wasn't long before Eddie realized he didn't much care about selling cars. He was going where the real money and excitement were.

GOD I had left Edward largely to his own devices—on cruise control, as it were. Nevertheless, he had developed nicely into the ruthless, aggressive specimen I desired. Now it was time to see if he could gladiate his way to fame and fortune, and, in the process, inspire the multitudes to commit acts of mass production, help them become addicted to mindless travel between identical urban centers, and lead them into a future of air pollution, MacDougall burgers, and mega-perdition. I needed cheerleaders. Rickenbacher and his ilk were integral to my determination to remain a progressive, forward-looking Diety. What I had once done with snakes and apples, I would now accomplish through Turbohydromatic, broad vinyl-trimmed backseats, and complimentary California champagne on flights exceeding 200 nautical miles.

• • •

I had become increasingly disillusioned with CBC. Its leadership was made up exclusively of men over fifty, and none had made the transition into the age of the automobile. Time was also leaving Lee Frayer in the dust. Back in Columbus he proudly showed me his new racing machine, the Red Wing Special. It had 50 horsepower at a time when the big FIATs and Benzes were topping 120. Still, he wanted to enter the thing in the 500-mile race scheduled for Memorial Day 1911 at the big new Indianapolis Speedway, and he asked me to be his relief at the wheel. I knew we had no chance of finishing anywhere near the money; still I jumped at the opportunity to run with the likes of Wild Bob Burman, Ralph DePalma, Louis Chevrolet, and Ray Harroun, not to mention society sportsmen such as David Bruce-Brown, and Spencer Wishart, the Millionaire Speed King from Philadelphia. That first Indy 500 was a great day of racing, cool and fair, with almost 100,000 in attendance. On the 133rd lap, Art Greiner's Amplex suffered twin blowouts at high speed, and his mechanic was thrown out and killed. He was the first man I saw die on the track. Other than that the race went smoothly, and we managed 11th place largely due to steady driving. But I never had a chance to challenge for the lead. The Red Wing was just too slow. I liked to race, and I wanted to pit my driving skill and guts with the best. But as long as I stuck with CBC, Lee Frayer, and their underpowered cars I would never have the chance.

AUGIE DUESENBERG Never liked him. Worked his way on the team, so's he thought he was runnin' it. One of those guys who knew everything. My brother was a genius; that was pretty obvious after a while. But I hafta give it to Rickenbacher, he was one of the first to figure it out.

FRED DUESENBERG I first met Eddie in Des Moines. Up to that time we had been building little two-cylinder jobs for Mason over in Waterloo, runnin' them all over the Midwest. But now—this was the summer of 1912—we were getting into the side-valve fours, still simple, yet compact and powerful—"Giant Killers," the press called 'em. Well, Eddie must have gotten wind of this. Walks into the shop and asks for a job as a mechanic. Hired him on the spot. He didn't exactly earn his keep with a wrench. But behind the wheel was another story entirely. He did some testing for us, and his times were consistently faster than anybody else we had.

He was a little crazy and hard on the cars, but we'd have been fools not to run him.

EDDIE O'DONNELL, RIDING MECHANIC He was good, damn good, 'specially on the dirt. Probably the first driver to really perfect the four-wheel drift. That was why he could go into the turns a little faster than everybody—except maybe DePalma. It made him look reckless and he got that reputation. But inside the car he was always in control . . . knew everything that was going on, and where everybody else was on the track. Like he had eyes in the back of his head. I always felt safe ridin' with him.

Not a bad guy neither . . . once you got to know him. Back then I was pretty ambitious, wantin' to drive an' all. He took me aside and encouraged me. Gave me time at the wheel, helped me with my technique. When he left the team I inherited his seat. Didn't do bad neither, till Lady Luck caught up with me in '20.

Nineteen-thirteen, my first full season with Duesenberg, was tough. We had the new 350-inch fours and the cars showed a lot of speed. But they were unreliable. To make matters worse, we were continually strapped for cash. Our chief competitors, Stutz and Mercer, were the products of profitable commercial enterprises. We were just a racing team. So campaigning the cars at a distance was a continuing problem. Even at the Elgin Trophy Race, just over in Chicago, we couldn't afford to send more than one car. Shipping racers out to the West Coast, where the whole winter season took place, was just not in the cards. So Mercer and Stutz cleaned up.

But just as it always does, adversity brought us together. Though poor, our team was rich in loyalty. Once that summer the tread of one of my right rear tires ripped loose in a long strip, which then acted as a whip thrashing my arm with each rotation. The pain was so bad I thought I might lose control of the car. Then, as quickly as it started, the beating stopped. Eddie O'Donnell, my riding mechanic, had reached around me and was absorbing the pounding himself.

FRED DUESENBERG Used the long off-season to shore up the operation. The cars were basically sound, just in need of development. Simplified the manifolding, reinforced the frames, and went to 35X5 tires on the rear to boost the gear ratio. Also, I appointed

Eddie team captain. Augie wasn't too happy, but Rickenbacher's business experience was something we needed. He was organized and worked like a dog—nonstop sixteen-hour days. Rubbed off too. Tact wasn't his strong suit; but by the time May rolled around he had forged the team into a disciplined unit committed to Giant Killing on any track within reach. Problem was, we were still broke.

ELIZABETH   More to vorry about. Everything vas going fine, and then ve hear Edward has quit Mr. Firestone to go vith the racing cars. I felt like giving Lee Frayer a piece of my mind for ever getting him involved vith such things. It vas bad enough he had thrown away his vunderful job, but now all the time he is facing danger. I vas really frightened for my boy. Then I remembered about the bat's heart, and if you tied it to your middle finger with a red silk string, it vould protect you. I wrote Edward right away and told him to find one quick. After that I vas feeling better.

We ran Indianapolis again and I took a tenth place. Augie and Fred were happy enough, but I was dissatisfied. One slot better than the lame-duck Red Wing the year before didn't seem like much progress.

The next big race of the season was on the fourth of July at Sioux City—300 miles on the brand-new two-mile dirt oval, with the winning car slated to receive $10,000. All the big names were there: Ralph Mulford and Wild Bob Burman, favorites in their powerful Peugeots; my friend Spence Wishart and his soon-to-be brother-in-law, Dario Resta, the Italian aristocrat, both in Mercers; Harry Wetmore with his Chalmers Six; and as always Barney Oldfield, who some called the King of the Racers. Yet in spite of the quality of the field I thought our cars stood a good chance. They were lighter, more nimble, and thoroughly tested. But we remained desperately short of funds, so short we couldn't even pay for a garage, but had to park the cars underneath the stands. The crew slept right there on bedrolls, and ate at any hash slinger's that would feed them on promises. I struck a bargain at a local boardinghouse, room and two meals a day for two-fifty a week . . . payable on departure. But as broke as I was, I told the proprietor's two boys I'd pay them a silver dollar for a bat dead or alive. I didn't like gutting the little creature, and I may have gotten the liver, not the heart. But with that thing tied around my finger I felt as though I was immortal.

Excerpt from the *Sioux City Iowan,* July 2, 1914

Young Rickenbacher has a savage style behind the wheel. But he is also a clean-living athlete. "My mother is still my best girl. And if I were to get hitched, I'd quit the racing game in a minute." So it's early to bed, early to rise for this dedicated competitor. "Cleopatra herself couldn't keep me up past 8:30 until after I've run this race," he told our reporter.

AUGIE DUESENBERG That day everything went according to plan. My brother had the cars tuned to perfection, and the drivers were completely familiar with the track. We went out slow, letting attrition take its toll. Oldfield led for the first hundred miles, then dropped out with radiator problems. For the next sixty laps it was between Wishart and Burman. Rickenbacher was cruising along in fourth, biding his time. Around lap 110 Burman went out with a fuel line. From that point on it was Rickenbacher and Wishart. Wishart would edge out on the straights, and Eddie would catch him in the turns. Finally, Rickenbacher got by. About five laps from the finish Eddie O'Donnell, the riding mechanic, got konked on the head with a dirt clod and went unconscious. But Rickenbacher never slowed and won by forty seconds. Tom Alley from our team also took a third for $2,500, so we had won a total of $12,500. We were rich, or so we thought. Next day Rickenbacher picked up the checks, and, before we knew it, tried to chisel us out of part of our shares. We finally got what was coming to us, but it left hard feelings. All and all though, it was our first big win. For the rest of the season we racked up thirty-four firsts, seven seconds, and fourteen thirds out of seventy-three starts. We had become a force to be reckoned with, and you'd hafta say he put us on the map.

MARION WISHART It all seemed so glamorous when we first met. Then after the wedding it dawned on me; racing was a form of suicide. I begged Spence to stop. After David Bruce-Brown was killed, I was frantic. But he seemed oblivious. I think he thought he was in some sort of fraternity. Of course, my brother-in-law Dario was Italian and from a very old family. But most of them were just glorified grease monkeys. On the track they had nothing to lose, Spence had everything.

Rickenbacher was the worst. From the first time he set foot in our house he frightened me. If there ever was such a thing as a lean and hungry look . . . my God! And this was the man my husband chose to befriend. You know he had the gall to come to the funeral. Didn't he think I'd heard the rumors? It gets worse. Years later, after the war, he called and asked me to dinner. I think he actually wanted to court me. I suppose you can't blame a tiger for his stripes. But that doesn't mean I don't hate him.

SPENCER WISHART Blame Eddie? No, I blame myself. I simply lost track of reality. Ultimately, I think practically all of us were killed. But Lord, how I loved it while it lasted. The speed, the attention, the feeling you were doing something out of the ordinary. Also, I relished the fact that we were all equal on the track. I was a product of privilege . . . separation. This was different. Your skills and your courage, nothing else mattered. Certainly we were rivals, but there was also real camaraderie. Of course, in the heat of competition there was a tendency to go overboard. At the Elgin race, a lap before the wreck, Eddie and I were both diving for a corner and came together with a jolt. Obviously, I thought the car was intact or I wouldn't have continued. But then out of the blue I lost control. Who can say what really happened? After all, Eddie crashed that day too. I do wish I'd lived long enough to have a son.

Newspaper excerpt cited by John Dos Passos in *The 42nd Parallel*
> His speed it is thought must have been between a hundred and a hundred and ten miles an hour. His car wavered for a flash and then careered to the left. It struck a slight elevation and jumped. When the car alighted it was on four wheels atop of a high embankment. Wishart turned the car off the embankment and attempted to regain the road. The speed would not permit the slight turn necessary, however, and the car plowed through the front yard of a farmer residing on the course. He escaped one tree but was brought up sideways against another. The legs being impeded by the steering gear they were torn from the trunk as he was thrown through.

A cold rainy night early in 1915 finds Eddie in the midst of an existential *cafard*. Driven from sleep by dreams of unavoidable collisions, he sits in a straight-back chair, wrapped in a blanket, shaking. The smell of death is all over him. He pans back over his short existence, which now seems nothing more than a string of life-threatening experiences—fourteen in all, five in his youth and eight on the track, their frequency steadily increasing. It isn't hard to catch their drift or project an outcome. Other men might have vowed to step back and save their sweet asses. Eddie found Inspiration.

After hours of fearful contemplation, I suddenly realized that there was a lesson to be learned from my past. I concluded that the Good Lord must be paying close attention to me, and only His hand could have guided me through so many brushes with death. But I had grown lax in showing my gratitude. That was why I could not sleep. So I promised that very night to begin anew my boyhood regime of nightly prayer and thanksgiving. Also, I vowed from then on to strive diligently to improve the condition of both the body and the mind the Lord seemed so interested in preserving.

GOD Touching . . . at least he wasn't completely oblivious; but then neither was Iscariot. Too bad about Wishart. Yet I was interested in observing Edward at the lethal edge, curious to know if he would kill without hesitation, and how he might deal with the aftermath. So Wishart's death was really quite useful. Besides, the nice thing about humans is that there are always more of them.

EUGENE MEYER, PRESIDENT, MAXWELL MOTOR COMPANY I first got to know Eddie in the latter stages of 1914. He was a pleasant young fellow, with the knack of coming right to the point. The Duesenbergs may have built excellent racing cars, but they ran a shoestring operation, and Eddie understood that to remain in the front rank of drivers he needed adequate financial backing. This dovetailed nicely with our own objectives. We had only recently moved into racing, primarily as a means of advertising our passenger vehicles. But in spite of a large technical budget and an expensive contract with Barney Oldfield, we had gone basically nowhere. Eddie seemed like the fellow to provide the necessary impetus. So, on my recommendation, we brought him on board to run the team.

BARNEY OLDFIELD I'd been racin' deathtraps for well nigh fifteen years. And the days was long gone when I'd stick my neck out to pass some wingnut, only to see him break down two laps

later. I had a pretty sweet deal with Maxwell. The cars was slow,
so's nobody expected you to challenge. But they was reliable an'
often enough you could pick up a few bucks on that score. Well,
along comes Rickenbacher, loaded for bear an' aimin' to turn us
into a bunch of front runners. I had a year left on my contract,
so's I kept my mutt shut. But ole Barney was not about go out in
a blaze o' glory for Maxwell Motors an' some punk kid.

Edict posted in the Maxwell Team Headquarters
  The trouble with most people is they are not ready to do the
  things necessary to succeed. Don't be shy. Step up and show
  what you've got. Always be prepared. Whatever your job, however lowly, it could lead to the driver's seat. And if you still don't
  like the way this team is run, then get out and find another
  opportunity. That is my recipe for achievement. I know it works,
  because it worked for me.

                                                —E. Rickenbacher

BARNEY OLDFIELD   First thing, he gives us this little book a'
rules filled with shit like "Always conduct yourself as a gentleman,"
an' "Don't reflect discredit on automobile racing." Even had a
rule 'bout goin' to the toilet before a race. Made you wanna puke
. . . or better, piss on his foot.

BILL TEAGARTEN, MAXWELL DEVELOPMENTAL ENGINEER   He
was full of ideas about improving the performance of the cars, and,
since he had the ear of the boss, we had to listen. Not that it was
all bad. He was on the mark as far as increasing the compression
of the engines and streamlining the bodies. But he didn't seem to
understand that the cars were based on production components
never intended for racing. So there was always a trade-off. Sure
you could increase the horsepower and the speed, but with every
gain came an equivalent loss in reliability.

EDDIE O'DONNELL   Didn't see Rickenbacher until Sioux City in
July. He'd been with the Maxwells in California, an' hit a dry spell.
Cars kept breakin' down. Meantime, we was high-hattin' it, Due-
sies winnin' everything in sight. Kidded him a little 'bout leavin'
too soon. That grin of his drops right off his face. "O'Donnell, I
like you," he says. "But stay the fuck out of my way today. I got
some scores to settle." I guess he did. Charlie Cox in the Ogren

Special went out real smart and grabbed the lead. Track was wet, an' the cars was rooster-tailin' mud every which way. It was hell to pass, so I just tried to stay clear. But Eddie kept after Cox, finally catchin' him around mile 140. As he went by, Tom Alley saw Rickenbacher throw the rear out an' bury Cox in mud. Right away Charlie loses control an goes flippin' off the course, killing Vic McGraw the mechanic an' leavin' himself all busted up. After that Eddie won in a walk. Later we heard the organizers accused him of "foul driving." But he got his check anyway, loaded up his cars, an' left without ever visitin' Cox in the hospital. Didn't matter much, Charlie died that Sunday. It was the last big race they held at Sioux City.

Although I was fully involved with my racing duties during this time, I also made it my business to meet and cultivate men in high positions—bankers, industrialists, and other power brokers. As they spoke I paid close attention and studied how such men organized and expressed their thoughts. I kept a dictionary and practiced certain phrases repeatedly before a mirror. This led to an understanding of the importance of looking directly into a person's eyes when speaking to them—not a stare, simply a straightforward attentiveness. A number of people mentioned that I had an engaging smile. Therefore, I made it a habit to wear a smile whenever possible, particularly when I was being photographed. Handshakes were important too—firm, but not like a vise, grasping the elbow lightly with the other hand for special emphasis.

I continually worked on my weaknesses. At dinner parties, for example, I tried to concentrate on how the well-bred ate—what knives and forks they used for what courses. I worked hard at remembering names, compiling a comprehensive list of acquaintances and reading over it regularly to keep them fresh in my mind. I even gave myself a middle name. "Edward Rickenbacher" was too dull. I wrote out my name repeatedly, each time inserting a different moniker. "Edward Vernon Rickenbacher" had the best look and feel. It was dignified without being stuffy. And it didn't hurt a bit that the dancing Castles, Irene and Vernon, set the tone for style and elegance at the time.

BOO HERNDON, THE GHOSTWRITER   When he told me the story of the middle name, I said something like, "This is background, right? You don't want me to include it, do you?"

"Of course I want you to include it," he shoots back. "Why the hell do you think I told you?"

My wife, Bonnie, who really didn't like Rickenbacher, wasted about three dollars of a long-distance phone call laughing when I read her my notes.

EUGENE MEYER   At the end of the 1915 season, Maxwell decided to withdraw support from racing. With the exception of Sioux City, the year had brought no notable successes. And we felt the continual deaths and injuries stemming from the track reflected negatively on the image of safety and security we wanted to project for our passenger vehicles. Consequently, we informed the team that their employment was terminated. The following Monday morning I received a message that Eddie was at our Detroit headquarters, seeking an appointment. Although I expected some unpleasantness, I agreed to meet with him. I was surprised by his demeanor. Rather than complaints and accusations, he presented me with a simple proposal to purchase the four racing cars and spares for $25,000 cash. We had a great deal more invested, but I readily acceded, since the cars were now of no use to us. Although I was somewhat dubious of his ability to finance the actual operation of the team, my already high opinion of Eddie rose still further as a result of this transaction.

CARL FISHER, CO-FOUNDER OF THE INDIANAPOLIS MOTOR SPEEDWAY   Jim Allison of Allison Engineering brought Eddie over to my office at the track. I'd known him just as a driver. But now he was proposing that we back a racing team under his name. The war over in Europe, he said, had greatly reduced the number of foreign racing cars in America, both lowering the competition for prize money and potentially creating a shortage of entries. Eddie argued that a four-car team based on the Maxwells would not only help fill out the field, but stood a good chance of capturing significant earnings. The whole thing made a lot of sense, both financially and because it would be good for racing. Without much further thought or discussion we decided to jump in.

Finally I had my own racing team. The first thing I did was to get rid of Oldfield, who was by now a no-account. Besides myself driving, I brought in my old sidekick from Duesenberg days Eddie O'Donnell, and also Pete Henderson to replace Bill Carlson, who had been killed on the West Coast. Rather than bringing all of our cars to each race, my plan was to run two two-car teams, sending them out in different directions so that we might make every major race in the country.

We radically modified each car, taking special note of the parts that had failed us the year before and making sure to strengthen them. I added special streamlined bodies, a move that increased the top speed by ten to twelve miles an hour. But I also believed that this was not necessarily how races were won or lost.

In event after event I had observed precious time slipping through the fingers of practically every team in the pits. As often as not confusion reigned supreme. I had concluded that the secret to success was scientific analysis—breaking the pit stop apart into a designated number of tasks, which then could be assigned to specific crew members to perform in a set sequence. Relentless practice would hammer home the routine. I still remember the crew's grousing as I led them through pit stop after pit stop with a megaphone. To cheer them up I brought out a Victrola and played a catchy tune, "I Love California"—years before Muzak, mind you. But the real payoff would be on the track when our cars came and went in under thirty seconds, while the others wasted up to two minutes. It was this sort of attention to detail that convinced me that 1916 would be a banner year for our Maxwell Specials, which by this time might as well have been called Rickenbachers.

RICKENBACHER WINS AT SHEEPSHEAD BAY

In a race marred by the death of two competitors, Eddie Rickenbacher raced to victory over a star-studded field in the Metropolitan Speedway Championship here yesterday. Tragedy struck on the fifth lap when the Delage of Carl Limberg suddenly lunged into the wall, pitching both driver and mechanic 50 feet in the air, killing them instantly. . . .

—*New York American*, May 14, 1916

RICKENBACHER OUTLASTS DePALMA!

Edward Rickenbacher won the 300-mile event held yesterday at Raceway Park, beating favorite Ralph DePalma by a scant 30 seconds. In a victory which remained in doubt until the last laps, Rickenbacher's Maxwell Special edged DePalma's more powerful Mercedes through a combination of better tire wear and shorter pit stops. . . .

—*Tacoma Oregonian*, June 27, 1916

O'DONNELL AND HENDERSON 1, 2 IN RECORD TIME . . .

—*Kansas City Post Gazette*, August 14, 1916

RICKENBACHER WINS 100-MILE RACE

Eddie Rickenbacher, driving like a man possessed, won the Labor Day Special yesterday, edging Tommy Aitken's Peugeot. Entering the last lap on a badly damaged left rear wheel, Rickenbacher suffered multiple blowouts, resulting in a spectacular spin just short of the checkered flag, forcing him to finish on his brake drums. . . .

—*Indianapolis Sentinel*, August 14, 1916

RICKENBACHER TEAM WINS SEVENTH RACE OF SEASON!

Peter Henderson drove his Maxwell Special to a first-place showing in Santa Monica yesterday, putting a cap on a splendid racing campaign under the leadership of local hero Eddie Rickenbacher. At her home on East Livingston Street, the driver's mother, Mrs. Elizabeth Rickenbacher, stated, "Edward is the best driver in America, and also the best son. . . ."

—*Columbus Dispatch*, September 24, 1916

Eddie was now what he had dreamed of becoming—famous. It was a mantle new to his broad shoulders, and he was not yet fully schooled in its care and maintenance. But certain things were obvious. In New York, among the cold granite spires, doors were now open to him. Not necessarily the most formidable doors, but the sleeker, more approachable portals of the younger set whose money had come quickly. "Hello, Eddie . . ." "Good to see you, Eddie, how's the boy?" The path to his future lay here, among the money changers, the suites, the penthouses, the endless clubs. He understood that. But his instincts led him elsewhere. Like a moth he was drawn to the golden glow of Hollywood, where fame was being manufactured with what amounted to empirical precision. Here among the other beautiful creatures of the moment he might flutter and mate and revel. For he possessed a special gravity in the world of the evanescent; his end was likely to come in a flaming bone-splintering wreck, theirs merely in a string of bad reviews and disappointing box office receipts. So they took him into their rollicking flock, let him drink their elixir, and he in turn provided a certain grittiness for which they longed but seldom could deliver.

MACK SENNETT Initially I think he was a friend of Fatty's. Good-lookin' chap. I met him out at the track. Took me out for a couple of laps. What a ride, scared hell out of me. Started coming over to the studio, hangin' around the set. Seemed real interested, everybody liked him. Before long he was makin' the rounds with the rest of us.

MABEL NORMAND I remember we were all at a roadhouse up in Malibu drinking Rusty Nails. Those things were strong, and he was pouring them down like water. But they didn't seem to have any effect. Finally, I said something stupid like, "You must be an experienced drinker, Mr. Rickenbacher." He looked at me kinda funny and said that he hardly ever drank before coming to California. The party went on till the wee hours, and practically everybody was hideously boiled. I remember thinkin', I'm getting in his car. Well, sure enough, he drove sober as a judge. He got that reputation—"No matter what happens, Eddie will get you home." I guess it made sense. After all, he was a race driver.

ROSCOE "FATTY" ARBUCKLE Rick was making quite a name for himself as a stickman. So I decided to fix him up with Constance Boyd, who everybody knew couldn't get enough—a match made in heaven, I thought. Anyway, I assumed all went well, and in a sense it had. The next day Connie shows up looking very haggard. "Fatty," she says, "you know I like to fool around. But that was ridiculous. The guy literally didn't stop." After reports of a few more similar episodes, I got an idea. Now Charlie Murray was known to be able to fuck a stump, an' make it scream. What about a contest, I thought. Most in an hour, a night, a week, you name it. Ten thousand on the head, you might say. Charlie was game. But when I broached the subject to Rickenbacher he turned purple. "What if any of that got out?" He was literally terrified. At the time I just laughed it off. But considering what happened to me later, I probably should have taken him seriously.

CLIFF DURANT   I first met Rickenbacher at Ascot Park. I was doing a little racing back then. But primarily I was looking after my father's West Coast interests—building up Chevy dealerships (this was right around the time he regained control of GM) and making sure our cars got the right publicity. Rickenbacher was helpful that way—used him for promo shots, brought him around for dealer openings. Affable enough, always smiling, could give a decent little pep talk. Gradually worked his way into our social set. We had a house in Beverly Hills—big place—used to have parties practically weekly. Everybody came . . . him too. Adelaide was always trying to fix him up with her friends. Must'a liked him herself considering how things turned out. He returned the favor. I'd meet him for a drink occasionally . . . never failed to ask, "How's Ma?"—that's what everybody called her. Always gave him the same line: "Fine as silk, Eddie old man." Whatta laugh. If there ever was a burlap broad, it was Adelaide.

CHARLIE CHAPLIN   Yes, I was introduced to him several times. But I was more aware of him as someone in the public eye—newspapers, that sort of thing. Struck me as loudly and obnoxiously pro-German.

W.C. FIELDS   Edward Vernonnnn Rick-en-bach-er . . . Bap-tized him my-self . . . Liked the ladies, liked to bend an elbow . . . Man after my own hearrrttt . . . At this point though, clearly treading on dangerous grounnndddd. Hollywood always was a provincial burg—barely aware of the biggest war in history . . . 'long as we weren't in it. But even then there were certain things you didn't doooo . . . like rooting for Kaiser Biiilll. Though new in townnn, I took him aside my-self . . . told him to can that shit.

It was the Santa Monica track publicity man who dreamed up the story with an *L.A. Times* reporter. I was supposed to be a German nobleman—Baron Edward von Rickenbacher—whose father, a colonel in the horse guards, had disowned him. So I was racing in America to show my Prussian patriarch I could make a go of it without his help. When the story broke, I just went along with the gag. Who would have thought anybody would take it seriously?

GLENN MARTIN   One day this big Cadillac touring car pulled up to our hanger in Riverside. The driver was Eddie Rickenbacher. I recognized him from the papers and introduced myself. He said he'd never seen an airplane up close, and thought he'd pull over and have a good look. "I'll go you one better," I said. "How about a ride?" Well he acted as if I'd invited him for a game of Russian roulette. Started hemming and hawing. "I wouldn't want to put you to any trouble . . . ," et cetera. Finally—I guess it was because I'd recognized him—he very reluctantly climbed into the rear seat, pale as a ghost. Well . . . the flight was completely un-eventful, and after we landed he was sky-high, only then telling me he was normally terrified of heights. That wasn't exactly a surprise, since he had thrown up all over my extra flight jacket. But I think he felt really good about conquering his fear, and left wanting to know if I would take him up again. Nice guy, but he didn't make much of an effort to clean up the jacket.

Another time, I was out for a drive in the country outside of L.A. and spotted a small military aircraft stranded in a field. The pilot was fooling with the engine, apparently without much luck. I stopped and walked over to see if I could help. The fellow intro-duced himself as T.F. Dodd, a major in the Army Air Service. "Motor runs, but I can't get enough power out of it to remain in the air, much less take off." I suspected that the problem was with the ignition, and after a few minutes of looking I found a coupling that had partially separated from the magneto. It took me just a few minutes to set it right. "Let's see if it works," I suggested. He jumped in the cockpit and I gave the prop a good spin. The motor caught immediately and it ran perfectly. "Thanks a lot," he shouted. "You're a genius." With that he took off, and I walked back to my car. Little did I know how useful that chance encounter with Major Dodd would prove in the very near future.

LOUIS COATALEN, MANAGING DIRECTOR, SUNBEAM MOTOR WORKS Automobile racing, which had been a remunerative sideline for us, had recently been halted in England, presumably for the duration of the War. Having already invested heavily in advanced machines for the coming season, we intended to press on with the program in North America. Mr. Rickenbacher, apparently having liquidated his own team, seemed an ideal candidate to spearhead the effort. We therefore extended to him an invitation to come to England to help with final development of the vehicles, with the understanding that he would subsequently bring them to America and campaign them there. Unfortunately, the path to this objective proved to be strewn with difficulties we could hardly imagine.

STRICTLY CONFIDENTIAL

His Imperial Majesty's Secret Intelligence Service

MEMORANDUM FOR RECORD: February 10, 1917

FROM: Vincent Kell, Chief MI-5, Counter-Espionage
TO: Special Counselor on North America, Ministry of Foreign Affairs, Whitehall
SUBJECT: Activities of Edward Rickenbacher (alias Edward Vernon Rickenbacher, Baron Edward von Rickenbacher) whilst in the U.K. 12/21/16–2/3/17.

1. Pursuant to the Defense of the Realm Act of 1914, surveillance was mounted on the SUBJECT upon embarkation of the SS *St. Louis* on December 11, with the intent of barring entry upon arrival in Liverpool. After a three-day confinement aboard ship, however, the U.S. consul was able to produce a valid invitation from Mr. Louis Coatalen, Sunbeam Motor Works, Wolverhampton, and on these grounds insisted that the SUBJECT be allowed to enter the country. It was judged prudent to accede, and the SUBJECT was allowed passage to London on December 24 under heavy surveillance, both overt and covert. His baggage and personal effects were carefully searched, and no incriminating evidence was found

2. During the weeks that followed, the SUBJECT's activities consisted primarily of four sojourns at Wolverhampton, each lasting approximately five days, during which time he was required to check in with the local constabulary thrice daily. Although he gave all appearances of being fully occupied here with legitimate activities, he would invariably return to London on the weekends, where he was observed engaging in suspicious behavior. The SUBJECT repeatedly plied agents Robinson and Warren with drink, and then attempted to elude them while ostensibly returning to the Hotel Savoy. Mistakenly assuming success, he then proceeded to Piccadilly Circus where he attempted to establish liaisons with prostitutes. On those occasions when he succeeded, the women involved were closely questioned and reported no attempts to employ them as intermediaries and nothing unusual with respect to his demeanor save an abnormally high sexual appetite. During his entire stay the SUBJECT was rude, uncooperative, and disdainful of His Majesty's laws and officialdom.

3. It is the conclusion of MI-5 that the SUBJECT is almost certainly sympathetic to the enemy, but not probably one of their agents. Since he is a well-known sportsman, it was deemed not in the interest of Anglo-American relations to incarcerate him, and he was allowed to leave the country shortly after the United States Government severed relations with Germany. The Sunbeam Motor Works was notified forthwith that they were to have no further contact with the SUBJECT, and it is strongly recommended that he not be allowed to reenter the Realm.

STRICTLY CONFIDENTIAL

DRIVER CALLS FOR AUTO RACER SQUADRON

Eddie Rickenbacher, recently returned from an extended stay in England where he consulted with a number of British officials, today called for the formation of a flying squadron composed exclusively of professional racing drivers. "I was told that in the sky against the Germans we will need men accustomed to speed and danger and possessing lightning-fast reflexes," Rickenbacher told reporters. "Such men already exist, racing on the many sanctioned tracks across this country. They understand engines;

they understand engineering; what better way to utilize their skills than to train them to fly together in a pursuit squadron?" Rickenbacher went on to state that drivers including Ralph DePalma, Ray Harroun, Ralph Mulford, and Eddie Pullen had already contacted him expressing an interest in serving in such a squadron. . . .

—*Philadelphia Inquirer*, March 23, 1917

The racing squadron might not pan out, but I was positive that one day I would fight in the skies over the Western Front. On these grounds I decided to take care of the tonsillitis which had been troubling me for years. Dr. Harold Foster, a New York ENT friend of mine, recommended a tonsillectomy.

The operation appeared to have gone smoothly, and I came out from under the anesthetic groggy but satisfied that I was in good hands. Gradually, though, I began to realize that I was bleeding slightly from the throat. Assuming it was not anything to worry about, I said nothing. Through the night the flow increased noticeably, and I began to sense my life ebbing away with my blood. Vivid images took control of my brain. I witnessed a series of events from my childhood. Blanche Calhoun appeared. Mysterious forms and beautiful hues floated before me. How comfortable it was to let death gradually overcome my will to live.

Finally, it dawned on me that I had never given up without a fight. Now I was faced with the toughest fight there is, and I was damned if I was going to lose. From somewhere down deep I summoned the strength to order the nurse to call my doctor. After she left, I knew the moment of truth had arrived. But I was not alone. I called out for God's assistance, and together we fought the sweet deceptive call to oblivion.

I was barely conscious when Dr. Foster arrived at my bedside. He wrenched open my mouth, applied a sponge, and strained to see what had gone wrong. During the operation he had accidentally grazed an artery with his scalpel. He clamped it with a hemostat and instantly stanched the bleeding. I would live.

In the period when I was regaining my strength I thought a great deal about the incident. Death was always there lurking, behind even the most mundane activities. You might be taken when you least expected it. Beyond a certain point, avoidance was useless.

I had been subject to a great deal of danger, and undoubtedly would be subject to more. That was the fate God had chosen for me. Now I must accept it.

GOD   He was ready at last. My chosen instrument.

Chapter Three

GOD You can't say they weren't asking for it. Pipsqueaks with attitude. Well, My first experiment with bipeds, carnivorous dinosaurs, hadn't worked out either. All they ever did was grow. What I ended up with was big goofy-looking eating machines, and more wallets and belts than I could ever use. Now these humans seemed almost as dense . . . just more manual dexterity. Science, technology, the Industrial Revolution. What a bunch of crap. Einstein, Planck, Heisenberg, cribbing *My* owner's manual. All they were doing was saving Me the trouble of picking out a good meteor.

Meanwhile, there was this futile obsession with laborsaving devices. Why in hell did they think I made so many of them? Factories belching smoke, clogging up their lungs. Inoculations prolonging their agony. Electricity screwing up their sleep. Of course, I knew from the beginning I'd have to go along, even encourage it with shills like Rickenbacher. These humans were that lazy and selfish.

But weapons improvements! How could they be such morons? What did they think the Thirty Years' War was all about? Didn't they remember that their dopey arquebuses and cannon had something to do with the population of Germany dropping by a third in three decades? Well . . . actually they did seem to get the point for a couple of centuries. But now they were back at it again, big time. Damn Europeans, always causing trouble. Repeating rifles, machine guns, shrapnel, crucible steel artillery tubes, dynamite . . . that last guy had the nerve to set up a Peace Prize! What the hell did they think would happen when they used all that stuff? They had no idea. Nada. I thought about just washing my hands of the whole mess. But I'd already made the mistake of casting them after my own image so they wouldn't turn out with scales and big ugly teeth. Probably the most embarrassing thing I ever did. Had an investment though; I couldn't let 'em go down without some kind of warning.

I'd give them a warning, all right. Make the rest of their wars look like a cotillion. It wasn't hard. They'd all been planning for it anyhow. That fellow Schlieffen, his last words were: "Don't weaken the right flank" . . . not five minutes before he'd be giving his final accounting to all-merciful MOI. In August of '14, after I had Princip pop the Archduke and his wife, Sophie, Europe just went on cruise control. One after another they mobilized and declared their belligerency. Crowds gathered in capitals. They cheered and danced around and got drunk. It was going to be fun. A short glorious war would be had by all.

Fat chance with Maxim guns and French 75s. Within six months I had a million new visitors in uniform check in, and the rest had been driven into trenches stretching from the North Sea to Switzerland. Human moles, here they would live and die and eat and shit for four years in the company of an equal number of rats. Periodically they'd venture out in great waves, only to be mowed down before most got even a hundred yards. Verdun was good, but my personal favorite was the Somme. Thirty thousand Englishmen in one hour. I even thought about widening the Pearly Gates that day.

Still, I can tell you it was no easy job keeping this extravaganza going. Officers were no problem, true professionals, lemmings to the core. But right from the beginning enlisted men were regrettably short on the kind of enthusiasm I expected—persistent grumbling and malingering in the face of certain death, nothing worse for morale in the trenches. I tried several experiments with divine inspiration . . . Angel of Mons, that sort of thing. Wasn't really My style though, a bit too flamboyant and direct. After all, I had to maintain a certain distance in case wiseacres started asking too many questions about what sort of Diety would allow such a thing . . . plausible deniability it's called.

Then one day, shortly after the first corpse harvest at the Marne, it hit me—Air Combat! It was perfect! A grand divertissement, true entertainment for the huddled masses. After all, in a trench there was but one way to look, and that was up. Meanwhile the props and the players were just about in place. Flying machines—actually crashing machines—were all the rage. Meanwhile, I had this cadre of stone-cold killers I'd been saving for special occasions. Edward, of course, was one of my favorites; but I had others stashed all over—the Richthofen brothers, Immelmann, and Boelcke in Germany; then there were Georges Guynemer, René Fonck, Nungesser, and Raoul Lufbery in France; Albert Ball and Mick Mannock in the U.K., even Billy Bishop from Canada and Frank Luke in Arizona, to name just a few. Magnificent specimens one and all, it had seemed like such a waste to let 'em get chewed up and spit out in the mud. Now I had the perfect outlet. Knights of the Air! Challengers of the Wild Blue Yonder! Dogfights and gruesome flights! Broken necks and flaming wrecks! High adventure and terrestrial indenture! Over the top, boys! Just like the Red Baron! For England! For Germany! For France! Into the void ten million would rush. . . . Now that's Show Business!

ROLAND GARROS   The question, you see, centered on finding an efficacious mechanism for destroying enemy aircraft. At first our methods were crude to the extreme. Pilots and observers armed themselves with pistols, rifles, even darts. In one case an English biplane was apparently downed with a brick. In most instances, however, hitting a target moving rapidly through three dimensions was difficult to the extreme. Without doubt, machine guns were required. But how and where to mount them? The obvious answer was directly in front of the pilot, so as to enable him to aim simply by pointing the plane itself. Unfortunately, such a procedure was bound to shoot off the propeller.

In the fall of 1914, myself and my mechanic, Jules Hue, were struggling unsuccessfully with a synchronizer gear, when it occurred to us that simple steel plates mounted on the inner blades of the propeller might suffice. It was somewhat dangerous, scattering bullets in all directions. But enough went through to enable me to destroy four enemy machines, before I myself was shot down by ground fire on April 19, 1915. The wreck of my plane was recovered by the Boche, encouraging Anthony Fokker to perfect the interrupter mechanism that would prove the key to reliable forward fire through the arc of the propeller.

Meanwhile, I, Roland Garros, would be declared a hero of France, and one day a great stadium for tennis would be dedicated in my name. To this day it is the site of the world-renowned French Open, and each year hundreds of thousands come to view the competition. None of them have the slightest idea who I was.

MAX IMMELMANN When Fokker's Eindecker (monoplane) reached the front in June, practically nobody could fly it. They were all used to heavy, stable craft. I took to it immediately. It was light and responsive. At last I could fly the loops and delicate maneuvers I had dreamed of. Three days later I downed my first victim, an unarmed English biplane. It was an exciting experience, but I always preferred the aerobatics to the actual shooting. Oswald, he was different—a real battle flyer.

OSWALD BOELCKE   I had been flying the two-place Aviatik crates for almost a year when they gave me my first Fokker single-seater. It was my ideal; I could be pilot, observer, and fighter all at once. By this time I was used to flying observation missions over enemy lines. Now I would take Immelmann and the pair of us would hunt early in the morning. There was nothing I liked better than an Englishman for breakfast.

MAX IMMELMANN   Oswald remained extraordinarily calm and deliberate, never gave the slightest indication that we were risking our lives. But I began to have second thoughts after examining the wreck of an English Avro I had picked off from within a hundred meters. The pilot had received three bullets to the head which had exploded. As they carted him away the leather helmet seemed to float over his broken skull. The observer had fallen out and was impaled high in the branches of a tree; his body was entirely broken, just a bag of ooze.

OSWALD BOELCKE, *letter to his parents, November 12, 1915*
> As long as one stays calm and deliberate, an air fight in my fast, maneuverable Fokker is scarcely more dangerous than driving an automobile.

MAX IMMELMANN   Tony Fokker was an oily little shit. He would take us to Berlin, put us up in the best hotels, and show us off to the Grosser Generalstab. But as to coming up with an answer to the French Nieuports which appeared the following spring, he could do nothing. His E-4 didn't climb and the new biplane was so inertia-bound that you could have danced on the wing with your grandmother. I had no choice but to cling to the E-3 and hope my flying skills would carry me through. I lasted one month more. On June 18, 1916, the synchronizer failed and the guns shot away part of the air screw, which then shook the plane to pieces. All Germany had called me the Eagle of Lille, but that day I dropped like a stone. Occasionally pilots still perform a half-loop, half-turn known as the Immelmann. This is all that is left of me.

GEORGES GUYNEMER   I hated the Boche. But my health was not good. My father had to use all his influence simply to secure me entry into the air service as an assistant mechanic. They were desperate for pilots, so I received air training. Within four months of my initial flight I scored a victory. By Christmas I was Knight of the Legion of Honor. I loved to fight them at close quarters . . . in part because I would not miss, but also so as to see them die. The day after my twenty-first birthday I closed to within ten meters of a Fokker, and directed fifty rounds into the cockpit. My victim was so riddled that vaporized blood sprayed on my windshield, cap, and goggles. I felt as if I had been baptized.

DAVID LLOYD GEORGE, BRITISH PRIME MINISTER, cited in Ezra Bowen, *Knights of the Air*
> "The heavens are their battlefield. Every flight is a romance; every report an epic. They are the Knighthood of the War, without fear and without reproach. They recall the legends of yore, not merely the daring of their exploits, but by the nobility of their spirit, and amongst the multitudes of heroes, let us think of the chivalry of the air."

ALBERT BALL   There was no sportsmanship; it was simply killing. You looked for the new boys, the frightened ones with as little experience as possible. My best trick was to dive through a flock, and see who fled. He was my prey. My motto was "Shoot them before they learn enough to be dangerous." In my forty-seven so-called "victories," I don't think I was involved in more than two or three fair fights. One of them, it turned out, was with the bloody Red Baron's brother; would have liked to have killed that bastard.

FIELD MARSHAL SIR DOUGLAS HAIG   The significance of air combat was vastly overrated. Aviation's decisive contribution was the ability to observe from above—spotting for artillery and providing advance warning of enemy troop concentration. Bombing also played some positive role through the limited interdiction of supply. There was perhaps some justification for direct operations against craft devoted to these functions. But fighting between aircraft came to exist as an end in itself, thereby leading to tremendous waste and misdirection of resources.

CORPORAL HORACE WHEATON, INFANTRYMAN, 4TH BATTALION, GORDON HIGHLANDERS   Scraps in the air almost always took place to the rear of Jerry's front lines. But all that twisting and diving often enough drove 'em down far enough so's you could get a good look from the trenches. Nothing much to it. Sometimes one'd catch fire or start spinnin'. But seeing an actual crack-up was rare. On the way back our boys often flew pretty low. Jerry would fire up at 'em, and we'd fire at Jerry. Always cheered as they went over. Don't know why really. Fortunate bastards. Got to fight up there out of the muck. Slept under clean sheets every night, nice and cozy. Some blokes had all the luck in the war.

"The Dying Airman," a song popular among British pilots

> *The young aviator lay dying*
> *As in the hangar he lay, he lay*
> *To the mechanics who 'round him were standing*
> *These last parting words he did say*
>
> *Take the cylinder out of my kidneys*
> *The connecting rod out of my brain, my brain*
> *From the small of my back take the camshaft*
> *And assemble the engine again.*

GUSTAVE DELAGE, CHIEF OF DESIGN, NIEUPORT S.A.   Single-seaters fell into two distinct categories, largely determined by motor type. At one end of the scale were what I call "corkscrews," aircraft powered by rotary engines—air-cooled, composed of a radial bank of cylinders rotating around a fixed crankshaft at the same speed as the propeller. Such power plants were durable and compact, though limited in power. It followed that appropriate airframes must be as small and lightly constructed as possible. They were thus extremely maneuverable, characteristics enhanced by a biplane or even triplane configuration and a generous dihedral. Then there was the torque effect of the rotary, rendering them sluggish in left turns, but lightning quick in the opposite direction. In the hands of a pilot experienced enough to exploit these qualities such a craft might carve a series of tight spirals until it was in a completely dominant position. Top speed and ability to withstand steep dives were not strong points. There were even those who maintained that my Nieuports persistently shed their wings in precipitous descents . . . charges that were greatly exaggerated.

But they do bring me to the second type, the "stiletto." Such planes invariably employed motors identical to automotive designs. They paid a significant penalty in weight, and water cooling rendered them vulnerable to penetration during combat; but they were inherently more powerful and economical. Thus speeds were higher and frames could be reinforced to withstand radical descent. Prudence dictated that such machines avoid prolonged combat with more agile foes, but instead strike suddenly from on high. The SPAD series exemplified such qualities amongst our own *chasse* craft. But I should emphasize that these categories extended beyond borders. Thus, English Sopwiths, the Pup and the Camel, excelled in the role of "corkscrews," while the S.E. 5a and Bristol F.2B were wonderful daggers. So too among the Hun—the Dr. 1 triplane being the archetype of maneuver, and the Fokker D VII operating most effectively as a "stiletto."

The careers of pilots rose and fell with the craft they flew. Amongst the English, Philip Fullard and William Bishop were masters at the controls of their Camels, while the opportunism and marksmanship of Albert Ball and Mick Mannock were fully rewarded by the S.E. 5a. Of my countrymen, Guynemer was an artist of flight and the Nieuport *chasse* his supreme instrument. René Fonck, who took no unnecessary risks and hunted prey with the cold precision of a panther, flew best in SPADs. The Hun followed suit, Immelmann and Boelcke excelling in Fokker monoplanes and Werner Voss in the tri-wing, while Udet and Goering thrived on D VIIs. There was but a single exception, one in all the war who flew everything with equal facility. Attacking suddenly, maneuvering endlessly . . . it did not matter. That was the Boche Red Devil.

RITTMEISTER MANFRED FREIHERR VON RICHTHOFEN
Boelcke taught us everything. It was the most beautiful time of
my life. He handpicked each one for the first big Jagdstaffel
and showed us how to hunt. He gave us our credo, the Dicta
Boelcke—"Keep the sun at your back; attack from the rear; fire
only at close range; fly to meet any onslaught; never forget your
line of retreat." "If you will only remember these simple rules,
Manfred," he told me, "you cannot be defeated. You will never
die in the air."

ERWIN BOHME   Boelcke and I had an Englishman pinned between us, when another opponent pursued by friend Manfred cut
in front of us. During the simultaneous evasive maneuvers our
wings touched. Boelcke immediately went into a wild spin. After
a while his wing flew off, and the crate dropped in a rush. His skull
was crushed on impact.

MANFRED VON RICHTHOFEN, *letter to his mother,*
November 3, 1916
> You ask me why I risk my life every day. I tell you frankly; it is for
> our soldiers in the trenches. I want to ease their hard lot by keeping
> enemy flyers off them. Fortunately, my nerves have not yet suffered
> as a result of the bad luck of others.

LOTHAR VON RICHTHOFEN   There was always brotherly competition between us. But when I finally reached the Jagdstaffel,
Manfred had already bested Hptmn. Boelcke's tally of forty; so for
once we could be easy with each other. Still, my brother was in-
tensely aware of the scores of others, particularly Voss. He need
not have worried. One by one they went down—Allmenroder,
Muller, Festner, Dostler, little Wolff, and then Voss himself. All
dead before age twenty-five. It was quite ironic that I should survive the war. Manfred was always the cool and calculating one.

MANFRED VON RICHTHOFEN   For whatever reason, one fine
day I came upon the idea of having my crate painted glaring red.
I wanted my opponents to understand who they were engaging,
so their fear might distract them. To them I was the Crimson
Angel of Death.

HERMANN VON DER LIETH-THOMSEN, COMMANDER, IMPERIAL
GERMAN AIR SERVICE   April 1917 was a critical time for us. The
prospect of the other Anglo-Saxon power's entry into the war demanded that we redouble our efforts to end the war quickly. This
was the genesis of the so-called Amerikaprogramm to maximize
production of aircraft and motors at the expense of new models.
At the front our pilots were ordered to meet the growing aggressiveness of the English with increased flying time and also ruth-
lessness. It would come to be known as Bloody April.

MANFRED VON RICHTHOFEN
From battle report, April 10, 1917
   "I had shot the engine to pieces. . . . I no longer knew any mercy
   [and] for that reason I attacked him a second time, whereupon the
   aeroplane fell apart in my stream of bullets. . . . The fuselage went
   roaring down like a stone on fire. He fell into a swamp. The aircraft's tail simply burned up, marking the spot where he had dug
   his own grave."

Report to Aviation Inspectorate, July 17, 1917
   "Our aircraft, quite frankly, are ridiculously inferior to British Camels and 200hp SPADs. . . . The people at home have brought out
   no new machines for a year, while [we] remain stuck with these
   lousy Albatrosses."

Diary entry, January 23, 1918
   "It is a strange feeling. There, once again a pair of men shot dead;
   they lie somewhere all burned up and I myself sit here . . . and the
   food tastes as good as ever. I once said that to His Majesty . . . who
   said to me only: "My soldiers do not shoot men dead; my soldiers
   annihilate the opposition."

Diary entry, March 21, 1918
   "I am in wretched spirits after every aerial combat. . . . When I put
   my foot on the ground again . . . I go to my four walls, I do not
   want to see anyone or hear anything. I believe that the war is not
   as the people at home imagine it, with a hurrah and a roar; it is
   very serious, very grim. . . ."

KUNIGUNDE FREIFRAU VON RICHTHOFEN, MOTHER   It was
his last visit home and we were looking at a photograph of Jasta

11. I pointed at the image of a young flier and asked what had become of him. "Fallen in battle." I pointed to another, and Manfred replied: "He died also." Before I could say another word, his voice suddenly grew soft. "Mother, don't ask me more. All of them are dead." Within a month he was gone, shot through the heart the day after his eightieth victory.

MANFRED VON RICHTHOFEN In retrospect, I was a fool to think I could survive. Combat wore us all down; left us hopelessly impulsive. A fatal mistake became inevitable. The future was with the Americans. Just because they had no experience. The most ruthless would do well. But caution remained imperative. Some might even survive. For the war was near its end, and their time on the cross would be short.

It was a critical moment indeed. The Russians would be driven from the war, freeing a million Germans to throw at the Western Front. A bigger, dumber, more muscle-bound son of Schlieffen would lurch once more toward Mademoiselle Paris, threatening to contaminate her bistros with bratwurst. The entire French nation girded itself for the final test, voices joined in a single determined cry: "Deefense!! Deefense!! Deefense!!" Would it be enough? Probably not. But salvation was on the way in the form of the laggard Yanks. Jaws set, all apple-cheeked and freshly scrubbed, they greeted their Gallic allies with similarly inspiring words: "Lafayette, we're . . . uhh . . . here."

BURGESS LEWIS I gave Rickenbacher a call. He was in Cincinnati getting ready for the Decoration Day race out there, set to drive a Mercedes, of all things. "Look, Eddie," I told him, "we're sending an advanced staff over to France. We need some good men. How'd you like to be General Pershing's driver?" "The hell with that," he said right off. Kept going on about not wanting to be anybody's chauffeur and wanting to fly in combat. Finally I said, "Look, if you can't be in New York tomorrow, you might as well not bother coming."

After the brass hats put the kibosh on my idea of a squadron of race drivers, I tried to apply directly for flight training, only to be disqualified for not being a college man and under age twenty-five. Now I figured, if I go overseas where the fighting is, I might get around their ridiculous regulations. So I found myself, at noon the following day, a sergeant in the U.S. Army. The next morning I sailed as part of the initial contingent of the American Expeditionary Force. The adjutant was a barrel-chested captain by the name of George S. Patton, and also aboard was Colonel T.F. Dodd, acting as Pershing's aviation officer—the same Dodd whose airplane I got running back in California not so long ago.

COLONEL T.F. DODD On the first day out, Rickenbacher came storming up to my cabin fulminating about how he was stuck down in steerage. "Well, where the hell do you think they billet sergeants?" I came right back at him. "That's ordinary sergeants, I'm Eddie Rickenbacher." Well, his approach was so outrageous from a military perspective that it actually got me laughing. "Look, Eddie, I owe you a favor. So I'm going to give you a field promotion to top sergeant, and get you second-class passage. How's that?" "Why not first class?" With that I threw him out. What a character!

GENERAL JOHN PERSHING Rickenbacher? A malcontent, a loudmouth, and an insubordinate son of a bitch. It was all I could do not to strangle Lewis for digging him up. We had a war to fight, and that lunatic seemed intent on getting the both of us killed. He kept bringing up flying, and when I told him it was none of my concern, he would drive all the faster. Yet I couldn't just get rid of him, the reporters would have had a field day. But the story of the bobby pin was the last straw.

The French weren't the French for nothing. So it didn't take them long to peg Pershing, and make sure he was supplied with a string of observant cupcakes—stenographers, interpreters, girl Fridays. One day we were out in the Hudson, and he's in the back with some cutie. Before long he orders me to stop and take a hike, so she can take some dictation. About an hour and ten cigarettes later, I'm back in the car and it won't start. I tried everything. Finally I found the trouble, a bobby pin jammed underneath the throttle . . . maybe in the throes of passion. I thought the whole thing was funny, and made the mistake of telling a few fellows I trusted back at headquarters. The next thing I knew, the story was all over, and I was up to my neck in hot water. At least I didn't have Black Jack to drive anymore. It might have been a whole lot worse; but once again Dodd stepped into the picture, getting me designated his driver. One day we were out and about, when we came across another staff car stalled by the side of the road.

BRIGADIER GENERAL WILLIAM MITCHELL   The Packard had been dead in its tracks for almost an hour, when from out of nowhere come Dodd and his driver. This fellow jumps out of the car, Johnny on the spot, takes a quick look at the engine, and starts taking the carburetor apart. Turns out the gas filter was clogged. In five minutes he had the thing running like a top.

"Say," I said to him as he got back in Dodd's car, "I could use a fellow like you."

"I bet you could," he shot back, sporting a big toothy grin that was anything but military. As soon as I found out he was Eddie Rickenbacher, I had him detailed over to me, figuring if anyone could handle those narrow French roads, it was him. Well, I was right about the roads; but how in the hell was I supposed to handle Rickenbacher?

I knew right away this was my main chance. Billy Mitchell had just been put in charge of the entire U.S. air effort. If anybody could get me flight training, it was him. But driving for Mitchell was no picnic. In the asshole department he wasn't even close to Pershing, but as far as nooky went he was worse. Didn't even bother making me get out of the car. Just kept me drivin' in front, while he was drivin' in back. "Keep your eyeeees on the road, Eddie," I'd hear him chortling back there. And if that wasn't bad enough, every time I brought up flying he found a way to change the subject. After two months of this I was thoroughly steamed. I figured that if I was ever going to get the bastard's attention, I was going to have to do something pretty dramatic. I knew he had a hot temper, but I also knew I didn't have much to lose. So I bided my time.

BILLY MITCHELL   One day—it must have been in the middle of November '17—I had a critical meeting back in Paris, and we were running late. I told Eddie to step on it, and he was making pretty good time. Then, without so much a warning sputter, the engine cuts out completely, and the Packard rolls to the side of the road. I yelled up to him to get a move on and fix the goddamned thing, while I went back to my paperwork. Well, I looked up after about five minutes, and there's Rickenbacher leaning against the front fender having a cigarette. The hood's not even up. I got out to read him the riot act, and he just looks at me, grinning. I swear, if I'd had my sidearm I might have shot the son of a bitch right then and there.

"I know you fucked this thing up somehow," he said. "Now you get it started, and that's an order." I held my ground. He threatened me with everything from a court-martial to burning at the stake. "What the hell is the matter with you?" he said finally. I saw my opening.

"I'll tell you what's the matter. You've got me rotting behind the wheel of this vehicle, when I should be out over the Front killing Fritzes."

"I've told you a thousand times, you're too old to fly."

"Bullshit, nobody at the track ever had the nerve to tell me I was too old to run their ass off the road."

"You know how long the average pilot stays alive at the Front? Three fucking weeks, you insubordinate idiot."

"Right you are! But I'm not average, and I'm used to playing rough—not like your namby-pamby college boys."

"All right, all right. I just realized how much I want you dead. If you'll get this thing running, I'll make sure you're transferred over to air training. Get you out of my hair once and for all."

BILLY MITCHELL   In wartime you have to know when to improvise. A year later American aviation would have its Ace of Aces, and, in the meantime, I would make the meeting with time to spare.

The basic flight training center was run by the French at Tours. Everything was French—French trainers, French aircraft, and . . . you guessed it, only French spoken. There were fifteen of us Americans in the class, mostly former drivers for the Red Cross who, like myself, had jumped at the chance to get to the War Zone ahead of the main U.S. contingent. Initially, practice time was spent in little craft called "penguins," monoplanes with their wings cut in half so they couldn't actually take off. Because of my experience with cars, I was accustomed to steering with my hands; but "penguins," like other aircraft, had rudders meant to be steered with the feet. Once the little engine had built enough revs there was a control stick to lift the tail up off the ground. Basically, everything felt just about the opposite of what it seemed it should be, and it took a good deal of concentration to overcome old habits.

In about a week I graduated to Caudrons, dual-control aircraft with huge wings making them easy to fly. After two sessions with an instructor jabbering absolutely nothing I could understand, I got my chance to solo. I was as jumpy as a cat on fire, and almost hit the hangar on takeoff. Landing was worse. I made what I thought was a perfect approach, eased back on the stick, and waited to touch down. Nothing happened. Finally, I looked over the side, only to find I was still about fifty feet off the ground! Lucky the practice field was enormous and I was able to gradually work my way down. Others weren't so fortunate. In the seventeen-day course we had four bad crashes and two fellows were killed. But at the end I had twenty-five hours of flight time, and emerged as a second lieutenant ready for advanced training . . . or so I thought.

MAJOR JAMES MILLER, TEMPORARY COMMANDER, ADVANCED FLIGHT SCHOOL AT ISSOUDUN   He hit the ceiling when he found out. "Engineering officer! Engineering officer!" He was literally screaming. "You're telling me my job is to keep those flying jalopies running for your precious Ivy Leaguers. Four-flushing bastards! If I wanted to be a mechanic, I'd still be working for Fred and Augie Duesenberg," etc. etc. Most officers would have had him placed under arrest. But I'd only been a major for a couple of weeks, and besides, I knew Eddie. So I just let him blow off steam until I could talk some sense into him. I explained that because of his age we had to slip him in the back door, and that there'd be plenty of flight time under "other duties as assigned." Finally, he calmed down and went off grumbling. But he got that shop running in nothing flat. Brought in a hundred thousand dollars' worth of equipment, and turned it into a first-rate operation. As for me, I lasted about two months. Forgot to salute "Tooey" Spatz and they shipped me back to disbursement in Paris . . . always a better banker than an officer.

So Eddie looked after his motley brood of training aircraft, flew whenever he could, and watched as progressively larger waves of cadet birdmen broke over Issoudun. He greeted them with profoundly mixed emotions. The English boots, custom-tailored uniforms, and polished Sam Browne belts, the endless chants of "Boolah Boolah" and "Bahh Bahh Bahh" that rose over the barracks at dusk, all served to confirm what he already knew . . . the Halls of Ivy had reserved a special spot in the sky for America's young thoroughbreds. "I'll give them lost sheep," he muttered as he commandeered a brigade's worth of buckets and sent them out in the mud to pick up rocks. To them he became the Prussian, to him they remained Ivy League Assholes . . . and yet, and yet . . . As he looked into their soft eyes, he caught reflections of the young faces he had once seen at tracks everywhere. At times like this he took no pleasure from his own hardened visage. He had glimpsed death and learned to live with it. But it had changed him. Now it was their turn to look. Some would live. Some would die. None would ever be the same. And in this he felt a great welling sadness, and continued to wonder how many had any idea what they were getting into.

2ND LIEUTENANT JOHN MCGAVOCK GRIDER, *war diary,*
September 20, 1917
"I haven't lived very well, but I am determined to die well. I don't want to be a hero—too often they are all clay from the feet up. . . . Thank God I am going to have the opportunity to die as every brave man should wish to die—fighting—and fighting for my country as well. That would retrieve my wasted years and neglected opportunities."

EUGENE "JACQUES" BULLARD I *was* a combat aviator. After a mob a' crackers almost lynched my papa in St. Louis, I got the hell out and came to France in '11. When war broke out I caught on with the Foreign Legion—wounded twice at Verdun. During my hospital time I wrote about flight trainin' and was accepted. Flew with Spa. 93 and 85. By this time Wilson had us in the war, and I offered my services. Over 200 Americans flyin' for France—every single one 'cept me accepted into the Air Service. Said I could work in the Transportation Corps. Otherwise Negroes need not apply.

LIEUTENANT QUENTIN ROOSEVELT, *letter to his father,*
January 14, 1918
Pilot training is almost over and I will soon be flying against the Hun. So as you used to say of San Juan Hill, I am on the verge of my Busy Time. My only fear, Papa, is not living up to the ideals you have set for us, and not proving myself worthy of this magnificent band of brothers who will soon sweep the skies of Boche. They are truly a wonderful crowd, their gaze set far above the nar-

row bounds of self-interest and firmly fixed upon the ultimate good
of mankind. I am honored just to be here among them. If you
could only join us, I know you would share my pride. Please give
Mama my love and tell her not to worry. The Lord Above looks
after me, and is my shield.

2ND LIEUTENANT FRANK LUKE, *letter to Bill Elder,*
March 22, 1918

Just a note to let you know how I am getting along. Well, there's
sure no doubt about it. I'm in the Army. They get me up early,
and put me to bed even earlier. The chow's not bad though, and
they give you plenty of it. Most of the fellows here speak some
French so they can translate what the instructors are saying. So far
I've wrecked two planes, which everybody says is a good sign of
being willing to fly on the edge. I sure hope so. I even gave up
smokes getting ready for Fritz. I'm sorry you can't be here; I miss
you like hell. I swear, when I get to be Ace of Aces, I'll make them
bring you over as my Orderly.

None of us had any idea what a real fight in the air might be like.
Instructors were some help, but mainly we were left to pick up
whatever tricks we could manage during free flight time. The cadets spoke about one stunt in particular, the tailspin. It turned out
to be a very valuable maneuver, since a plane spinning in this manner was not only hard to hit, but also looked like it was out of
control. Many an out-flown aviator would escape death's clutches
with a tailspin. But it wasn't easily learned. The pilot had to first
stall his aircraft, then kick the rudder all at once, allowing the nose
to fall and the tail to start swinging around building momentum.

With nothing more to go on, I took a Nieuport about twenty
miles south of the base and began private practice. The first day I
couldn't manage even one. But through sheer persistence I reached
the point that I could spin it like a top. I heard students boasting
about how many revolutions they managed before pulling out, but
I said nothing.

Now it just so happened that on Sundays the college boys were
in the habit of putting together a baseball game, which often attracted the top brass from Paris. It was also my chance to treat
everybody to a tailspin deluxe. I came in over the diamond at about
500 feet, stalled the plane, and pushed it into a spin right over the
pitcher's mound. Down it came, right on top of the players and

spectators, lower and lower until everybody ran. Only then did I break it off—knowing I had made a real impression.

MAJOR CARL "TOOEY" SPATZ, COMMANDER, ADVANCED FLIGHT SCHOOL AT ISSOUDUN   They just about ripped me a new asshole for that caper. Jesus Fucking Christ, we had three BGs drivin' their dicks in the dirt trying to avoid that maniac. Grounded him for thirty days, but I knew there'd be trouble so long as we kept him here. There was one place for Rickenbacher, and that was at the Front. So, after a decent interval, we shipped him to the gunnery school at Cazeau with the rest of the Cadets.

I'll tell you though, that was one helluva spin. He was no natural flyer, but he learned what he needed to stay alive.

ELIZABETH   I never vorried ven Edward vas overseas. It vas the racing that vas really dangerous. He wrote me that there vas plenty of room in the sky, so I told him to be sure to fly slow and close to za ground. Vun thing I didn't write vas about the war. Vy was we shooting at Germans, ven everybody knew it vas England's fault? The English treated my son like a criminal ven he vent there, and I knew he didn't like them. But this I kept to myself.

Cazeau was a pretty, out-of-the-way place set on a lake. At first they had us out in little boats blasting away at targets with .30-caliber rifles, while we bobbed up and down. I don't remember anybody hitting anything. Next, they gave us a technical introduction to Lewis guns and Vickers .303s. Finally, they sent us up in Nieuport 11s with a single machine gun. The idea was to hit a sock towed by a Caudron. The first time I got too close and cut the tow rope in half. After I landed a Frenchman ran up yelling, "*Tirez là*," pointing to the sock, "*pas là, pas là*," gesturing at their plane. "What the hell," I thought, "I'm not going to be shooting socks at the Front."

LIEUTENANT DOUGLAS CAMPBELL   We all struggled at Cazeau. Rickenbacher in particular was no Hawkeye. But his ears pricked up when we got a hands-on with the machine guns. He wanted to know exactly how they worked, and how to keep them working. Considering how the things always seemed to jam up in combat just when you needed them, I'd have to say that Eddie was probably the only one of us who got anything at all out of the school.

But technically at least we could now fly and we could work the guns, so it was off to try our hands against the Boche.

JOHN MCGAVOCK GRIDER, *war diary, May 13, 1918*
"I'm either coming out of the war a big man, or in a wooden Kimono. I know I can fight, I know I can fly, and I ought to be able to shoot straight. If I can just learn to do all three at once, they can't stop me."

2ND LIEUTENANT JOSIAH P. ROWE, JR., *letter to his mother, June 28, 1918*
Well, there are lots of things you won't understand until I get back home, but I will say that we took the course that would enable us to get to the Front with the least possible delay. I would go to Borneo if it would hasten the time when I could take an active part in the fight.

MAJOR RAOUL LUFBERY To the U.S. Army the Lafayette Escadrille meant nothing. We had flown together against the Boche for nearly two years, and now they scattered us to the four winds. The only American pilots with the slightest combat experience and the best they could think to do was to have us read eye charts and check our blood pressure to determine whether we were fit to fly. It was said that I was to be one of the fortunate few. After I manned a desk at Issoudun, they made me a major and dispatched me to the 94th Pursuit Squadron at Villeneuve, where I would find a flock of downy goslings I was expected to keep alive. *Merde!*

Lufbery was actually a French soldier of fortune, who had picked up U.S. citizenship before the War through a hitch with the Army in the Philippines. He was barely five feet tall, but barrel-chested, with a look to him I hadn't seen since the racing circuit. No personality, none—but he had fourteen confirmed kills with the Escadrille. So I made it my business to get to know him, and pump him for as much information on air combat as I could.

RAOUL LUFBERY The situation in the 94th was abysmal. None of them had more than a rudimentary knowledge of combat flying, and only a few appeared capable of learning. Yet the command elements were pressing for a commencement of purely American patrols. Our Nieuports hadn't even been fitted with their guns!

The situation was impossible . . . but unavoidable. I chose Rickenbacher and Douglas Campbell for the premier mission over the Boche lines. Both had taught themselves to fly, and appeared to have at least some instinct for survival.

The results were predictable. The neophytes had trouble keeping formation, lurching wildly when they came under Boche anti-aircraft fire, or Archie as the English say. Back on the ground, they nonetheless seemed quite pleased with themselves. Pleased until I questioned them in front of the others as to what they had seen. "Nothing, no planes, eh? But of course you saw the flight of five SPADs which passed underneath us as we crossed the lines, or perhaps the second group of five that went by not 500 yards in front a quarter hour later. And what of the four Albatrosses, and the single Halberstadt? Note please also, Lieutenant Rickenbacher, the holes in your wing where Archie passed through. Hadn't noticed, eh? Is it not a rare privilege to fly with the blind?"

On the track I'd never missed a thing; now I was faced with learning to see all over again if I wanted to stay alive. And that wasn't all. A session stunting with Lufbery—snap rolls, barrels, and Imelmanns—convinced me I wouldn't have the slightest chance with any Hun worth his salt. But if life had taught me anything, it was that practice makes perfect. So I flew as much as possible, working on every crazy evolution I could think of, and coming home all too often with vomit dripping over myself and the cockpit. And to add to my misery, while I was building for the future others in the 94th were cashing in immediately. By April 15, Doug Campbell and Alan Windslow each had bona fide kills, while the closest thing I could point to was an aborted dogfight with Charley Chapman, who I mistook for a Hun. I kept telling myself that lucky kills and instant fame could be dangerous, and that all comes to him who waits. At long last, after almost a month of searching, I found my first cooperative Fritz.

FLIEGER (PRIVATE) HERMANN MEISE Two years in the trenches convinced me that I was invincible; besides, flying would help me at home with the girls. So I jumped at the chance. Barely six weeks of training and I found myself in a new Pfalz high over French territory, having lost my staffel and become hopelessly lost. I thought of simply landing my craft and surrendering to the nearest poulis. But then I looked up to see two Nieuports already firing.

I remembered only to dive, hoping they dare not follow lest their wings fall off. I had no such good fortune. Each time I looked back they were closer to my pig of a Pfalz. Then I heard shots hitting the fuselage, and felt a terrible pain in my legs and chest. They were gone, but I could not catch my breath. I thought at the last of my mother, who I loved very much.

I had my Hun. My wingman, Jimmy Hall, and I swooped down on the field side by side, and taxied our machines to the hangar. I can't think of a better moment in my life. Victory! Almost immediately we were surrounded. The French had already telephoned to confirm the kill, and the whole of the 94th turned out to offer me their heartfelt congratulations. Though news of my first victory went directly back to America and letters and telegrams flowed in by the hundreds, the approval that matters comes from your comrades. Never has there been a closer bond than the one that was built among the American aviators fighting in the skies over France. And no band of brothers had a greater élan than those of the 94th.

But Squadron 95, which also occupied our aerodrome, contained much the same quality of material. One of the newly assigned fliers there was President Theodore Roosevelt's son Quentin. His commander, perhaps with this in mind, named him Flight Leader before he had even made a single trip over enemy lines. Quentin accordingly tried hard to avoid the honor, but was directed to obey orders. So, on the night before his first patrol, he pulled his pilots aside. "Look, any one of you knows more about this game than I do. So I've made up my mind that tomorrow morning you, Buckley, will take the lead. I'll drop back into your slot. They may be able to name me Flight Leader, but rest assured the best pilot is going to be in charge."

CAPTAIN JAMES NORMAN HALL That trigger-happy lummox shot me down—Rickenbacher. I can't prove it, but all signs point in that direction. At around eight in the morning of May 7 we got a call that two Hun aircraft were over Pont-à-Mousson heading south. Eddie Green, Rickenbacher, and I jumped into our machines, and headed off in hot pursuit. We found them without much trouble, two-seater Albatrosses, and set up for an attack. Not surprisingly it was a trap; I caught sight of four Pfalz scouts lurking in the distance waiting to bounce us. But they were too far off, and I calculated that we could dive through the Albatrosses with time and distance to spare. Signaling the others, I went in ahead, guns blazing, Rickenbacher close behind. The next thing I knew the rudder went dead, controls completely shot away. Conceivably it could have been observer fire from the Albatrosses, but more likely it was him. I went into a spin immediately, and ended up crash-landing with a badly broken ankle. The Germans took good care of me, and I spent the rest of the war in the hospital in Metz. By the time I crossed over after the Armistice, Rickenbacher was a national hero. So I buttoned my lip. I never saw him again. But shortly after Nordhoff and I published *Mutiny on the Bounty*, I received this sheepish congratulatory letter, hinting that although my "accident cost the Air Service a fine pilot, it also may have saved the reading public a great author!" Imagine that.

2ND LIEUTENANT REED CHAMBERS Although Jimmy Hall survived his crash, the immediate impact of the news set off a tragic train of events. Raoul Lufbery was a pal of Hall's from Escadrille days, and when he heard of his friend's apparent death he went on a one-man rampage, chasing every Boche plane he could find, regardless of the odds. Well, four days later an unsuspecting Halberstadt wandered over the aerodrome and Lufbery was alerted by our Archie blasting away. He commandeered a motorcycle, and roared over to the hangar. His own machine being down for repairs, he grabbed the first flightworthy Nieuport and took off. In plain sight of everyone, he worked his way up to the Boche, and began a determined assault. But on his second pass, the Hun gunner put a long burst into his fuel tank which ignited just in front of the cockpit—every pilot's nightmare, being roasted alive. Luf squirmed out of his seat, and straddled the fuselage. But the flames swept back over him after several seconds, and he jumped. We got a car and raced off in the direction of his fall. We arrived to find him impaled on a picket fence, a French shoemaker's wife holding a bloody stake she had already pulled from Lufbery's throat. That was the end of America's first Ace of Aces and our greatest teacher. We were on our own, literally and figuratively without parachutes.

Hell, the softest thing we had to land on were those nurses. God! Talk about Angels of Mercy.

LENORA TOLES, 2ND FIELD NURSES' DETACHMENT When we arrived at the hospital at Villeneuve the only thing we were expecting was a mountain of work in the grand tradition of Florence

Nightingale. Imagine our surprise when we discovered the 94th and 95th. Pursuit squadrons they certainly were. By the end of the first week there was barely a foolish virgin left among us. What were we to do? We were surrounded by handsome, well-bred young men, many of whom would soon be dead; it was practically our patriotic duty! Unlike most young women of our generation, we knew exactly where babies came from and the dangers of disease. So prophylactics were the rule. But other than that—as they say in the song—"Anything goes" . . . or went. One minute you were on the ward, all prim and starched, the next you found yourself in a virtual seraglio. Except that we ran it. That was the marvelous part. We chose whomsoever we pleased. And most of us were pleased by practically every one.

Rickenbacher? No, not me. That jack-o'-lantern grin put me off a bit. But plenty found him attractive, especially if a girl was really in the mood. You see, he had a reputation for being nobody's one-trick pony.

CORPORAL BLANTON EDWARDS, CREW CHIEF, 94TH SQUADRON　Lieutenant Rickenbacher watched us like a hawk—engine mechanics, riggers, any swingin' dick with a wrench. Not like them college bozos, knew the planes inside out. Abe Karpe, little Jew gunnery chief from Brooklyn, really had it rough, especially if the lieutenant's guns should happen to jam. He'd have him filing down the slides, coatin' everything that moved with Vaseline. Christ, at one point he had Abe measuring bullets with calipers. It's a wonder anybody got any sleep.

REED CHAMBERS　Eddie liked to do his hunting in the morning, and he dragged me along for company. Three-thirty, I'd hear him like the Grim Reaper banging at my door. By five we'd be behind enemy lines circling at 20,000 feet, waiting for the sun to rise and the first Boche patrols to take off. I've never been colder in my life. It must have been fifty below up there. After an hour or so, I'd get to the point I couldn't stand it and head home half-frozen. When he finally rolled in, he was always furious. "Why'd you leave me? If I'da nailed one, who in hell was going to confirm my kill?"

In late May, one of my early morning forays had unexpected results. I'd spent most of my fuel drifting around over the Metz aerodrome, but the Heinies there simply weren't biting. So I tried my luck over the field at Thiaucourt. After climbing to 18,000 feet, I shut down the motor to conserve fuel. While I circled with just the wind whistling through my struts, I spotted three tiny Albatrosses taking off. Apparently having no idea I was there, they flew directly south, single file. I dropped my Nieuport into a shallow dive to get some momentum, and then switched on the ignition. As soon as the motor caught I opened it up and headed straight down toward the last Albatross. What seemed like minutes passed. Finally, the pilot turned his head to look up. He saw me and panicked, trying to dive out of range. But I was too fast. At fifty yards I pulled the trigger. I saw the tracers hammer into his torso. I felt no pity, only grim satisfaction. He had been a fool to dive rather than maneuver. Now he was paying the price.

It was only when my victim fell out of control that it crossed my mind to break off the dive. I must have been doing at least 150 mph when I eased back on the stick. A sickening ripping crash followed almost immediately. The cloth covering of the right upper wing had torn away. The Nieuport immediately flipped over on its side. Then the tail jerked up and began spinning. It was my old friend the tailspin, only this time I had absolutely no control. It was a death sentence, and just to make sure the two remaining Albatrosses were diving on me, pouring a stream of lead into my crippled ship. "Why bother?" I remember thinking. "What bird plays possum with a broken wing fluttering in the wind?"

Down and down I fell, waiting for the plane to shake itself apart. All the chapters in my life, both large and small, began flashing before me. I thought of those I had disappointed, and prayed for another chance.

"Oh God, help me," I screamed into the wind.

The ground raced up to get me. Then, as though something took my hand, I spastically gunned the throttle. The sudden burst pushed up the nose. I reversed the rudder, and pulled back on the stick. Like magic the spinning stopped. Sinking steadily, engine coughing, controls shoved full over, I somehow crossed our lines and lurched home for a landing. After I taxied my bullet-riddled, nearly wingless craft to the hangar, I was determined to maintain my composure. But as soon as I set foot on the ground, my knees melted and I found myself sitting in the grass.

GOD   Lucky for him I was paying attention. Also, he didn't mention that he shat his pants.

JOHN MCGAVOCK GRIDER, *war diary, June 10, 1918*

"I'm beginning to understand the term 'Anti-Christ.' . . . What a joke it must seem to Him to see us puny insignificant mortals proclaiming that we are fighting for Him and that He is helping us. . . . The heavens must shake with divine mirth."

JOSIAH P. ROWE, *letter to his mother, June 21, 1918*

These Nieuport planes we use in the 94th are wonderful little machines and the mechanics keep them in excellent condition. Seldom is there a forced landing on account of motor failure, but quite a few fellows get lost in cross-country trips. . . .

OUR EDDIE AN ACE, SCORES FIFTH VICTORY!

Famed racing car driver and local resident Lieutenant Eddie Rickenbacher is carving a name for himself in the skies above the Western Front. A member of the 94th Pursuit or "Hat in the Ring" Squadron, Rickenbacher took his place among the war's elite pilots or "Aces," when his fifth aerial victory was confirmed on June 1. In less than two months of combat flying Rickenbacher has already won three Distinguished Flying Crosses and the coveted French medal for valor, the Croix de Guerre. Interviewed at her home on East Livingston Street, the pilot's mother, Mrs. Elizabeth Rickenbacher, stated, "Edward is the best pilot in America, and also the best son. . . ."

—*Columbus Dispatch*, June 12, 1918

FLYING ACE TAKES HUN OUT OF NAME

The Army Air Service's most famous pilot, Lieutenant Eddie Rickenbacher, is spelling his name differently these days. His many friends are receiving letters from the Front signed Eddie Rickenbac*k*er—the Germanic sounding "H" having been dropped for an All-American "K." For some this may seem an important clarification. But this reporter doubts that the Hun Flying Circus ever had any question whose side he is on.

—Damon Runyon's "Around and About,"
New York American, July 1, 1918

BILL RICKENBACHER   It was hard to believe that little squirt who was once my kid brother and this fellow in the newspapers were one and the same. Never ceased to amaze me. I'd get used to him being one thing, and then I'd look up and he was something else. Always a success. I'd go back to our childhood and try to pick out one single thing that made the difference. But I never could. It was as if somebody or something was looking out for him, pushin' him along.

On the face of it, things were going like clockwork. After Jimmy Hall's crash I became deputy squadron commander, and Mitchell told me he had higher things in mind. But with rank came responsibility—watching over young pilots; making sure that everybody's machines were properly maintained—and less time to look for trouble and score kills on my own. Then there was the matter of the earaches. The constant changes in altitude and temperature cause most pilots trouble. But mine settled into a deep infection which made every mission agony and even began to affect my balance on the ground. One morning I awoke to find myself covered with sweat and shivering uncontrollably. There was nothing else to do but let the doctors ship me off to the hospital. That stay probably saved my life.

I responded to treatment almost immediately, and was quickly on the mend. But the quiet of the hospital gave me the time for thought and self-analysis, my first since the rush of war began. As I looked back in detail over each of my aerial combats, the tremors of fever were replaced by tremors of fear when I began to realize how many foolish errors I had committed. I stopped right there and prayed for my deliverance. But I also knew the Lord helps those who help themselves, so I continued thinking. Some questions, like the skill of my prospective opponents, were clearly beyond me. But I was able to grasp that there had been a pattern behind my mistakes, that I was making the same ones over and over. Now I saw that in the heat of combat I had repeatedly cast caution—my best friend—aside. I knew . . . we all knew the Nieuport's wings were fatally flawed. Yet I had persisted in diving with reckless abandon in hopes of obtaining a quick victory. I longed for the sturdy SPADs we had been promised. But until that time came, I vowed to fly within my Nieuport's limitations, no matter how many kills it cost me. I understood at last that the key to becoming a better pilot was survival. And with that realization I dropped off to sleep, and awoke with a feeling that a great load had been lifted from me.

GOD Go, Eddie! Go, Eddie! Go, Eddie! Go . . . go, go, Eddie! Go, Eddie! Go, Eddie! Go . . . go, go, Eddie! Go, Eddie! Go, Eddie! Go . . .

BILLY MITCHELL Back home, Rickenbacker was hotter than Krazy Kat. Like it or not, in the eyes of the man on the street, he was the U.S. Air Service. So I made it my business to take him under my wing, made sure he met the right people, and above all said the right things to the gentlemen of the press. When he took sick I was more than a little concerned that he might be losing his nerve. I visited him at the hospital, and talked to him carefully. He seemed okay, but definitely down in the mouth. So when he started feeling better, I decided it was time for a pick-me-up. Took him over to Orly to have a look at the latest SPAD XIII—220-hp Hispano-Suiza engine, wings so strong you couldn't blow 'em off with a hand grenade, guns mounted on top of the manifold to keep 'em warm and jam free, the works. I swear, he was like a kid in a toy store, picking over every detail. Finally, I left him there and started walking back to the car. Before I got very far I saw these two French officers yelling and waving their arms. God-damned if he hadn't jumped in the plane and taken off. At first I thought he'd just circle the field; but the last we saw of him he was headed due east toward the Front. Just took the thing back to the 94th like some sort of trophy. Believe me, it took some fast talking to head off a court-martial, not to mention an international incident. But it was the last time I worried about Rickenbacker losing his nerve.

JOHN McGAVOCK GRIDER, *war diary, July 23, 1918*
"I have learned many things, especially that discretion is the better part of valor."

QUENTIN ROOSEVELT, *letter to his father, July 6, 1918*
I am writing you on the occasion of my first combat victory. You will be gratified to learn that it has come about as a result of the fabled virtue of Caution, which you and my commanding officers are continually urging upon me. The episode began this morning

over enemy territory, when I reluctantly departed from my formation to investigate a flight of enemy machines, which my squadron-mates persisted in ignoring. Upon discovering they numbered twenty to my one, I immediately—though not instinctively—resolved prudence in the matter and reversed direction, seeking to rejoin my fellows. Flying alone for a time, I caught sight of what I supposed to be my formation and dropped in behind. Here I remained, flying serenely for the better part of fifteen minutes until the leader began a leisurely bank to the left. One by one each successive machine revealed a large black Maltese cross stenciled upon its wing. It seems I had fallen in with the wrong crowd, and Dame Caution urged me to eschew my new companions. Putting a long burst of lead into the nearest Hun (who obligingly burst into flames) I dropped my nose and streaked for home. Friendship in war being fleeting, none of my erstwhile comrades chose to follow.

Cable to all Embassies, July 14, 1918
The Imperial German Air Service announced tonight that Lieutenant Quentin Roosevelt, son of President Theodore Roosevelt, has been killed in aerial fighting over the lines near Chateau-Thierry. Lieutenant Roosevelt died valiantly in combat with Jagdstaffel No. 11 (Richthofen), during which time he was shot down by Obltn. K. Thom, who has now twenty-four victories to his credit. Lieutenant Roosevelt will be buried with full military honors.

JOHN McGAVOCK GRIDER, *war diary, July 23, 1918*
"I can't write much these days. I'm too nervous. I can hardly hold a pen. I'm all right in the air, as calm as a cucumber, but on the ground I'm a wreck and I get panicky."

JACQUES BULLARD I was still stuck in own my personal Jim Crow no-man's-land, when I heard through the grapevine that the Americans was finally gettin' SPADs. Now the SPAD was *my* plane, I'd flown 'em for almost a year. And I was dumb enough to think this might be my chance to get to be flyin' again. So I wrote everybody I could think of in the Air Service, includin' Eddie Rickenbacker. Nuthin' happened of course. But of all those white bastards, he was the only one who had the courtesy to reply.

Things seemed to be going to shit. By July we all had the SPADs, but they weren't doing us any good. We couldn't buy a fight with the Boche. Our one good chance, a seven-on-seven with a flight of Fokkers, came to nothing. I had one dead to rights, but right on schedule, my guns jammed. And all the while my ear was killing me, acute mastoiditis the quacks grandly called it. All I knew was that if a Fritz had put a bullet in my brain I probably wouldn't have noticed. It got so bad I went into a sort of semicoma in my room, and they grounded me for a month. Mitchell was becoming a real pest. It seemed like every time I talked to reporters, he was there interrupting me and generally screwing things up. Meanwhile, he was always after us to round him up some nurses, who didn't particularly like the idea of a brigadier general close to forty. Then, to add to all my troubles, there was the matter of Luke.

FRANK LUKE, *war diary, July 26, 1918*
Here at last, my first combat unit! Near midnight when we shipped in. HQ First Pursuit Group. Adjutant lined us up, then nuthin. "Hurry up an' wait. Always a shavetail's sad fate." Finally began processing in. Blah! blah! blah! blah! Think they'd know my name an' rank by now. All the while there's this rangy jasper lookin us over, grinning. The boys in front told me it was Rickenbacker. Didn't look so tough. Thought about saying howdy, but he smelled like a still. I figure he's going to get to know me fast enough when I start sending Heinies to Heaven.

MAJOR WILLIAM HARNTEY, COMMANDER, 27TH SQUADRON, FIRST PURSUIT GROUP Luke was trouble from the beginning. That first morning I gave the kids my "Survive the first two weeks, an' you're home free" speech. The others listened close, but Frank just stood there with that insolent smile pasted across his puss. It ruffled me. Yet the moment he got into a plane I realized he could back it up. God, how that boy could fly! Also, he was very likely the best aerial sharpshooter in the War. But what really caught your attention was his moxie. I've never met a lad—and I've met some brave ones in my time—with more arrogant courage than Luke. Too bad he was such a misfit.

On his first patrol he just drops out of formation and sails off on his own. Engine trouble, he claimed. I let it pass. But on the second he does exactly the same thing, and comes back claiming he got a Hun. No confirmation, just writes a combat report to that effect. I lowered the boom; grounded him for a week. Had to; the

Squadron was calling him a liar and a four-flusher. His reaction was bitterness and contempt for us all.

CAPTAIN JERRY C. VASCONCELLES It was sometime early in September. We were sitting around the mess room after supper and the talk turned from condoms to drachen, the observation balloons the Jerrys used to float over the trenches to spot for their artillery. I remember saying that they were the toughest nut to crack, and that any pilot who got one had to be good, or he'd die in the attempt. Luke had been sitting alone as usual. But suddenly he was in the middle of the conversation, grilling me for information. It was like somebody had turned on a lightbulb over his head.

FRANK LUKE, *war diary, September 12, 1918*
> I got my first gas bag. Wasn't easy. Archie was everywhere. Shot the thing full, but couldn't get her to burn. Heinies winched it down and almost had her on the ground. Made one last pass an' really raked it. Who-o-o-mp! Huge ball of fire, knocked me a hundred feet up an' fell right back on the Heinies. Looked like burning rats scurrying around. Got back an' asked the crew chief if he'd seen it. He laughed, said it lit up the whole sky. Nobody's going to question my kills from now on.

2ND LIEUTENANT JOSEPH WEHNER For all his cowboy bravado, Frank was a sensitive soul. We were both outcasts, and that initially brought us together. But we had a great deal more in common. Frank was the only person with whom I could really communicate. But as our friendship deepened, it simply drove the wedge between us and the unit deeper. Then Frank discovered drachen, and suddenly became the toast of the hoi polloi, the Arizona Balloon Buster. I fretted that it would end our relationship. But quite the contrary. The night of his third victory he came to my room: "Wanna go sausage huntin' tomorrow?" It was all I could do to keep from weeping. "We're gonna go on a rampage, Joe. Set the whole damn Front on fire." So that night we became truly brothers in arms, and what a sweet rampage it would be.

Eight balloons in five days, Mitchell was out arranging for mobile searchlights so Mr. Arizona could fly past dark, and I'm on the ground with my thumb stuck up my ass. If I was ever going to get out of this war with any kind of reputation, I realized I'd have to get down to business fast. The ear was better. But the medics were still hemming and hawing. Finally I just started flying, dared the sons of bitches to come and arrest me. Fortunately, my luck turned almost immediately. The SPAD was a real killing machine, and suddenly there were plenty of fresh young Fritzes to be had. On my first two days back, September 14 and 15, I bagged a matched pair of Fokker D VIIs. Now I had seven, but Luke was still going wild. On the 18th he got three planes and two balloons in less than ten minutes, and Pershing put him in for the Medal of Honor. Why not? He was Ace of Aces with fourteen, and I was eating his dust.

MAJOR BILL HARTNEY   The death of Wehner pushed Frank Luke over the edge. One look convinced me he was in trouble, and I packed him off to Paris for a week's leave. He was back in three days, claiming there was nothing to do. The worst sign possible. The boy should have been grounded then and there. But he was the hero of the hour, demanding the opportunity to down more drachen. What the hell were we supposed to do? So his behavior was left to degenerate, until every trace of military discipline had disappeared—leaving the squadron without permission, flying unauthorized missions with the French, taking every unnecessary risk imaginable. God knows what was going on inside his head. When he took off that last time, he was literally facing a court-martial. It never convened. The Boches were waiting for him, an entire squadron. He got three more balloons; but they got him. Crash-landed near Murvaux, strafing German infantry on the way down. They finally cornered him in a churchyard. He could have surrendered, but chose instead to shoot it out with twenty of them. That was the end of Frank Luke. America called it heroism of the first order. I call it suicide.

JOHN McGAVOCK GRIDER, *war diary, August 27, 1918*
   "It's only a question of time until we all get it. I'm all shot to pieces. I only hope I can stick it out. My nerves are all gone, and I can't stop. . . . It's not the fear of death that's done it. I'm still not afraid to die. It's this eternal flinching from it that's made a coward out of me. Few men live to know what real fear is. It's something that grows on you, day by day, eats into your consti-

tution and undermines your sanity. . . . At night, when the colonel calls up to give us our orders, my ears are afire until I hear what we are going to do the next morning. Then I can't sleep for thinking about it all night. . . . Oh for a parachute! The Huns are using them now. I haven't a chance, I know it and it's the eternal waiting that's killing me."

MAJOR PETER D. SPRINGS, COMMANDER, 17TH SQUADRON, 5TH PURSUIT GROUP, *letter to Mrs. Beauregard Grider,* *September 23, 1918*
I know that nothing I might say will wash away your pain and sadness in this time of trial. I do, however, hope that your burden of grief will be lightened by the knowledge that John sacrificed his life for a cause in which he fervently believed. I am certain of this because he visited with me shortly before his last mission, and spoke at length of his unwavering sense of duty and his deep pride and gratitude for the opportunity to serve his country. . . .

ELIZABETH   It vas za first time Edward stopped writing me. I vorried because maybe he vas becoming too big and important to think about his mudder. But later he told me it vas because they had him vorking all za time, just like in za glass factory.

RACER UPS SCORE

Barely a day goes by that former racer Eddie Rickenbacker doesn't bag himself another Hun aircraft. Remembered here for his fearless driving, Rickenbacker has displayed skill and daring that recently paid big dividends along the Western Front. "These German boys are good," Rickenbacker told reporters in Paris, France, "but our superior pilot training and these new SPAD XIII aircraft make combat with them like shooting fish in a barrel. . . .

—*Indianapolis Sentinel,* October 2, 1918

RICKENBACKER NEARS LUKE

Captain Eddie Rickenbacker is building his personal score of victories quickly. Recently promoted to commander of the much-decorated Hat in the Ring Squadron, Rickenbacker now has 16 confirmed kills compared to the 19 tallied by Phoenix resident Frank Luke before he disappeared behind enemy lines on the 28th of September. While Rickenbacker's score seems impressive, it consists largely of enemy aircraft and only three observation balloons. Luke's record is made up overwhelmingly of balloons, generally considered by far the more difficult target. Therefore, should Rickenbacker surpass Luke and lay claim to the title American "Ace of Aces," the authenticity of this distinction will remain forever open to question by those who truly understand air combat.

—Editorial, *Phoenix Sun*, October 5, 1918

October 1918 remains in my memory a blur of endless combat and fatigue. I can recall doing very little else but flying and leading the 94th. One incident, however, stands out in my mind. It took place during the Allied push into the Argonne forest. We had the Hun on the run, and I wanted to make sure that the Hat in the Ring squadron did its part. I pushed morning patrols back to well before dawn so that we would be waiting when the Heinies took to the sky. On this particular mission we found ourselves hunting drachen in the near-darkness. Suddenly a sausage-shaped object loomed up, dimly outlined by the artillery flashing in the distance. I fired immediately and no sooner had my tracer rounds entered the thick bobbing mass than it burst into a huge ball of flame, lighting the vicinity with its lurid glow. There was no chance to celebrate. I looked right and there, precisely outlined against the orange inferno, was a Fokker D VII ready to fight.

He roared ahead, and then cut sharply around so as to come directly at me. I was not about to refuse the challenge, and flew to meet him head on. We began shooting simultaneously. In the darkness it looked as if our machines were joined by two gleaming cords of tracer fire. We were converging at over 200 miles an hour, an aerial game of what kids now call "chicken." Closer and closer we came. I seemed to be surrounded by flashes. I could feel my SPAD stagger as we drew near point-blank range. It seemed that we must collide. Then, without warning, his machine erupted in flames and fell away.

An instant later I was left alone in the darkness, only the lurching of my wounded SPAD left to remind me of what had just happened. I backed off the throttle and crossed my fingers that the thing would stay in one piece long enough for me to get back to Allied territory. There was an emergency field three miles past our lines. I made a beeline in that direction, and staggered in for a landing.

As soon as I climbed out I saw that substantial chunks of the propeller had been shot away. Bullet holes were everywhere, a dozen within a three-foot radius of the plane's center line. Closer examination revealed that a single shot had passed through the isinglass windshield not two feet ahead of my face. I pulled off my helmet. An evil-looking black scar branded the entire left side. It's time to go to Paris, I thought.

ANNA LEE HUTCHINSON   I'd been with the Red Cross in Paris for maybe six months. Just like everybody else, I was taken with his heroics. But I never thought I'd see him again, or that he might recognize me. Then one fall day I was lollygaggin' down the quai de Tournelle, and there he was, smilin' and talkin' to me as if he'd known me all his life. I'd pretty much forgotten how tall an' good-lookin' he was. And in the uniform, with all those medals . . . I was smitten.

Over a glass of wine he asked me if I was free for dinner. I said I was, but that back in Texas he hadn't exactly acted like a gentle-man. I made him promise to be on his best behavior. It was all a silly girl's hoax. I'd already made up my mind to sleep with him. I was still a virgin, but I was sick of it, an' this seemed like fate intervenin'. So after supper I took him back to my apartment, an itty-bitty place on the rue de Bussy.

It turned out to be a fiasco. I realized later that he must have been under a great deal of strain. But, to make a long story short, he couldn't perform. I was so naive that I wasn't sure what was goin' on. He seemed to be almost in shock, an' kept on apologiz-ing. Finally he left—fled is more like it—and I never heard from him again.

Years later, I was with my husband at some function in Tulsa, and he was the speaker. I went up to him. He looked as if he'd seen a ghost, and insisted he had no idea who I was. It was all very sad and embarrassing.

GENEVIEVE JOUBERT   To me he was just another American avi-ator in Montmartre . . . though perhaps more heavily decorated. I brought him up to my room, and asked for twenty francs immediately. He paid, but seemed preoccupied and morose. Since he had next to no French I removed my things straight off, and lay down on the bed. He simply stood there fidgeting. With some persuasion I got him to sit next to me and fondle my breasts, while I worked to make him erect. As soon as he was the least bit stiff I took him in my mouth, all the while stroking his testicles. In this manner I brought him quickly to a climax. He was pleased and peeled off an additional forty francs, saying he wanted to meet me the next day. I was wary of this, and made some excuse. You see I knew his kind, I had been with them many times before. Their time at the Front had already killed them, they simply did not realize it. This part is the first to die; the rest would soon follow. My little trick worked just once, after that I risked a beating or worse. It could not be otherwise, Monsieur.

The tension became greater as the war drew to a close. Every mission was more taxing and dangerous than an entire 200-mile race, and they came twice a day, not once a month. I was haunted by our lack of parachutes. Toward the end of October we heard that Germany was suing for peace on Wilson's terms. But it turned out to be a false alarm, and the fighting went on. I preached caution to myself and everybody else on the ground. But in the air I took more and more chances. I had already surpassed Lufbery and Luke . . . nobody was even close. But I remained determined to up my score. At one point I was concentrating so hard on finishing off an Albatross that I failed to notice a flight of five Boches lying in wait. A rookie mistake almost cost me my life. Another time I flew straight into a barrage of Archie with Ham Coolidge, only to see him blown to bits in the wink of an eye. It seems to me now that I was in a trance. I didn't know whether I would live or die. And I'm not sure I cared.

GOD   Actually, I was tempted to kill him. But I enjoyed his antics, and kept putting it off. The others, virtually all of them, were completely shot and useless. But a few—Goering, Udet, Fonck, and Edward—seemed to still have possibilities. So I thought, "Why not let them live, and play out their meager little hands?" After all, isn't that what being a benevolent Deity is all about?

• • •

Our mission had been canceled and all the pilots were grounded in anticipation of the cease-fire. But I wasn't buying. Around 9:30 that morning I wandered out to the hangar and told my mechanics to get my ship ready to fly. When it was warmed up, I climbed in and took off. I headed toward the Front, flying low. Soon I could see both lines—Germans and Americans peering out over the top of their trenches. Periodically a German took a potshot at me, but nothing came too close. I looked down at my watch. It was exactly 11:00 A.M.—the eleventh hour of the eleventh day of the eleventh month. Men on both sides began pouring into No Man's Land until gray uniforms mixed with brown. I could see them hugging each other, dancing, jumping. I banked my ship back toward home. The Great War had finally ended.

FINIS FARR, *Rickenbacker's Luck*

"Rick's diary entry for November 11 tells a plain tale. It records that he went up at five minutes of eleven in the morning, 'trying to get to the front, was unable.' "

American Ace of Aces. Four men had held the title before me. They were dead; I had survived. There was luck involved, that I don't deny. But ultimately air combat was about competence, daring, and persistence in the face of the odds. As a pilot I never thought of killing an individual, only of shooting down an enemy plane. And that was a matter of skill.

VICTORIES

NAME	DATE	AGE	INJURY SUSTAINED
Flg. Hermann Meisse	4/29/18	22	Dead—Bullets to legs, heart, and lungs
Ltn. Otto von Breiten-Landenberg	5/17/18	21	Dead—Broken neck
Hptmn. Kurt Lischke	5/22/18	24	Dead—Multiple bullet wounds
Obltn. Kurt Doring	5/22/18	21	Broken back
Hptmn. Walter Goos	5/27/18	19	Uninjured
Vzfw. Eduard Festner	5/30/18	26	Dead—Burned alive
Oberst. Petre Egli	5/30/18	25	Dead—Burned alive
Flg. J. Brichta	9/14/18	17	Dead—Bullets to head

Hptmn. Victor Carganico	9/15/18	24	Two broken legs, broken arm
Flg. Hans Behr	9/25/18	19	Dead—Bullets to head and torso
Ltn. Werner Stenhauser	9/26/18	24	Dead—Bullet wounds and burns
Flg. M. Zander	9/28/18	19	Dead—Burned alive
Flg. Petre Schmutz	10/1/18	20	Dead—Burned alive
Flg. S. Todter	10/1/18	23	Dead—Burned alive
Obltn. Georg Zimmer	10/2/18	24	Dead—Spinal column severed
Ltn. Wilhelm Hohs	10/2/18	29	Uninjured
Flg. A Niederhoff	10/2/18	20	Uninjured
Oberst. Fritz Bopp	10/3/18	26	Dead—Burns and bullet wounds
Flg. Franz Salzmann	10/3/18	16	Dead—Bullets to torso and head
Hptmn. Otto Putzer	10/6/18	20	Dead—Multiple wounds
Obltn. Raul Henning	10/9/18	24	Dead—Burned alive
Flg. Petre Zunt	10/9/18	19	Dead—Internal injuries
Hptmn. P. Milch	10/10/18	20	Dead—Bullet to right eye
Flg. Kurt Rabe	10/10/18	18	Dead—Bullets to lungs and liver
Ltn. Manfred Lutz	10/12/18	24	Dead—Multiple bullet wounds
Ltn. G. Rudorffer	10/22/18	26	Uninjured
Oberst. Georg Gill	10/23/18	23	Dead—Burns and broken neck
Flg. Ernst Nekel	10/23/18	19	Dead—Decapitated
Flg. Hans Coll	10/27/18	18	Dead—Bullets to head and torso
Ltn. Wilhelm Berr	10/27/18	24	Dead—Legs severed
Obltn. Ernst Althaus	10/30/18	27	Dead—Burned alive
Flg. Hans Weiss	10/30/18	20	Multiple burns
Hptmn. Max Sorg	10/30/18	22	Dead—Multiple bullet wounds

CHORUS O Lord, why hast Thou forsaken us? Why hast Thou torn us from our families and those others we love? Why were we cut down in the springtime of our lives, nevermore to see even one flower or the sun rising? Why now are we cast beyond the pale of warmth and affection, and plunged into this black endless night? What have we done? How have we failed You? Why is our killer left free to roam the earth bathed in the praise of his countrymen? Why, Lord? Why?

GOD Because I felt like it. Besides I liked him better than any of you. Whine! Whine! Whine! Who the hell told you to go to war in the first place? Show me where it says in the Bible: "Thou shalt climb into contraptions, disobey the law of gravity, and kill thy fellow man." Besides, how bad was it? You got to grow up, walk around for a while. Most of you got laid. What the hell did you expect from life? I could have made you cockroaches, or worse, cocker spaniels. If I were you I'd shut up, and hope I don't decide to reincarnate the lot of you.

Chapter Four

BILLY MITCHELL   It didn't take me long to realize that we had
to get him home . . . the quicker the better. After the Armistice it
was decided that the only sure way to prevent the German Army
from reconstituting was to move our own forces immediately east,
right on top of them. Because of their mobility, air units were a
vital part of the scheme, and I pushed Pershing hard to make sure
our key combat squadrons leapfrogged across the Rhine as quickly
as possible. This was strictly a military operation, as vital strategi-
cally as any during the war, but a few clowns were intent on
turning it into a goddamned fraternity party. Regrettably, Rickenbacker was one of them.

   Now at this point, a number of the German aircraft manufacturers, anxious to curry favor with their conquerors, gave me and
my staff the opportunity to examine their latest hardware in Berlin.
It made sense to bring Eddie along as a test pilot, so I proceeded
immediately to Coblenz where the 94th and 95th were headquar-
tered. What I found was in no way reassuring. Rickenbacker and
a few of his cronies had succeeded in pulling enough strings to
have a bevy of Red Cross girls attached to the squadrons on a co-ed
basis. To state that military discipline had deteriorated to the point
of nonexistence is putting absolutely the best face on it. And in
the midst of this little Gomorrah I discovered America's Ace of
Aces holed up in a hotel with three young women—I use the term
loosely—a case of Johnny Walker Black, and a writer named
Driggs, who was apparently under contract to compose a tome
under our boy's name, to be titled *Fighting the Flying Circus*. Well,

I wasn't in the business of supporting the arts. So I cornered Rickenbacker and ordered him to report the next morning at 0600 to the local bahnhof, in full uniform with neither literary nor feminine companionship, ready to proceed east.

Our trip proved highly informative. We were met by a delegation that included every major figure in German aviation, each intent on hawking what just a few weeks before had been their nation's most closely held secrets. No doubt about it, they had made vast strides with airframes. Most impressive was the Junkers D.1, an all-metal monoplane with a stressed duralumin outer skin and total internal bracing. The thing was completely clean of external supports and decades ahead of its time. But Rickenbacker missed it completely. Instead, he harped on their weak engine technology, and told war stories with Hermann Goering and Ernst Udet, who had seventy-two kills. When the conversation turned to fräuleins, and what a supply of good Scotch might buy on the black market, I decided that the time had arrived for a triumphant homecoming. He was simply too hot a property to risk in such an environment. Rickenbacker was the best thing we had going for us, in some ways the very future of American Air Power. But if he didn't keep his nose clean, he would become useless. So the answer it seemed was a giant helping of Motherhood and Apple Pie.

Fast Eddie Rickenbacker stood on the deck of the liner *Adriatic* with a hell of a hangover, looking out at the skyline of New York. His tongue felt big and dry, like a kitchen sponge, and there were spots—blue and green ones—dancing around in his eyeballs. He squinted at Manhattan's mound of stone-sheathed towers, trying to figure out what they might portend. Granite pointers maybe, directing him toward the sky; or Gotham's middle digits raised en masse to flip him off; or maybe just testimonies to the speculators' infinite knack of jacking up land prices and structural steel's tensile inclination to play along. Who knew? Was he just one of a million other doughboys, lucky to be greeted with a handshake and a nod? Or would he be the one scooped out of the crowd and plumped down permanently at a long walnut table on the forty-first floor? One thing was sure, he was through being a circus freak. War had taught him a single big thing . . . danger inevitably equals death. It had made him famous and put clothes on his back. But now he realized that survival demanded that he figure out a way of transmuting exploits into gold . . . a steady substantial means of getting people to give him money simply for being Edward Vernon Rickenbacker. There was more, of course. He wanted to be an insider, not just an ornament. . . . a doer, a decisionmaker; the pavement should shake a bit when he strode down the boulevard. It was his birthright, the birthright of every striving American male of the era worthy of his own Johnson. Yet what separated Eddie from the other rodents in the pack was the understanding that his very life depended on it . . . that was his edge, that was his goad, that was his future.

JOHN DOS PASSOS   For the record, I admit it, Charley Anderson was Rickenbacker. Not initially, in the *The 42nd Parallel*—that character was plainly moving in another direction. It was only later in the third book of the trilogy, *The Big Money*, that I started using the real Rickenbacker as a model for Charley. But it got out of hand, things I invented earlier seemed to be happening to Rickenbacker subsequent to the book's publication. It might have been rather satisfying—life follows fiction, etc.—had not the real man been such a lunatic. I'd get these calls in the middle of the night, drunk of course. He'd go on and on, threatening me, then trying to wheedle information about his "future." For the longest time I denied everything. Finally, he really got my goat, called me a pinko Devil worshiper. So I told him I had a manuscript in a safe deposit box called *Charley Anderson in Hell*, and unless he left me alone I would publish it immediately. That must have been in the late forties; it was the last I heard of him.

GOD   Dos Passos? Yeah, I know who he was—back then everybody did. What of it? You know, it's not always easy to come up with original material. History is a complicated business. Sometimes you have borrow a few odds and ends to keep the various plotlines moving. Remember, I'm the Director, not some two-bit scriptwriter. Now if I were you and didn't want to worry excessively about lightning bolts, I'd get back to the story.

ELIZABETH   Such a big shot he had become. All the vay from Columbus the authorities brought me, just so I could meet him at za boat. Such a big boat it vas! And za crowd, there must have been thousands, all for my boy. Edward he looked so tall und straight, dressed in a big camel's hair coat over his uniform with all the medals. In the car I told him zat prouder of him I could not be . . . except maybe he fought for the wrong side. He looked at me very serious. "Mother," he said, "you must never say this again, not even in private. From now on I am what people think I am. If they get the wrong idea, I can go from hero to zero in just one day."

ALICE WHITNEY PAYSON   It was certainly a bizarre turn of events. We went out for drinks with the Sheets and Billy Astor, and the next thing I knew I found myself sitting in the grand ballroom of the Waldorf at a testimonial dinner for Edward Rickenbacker! My God, ten years before the man was nothing more than a mechanic. Now Newton Baker, the Secretary of War, was fawning over him before the assembled masses. To make matters worse, I made the mistake of relating to our table the story of meeting him at the Vanderbilt Cup, which I thought was quite droll. Instead of laughing, Helena Sheets began yammering, "You know him? You know him? Can you introduce us?" Fortunately, her very limited attention span was drawn immediately to the front of the hall, where the man-of-the-hour was having problems of his own. You see, the time had come for him to speak, and as usual he had absolutely nothing to say. He stood there squinting at the crowd with that disgusting grin of his, utterly tongue-tied. It was all I could do not to fall over laughing. But then, without a bit of warning, he held up this jeweled set of wings they had just bestowed upon him and yelped, "For you, mother!" It brought down the house. Vox populi. Another precious anecdote of democracy in action. Really, Mencken was an optimist.

Mrs. Henry M. Humphreys
243 Gateway Blvd.
Milwaukee, Wisconsin
February 10, 1919

Captain Edward Rickenbacker
Plaza Hotel
New York City, New York

My dear Edward:
Please do not think me a silly old fool for writing you. I was your third grade teacher at East Main Street School in Columbus. You would have known me as Miss Alexander. I have

followed your career carefully, and could not be prouder of your accomplishments. The holiday season in particular always brings you into my heart. You see back then you and your classmate, John Weissinger, brought identical angels to decorate our school Christmas tree. When we removed it, John took his ornament home, but you wanted me to have yours. So I have kept it these many years. And each Christmas your angel has found a prominent place on our own tree, an object of pride for all of us. Now I want you to have your angel back, so you and your family may enjoy it as much as I have.

> May God bless you,
> Mary Alexander Humphreys

DAMON RUNYON Now Eddie I always liked. Had him scatter my ashes over Times Square when my number came up. But we are not talking a great mind here, nor are we talking a great mouth. There was plainly lucre in this hero business. Yet this required a speaking tour on the part of a hero who could not speak. The best I could do was write him a piece that said absolutely nothing in words of three syllables or less. He managed to memorize it, but believe me my Underwood sounded more convincing. So we sent him over to Madame Amanda, the elocutionist and seriously large broad. She has vowed revenge ever since, something I do not take lightly. Nevertheless, Amanda did what she could. Took him over to the empty Metropolitan Opera House, put him on the stage, and then climbed to the top balcony, from whence she gave birth to this modern Demosthenes. What a sight it must have been. "Throw out your right arm. Roll your Rs. Throw out your left arm. Pause for effect. Rise to a crescendo. God . . . shut up."

"I have taught dogs to talk," she maintained years later, "but nothing was worse than Rickenbacker." This may be true, but I have no way of judging, since most of the dogs I know do not talk.

SPECIAL EDITION
THOUSANDS GREET WINGED KNIGHT!

The special train carrying Captain Eddie Rickenbacker, America's Ace of Aces, back to Columbus was met by a sea of friendly faces as it pulled into North Square Station this morning. "There is no place I'd rather be than among friends and neighbors. And I thank God, who has always watched over me, that this day has finally come," said the beaming Rickenbacker as he stepped off his private car accompanied by his mother. Later, at a testimonial dinner attended by Governor James M. Cox, ex-President William Howard Taft, and 1,500 honored guests, Mayor Allen presented Captain Rickenbacker with a set of cuff links in the form of platinum wings encrusted with sapphires and diamonds. "America's most valiant warrior deserves nothing less. . . ."

—*Columbus Citizen*, February 17, 1919

A HERO AND HIS GAL

Mother and son—those of us who were privileged to watch them on the train during the long ride home learned a great deal about this blessed pair. Whether it was in their little arguments or in the words that did not have to be said, their splendid devotion was obvious. This tiny woman was still the "boss," but she ruled with a loving heart alone. She agreed with the big fellow in most instances; he had his way as he presumed. But behind her every word and gesture was a mother's authority—the most beautiful authority there is. To her it was no battle-scarred warrior who sat beside her, but simply her boy. He could lord it over his opponents. But here, in this frail mother, was more than his master—and he felt it without ever realizing it.

—Editorial, *Columbus Dispatch*, February 17, 1919

TO OUR BRAVE BROTHER MOOSE

Let it be Known, on this the 22nd day of February in the Year of Our Lord MCMXIX, that the Loyal Order of Moose of the Great State of Ohio Commemorates the Unparalleled Bravery, Patriotism, Piety, and Otherwise Sterling Virtues of Brother Moose Captain Edward Vernon Rickenbacker. Your Unexcelled Feats of Daring, Skill, and Technological Wisdom have brought to you the Universal Love, Recognition, and Admiration of All Moose Everywhere. May your life hereafter be paved with the golden bricks of happiness, and may your broad shoulders continue to bear the burdens of responsibility, duty, and honor, which are the inevitable results of the trust you have earned from your fellow man and Brother Moose.

Amos "Doc" Waddell, Grand Master

ELIZABETH   If Edward vould live in Columbus, they vas going to build him a big new house by the University for free. "As much as I vant to be close to you," he told me, "I can't do it. I'm beyond this place; I belong to the whole country now." I thought maybe he could take za house for a little while, zen sell it. But he said someone in his position could never do zat sort of thing. Such a shame. My boy vas a hero; yet he couldn't settle down and rest.

(For Release: 1 March 1919)

B.P. POND LYCEUM BUREAU PROUDLY ANNOUNCES: THE NATIONAL SPEAKING TOUR OF

CAPTAIN EDDIE RICKENBACKER

in Conjunction with the Publication of His Book
Fighting the Flying Circus

by Frederick A. Stokes & Company, New York.

DATES AND LOCATIONS:

23 March	Faneuil Hall, Boston, Mass.
24 March	The Coliseum, Hartford, Conn.
1 April	Metropolitan Opera House, New York, N.Y.
6 April	Hay-Adams Hotel, Washington, D.C.
12 April	Academy of Music, Philadelphia, Pa.
15 April	Gould Pavilion, Utica, N.Y.
17 April	Tonowanda Hall, Buffalo, N.Y.
22 April	Michigan Avenue Auditorium, Chicago, Ill.
2 May	Jackson Hall, Ann Arbor, Mich.
4 May	Pontchartrain Hotel, Detroit, Mich.
6 May	R.E. Old Auditorium, Flint, Mich.
17 May	Atkins Museum, Kansas City, Mo.
19 May	Omaha Club, Omaha, Neb.
20 May	The Cow Palace, Sioux City, Iowa
25 May	Civic Center, Toledo, Ohio
29 May	Indianapolis Motor Speedway Pavilion, Ind.

BOO HERNDON, THE GHOSTWRITER   Neither the book nor the speaking tour was any too successful. In the autobiography he insisted on maintaining that the tour was intended to sell Liberty Bonds, when in fact it was all about selling Rickenbacker—which it plainly failed to do. I came across a ledger with his share of the gate receipts. Some weren't bad—$460 in Boston; $800 in New York; $900 in Philadelphia. But there was also—$36.50 in Utica; $83.40 in Toledo; and $23.10 in Buffalo. Under Omaha there was just a penciled notation: (free dinner). The book did somewhat better—sold nearly 6,000 copies. But this was far below expectations. Too bad, since my fellow Mouthpiece Driggs did a rather nice, if unattributed, job. The problem was that Rickenbacker was a war hero at a time when people wanted nothing to do with war. They simply wanted to forget the whole mess and him with it.

WARREN GAMALIEL HARDING, *Boston, July 1919*
   "America's present need is not heroics but healing; not nostrums but normalcy; not revolutions but restoration. . . . "

REED CHAMBERS   I came to New York; it must have been early in June. Since the Armistice I hadn't done much beyond being glad I was still alive. I rounded up Eddie and two complaisant lassies, and we headed over to Princeton to watch Yale lose the big ball game on University Field. Eddie barely said a word all day. I was ready for a night on the town, but he maintained he wasn't feeling well and dropped out early. I was back after him the next morning, and we took a long walk around the city. He didn't say much until we came upon this panhandler on 42nd Street, dressed in a ragged Air Corps tunic. We both realized at once that it was Josiah Rowe, one of the fellows from the 94th. It was an embarrassing moment to say the least. He kept stammering that he was on his way back to Fredericksburg, Virginia. I didn't know what to say. Finally, I stuffed two tens in his mitt, grabbed Eddie's arm, and basically fled. Rickenbacker looked like he'd seen his father's ghost. There was absolutely no color in his face. He kept shaking his head and muttering, "Hero to zero. Hero to zero." I tried to talk some sense into him. My God, after Alvin York he was the most famous and beloved figure to come out of the war.
   "Sure, some of us are having a bit of trouble getting reintegrated. But basically the future is wide open, opportunity's everywhere. Things are bound to settle out."

He wasn't buying. "That's okay for you to say, Yale man, born with a silver spoon stuck up your ass. All I've got's a name. And every day goes by it's getting dimmer and dimmer. I'm fading away, Reed." It was a revelation, I'll tell you. All his confidence and bullshit. It was probably the only time I got a glimpse of what was really going on below that hard outer shell.

MARION WISHART Rickenbacker the world-famous killer; it made a certain sense. After all, he had killed my husband. When he appeared at the Academy of Music, part of me wanted to go right over there and tell the world exactly what he was. I didn't, of course. But then, about a month or so later, I received this note from him "requesting the pleasure of my company at dinner." It literally sent shivers down my spine. It would have been even more frightening had it not been so transparent. "Air Ace to Wed Widowed Heiress. . . ." You could see the headlines in his twisted, lower-class imagination. I burned the note, and ordered the servants to never let him on the premises. Fortunately, it was the last I heard from him.

W.C. FIELDS Rick-en-back-er headed west, summer a' '19. Biiig welcommme . . . Rolled him arounnnd in a SPAD made a' peonies . . . All L.A. turrrrned out, 'cept the hay fever sufferrrrrs. Come a long way since his pro-Kraut days . . . Took my adviiice, killed a pack of 'ummmm. Stillll ready to fuck at the drop of a drawerrrr . . . Drank anything liquid, with the rest of us fishieees . . . seemed a little tight though . . . a little tight . . . sniffin' here an' there, like a dog on the runnnn. . . .

MACK SENNETT Rickenbacker had definitely changed. For one thing he didn't want to be called Eddie any more, but Rick. It seemed idiotic, but he insisted. "I hate Eddie, it makes me sound small. If you're my friend, you'll call me Rick." Also, before the war he seemed fascinated with the business. Now Universal wanted him to do a film; Thalberg was following him around with a certified check for a hundred grand. But he hesitated. Talked to me about his stature and not wanting to ruin his image. Shit, we were the image makers. I didn't know what the hell he was talking about. But he never did the movie.

CLIFF DURANT   Yeah, he made a beeline over here as soon as he hit town. Ended up staying with us. Guess I felt pretty flattered; he was a big shot now. Or at least thought he was. Remember asking him what he was gonna do. Gave me that grin of his, an' said he thought I might be able to help him. I guess he did. He wanted to meet my father in Detroit, which was fine. But what I didn't know was that when I was out, he was upstairs banging Adelaide, which was not so fine. Sure, I was through with the bitch; but there's such a thing as wearing out your welcome.

ADELAIDE FROST RICKENBACKER   Things had already reached rock bottom between Clifford and myself. He had ceased even trying to hide the fact that he was seeing other women, and we were barely on speaking terms. When Edward arrived he seemed like a knight in shining armor. There was nothing between us at this point; but I will admit that the comparison between the two probably had something to do with my decision to finally seek a divorce. In retrospect, I don't know how I managed to last that long. Clifford was as close to a monster as any man I have ever met.

While I was on the West Coast, officials from the Curtiss Aviation Corporation got in touch with me, suggesting that I join forces with them. America's premier aviator and America's leading aviation manufacturer—they argued it was a combination that could not be beat. There was no doubt in my mind that one day air transport would be a major industry. But had that day yet dawned? War's end had also brought an end to the large military orders that had initially caused the industry to boom. Now there was clearly a future in aerial mail delivery. But only a large-scale passenger business could sustain the kind of aircraft research and infrastructure development necessary to create a sound and substantial civil aviation sector. Was the public ready for air travel? I did not know. But there was one surefire way to find out—float the idea right before the nose of John Q. Public.

AIR ACE GIVES STRANGE SPEECH

Captain Eddie Rickenbacker came to town last night intent on portraying a world of the future which literally defied gravity.

Maybe it came from breathing all that thin air high up, or perhaps from the loco weed we always hear is being smoked down in South California; but whatever the source, America's leading wartime ace presented the crowd gathered in Stoner Auditorium with a vision of air travel that stretched their imaginations to the breaking point. "Here I am in Seattle. I feel that I am living in a new era ten years hence, and that the North Star is actually the shining headlight of a large passenger plane just arriving from Alaska. Then I see other headlights not so bright, far out over the Pacific—meaning more planes coming from the Orient, possibly Japan. I wait until they land—one, two, three, four, and five of the ordinary size, carrying an average of from two to three hundred passengers. Then at last, the sixth, an immense airship—down it comes slowly landing like a bird. From the top deck I hear a voice shouting, 'Hello, Rick!' " . . . Possibly, if there were any Wobblies in the audience, they may have thought that was Edward Bellamy calling out this greeting, but for the rest Captain Rickenbacker was just hearing voices. . . .

Critic at Large
Seattle Sentinel, August 12, 1919

It had been a long seven months. Red Fokkers had been replaced in my nightmares by auditoriums filled with red faces, or worse, no faces at all. I needed a break, some time away from the rest of humanity. No place was more silent and solitary than the high desert of New Mexico. It was here I took refuge as the summer of 1919 drew to a close, wandering across the stark landscape with no idea of a destination. At night beneath the black dome and bright stars I would calmly chart my future. This hero business had plainly become a detour from the true path of achievement. My life had become a three-ring circus. Huge sums of money were proffered simply to use some product I didn't care about. Playing myself in a movie would be degrading. By this time I realized how little I really knew about public speaking. There was a pot of gold waiting for me in auto racing; but I had promised myself never to race again. I was essentially a builder, a creator, and I wanted to do something worthy of these ends. Aviation continued to attract me. But it was an infant industry and not yet ready for men of real stature. So, my thoughts turned again to the automotive industry, which was now turning out literally millions of vehicles. Surely there was still a place there for me. For the moment, a position in the executive hierarchy would do. But I had bigger plans. Since my days at Frayer-Miller I had dreamed of developing and producing a motor vehicle exclusively of my own design. It would be in the vanguard of all others—fast, high-powered, safe, reliable, and priced within reach of discriminating consumers. So at last I left the desert of New Mexico armed with a plan.

GOD   Alpha types often wander off in the wilderness. Seems to do them some good. Moses brought back the Ten Commandments. Christ emerged after forty days renewed and ready to preach the Word. Rickenbacker, he was going to bring forth a midrange vehicle with the performance and sex appeal to separate the suckers from their money. Kind of gives you goose bumps, doesn't it?

Today it's easy to dismiss Detroit. A relict . . . a raggedy-ass agglomeration of urban entropy, pollution, and corporate malfeasance—all of it suffused with the stale aroma of chitterlings, kielbasa, and two-day-old Pabst. What other major metropolitan center tries to burn itself down every Halloween? And yet this shattered crack-head of a city once had a youth that was the envy of all. During the first several decades of the twentieth century the Industrial Revolution took up residence right here on the banks of Lake St. Claire. For Detroit was the epicenter of all things automotive, the high altar of absolutely the hottest technology on the face of the globe . . . the Silicon Valley of the Jazz Age.

And as Motor City revved itself up, it drew into its combustion chambers a mix of high-octane talent so potent as to not only wrench folks everywhere out of their buggies into flivvers, but to change the way things were made in a manner so fundamental that it would supply the key economic and organizational metaphors for an entire era. Here was Henry Leland, the bearded patriarch of Cadillac and Lincoln, and prophet of tolerances so close that he once threw Alfred P. Sloan out of his office for being a thousandth of an inch off. There was Ransom Olds, who took to driving his snappy little Curved Dash runabout up the Court House steps, and in doing so generated the first mass market for motor vehicles (nearly 20,000 sold), and the first really cool car tune, "My Merry Oldsmobile." Then there were the rambunctious Dodge brothers, who constructed engines and transmissions for Ford by day, and deconstructed Detroit's saloons by night. Up in his lab was Boss

Kettering, GM's Merlin, replacing the crank with the self-starter, taking the knock out of the engine block, and brewing up a rainbow's worth of paints so fast-drying that every car no longer need be black—all the while stampeding the ladies into the driver's seat.

And looming over these and hundreds of other tinkerers busy transforming the horseless carriage into the century's number-one big-ticket consumer item were the great organizers, the industrial Bigfoots who hammered out the principalities of Ford and GM. They were the plungers, crammed full of energy, a few good ideas, and the unwavering determination to risk everything to make their dreams real.

Henry Ford was a scrawny bundle of contradictions. Ever the country boy, he hated the family farm, and turned to machinery as a way out. A pacifist and humanitarian, he hired thugs to beat the hell out of his workers, and grew so anti-Semitic that he inspired Hitler. A family man who drove his only son, the eponymous Edsel, into an early grave. Boss of the world's biggest and most integrated industrial enterprise, he never bothered to install a management system.

And much of this was reflected in the cars he built and how he built them. In 1908, after years of trying, Henry believed he had perfected the automobile. When introduced, the $950 Model T was the most advanced car available anywhere at any price. Light tough vanadium steel construction, a monoblock four-cylinder engine, a planetary transmission that was granddaddy to the automatic—the list of firsts went on and on. And here they stayed. Through nearly twenty years of production, Henry vetoed changing even one major system. The T was good enough.

His focus now was on producing more to drive the price down, so more folks could buy them, so he could produce even more, so he could lower the price still further. He ended up selling Ts for $240 in 1925—the rolling equivalent of disposable lighters—and in doing so put America on wheels—over 15 million went out the door, the most until the Beetle. To build this many, Henry had to stay busy and gin up a few innovations, like the assembly line and a five-dollar-a-day wage for every worker. The plants got bigger, the lines got longer, machines were everywhere, and everything became more self-contained.

His masterpiece was River Rouge, the biggest industrial complex in the world, by a long shot. At one end, in came ore and coal from Ford mines, rubber from Ford plantations, wood from Ford forests, and hides from Ford ranches. At the other end, out popped finished Ts, up to one every fifteen seconds. Inside was a living hell—a Midwestern Gulag. Everybody stood, nobody talked, the line went so fast you couldn't take a piss, armed guards were everywhere, the men hated their lives and Ford even more. Henry didn't care. He was too busy hating Jews and becoming a bitter old man.

William Crapo Durant was different. He liked people. Liked them so much that he was going to make them all rich—if they just listened to him and took a few chances. He started off small in the horse buggy business up in Flint. Billy could sell anything, and he would buy anything. So he gobbled up competitors and soon owned the biggest market share in the industry. The future looked bright. Then his pal A.B.C. Hardy warned him to "get out of the carriage trade, before the automobile ruins you." Billy wasn't worried, but then he took a few rides and decided to make the switch—mostly out of restlessness. He was always restless.

A fellow named Buick had invented a superior valve-in-head engine, but the company was floundering in Flint. So in 1904 Billy grabbed it and began building. Buick boomed. Factories spread across Flint like magic. Durant was practiced in the arts of weird finance, and left pyramids of paper and brick wherever he went. Everybody bought stock, and everybody made money. And he didn't stop there. He latched on to Oldsmobile, then Cadillac, and then launched General Motors on a sea of hot air and hope. Billy Durant could capitalize a toothpick. You see, people loved him, and he loved them right back.

That's how he came to marry his second wife, Catherine, a babe if there ever was one. She was twenty-one and he was forty-six, but nobody thought the less of him. A young woman at his side only made Billy Durant look better. It worked out so well, in fact, that he pushed one of Catherine's cute friends, Adelaide Frost, right into the arms of his asshole son Cliff, hoping to set the kid straight. That never worked out. But Billy never blamed Adelaide, and did what he could for her. He was that kind of guy.

Meanwhile, GM just grew and grew and its stock kept climbing, allowing Durant to buy companies and recapitalize again and again. Stock issue followed stock issue, and company followed company, until Billy had no idea what he owned or owed. But it all went down fine enough until sometime in 1910 when GM hit a snag in its cash flow. The bankers were willing to loan 15 million at inflated rates, but the price also included Durant's resignation.

It hardly fazed him. He just invented Chevrolet and came roaring back. In 1916 he buried the bankers in a avalanche of Chevy stock, and took the wheel at General Motors once again. He was no more cautious than before. Ever the player, he bought and bought again. What Ford could do with one company, Billy would do with many. "Saturation point? When it comes to the automobile market there is no such thing as a saturation point." But there was, and early in 1920 GM's product inventories started to climb alarmingly. And as the stock of unsold vehicles rose, the company's stock moved in the other direction. Billy sought to stem the tide by buying huge blocks of GM long, only to see the price sink further and corporate debt grow heavier. He might have ridden out the mess had he owned the company, like Ford. But the real owners were the du Ponts and the bankers, and they were closing in. And just behind, almost invisible in the corporate weeds, was an asp among tycoons, a viper Billy had unwittingly drawn to his breast in one of his many acquisitions. His name was Alfred P. Sloan.

Sloan had a reptilian look. In group photos with his bullnecked underlings, you notice the enlarged nose, lips, and hands attached to a slender elongated frame, like a serpent standing tall among beef cattle. Nobody ever called him anything but Alfred, not even his mother. He went to MIT, then bought the Hyatt Roller Bearing Company with money his father loaned him. After Henry Leland chastised him just once for that bum bunch of bearings, Alfred was never anything less than precise. Indeed, he became the functional equivalent of a good roller bearing—absolutely reliable, without edges, buried deep in the machinery, ensuring everything ran along lines of least resistance. After GM took over Hyatt, he slithered up Billy Durant's rickety corporate ladder with barely a rustle, slipping poisoned memos to Pierre du Pont on how the shambling giant might be reorganized to run smoothly. After Billy's defenestration, he worked soundlessly under Pierre, tidying the corporate structure, eliminating friction, lubricating squeaky wheels, or getting rid of them. When du Pont retired, he slid into the driver's seat virtually unnoticed; for decisions at the top, Alfred's, that is, were henceforth intended for group attribution.

Meanwhile, he was watching the competition with unblinking eyes. Henry Ford, stubbornly digging in his heels, churning up clouds of dust, and doing what he goddamn well pleased, became a target of opportunity. If Henry insisted on purveying unchanged Ts, all of them dressed in widow's black, then Alfred would give the public what it really wanted—style, color, and sex appeal—just like Eve and the Apple. He instituted the annual model change, planned obsolescence, installment buying, Oxford green, sandstone gray, ruby red, and Plantagenet purple. Soon GM's product line came to mirror its neat corporate pyramid. A young man on the rise might get started in a Chevy, jump to a Pontiac after that first promotion, hop into an Olds with that big bonus, and slip into a Buick when he made regional sales manager—all the while dreaming of the executive vice-presidency and the Caddy it would bring him. Cars came to track success with the accuracy of an electrocardiogram, and Alfred's fortunes rose on envy and expectation.

And through it all, it was hard to know he was even there . . . a quiet word spoken here, a string pulled there, a knife deftly inserted between the third and fourth rib. Alfred's office was very large and dark, dominated by a long table where the Group Executives sat when he called them. But he preferred to sit in the shadows, in an easy chair lit by a single Tiffany lamp, positioned so its light played over his features. Here he watched and waited and planned and built, never in a hurry but always ready to move. And as GM dropped into passing gear and sped past Henry's wheezing T-grinder, Alfred became Master of Motor City. Yet only a few on the inside had any idea how he had managed it.

Back in the fall of 1920, Eddie Rickenbacker was on the outside. Things had changed in the auto industry since he went to war. He may have been tough, and brave, and determined to squeeze a fortune out of Detroit, but learning the ropes would still take time. He barely knew who Alfred P. Sloan was. His money was on Billy Durant.

FINIS FARR   This can't have been a pleasant period for Rick. Just as Dos Passos said of Charley Anderson, he was "ready to go to Detroit anytime." Yet the reception he received was far from definitive. An assortment of notables greeted him, and spoke vaguely about his future. He was steered to Henry Leland. But when Leland realized Rick had neither capital nor a firm position, he too became vague. The simple goal of finding a man with the guts and power to make a hiring decision kept eluding him. A fellow would be extremely receptive, but later wouldn't answer his calls. Another would say, "Rick, we ought to be able to bring you aboard," but that he should talk to so-and-so before finalizing things. Yet when this was arranged, some stuffed shirt inevitably came up with something like . . . "I don't know anything about this Captain Ricken-backer, and even if I did, I couldn't approve it." Yet there was no quit in the man. He continued to track down every lead, a trail that sometimes had him riding the Dearborn Limited between New York and Detroit as many as three times a week. It was expensive traveling first class, especially since he had nothing coming in. But in this era, big-name trains were the terrestrial equivalents of ocean liners in terms of providing access to important people. And one night, in the club car, he ran into exactly who he had been looking for.

WILLIAM CRAPO DURANT Impressive? Well, I suppose he was. Large physically, a military bearing, and, of course, there was his reputation. But I was surprised what a likable chap he seemed to be. Very easy to talk to, always smiling. We spoke of business conditions in California. He had recently been out there, and I was surprised to find he knew Clifford and Adelaide quite well. All in all, a very pleasant encounter. I told him, when he had the chance, to stop by the GM building, which was then up near Columbus Circle.

In a week or so, I followed this up with a note inviting him over for lunch. This proved a bit awkward, since he was apparently expecting a job offer. He brought up the subject of overrides—a general commission GM sometimes gave to individuals capable of exerting a positive effect on sales. Now overrides were a tremendous plum, since they amounted to a percentage of every vehicle we sold in a particular market. He wanted New York City. This was out of the question. Young Rickenbacker had neither the influence nor the acumen to warrant such a perquisite. But more to the point, this conversation took place late in 1919, and I was already having my troubles with some of the larger stockholders. I could ill afford to be seen as handing out valuable commissions in an impetuous fashion. I was quite frank with him on this. But I must say he took it well. He must have been disappointed, but he said nothing to lower my opinion of him. I told him I would keep him in mind, and I meant it . . . although he may not have thought so at the time.

ALFRED P. SLOAN Approximately eight months before he left the company, Mr. Durant came to my office and suggested that Eddie Rickenbacker could be useful to us. He asked me if I could find something for him to do. I certainly knew who Rickenbacker was, but this was a period of considerable turmoil, and Mr. Durant made a great many requests. Therefore, when I was unable to locate an immediate fit, I let the matter drop. Then in November of 1920, at the very height of the company crisis, Mr. Durant brought the matter up again. He requested that Rickenbacker be named California sales chief for Sheridan, a four-cylinder job we were just then introducing. I had reservations about the Sheridan. Yet the fact that Durant thought enough of Rickenbacker to remember him at the height of his own troubles impressed me. I made sure Rickenbacker got the job. And from this point I followed his career with some interest.

DAMON RUNYON   The good Captain during this period was in a position to chart a course between the legs of some excellent dolls. Like all great navigators he took this charge seriously. You see, he was of the mind that a good cunt can only be improved by fucking. And by all reports his capacity and magnanimity in this area exceeded even legendary benefactors such as Joe Adonis and Willie the Weasel.

PRISCILLA DEAN   If ever there was an hombre built for sex, it was Rickenbacker. . . . Stupid though. We palled around some in L.A. between shoots, but the newshounds was keeping a close watch on the both of us. It so happened I had to do some publicity shots up in Vancouver. So I invite Rick to come up and keep me warm at the Excelsior. Well, I arrive to find the dumb cluck in the process of registering . . . in the same goddamned hotel! Jesus, the whole thing flashes before my eyes—house dicks, pix, headlines in the tabloids . . . "*Love Nest Discovered!*" Lucky I managed to get out of the lobby without anybody noticing. Left that moron to play with himself.

GOD   I liked to do this from time to time. Remind him of waiting for Sally Zarnetski outside Olentangy Park.

BILLY MITCHELL   We were banking on Rickenbacker spreading the gospel of Air Power to the great unwashed. He started off well enough, but then just seemed to tail off. I had him down to Washington a couple of times, tried to show him how important public relations was going to be in the brewing fight with the brass hats over an independent air force. He seemed to buy in, but not much ever came of it. At least these meetings were businesslike. When I came to New York, I saw a whole other side of him.

Some of the boys from the Detroit Athletic Club were in town for the World Series. We rented a couple of suites at the Commodore and had box seats over at Ebbets Field. There was one extra, so I wired Mitchell, who was always pestering me about coming up. Well, he arrived in full uniform, hotter than a two-dollar pistol. We had cocktails before lunch, beer at the game, and then a couple rounds of highballs back at the hotel, when Mitchell gets it into his head that he wants to go out on the town. All day he had been treating me like I was still his driver back in France, and I was steamed. "To hell with that," I said. "You're dressed like you're the Emperor Jones. Get some civvies and I'll think about going out with you," knowing he didn't have any. But then one of the boys from the DAC around his size fixed him up with soup an' fish—top hat, cane, the works. So off we went.

We must have hit ten clubs that night. Wound up out in front of this Greenwich Village gyp joint, both deep in our cups. I was still fulminating over the rank business and just about to let him have it, when Mitchell turns to me:

"Eddie, there's something we've got to get straight. You're our country's greatest hero, and I haven't been treating you right. I consider you my friend, and from this day on I want there to be a clean slate between us."

"Bill, you sonofabitch! I was just gonna tell you, you owed me some kinda apology. But now we're square. It's all in the past. Let's shake on it."

"Hell, Eddie, let's drink to it!" So we marched into that speakeasy—right out of the frying pan and into the fire.

DAMON RUNYON There are several versions on the street of how the Ace of Aces lost, then regained, the Watch of Watches. The standard account, related to me by Abadaba Berman but subject to revisionist critique by Dave the Dude, has Rickenbacker and Brigadier General William Lendrum Mitchell, scourge of the U.S. Navy, wandering into the aptly named Red Letter Café, both of them snockered to the gills. After a brief period of libation, the celebrants make the acquaintance of two damsels of dim repute, creatures for whom this establishment is justly famous. The parties enter immediately into financial negotiations, and upon reaching acceptable terms, repair to a brownstone conveniently located next door. There the couples transact their business in a mutually satisfactory manner, and the swains having just bid adieu to their respective fallen flowers, Rickenbacker realizes something is terribly amiss. As the cab roars off, he howls into the night: "My fucking watch is gone." Gone it was.

Exactly how the good Captain, justly renowned for his situational awareness, should have allowed such a thing to happen has never been adequately explained. But one thing is certain. This was no ordinary Benrus or Hamilton. It's one of a dozen platinum tank watches, specially designed by Monsieur Cartier and given by the Frenchies to those Americans deemed most heroic in the Great War. Not even Mitchell has one of these little darbs. Nevertheless, the General, being a leader among men, tries to put matters in perspective for his friend, who is now beside himself with remorse. He explains that the proprietors of the Red Letter, once they hear what an injustice has been wrought, will move heaven and earth to retrieve the errant timepiece. As good as this sounds, reality is and always will be more difficult than it sounds.

"Look, I don't know nuffin' 'bout no watch. But I can let youz tawk to the owna if y'd just cool yer heels at dat table ovuh dere," advises the helpful majordomo. As good as his word he returns within minutes accompanied by a tall notably good-looking stranger.

"Dis is Mista' Diamond, Mista' Jack Diamond. Maybe you hoid a' him." In fact, neither side exactly traveled in the same circles, so the conversation proceeded unhindered by reputation.

"Now look, fellas. You come down here lookin' for a good time. You pick up some frail, an one of 'em lifts your watch. What am I supposed to do? Lots of people come in here, too many to count . . . includin' rubes from the suburbs who probably shouldn't be here in the first place . . . if you catch my drift." Well, no sooner do these words leave Legsy's mouth than he realizes these guys are not about to be scared off by mere words, and that sterner measures are in order. So he reaches into his well-tailored tux and out pops a piece . . . a very large piece, a forty-five built to blow big holes in little people. He lays it down on the table with a clunk and then smiles.

"I used this on a guy in here last year. Took the help all day to clean up the brains." Rickenbacker is beyond words, but Mitchell remains determined to clarify the situation still further.

"You're a two-bit punk used to shooting other punks in the back. This man in front of you was in 134 aerial combats and killed 26 men in fair fights . . . something you know nothing about. Let me tell you what will happen if you were to harm even one hair on his head. A crowd would gather in Times Square and march down here and rip you limb from miserable limb. Then they'd drink your blood and eat the pieces. You got that, Mr. Diamond?" Now, when Billy Mitchell spoke, people had a way of listening. But in this case Legsy was more impressed with the murderous look in Eddie Rickenbacker's cold blue eyes. He stared at them for a long, long time . . . killer to killer . . . eyeball to eyeball . . . and believe me, it wasn't the other guy who blinked.

"Come back tomorrow, gents. Your watch'll be here."

ELIZABETH   Edward, he came to visit me before it vas time for him to go to California. All he does vas mope around za house, not saying much and sleeping all za time. Me, I couldn't understand. He is famous. He has za new job vith the General Motors. Vat could be wrong?

"It's a woman, Mother." Vell I already know zat Blanche Calhoun took sick und died. But zat vas almost a year past.

"It's nobody you know. . . . She's a society lady, married to the son of a big wheel in Detroit," he says.

"Married? Married, you say? Zis not right," I tell him. But then he tells me the lady is getting a divorce. By now my head vas spinning. My boy mixed up vith somebody who is divorced. I'm only thankful zat his father did not live to hear these vurds.

REED CHAMBERS   The change in Eddie was amazing. It was over a year since I'd seen him. I had been talking up aviation around the country, and I brought a SPAD out to Selfridge Field in Detroit. Eddie was there with a crowd of auto execs, but he took me aside right away and told me he was in love with Adelaide Frost, who I knew from the papers had just gotten a divorce from Old Man Durant's son. This sounded fine to me and I told him so. But then he started with his usual tale of class differences and lowly background. I'd heard this just once too often, and basically read him the riot act. Christ, the guy's a national hero and he's worried where he did or did not prep.

The next thing I knew he wanted to fly the SPAD, I guess to impress his Detroit buddies. I warned him that Hobey Baker had gotten himself killed doing the same thing. But Eddie was Eddie, and he laughed in my face.

God, what a flight . . . up and down and every which way. Tops it off with a tailspin that had them running for cover. I couldn't help thinking, as he pulled out, that this was a plane flown by a man in the clutches of Cupid.

JOHN DOS PASSOS, *The Big Money*
The bar was full of men and girls halftight and bellowing and tittering. Charley felt like wringing their goddamn necks. He drank off four whiskies one after another and went around to Mrs. Darling's. Going up in the elevator he began to feel tight. . . . Once inside he let out a whoop. "Now Mr. Charlie," said the colored girl in starched cap and apron who had opened the door, "you know the missis don't like no noise . . . and you're such a civilspoken young gentleman."

"Hello, dearie." He hardly looked at the girl. "Put out the light," he said. "Remember your name's Doris. Go in the bathroom and take your clothes off and don't forget to put on lipstick, plenty of lipstick." He switched off the light and tore off his clothes. In the dark it was hard to get the studs out of his boiled shirt. He grabbed the boiled shirt with both hands and ripped out the buttonholes. "Now come in here, goddamn you. I love you, you bitch Doris." The girl was trembling. When he grabbed her to him she burst out crying.

He had to get some liquor for the girl to cheer her up and that started him off again. Next day he woke up late feeling too lousy to go out to the plant. . . .

WILLIAM CRAPO DURANT   Sometime after I left GM I asked Eddie to come up to Flint and have dinner with Catherine and myself. As was my habit, I immediately brought up the issue at hand, his friendship with Adelaide. Not surprisingly, his initial reaction was one of some discomfort and even hostility. I quickly explained it was not my intent to chastise him . . . quite the opposite. Catherine and I liked Adelaide a great deal. Nor were we under any illusions about the nature of her marriage to my son. It had not worked out and that was that. The whole point of having him to Flint was to inform him that we thoroughly approved of this alliance, and were, in fact, relieved to hear of its existence. I also thought it only fair to tell him that I had established a substantial trust fund for Adelaide, which, in addition to her divorce settlement, should remove any question of her financial independence.

Well, I certainly hadn't banked on his reaction. He virtually broke down at the table and began a lugubrious monologue on his own unworthiness. Catherine thought this quite charming, and I presume told Adelaide, who was in on this little charade from the beginning. I found it embarrassing. I felt badly for Rickenbacker, but I was also puzzled by this show of emotion. The man had faced death countless times, and was, by all appearances, utterly self-confident. I suppose it simply showed that when matters of the heart are concerned, there is simply no predicting human behavior.

ADELAIDE Edward was always very sensitive about the nature of our relationship before we were married. In his book he has us reunited by chance at a party in New York. This was ridiculous. Everybody knew we were close friends, and had been seeing each other from practically the moment the divorce papers became final. But it was really quite a romantic courtship. After Clifford any man would have seemed like a hero. But in this case my beau really was a hero. At times I had to almost pinch myself. And to make it all the better, Edward was just as inclined to place me on a pedestal. It seemed as if my earlier unhappiness was now being rewarded with an equal measure of bliss. He was really quite chivalrous, writing me poems, taking me on long walks, getting down on his knees to propose. I'm quite sure this was a side of him no one else ever saw. Almost a half century of marriage certainly dispelled many of my illusions. And, as it turned out, there were certain things I should have told him before we tied the knot. But I can tell you this without any hesitation. Till the day he died, I never stopped loving Edward Rickenbacker.

ELIZABETH Vedding? Vat vedding? They snuck up to Connecticut vere nobody vould know them. Only Pastor Pister und myself and a few of their smarty friends from New York. Edward should have been married in Columbus, with a church full of people. But

zis is vat happens ven you marry a fallen woman. Pastor Pister—
Edward brought him all zat vay to vash his guilty conscience—he
tried to tell me it vas not a problem. But I know better, and God
above, he knows better.

GOD   Actually, I always liked small ceremonies. Adam and Eve
. . . just the three of us. Mary and Joseph . . . had a good time at
that one too.

ADELAIDE   The wedding was very small, an anticlimax really. It
was the introduction of Edward's car the week before at the New
York Automobile Show that I remember as our real nuptial moment. September 9th, 1922. I helped him with all the decorations
and flowers and was on the platform when they unveiled the sedan
and then the roadster. They were the hits of the show. Crowds
swirled around us and the cars. And in this midst of it Eddie kissed
me and said it was the proudest day of his life. I don't think I ever
saw him happier.

HARRY CUNNINGHAM, AUTOMOBILE MAGNATE   A little after
Billy Durant and GM parted company, I had a talk with him. I
told him Walt Flanders, the production whiz, and Barney Everitt,
the body man, were looking to get something going in the way of
a new car, and did he want a piece. Well, Billy hemmed and hawed,
sayin' he was busy with Durant Motors but that he might be able
to grease the skids on Wall Street, should we be interested in pur-
suing an angle he had been kicking around. The deal was that we
enlist Eddie Rickenbacker as a way of getting across to the public
that this new job represented advanced design and engineering.
This was sweet indeed. I knew he was dead on as far as Rickenbacker's market appeal. Meantime, nobody could put together a
better automotive package than Flanders and Everitt, and with Durant involved you knew there'd be one of his patented stock of-
ferings at the end of the rainbow.

"Eddie's a little headstrong," Durant added as I got up from
the table. "But he won't bother you too much, since I have him
selling Sheridans out in California." And people wonder why they
called the man a genius.

BARNEY EVERITT   Things went off pretty much without a hitch.
Wally and I had got two key design objectives: smooth out engine

vibrations; and lower the center of gravity so the thing would hug the road. In other words, fit it into the middle price bracket through good engineering and not expensive materials. We went after the engine problem by using dual flywheels at either end of the crankshaft and setting the cam in its own separate oil bath, so's we ended up with a 60-horsepower six what run like an eight. Next we stepped down the frame four inches front and rear, usin' wide and very deep eight-inch channels and semi-elliptic springs. We hardly had to tune the suspension, the thing just ran like a charm. Rickenbacker wanted four-wheel brakes, his sole and only suggestion, but we put that on hold to keep production costs down.

Since I was on the West Coast setting up a sales network for Sheridan, I had to outline the necessary features of the car and let the designers carry out my wishes. My partners were professionals in every respect, and quickly produced a prototype which met my specifications on all counts except one—they failed to incorporate the four-wheel brakes that I had used in my race cars and knew were necessary for true safety. But when I visited Detroit and actually saw the first car, I vowed to become more directly involved with the final development. My partners suggested that I undertake an extensive series of tests, which took me over what amounted to multiple thousands of miles across the steaming panhandle of Oklahoma, the endless muddy tracts of Nebraska, and over the craggy peaks of Wyoming. It stood up to everything I could hand it.

While I was doing the testing, my partners, acting on a tip from Mr. William C. Durant, the automotive mogul, were able to secure thoroughly modern factory space at an excellent price from a firm that was giving up the fight. But as fortunate as this seemed at the time, it was easily topped by a development that none of us could have foreseen.

HARRY CUNNINGHAM   Now that we had the car, it was time to promote it. We got in touch with LeRoy Pelletier, best PR man in Detroit. Didn't come cheap, but as things turned out he was worth every penny. Right away he comes up with "The Rickenbacker—A Car Worthy of Its Name." Now Wally especially thought this was laying it on a little thick. But Durant knew better. "In the initial stages of a campaign you can't overdo it. The idea is just to get the name out." Well, you couldn't fault Pelletier on that score. Before we knew it he came up with "Cracker Jacker Rickenbacker," and had Leo Wood working on a song—"In My Rickenbacker," with lines like "She won't jar your vacation/Since there's no vibration." Then we had a press preview, sent photos of the car—complete with the Hat in the Ring insignia and a little SPAD radiator cap—to every newspaper we could find an address for. Within a month we'd blanketed the whole country. The Rickenbacker was just where we wanted it—not on the road, but in the imagination. Pay dirt was just around the corner.

Through it all Billy Durant stayed in the background, always the silent partner. But now it was time for him to work his magic. A quick trip to New York, a string of phone calls, and presto-chango we had our underwriters, Kuhn, Loeb and Company, top kikes on Wall Street. The offering would amount to 75 percent of equity, basically a million shares at five bucks per. They went like hotcakes. It was fucking amazing. Over 13,000 subscribers. A month and a half, and we had a cool five million in the till. Durant and the Jews split a million off the top. We applied two to operating capital, and divvied up the rest—half a million apiece. Not bad for a year's work. When we handed him his check, Rickenbacker looked like he was gonna drop his teeth. He had no idea what had been going on, or what to expect. Kept talking about the car this and the car that. Sure we were going to produce the car. But the stock offering was the whole point . . . that's where the money was. I don't think he ever caught on.

The Rickenbacker Motor Company was such a success initially that I felt I could take on the responsibilities of marriage secure in the knowledge that I had accomplished what I had set out to do. I was still just thirty-one. But I was now a man of affairs, with a substantial fortune behind me. After the overwhelming response to the Rickenbacker at the auto show, my partners reluctantly agreed to dispense with my services long enough for Adelaide and myself to embark on an extended honeymoon tour of Europe. For six weeks we wandered the Continent, the first real relaxation I had granted myself since I left for war over four years before. The passage on the *Majestic* and interludes in France and Italy were particularly restful. Adelaide proved to be just as I hoped—a delightful companion, a loving helpmate, and a thing of everlasting beauty. But she did have a frightening habit of losing valuable items . . . a $325 fur neckpiece, and a very costly diamond pin, which fortunately was recovered. But it served to remind me that, as lovely as she was, my new wife was a potentially very costly addition to my life.

Another ominous sign cropped up on our side trip to Berlin. I hadn't forgotten the all-metal D.1 monoplane the Germans showed me after the Armistice. Now the Junkers company had come out with a duralumin four-passenger version that, as a favor to my old friend John Larsen, I scouted out for potential airmail and passenger work. The people on Unter den Linden had a shabby discouraged look to them that I couldn't help contrasting to the advanced design of this plane and the self-confidence of my hosts. They were basically the same bunch who had seen us the first time—Junkers people plus Ernst Udet, Erhardt Milch, and Hermann Goering, who was obviously the leader. At dinner he got pretty tight and told me: "Herr Eddie, our German Empire will be regained from the air. First, our youth will join glider clubs. Then we will build a commercial air fleet using planes that we can transform into bombers. Then, when it is too late to stop us, we will build a real air force. We have no quarrel with your country, but we have scores to settle with the Anglo-Saxons and the French-men." This was something Mitchell and his boys needed to hear, and I made up my mind to tell him as soon as I got back. Unfortunately, I soon discovered that his scattershot mouth had finally gotten him into big trouble.

BILLY MITCHELL   My campaign for Air Power had started to draw reactionary blood. After I sank the captured German battle-ship right in front of the Navy's collective nose and Hughes went ahead and pushed through the Washington Treaty, stopping fur-ther waste of public funds by building more of those floating cof-fins, I knew the interests would come after me. But how could I back off? If we didn't have an independent air service, Air Power would never be given more than lip service. And if that happened, then our country would be completely helpless in the future. So I continued speaking my mind, and let the Devil take the hindmost. The bastards slowly ground me down—busted me to Colonel, transferred me to the boondocks, and, when I still wouldn't shut up, court-martialed me. Like always, Eddie stood up and spoke his mind, testifying that the nation owed me a debt of gratitude, not a court-martial, for speaking the truth. But with the likes of Drum and MacArthur on the Board he might as well have been whistling

Dixie. After the verdict, I remember telling him peacetime was bound to be tough on straight-shooters like him and me. He just laughed and offered me a job in that car company of his.

MARGUERITE SHEPHERD   I was already installed as his secretary when he arrived back from his honeymoon. His first words to me were: "Who the hell are you?" I told him my name, that I was from Hamilton across the river, and that I was a no-nonsense person who didn't appreciate profanity. He answered that he needn't bother learning my name, since I was probably just on the lookout for a husband, and in a few weeks he'd have to train another girl. I told him I had no interest in marriage. He then began to flirt with me. This had gone far enough. "Mr. Rickenbacker, I will tell you this just once. I am here to work and nothing else. If you persist in this behavior, I will contact the proper authorities." He looked at me for a very long time. "You're perfectly right in saying that. If I ever step out of line, I encourage you to call my wife Adelaide immediately. Now, may I call you Sheppy, as I don't like the name Marguerite?" I was never anything else to him . . . for forty-four years. He was the finest man I have ever known. And this became abundantly clear in the crisis which soon engulfed us.

I decided that the 1924 model year was the ideal time to introduce the first mass-produced passenger vehicle with four-wheel brakes. Under a cloak of secrecy we developed an all-wheel brake system—operated mechanically, not hydraulically, for simplicity's sake—and then tested it until it was as bulletproof as human hands could make it. When we built up a sufficient inventory of Rickenbackers with four-wheel brakes, we ran full-page advertisements all across the country. The reaction was immediate and overwhelmingly positive.

With one big exception. I had failed to consider the predicament of the other manufacturers. They had millions upon millions of dollars sunk into inventories of outmoded two-wheel-brake models. In order to unload these vehicles, a decision was made to convince the public that four-wheel brakes were dangerous—the exact opposite of the truth. A whispering campaign was begun. Dealers everywhere joined forces against the Rickenbacker. Some alleged that it would flip over in a curve; others suggested it would skid without warning, and still others gave the impression that a Rickenbacker would stop so fast it would throw its passengers through the windshield. While well-informed customers saw through this hail of propaganda, many did not, and the bottom fell out of our sales. Before I knew it the company was in trouble.

SHEPPY It was very difficult to watch. Every morning Mr. Rickenbacker would arrive at the office bright and chipper. Then he would sit at his desk all day long, conferring with people from the factory, telephoning dealers, and doing everything possible to instill confidence in those around him. Finally, in the early evening he would leave, gray and haggard . . . a little more so each day. Because I handled his correspondence, I had a special insight into the kind of burden he was bearing. During 1925 and 1926, Mr. Rickenbacker took out a series of loans to meet payroll amounting to a quarter of a million dollars, all of it under his own name. So as the company sank, it was dragging him down with it.

BOO HERNDON, THE GHOSTWRITER When he told me the story of Rickenbacker Motor's fall from grace, certain things didn't add up. I kept stopping him, asking for more detail and clarification. Eventually, he slammed his hand down on the desk and went into a regular tirade. He screamed and ranted . . . accused me of calling him a liar and threatened to fire me on the spot. Well, if my days as a newspaperman taught me anything, it was never to bite the hand which happened to be feeding you at the moment. So I said, "Look, it was your company. You know what happened. We'll write it just as you say." That quieted him down; but it left me wondering why he was so sensitive on this. I suppose he just couldn't stand any sort of failure.

HARRY CUNNINGHAM When the company hit the skids, Rickenbacker couldn't take it. Cooked up this wild story in his mind that the rest of the industry did us in because of four-wheel brakes. That was bullshit. The company went down for two reasons and two reasons only. In the fall of '23 Walt Flanders got himself tanked up on Canadian Club and drove his Packard into a tree . . . killing him. You don't lose a guy like Walt and not suffer for it. Then in '25 and '26 the auto market went sour. Like everybody, we cut prices—right at the time the suppliers was raisin' theirs. Charlie Nash warned us all we was cuttin' our own throats. But what the hell else could you do? So the big fish survived and the little ones got eaten. That's the way of the world.

But Rickenbacker couldn't see it. He took it personal, as if the whole thing was designed just to get him. And when things really got bad, he wanted us to go into hock—like it's a matter of honor or something. Now remember, we'd all made a pretty penny on this deal and weren't about to throw in good money after bad. So we told him if you think it's so important to save the company, then you borrow the money and we'll step aside. Well, that's exactly what he did, to the tune of a quarter million. But in the larger scheme of things, this was chicken feed. Finally, he panicked. Came to us lookin' for a way out. At this point there wasn't many options. Told him if he'd resign, we'd liquidate and get what we could. Didn't work out bad though. After all the money passed under the table was factored in, we got about forty cents on the dollar. Stockholders took a bath though.

They called him the Lone Eagle . . . everybody did. Always the solitary, even as a little eaglet navigating the hills of Minnesota or the alleyways of D.C., where his father C.A. was a congressman. His only friend was his mother, and he didn't like her that much. Lindbergh or at best Lindy . . . never Charlie, barely ever Charles.

Discounting movie stars and maybe Jack Kennedy, he was probably the best-looking American public figure of the century. The picture of him standing in his leather flight jacket flanked by the *Spirit of St. Louis,* just before he took off, melted a million hearts, including Anne Morrow's, whose father was a full partner at the House of Morgan. And why not? This exquisite man-child was about to die in an utterly quixotic pursuit, flying alone across the Atlantic—New York to Paris—and he didn't look the least bit concerned. "Okay, take your goddamned picture and get it over with, I'm busy." Except he didn't curse, and he didn't die. He made it all the way to Le Bourget and in the dark found a sea of faces waiting to make him a god. It was the same everywhere he went. "In the spring of 1927," wrote F. Scott Fitzgerald, "something bright and alien flashed across the sky. A young Minnesotan who seemed to have nothing in common with his generation did a heroic thing, and for a moment people set down their glasses in country clubs and speakeasies and thought of their old best dreams."

So Lindbergh would spend the rest of his life swinging on a trapeze wired so he could never fall off. The kidnapping death of his and Anne's baby only added a necessary measure of tragedy. Erudition? Without benefit of training or much education, he dubbed himself scientist and collected Nobel prizewinners as colleagues. Family values? When he took to wandering off on further adventures, the neglected Anne wrote books that made them both even more famous. Humanitarian? Jew-baiter and pro-German right to the Normandy beachhead and the gates of Auschwitz. The public held their noses and allowed that a few indiscretions should not obscure the larger picture.

Of course, Fast Eddie Rickenbacker, heretofore America's reigning aviator and just now getting used to being a former automobile manufacturer, saw the ascension of the Lone Eagle a bit differently.

REED CHAMBERS   As the curtain fell on Rickenbacker Motors, Eddie began to take a real interest in civil aviation. He was instrumental in getting the Junkers people to show the D.1 to Bill Stout, who used it as a model for his 2-AT, the first all-metal aircraft produced in the U.S. Henry Ford, who was already interested in fostering airlines, built Stout a factory for the 2-AT—which, incidentally, was the precursor of the famous Ford Tri-motor. Soon after, Stout and some of Ford's people came to Eddie and me offering to sell us four 2-ATs at a very attractive price, if we would bid on the Atlanta-to-Miami mail contract, CAM-10, and establish passenger service. That led us to set up Florida Airways, an ill-fated enterprise if there ever was one. Christ, during delivery from Dearborn one of our pilots managed to crash into the other three of our aircraft parked at the Nashville Airport. And things continued roughly in the same direction. Passengers were nonexistent, and to make any money on airmail by weight we had to send ourselves bricks back and forth along the route. But this didn't help much, and in less than a year Florida Airlines bellied up, leaving Ford holding the bag for four aircraft, only one of them in working order. That was the beginning of the bad blood between Ford and Eddie, but the experience also left Eddie bitten by the air-travel bug.

And that led the both of us to New York in the spring of '27 to see if we could work out something with Juan Trippe. You see, Trippe and C.V. Whitney, backed by Billy Vanderbilt and Averell Harriman, had just formed Pan American and were vying with our group, pushed mainly by Percy Rockefeller and Richie Hoyt, to grab the airmail contracts to Havana and later down into South America. The idea of the meeting was to merge our resources and gain enough momentum to have a chance of succeeding in what was a very ambitious undertaking. This eventually would go forward, although Eddie and I were pushed out at a fairly early stage by that skunk Trippe. Meanwhile, this particular meeting turned into a donnybrook.

We made the mistake of holding it in the bar of the Brevoort Hotel, whose owner, Raymond Orteig, had established the $25,000 prize for the first nonstop New York–to–Paris flight. Well, on this very day the Lone Eagle himself arrived from California in his storied Ryan monoplane, set to give it the old college try. All the papers, of course, picked it up, and the place was in a commotion, since about three other teams were also going to take off within a week or so. We never really got down to business. Instead, we started talking about how distracting these stunt flights were from the main job of getting the airlines going. But then the conversation shifted to Lindbergh, with Trippe and Eddie getting in a doozy of an argument. Trippe thought Lindbergh had a real shot at it, since his plane was light and simple and had big fuel reserves. Eddie said he was a dead duck . . . a sacrificial lamb about to be slain on an altar of newsprint. He kept going on about how this apparently fine young man was being exploited by the publicity hounds, and what a shame it was that they were going to cost him his life. Trippe said some pretty sarcastic things in return, and I thought for a minute that Eddie might jump him. It ended with bad feelings on all sides. Of course, all of this is pretty amusing now when you consider what really did happen, and how Eddie ended up feeling about Lindbergh.

BOO HERNDON, THE GHOSTWRITER   It must be obvious now that working for him was akin to tiptoeing through a minefield. And the record will note that I stepped on more than my share. Lindbergh, for example. We were going on one day about aviation in the twenties, and I made the mistake of interjecting something about how Lindbergh's flight must have given it a real boost. That was all he needed. "Lindbergh? . . . Lindbergh! That son of a bitch was a nothing, a phony of the first order. One flight . . . one fucking flight. All he had to do was stay awake. He wouldn't have lasted a week on the Western Front. A creation of the press, nothing more . . . 'Lucky Lindy,' the only true thing they ever said about him. And I had to read that crap till I choked . . . year after year. You make sure that there's nothing—not a word—about him in the autobiography. If I so much as see his name, you're done for, understand, Herndon?" So that's why the autobiography is blank on the subject. Only book that covered the airlines' early days and never mentioned the Lone Eagle.

It was pure envy, of course. Lindbergh had shoved him out of the public eye, obscured him. He was now America's favorite pilot and Rickenbacker could never forgive him that.

GOD   It's always the same story. Why do you think Cain whacked Abel? I thought of maybe giving Eddie back his SPAD. It might have been fun watching him go after Limburger, or whatever his name was.

ADELAIDE   Every marriage has its mutual accommodations. In our case they were probably greater than most. But I do think our ability to look beyond certain things actually strengthened the bond between us. Certainly it put it on a more realistic basis.

Edward was a strong man, filled with verve and energy. I knew this when I married him, and I'd been around men enough to know this could lead them into compromising situations. I won't say it didn't hurt to be aware of this. But Edward, unlike Clifford, never tried to humiliate me. He kept these things well away from the home. Sheppy, in her day, was quite an attractive woman. But there was never any question of an involvement. She was as much my friend and confidante as his.

And in the meantime our intimate life was always . . . well . . . very intimate. But there is a twist here. Clifford's tastes were, to say the least, varied. So much so that after almost ten years of marriage I probably experienced more than most wives of that time ever dreamed of. Most of this, of course, was absolutely disgusting and I submitted only because he physically forced himself on me. But I must admit there were certain things that Clifford exposed me to that I actually came to find quite pleasant. Edward, for all his worldly experience, was really quite naive. And when, in the course of things, I showed a certain willingness, it absolutely delighted him. He used to call me his little French courtesan. It became our special secret, something to come home to in the face of temptation.

Of course, there was something else . . . something I've never stopped regretting. Clifford hated children, absolutely abhorred the idea of having them. I always took precautions, and I think it was also behind his attraction to unnatural practices. But, in spite of this, sometime late in our marriage I found myself pregnant. I had no particular desire to have his child, and he was absolutely against it. So he found a doctor, and that was that . . . or so it seemed. Instead, I drifted into a state of extreme melancholy and had, I suppose, a nervous breakdown. My recovery lasted several months, and left me determined to divorce him. But in the meantime Catherine Durant came west to help get me back on my feet. She was my best friend, and I told her everything. I think this is why Mr. Durant established the trust fund, and why he and Catherine supported my marriage to Edward.

But I couldn't bring myself to tell him . . . that was my greatest mistake . . . until, of course, after several years of marriage, it became apparent that we might not be able to have children. We went to doctor after doctor. It was never clear one way or the other, but something must have gone wrong originally in California.

Eddie couldn't have been more wonderful. I offered him an annulment, but he wouldn't hear of it. He was obviously devastated. Yet he told me he loved me more than any child, and besides we could always adopt. We did, of course, and he proved to be a wonderful father to David and Bill. But he always insisted that we keep their adoptions hushed up.

Life is so strange. Edward never got the chance to have children of his own. And the Durants, after making every effort to clean up after Clifford, ended up losing all their money and living nearly in poverty. In the meantime, the reprobate son prospered and grew immensely wealthy. There's just no justice.

GOD   So ignorance has its say. First, it wasn't her at all. Rickenbacker had the sperm count of sandstone. And as far as justice goes . . . justice is what I want it to be. They seem to think I owe them something, that we have some kind of agreement. A covenant? I don't remember signing anything. Do they accord the same prerogatives to their inferiors? Is there a covenant of the wild? Did, at some point, representative sheep arrive in business suits lugging briefcases full of carefully inscribed parchment? Can wolves dutifully masquerading as dogs sue if they get shorted on the Alpo exchange? Did the passenger pigeons have recourse to the courts? How about the buffaloes? They want a merciful deity. But what the hell's merciful about an abattoir?

Remember, mercy is defined by those in a position to be merciful. So is justice. I may be just. I may be merciful. But that's for

Me to know. "Explain the ways of God to man. . . ." What bullshit. Do they attempt to explain quantum mechanics to orang- utans, who, incidentally, I cast after *their* image?

Why can't they leave it at this? They are what I made them. They amuse me. They keep me from being bored. The end is probably no worse than the beginning. The rest is my business, unless I choose to reveal it.

Chapter Five

ALFRED P. SLOAN Shortly after Eddie's company went bankrupt, I invited him over to my office in the General Motors Building for a chat. He wasn't in a very good mood. In fact, he seemed quite bitter. I began by telling him that I had been keeping an eye on him at Mr. Durant's request, and had been favorably impressed. But instead of waiting to hear what I had to say, he blurted out: "Then why the hell didn't you put a stop to the whispering campaign against my car?" When I told him that no such thing existed and that his car simply fell victim to the business cycle, he jumped to his feet, muttered something like "Nuts to that," and stalked off toward the door. As he went, I told him that if he left the office, he would never be allowed back in. This took some of the starch out of his sails, and he stood glaring at me from across the room.

"Now, Eddie, why don't you come over here and have a seat? I have some important things to tell you and not a lot of time."

"I'll listen, but I'm not promising a damn thing."

"I know that, Eddie. Now look, when I told you that your car fell prey to the business cycle I meant more than just that. Things have changed in the automotive industry. This business was started by visionaries, people like yourself. But it's matured, grown into huge organizations. The days when a fellow like you could just move in and start his own car company have passed. Look at me, Eddie, nobody would pick me out from a thousand other men on the street. I'm a bureaucrat, a faceless bureaucrat. That's why I'm sitting in this chair and not Mr. Durant. Cost accounting, organization, management, Eddie, that's what required now. Ford will learn eventually also, there's no other choice with something this big."

"If all this is true, why are you bothering even to tell me? You're saying I'm washed up."

"No, Eddie, I'm not saying that at all. Far from it. We still have a vital need for people like you. Simply in a different role. You're a pioneer, a trailblazer, and as this industry expands it will continue to demand men like yourself to push out ahead of the others. That's why I'm prepared to go to considerable lengths to enlist your services."

"I'd have to give that a whole lot of thought. I'm not about to—"

"You don't have to decide now. But what I'm proposing is that you remain primarily a free agent. At times we may want you to come on board to fulfill a specific objective. But for the most part you would remain your own man . . . but always with our backing. There are certain enterprises with which, for one reason or another, corporate involvement is deemed premature, but which could still profit from your participation. Others you might find on your own, and desire to take a position. Provided they are sound, we would sponsor you and ensure that you receive a line of credit. There will be times when we will want to take a more active role, but generally you would run these companies yourself. It is very important that you continue to be seen as an independent businessman, an entrepreneur. Do you understand how this might play out, Eddie?"

"Look, Mr. Sloan, I've got certain obligations I can't just walk away from—"

"I'm glad you like the concept. Now I've been led to believe that you and the principals over at Rickenbacker Motors didn't suffer too badly, but that there is this matter of a $250,000 personal debt. You should stop worrying about that. At some point in the future we will arrange things so you can pay that debt off in full. Your reputation is important to us. We can't have you carrying bad debts. But on the other hand, we want to show the public that you dug your way out from under this burden through your own hard work. Are we seeing eye-to-eye?"

"Well, as far as that goes, yes, but there are still a lot of details—"

"Good, now let's get down to real business. Recently I've had some bad news out of Indianapolis. As you know, the 500 has long been a prime test bed for new technology and a showcase for the industry in general. Heretofore, we've had a good relationship with management—but they're about played out. Frank Wheeler and Art Newby are both dead, Carl Fisher is spending all his time in Florida developing Miami, and Jim Allison wants out. Now the 300 acres the Speedway sits on has become quite valuable as the city has expanded. And rumor has it that a group of local realtors are putting together a consortium to buy the whole package, their object being to subdivide. Obviously the track will be razed, and that will be the end of the 500. We can't let this happen. I know you are friends with Jim Allison. We want you to cement that friendship by making him a generous offer for the Speedway. The realtors are talking in the neighborhood of half a million. I think you could go as much as two hundred thousand over that. We want Allison in particular to be satisfied, we have some interest in his aero-engineering business. But primarily we want the Speedway. Eddie, get us that track!"

"I think that could be arranged."

"Excellent. And as far as any misunderstanding between us, I hope we are friends now."

"Mr. Sloan, I've always considered you my friend. . . . In fact, uhh . . . well . . . my friends usually call me Rick. . . ."

"Oh, I see. . . . Well, Eddie, I'll try to remember that."

GOD   They're so cute when they do that.

FINIS FARR   As he shaved every morning, Rick saw in the mirror the image of a thirty-five-year-old male out of a job and in debt to the tune of a quarter of a million dollars. To other men this would have been daunting, but Rick took it as an asset. He pronounced failure beneficial, a lesson which taught you your limits and how to account for them in the future. Detroit's bankers could not fail to be impressed by this brand of intestinal fortitude, and Frank Blair of Union Guardian Trust made it clear that he would listen long and hard to any moneymaking proposition that Rick might present. This was a tribute to the man's force of personality and nothing else. By all appearances his cash position had not a thing to do with Rick's calculations as to whether a deal could be closed. Therefore, he did not hesitate to enter into serious negotiations with Jim Allison for the sale of the Indianapolis Motor Speedway, home of what was then called the Decoration Day 500. When Allison suggested a sum in the neighborhood of $700,000, Rick didn't bat an eye, acting as if he could easily meet such a price, should he be given a thirty-day option to buy.

The bargain having been struck, Rick next consulted Frank Blair. The banker told him that he believed a bond issue for the Speedway could be floated, but that this demanded legal wording, the approval of the Michigan Attorney General, and the vending of the paper—all of which took time. Days, then weeks passed, and Rick's option was slipping away like sand in an hourglass. Finally, with but one hour to go, everything fell into place and the money was delivered.

Through it all Rick had remained outwardly calm and confident. When a man has fought the Flying Circus, this sort of self-control comes as second nature. Still, there must have been doubts and even anguish. Yet all came out well in the end. Rick was now the proprietor of the world's most important motor race, and had proved beyond a shadow of a doubt that he was a true insider.

As a former racer myself, I looked at things from the perspective of the man behind the wheel. His needs, his interests, and above all, his safety remained uppermost in my mind. When I bought the Speedway, it was paved with bricks, a rough and very abrasive surface that was hard on tires. I had the oval completely redone with velvet-smooth Kentucky asphalt, allowing considerably higher speeds. But still, going over the walls remained one of the biggest hazards at Indy. I reconstructed the barriers using steel reinforcing and energy-absorbing chain-link fencing, so the racers could drive hard at all points and know they would not end up in the stands. I also had the curves revamped, increasing the banking so they could be negotiated faster and safer.

I firmly believed we were putting on one of the greatest shows on earth and that as many people as possible should have the chance to enjoy it. So at the first opportunity I arranged for my old friend Merlin H. Aylesworth, the head of the National Broadcasting Company, to be present in my box on race day. It didn't take him long to see the event's potential, and from then on there was start-to-finish coverage via a national hookup. Now Indy had millions rather than thousands of fans.

No sooner had I succeeded in putting Indy back on the map

than the bottom fell out of the stock market and the Depression rolled in. Yet the Speedway's bond issue remained afloat, and, unlike every other one of its kind in the State of Michigan, continued paying dividends.

Soon enough I had things straightened out sufficiently that I only had to devote several weeks a year to race promotion, leaving the day-to-day management in the hands of my subordinates. This arrangement proved satisfactory throughout the thirties and up until World War II, when I closed down the track for the duration. After the War, with my increased airline responsibilities, I decided the time had come to get out. Acting on the recommendations of Wilbur Shaw, one of my best drivers and a three-time winner, I sold the Speedway to Anton Hulman, Jr., scion of a monied Terre Haute family, for exactly what I paid in the first place, discounting totally the many hundreds of thousands of dollars' worth of safety improvements I had poured into the facility.

This was only proper. I always considered ownership a sacred trust. The true reward came from knowing we at Indy were pushing the automobile industry to improve the state of the art. For race day and its challenges were easily equal to years of routine testing. In other words, without the Speedway your brand-new car would be not much better than your neighbor's beat-up old jalopy.

MAURI ROSE, DRIVER He was a penny-pinching fuck. All he cared about was raising the speeds. If you crashed and burned, he'd toss your charred carcass over the wall and scream bloody murder until the stewards waved the green flag.

AUGIE DUESENBERG We knew Eddie too well. When he came in, we got out of Indy. Went to building passenger cars exclusively.

HARRY MILLER, DESIGNER OF THE REVOLUTIONARY MILLER 91 RACER Rickenbacker? Contributions? Well, I named my dog Rick. . . .

"Ace Drummond," now that was certainly my most offbeat undertaking, an action cartoon based on my own combat exploits in World War I. I was approached by a number of Detroit businessmen who offered to supply seed money, cartoonists, and take care of syndication. But I supplied the story and dialogue. At the height of the strip's readership, "Ace" appeared on the pages of something like 135 papers.

REED CHAMBERS It was late '29—I remember the date because it was right after the Crash—when a congressman from Michigan, Representative Clancy, began lobbying to have Eddie awarded the Congressional Medal of Honor. I don't know how or why this fellow took such a liking to Rickenbacker, but he surely was determined. A good thing too, because it was an uphill fight from the word go. First, there was trouble in the House with the Drys, who, like everybody else, knew that Eddie was not averse to taking a drink now and then . . . and any time in between, for that matter.

No sooner did Clancy have that smoothed over than he ran into a brick wall in the Senate. This time the problem was Hiram Bingham, the Yale man who had discovered the Inca stronghold Machu Picchu and then turned to politics. He let it be known that he was "unalterably opposed," citing Eddie's supposed commercialization of his combat record. That was a bum rap; Eddie had turned down all manner of endorsements after the War, including a big movie contract.

Anyway, Clancy got in touch with yours truly, urging me to talk to Bingham as a fellow Eli and a member of the air corps. I owed Eddie at least that much. So I went to see the senator in Washington. Right off he said that if I was there to plead that "damn Rickenbacker's" case, I might as well not waste my words. Well, I just sort of backtracked, and after about fifteen minutes of fast talking managed to get to the bottom of things. Bingham had been the Deputy Commander of Issoudun when Eddie scattered a whole damn baseball game by flat-spinning a Nieuport. I guess Bingham had ended up with his face in the dirt. As he told me the story, for some reason I started to laugh. I felt sure he was going to throw me out of his office, but I just couldn't stop. Luckily it must have been contagious, since by the time he finished we were both doubled up.

That was pretty much the end of it. Clancy kept working his end as if his life depended on it, and Eddie finally got his medal. I'll tell you, those folks in Michigan sure must have loved Eddie.

They did indeed. Eddie had slipped into a particularly sweet little niche in Detroit's feeding chain. With very little effort and practically no danger he was making simply being Eddie Rickenbacker pay for itself. Most citizens of a country mired in the worst economic depression in history would have killed for an equivalent spot. In fact, many killed for a whole lot less—like a two-dollar watch or a half-drunk bottle of muscatel. Eddie hadn't survived this long by playing the fool. When caught in an updraft he had learned to spread his wings, and, of course, his legs. Sure he was a whore. But so was practically everybody else. He just charged more and served fewer clients. And he never forgot the hooker's credo—"You got it. You sell it. And lo and behold, you still got it." Long before it ever dawned on Dirty Harry, Eddie realized that a man had to know his own limitations. But in those limitations were always possibilities. He might not be a captain of industry. He might be just a shill. But that was now, and there was always tomorrow. The trick was knowing what game was being played, not losing your concentration, and biding your time. Meanwhile, there was plenty of fun to be had.

GOD   Scribe, let me remind you that words don't cloud *My* vision. Are you feckless enough to believe justification signifies absolution? Has it occurred to you that his consorting with prostitutes may have rubbed off? Your utilitarian Rickenbacker is simply bouncing between degrees of damnation. And *My* scales don't round off to the nearest misdeed. There may be a tomorrow, there may be an eternity. But life for you air-breathers is finite, and the parking meter is running. So don't try to bullshit *Me!!!*

JOHN DOS PASSOS, *The Big Money*
  Charley laughed. "My what a sweet little girl! . . . But you must never be scared in a car when I'm driving. If there's one thing I can do, it's drive a car. But I don't like to drive a car. Now if I had my own ship here. How would you like to take a nice trip in a plane? . . .
  They were running along beside the railroad track. They were catching up on two red lights. "I wonder if that's the New York train. . . . Hell, I can beat him to the crossin." . . . The bar was down at the crossing. Charley stepped on the gas. They crashed through the bar, shattering their headlights. The car swerved around sideways. Their eyes were full of the glare of the locomotive headlight and the shriek of the whistle. . . .

SHEPPY   The accident was serious. The railroad engineer had seen him racing ahead. There was a woman in the car, and he had been drinking heavily. The police took photographs at the scene.

He tried to laugh it off. Even tried to play golf the next day. But the young lady had a broken ankle and was threatening to sue. I know this because I delivered a three-thousand-dollar check to her in the hospital in exchange for a waiver. We managed to keep it out of the newspapers. But I'm sure Adelaide knew the circumstances.

The situation was intolerable, and I marched into his office and told him so. "You think you are invincible, but you're not. Your reputation is everything; one misstep will destroy it. I'm no Pollyanna. I know you're a man and this is what men do. But if you must, do it carefully."

He simply nodded, and I left. But there were no more repetitions. Years later, for no apparent reason, he reminded me of my little speech and told me it was the best advice he had ever received.

AMELIA EARHART   I flew into Indianapolis from Chicago, for the race there. I had a minor crack-up and broke part of my ship's landing gear. He was waiting at the field. He was tall and angular, and wore a light herringbone tweed jacket, fawn pleated slacks, and two-toned wing-tips. His polka-dot tie was done in a very tight knot, and there was a monogrammed linen handkerchief peeking out of his breast pocket. He said very little on the way to the track, but was not unfriendly or condescending. He seemed to view me as an equal, and during the Triple-A ceremony before the start of the race gave me a conspiratorial wink.

He drank heavily at the banquet that night, but appeared completely unaffected. He was pleasant and listened carefully to what I was saying. I'm afraid I monopolized the conversation. As dinner was breaking up he asked me quietly if I would like to go for a ride in the country. It was a lovely clear night, and, frankly, I was flattered.

He drove what turned out to be a Rickenbacker, and told me about the rise and fall of his car company. I was so engrossed I failed to realize how far we had gone. He said he had a small hunting lodge a few miles further, and suggested we go there for a nightcap.

As soon as we entered he began making love to me. He was a very big man, sleekly muscled. There was an urgency to his passion.

He breathed heavily and seemed desperate to thrust himself even further inside of me. I felt as if I was being ravished by a stallion. I was very excited and climaxed long before him.

Between episodes—this went on for several hours—we talked and smoked cigarettes. He asked me if I thought I was a good pilot. "Not especially," I told him, "but I make good choices." He laughed and said that was his trick too. He told me I looked like Lindbergh, which unfortunately everybody noticed. He wanted to know if I ever made love in an airplane, and we agreed that something of this sort might be arranged between the two of us.

Then he brought up the autogiro. I'd just taken one up to 18,500 feet for a record, and planned to fly it coast-to-coast. "They're dangerous," he said. I begged to differ.

"They're the safest planes in the air, and they're going to bring a lot more women into aviation."

"I don't mean dangerous that way." He didn't explain himself further. We had one more brief meeting, but never managed the joint flight. I regret that.

ALFRED P. SLOAN The time had arrived to bring Eddie back into the fold. We wanted him to help market the new LaSalle and pep up the Cadillac dealers, who were running into some sales resistance. But more important, I wanted him to learn General Motors' system of cost accounting.

"We follow the money here, Eddie. On any given day I know exactly how much is being spent on what, and why. When others in the industry talk of dollars, we talk in cents. The Devil is in the details, and there is no better means of rooting him out than through strict bookkeeping. That is the secret of our success. And it will be the secret of your success, when you apply the lessons you learn at GM to aeronautics."

"Aeronautics?"

"Exactly. Eddie, as strong as the automotive industry appears today, it is our belief—Mr. Ford's and my own—that we face a severe challenge in the near future. That challenge will come from the small personal aircraft. You see, just as every man wants to own his own car, there will soon be a similar urge to own a plane. What could be more pleasant than traveling to work and making short trips in a personal flying machine? Such a device would seem to have the capacity of doing everything that an automobile can do, only faster and without the necessity of building and maintaining a vast network of roads. This, of course, is an illusion. . . ."

"It certainly is. The average man will always lack the reflexes and special skills necessary to fly a plane successfully. Why, during the War not more than one man in twenty . . ."

"Correct, Eddie. But before this becomes clear a great many resources could be misdirected, and the automobile business could suffer accordingly. That is why it is so important to get aviation on the right track. There is certainly a role for air transport beyond hauling mail. But the rapid transit of passengers demands large planes flown by professional pilots. A man should be able to drive his car to a regional airport and travel in the comfort and security which only a modern well-managed airline can provide. The government stands ready to do its part. Your friend Mitchell has made enemies, but he has gotten his message across. It is generally understood that a modern air force will be based on long-range bombers, and that this will require industries highly capable of producing and operating large aircraft. So the airlines have an ally in the Hoover Administration. But Washington can only do so much."

"That's for sure. If given the opportunity they'll stifle free enterpr—

"Yes, and this is where we come in. Mr. Ford and myself agree that a certain amount of support is well-warranted. We are already in the process of investing in promising ventures—not only airlines, but also aircraft constructors and related technologies. We will provide capital and we will also provide leadership. We are grooming you for such a role, just as Mr. Ford has taken an interest in Charles Lindbergh. Together, you represent the best aviation has to offer. You have the public's trust. Should you become involved in an undertaking, it will signify progress and the correct course of action. This is particularly important at the moment. We have indications that certain developments in small plane design—some of which you may be aware of—could divert attention and badly disrupt our plans.

"The autogiro?"

"Yes, Eddie, the autogiro."

This is the story of Harold Pitcairn. He was born rich in Pennsylvania, and grew up skinny, mechanically inclined, and obsessed with flight. The family discovered too late they had raised a bird-man. Still, they sent him to the Wharton School, and made him treasurer of the family holding company, a serious holder of things like Pittsburgh Plate Glass. But Harold only went to the office and set up a one-man aviation division in Bryn Athyn. There he put his friend Agnew Larsen to work designing airframes. Harold always took care of his friends, even if he didn't exactly take care of business. So one day his father stopped by to find him staring out the window in the general direction of Bryn Athyn. Knowing he was licked, the old man emancipated Harold from his corporate post and bankrolled Pitcairn Aviation.

Beginning in the summer of 1925, Harold and Larsen built a series of fast little aeroracers, which they campaigned with growing success. After one particularly sweet win, he took his designer aside and told him they were going to build a fleet of planes.

"A fleet?" Larsen asked. "Why in hell do you need a fleet?"

"So we can start an airline," announced Harold Pitcairn.

The idea was to carry the mail, and, at the going Post Office rate of up to three dollars a pound, not a bad one. They developed a fast, steady little biplane, the PA-5; bid successfully on CAM-19 (the route linking New York, Philadelphia, Washington, Richmond, Greensboro, Spartanburg, and Atlanta); and set about delivering the mail. Soon they grabbed CAM-10 and pushed as far south as Miami. By mid-1928, Pitcairn Aviation was flying nearly a third of the country's airmail mileage.

But the cost was higher than Harold ever imagined. Just two weeks into operations, pilot Ed Morrisey perished in a fireball that had been his PA-5. Eleven days later it was Jim Reid, field manager at Philadelphia. There were no more fatalities, but pilots kept falling from the skies with terrifying regularity, tearing up crops and crashing into barns—this is how aviators first "bought the farm." But nothing, nothing could buy back the lives of Harold's pilots. They were his friends, and he felt terrible. Others would soldier on, learn to fly on instruments, and gradually lengthen the odds in their favor. But Harold Pitcairn opted for a more radical solution. First, he sold the airline to an operator named Clement Keys, who renamed it Eastern Air Service and proceeded to mismanage the enterprise until it was ripe to fall into the waiting arms of Fast Eddie Rickenbacker. Meanwhile, Harold took his profits, which were substantial, and began looking for a plane based on entirely different principles, a plane that couldn't crash and hurt his friends.

He found it in the work and person of Juan de la Cierva. As a young man, Cierva had designed a bomber for the Spanish government, only to see it crash in a low-altitude turn. Repelled by the waste, he came away from the wreck of his airplane determined to explore the theory of flight in search of safer alternatives. In time he came upon the idea of a rotating wing—not a helicopter, which struck him as too complex and unstable—but a freewheeling airfoil that would supply lift from above while a conventional engine and propeller drove the craft through the air. There was a problem initially with balance caused by the uneven lift generated by advancing and retreating blades; but Cierva solved it with a series of hinges that allowed the blades to flex and thereby achieve equilibrium. By the time Pitcairn and Larsen arrived on the scene, lured to Madrid by rumors of an amazing flying machine, a prototype had already made a series of short but successful flights.

"What do you call it?" Harold asked.

"Autogiro," Cierva answered, referring to the blades' self-activated pursuit of stability. And that wasn't all. Cierva's design incorporated a tilting rotor hub, which not only replaced the elevator and ailerons in controlling roll and pitch, but could spin up the blades on the ground and then pull the autogiro straight up to a height of thirty feet where the propeller took over. Landing was not vertical, but close to it. And perhaps best of all, should the engine fail in flight, the freewheeling blades would maintain enough lift to deposit the autogiro gently on the ground. It was essentially a crash-proof aircraft, a flying machine with its own built-in parachute.

Cierva wanted to move to London to oversee further development and eventually production. But Harold Pitcairn thought he saw the Model T of the air . . . a chicken in every pot and an autogiro in the driveway. When the Autogiro Company of America opened for business the dream seemed about to materialize. Before you could say, "If God meant men to fly he would have given them wings," autogiros were landing on the roofs of skyscrapers, spraying crops, carrying newspaper photographers to natural disasters, and playing aerial billboard for chewing gum and spark plugs. "That's the answer," proclaimed Thomas Edison, when he saw a Pitcairn autogiro fly at speeds ranging from 20 to 115 mph and then land in a space no bigger than a baseball diamond. Now if anyone could recognize a good invention, it was Edison. The future was wide open.

But things started to go wrong. This was the Depression and most folks had trouble buying cornflakes, much less a personal whirligig. So Pitcairn pitched his ads to the country club set, with pictures of sleek couples in tennis whites about to disport in a waiting autogiro. But sales remained sluggish. Part of the problem was the aviators. Charles Lindbergh called them "fundamentally unsound." And Eddie Rickenbacker, after an apparently uneventful test flight, emerged claiming he had been "lucky to get out alive." Only Amelia Earhart stood behind them. But on her transcontinental flight in Beech-Nut's new autogiro, the engine failed over Kansas. Pitcairn maintained that he found water in the fuel tank, but the damage had been done as far as the press was concerned. Even Henry Ford weighed in, maintaining that the personal plane "had no future," and that as far as air travel was concerned "there is safety in numbers."

Trouble with the government followed soon enough. The Air Mail Act of 1934 specifically prohibited the transportation of mail by "unproven conveyances," and shortly thereafter the newly established Federal Aviation Commission ruled that autogiros constituted such a conveyance. Meanwhile, an amendment to the Air Commerce Act promoted by Senator Hiram Bingham made compulsory the inspection of flying schools, which in turn led to the autogiro being banned from such schools on the grounds that it was "potentially dangerous." When Pitcairn advised customers that his aircraft were so simple to fly that "no specific course of study is recommended," the government responded with licensing procedures for autogiros including completion of a "recognized course of study in a Federally certified flight school." Still trendsetters, Harold Pitcairn and the autogiro managed to fall into the clutches of Catch-22 nearly two decades before anybody outside of Sheepshead Bay ever heard of Joseph Heller.

Despite all the trouble, research continued, and almost 200 Cierva-Pitcairn patents were granted. Most significant were those related to changing the angle of the rotor blades in flight—not just for the autogiro, but also for the helicopter, which was the U.S. military's darling because it could hover and land vertically. As World War II progressed, millions and then hundreds of millions were poured into the complicated craft, and it was expected that the companies involved—Sikorsky, Bell, Kaman, and Hiller—would duly pay Pitcairn and Cierva licensing fees. But then the government reversed itself, and declared the helicopter manufacturers free of any potential patent infringements. Pitcairn, who had spent over three million dollars on rotary wing research, was outraged and intended to sue. But the government informed him he would have to wait until the War's end. In the meantime, Cierva was killed in an unexplained air crash, and Harold did not actually file until 1951. The case dragged on until 1977, when it was finally settled in his favor. But that was seventeen years too late for Pitcairn. In 1960 he was mortally wounded by his own handgun, during a nightly security check of his Pennsylvania estate. The exact circumstances have never been explained.

ELIZABETH I vas real sick. I vas thinking maybe it vas my time. I called Edward and told him to come to Columbus. But he says he can't because he vas in a big business deal vith za General Motors. Instead he vants me to stay vith him. "Nothing doing," I told him. "I vould rather God strike me dead than live under the same roof with zat Jezebel." Edward got real mad, and told me if I ever said this again he vould never talk to me. I knew then she had her hooks into him real deep. So I vent to California and stayed vith his brother Dewey, vere it vas varm. Dewey vas always a good boy.

ADELAIDE After the first few years of marriage Edward and I began to quarrel bitterly. It worried me a great deal at the time, and frankly I wondered where it was leading. But he said and did things that infuriated me, and after Clifford I was not about to hold my tongue. As it turned out, though, it was for the best. Edward was one of those people who would push as hard as you let him. In business and elsewhere he was used to getting his way. I gradually realized that he only really respected people who were willing to stand up to him when he was being ridiculous. I remember once he became so angry that I thought he might actually hit me. But instead he began chuckling and said, "You know, Adelaide, I'd never want you as my enemy." I think there are turning points in every marriage, and I'm sure this was one in ours.

Edward was never absorbed by the trappings of success. He dressed impeccably, and when we traveled it was always first class.

But unlike Clifford, who forever hid behind impressive facades, Edward didn't seem to feel the need to own expensive automobiles or a huge house. While we were in Detroit we had a lovely home in Grosse Pointe, but when it came time to move to New York, he happily traded it for a much smaller place in Bronxville. He also kept a room at the Roosevelt, but that was another matter entirely.

ERNEST R. BREECH, ASSISTANT TREASURER, GENERAL MOTORS
I was Rickenbacker's handler, working directly for Mr. Sloan. He was never much more than a front man, although he may have thought he was. The idea was for us to slide quietly into aviation, without tempting the antitrust boys to pour salt on our tails. The first move was to have Rickenbacker buy Allison Engineering from the estate of Jim Allison, who just died. He then sold it to the Fisher Brothers, who transferred it to GM as a subsidiary of Fisher Body. That gave us a base in aircraft engines.

Next we bought the American division of Fokker Aviation outright. That was okay, because the Government didn't want this German, who claimed he was Dutch, owning part of our aircraft industry. The plan was to move Rickenbacker in as executive vice-president for sales; but he put up a stink about having to work for a company that tried to shoot him down during the War. It took some convincing, but he did a pretty good job in that capacity until July '31, when Knute Rockne was killed in a Fokker crash and it hit every front page in America. I got a call from Mr. Sloan that very morning telling me to get Eddie out of that job quick. We cooked up some story that he was leaving the company because he didn't want to be transferred to Baltimore; but he remained on our payroll throughout. In fact, when we wired the purchase of Pioneer Instrument, which later became the Bendix Corporation, Mr. Sloan insisted that Rickenbacker be given a bundle in stock options.

FINIS FARR, *Rickenbacker's Luck*
" 'It can't be mentioned,' was all he would say later on. . . . It turns out that financial sleight of hand was involved, and Rick's commission for arranging the sale was 2400 shares of Pioneer stock. He sold enough of this at $95.00 a share to retire the outstanding amount of his loans in behalf of Rickenbacker Motors. Somehow Rick managed to freeze out the tax collectors, for which one can give him nothing but applause."

BOO HERNDON, THE GHOSTWRITER   Rickenbacker maintained that the failure of his car company in '27 prepared him early for the Depression, and in this way he had a jump on everyone else. But there was plainly something fishy about his career in the thirties. He'd describe his corporate maneuvers, jumping from slot to slot, and I'd fancy some hidden hand beneath the chessboard working a magnet. Of course, by this time I'd learned not to ask too many questions.

B.C. FORBES, *letter to Alfred P. Sloan, May 25, 1930*
. . . The opening was a great success, and Walter was in his glory. Everybody agrees Van Alen did a good job, and the Chrysler Building, gargoyles and all, dominates the New York skyline. The sole bright spot for our side came when Eddie Rickenbacker, who the emcee invited to the mike, waxed eloquent in praise of the Great Man and his Edifice. Ablaze with his famously predatory grin, Rickenbacker proceeded to congratulate Walter "on being the second-largest manufacturer of automobiles in America, which is entirely appropriate, since next year, when the Empire State Building is finished, he'll be the proprietor of New York's second-tallest building." I thought immediately about hiring him for the magazine, but then I realized you write all his material.

AVERELL HARRIMAN   Actually, I met him at one of the Swopes' alcoholic garden parties at Sands Point. His wife was the former Adelaide Durant, and the man was an absolute wizard at croquet. Steady, powerful, and deadly accurate. At one point, he managed to send Bill Paley's ball into Manhasset Bay. That was unheard of. Later, we got to talking about AVCO, the holding company Bobby Lehman and I used to put American Airlines together. He seemed knowledgeable and energetic, and of course he had the cachet "Ace of Aces," so I arranged a meeting with Bobby. He was less impressed, but we ended up offering him a position as VP. I certainly have made bigger mistakes. But as more than one of my wives has remarked, I did have a tendency to be overimpressed by a man's proficiency at croquet.

My most important responsibility at AVCO was developing and maintaining governmental contacts, and that demanded frequent trips to Washington. As a representative of the airlines, I traveled when I could by air. In those days the sole air link between Washington and New York was Eastern Air Transport, controlled by Clement Keys's holding company North American Aviation. Eastern wasn't much, basically a seat-of-the-pants organization; but being forced to fly it got me thinking. There was great potential in an alliance between American Airlines, which had an east-west route structure, and Eastern, which went north-to-south. American thrived in the spring and summer months, while Eastern, which reached all the way down to Florida, was busiest in the late fall and winter. Combining the two spelled year-round utilization. This was 1932 and the Depression had just about finished Keys. When I got word that he was on his way out, I strongly advised Lehman and Harriman to buy North American and in the process get control of Eastern and its access to the South. But high finance is seldom without complications.

ROBERT LEHMAN   It was a debacle, an absolute debacle, and Captain Eddie was the Spaniard in the works. Not to say Averell and I didn't deserve a substantial share of the blame. The initial mistake was ours. We were foolish enough to buy Century Airlines from none other than Erret Lobban Cord, and then compounded our error by paying him off in AVCO stock. Let the goddamned wolf right into the fold. Well, E.L. wasted very little time before thoroughly scrutinizing our books, and lo and behold discovered the thirty-million-dollar nest egg we had stashed for corporate development. This wouldn't have been so dangerous had it not been for the fact that we were controlling AVCO with less than 7 percent of the outstanding stock. Before we knew it, E.L.'s minions were out buying every share of AVCO they could lay hands on.

Enter Rickenbacker, the Bismarck of High Finance. He had been after us to buy North American Aviation as a means of getting ahold of Eastern's routes to the South. Now he recommended paying for the deal by issuing two million new shares of AVCO, thereby watering down E.L.'s holdings—the proverbial two birds with one stone. Like all truly bad ideas, it sounded good initially. But when E.L. got wind of the scheme, he not only got serious about the proxy fight, but began telling everybody who would listen just how much skullduggery was involved in airline finance. Meanwhile, Averell and I found ourselves on the losing side of an all-out war. Ever the loyalist, Rickenbacker took off for California, and returned only when our situation was hopeless. Fortunately, we marshaled our legal resources in the cause of liberating our thirty million, and conceded the somewhat desiccated plum AVCO to E.L. and his hungry men.

I wish I could say, as Mr. Fiske said to Mr. Gould, "Nothing was lost save honor"; but the publicity attached to this episode had the effect of alerting the do-gooders not only to the airlines' finances, but to their whole relationship with the Government. For this we have Captain Eddie to thank.

AUGIE DUESENBERG   Cord was a square guy. Sure did right by us. Under him we were building Auburns, the front-drive Cord, and he gave my brother the money to bring out the Model J Duesey—the best damn car ever made in America. Anyway, ran into Eddie right after the AVCO tussle. Couldn't resist jabbin' him a little about trying to cross E.L. and how he chose the wrong side. Just laughed and said, "Don't be too sure. I always land on my feet."

ADELAIDE   We were guests at the Breeches' for Christmas dinner. It was right in the midst of the AVCO battle, and all the men could talk about was business. Lorraine Breech and I took turns rolling our eyes across the table. I remember Edward saying that Cord was primarily angry over Averell's attempt to buy the company that at that time owned Eastern, and this was why he started the proxy fight. He told Ernie this left an opening for GM and that the company could now be bought for a song. I suppose it was good advice. But it was Christmas, and it certainly could have waited. Men never seem to be able to leave their jobs at the office.

ERNIE BREECH   There were some obstacles to be cleared. Colonel Deeds of United also wanted to get his hands on North American and tried to warn off Mr. Sloan. But then we got to Walter Brown, and in his last official act as Postmaster General he voided United's proposed acquisition of North American.

Still, it wasn't exactly clear sailing. North American was by now in receivership, and the lawyers proved to be assholes. The negotiations were going nowhere, and Eddie turned to me saying, "You guys are never going to agree—I'm gonna take a leak." While he was gone, their side finally went for our proposal to spin off Sperry Gyroscope, and just that quick the deal was made. I don't know whether it was just coincidence, or a tribute to Eddie's charm and bargaining skills. But anyway the transfer became official on the last day of February 1933, and GM now had its feet firmly planted in the airline business. Of course, little did we know the whole fucking roof was about to fall in.

WALTER FOLGER BROWN, POSTMASTER GENERAL, HOOVER ADMINISTRATION We were not buying peanuts and pencils; we were buying a service that was highly specialized and exceedingly hazardous, and there was no sense in taking the Government's money and dishing it out to every little fellow that was flying around the map. If transcontinental air service was going to work, it had to be in the hands of large corporations with the resources to invest in constant improvement. That was my policy and I make no apologies for using mail contracts and the consolidation of routes to bring about that end.

FULTON LEWIS, HEARST SYNDICATE It all began over lunch with Bill Briggs. He was bellyaching that his company, the Luddington Line, was on the edge because it failed to win the New York–to–Washington mail contract with a bid of twenty-five cents a mile, and now Eastern Air Transport was trying to ram through a buyout for a measly quarter-million. I remember thinking that's too bad, but things are tough all over. Then about a month after, I chanced to see a Post Office notice awarding Eastern the New York–to–D.C. route for eighty-nine cents a mile.

Something obviously smelled; so I started digging. What I found was a regular dung heap. In a supposedly competitive bidding process, four companies—United, AVCO, TAT, and Eastern—were given twenty out of twenty-two mail contracts. In the last three years of Walter Brown's term these same airlines were paid a total of fifty-six million to provide a service that by their own accounting cost them less than twenty million to deliver. And this was just the tip of the iceberg.

It was exactly the kind of story the Old Man loved. Fat cats bilking the taxpayers, chicanery at the top. He had me working on it full time, sending daily reports out to San Simeon. Then just as we were about to go to press, he sat on it. Citizen Hearst, fearless champion of the little man. They got to him. Well, I wasn't about to be shut up. So I went to Senator Black.

• • •

I wasn't surprised. In February of '34, I was at a party at Bill and Dorothy Paley's that included Bess Farley, wife of the new Postmaster General. Before long the situation with the airmail contracts came up. She looked me straight in the eye and said, "Mr. Rickenbacker, you ain't seen nothin' yet."

GOD I watch ants fighting over crumbs sometimes. When the crumbs are first discovered, there is the possibility of splitting them in a sort of orderly fashion. But this seldom happens. Instead, the ants go back to their respective nests, and bring in bigger, more important ants. Before long, there's a regular war going on. Of course, crumbs are of great concern to ants.

FRANKLIN DELANO ROOSEVELT Hugo Black had them chapter and verse. The Republicans and the monopolists. One hundred and twenty-three separate violations of Federal statutes, along with countless other questionable practices. The airlines had been running roughshod over the public interest. I must say, Jim Farley did counsel caution. But this seemed to me a matter of principle requiring prompt and decisive action.

We called in General Foulois and asked him directly if the Army Air Corps was capable of delivering the mail in the event we decided to cancel the Government's contracts with the airlines. Without hesitation he answered in the affirmative. I should have known that they always answer in the affirmative without hesitation no matter what you ask them to do. MacArthur was the only one of them who ever said no to me, and then promptly vomited on the White House lawn. So with the benefit of expert professional military advice, I continued charting a course leading to humiliation and disaster. I can only thank the good Lord that Postmaster General Farley had the wisdom and fortitude to plot for me a way out.

ALFRED P. SLOAN The New Deal had declared war on free enterprise. We were fighting for the soul of this country. The cancellation of the airmail contracts was simply one battle in a much larger conflict. But it was a very important battle. We had the opportunity for a clear comparison between the efficiency of the private sector and the waste and incompetence of big government. It was our duty to demonstrate to the public the differences between the two systems. Fortunately, we were able to do so.

Press release of telegram from Charles A. Lindbergh to Franklin D. Roosevelt, February 10, 1934
> "Your present action does not discriminate between innocence and guilt and places no premium on honest business. Your order of cancellation of all air mail contracts condemns the largest portion of our commercial aviation without just trial. . . ."

The New York reporters filed into my office to see what I had to say. It was a gray, fog-laden afternoon.

"What worries me, boys, is what's going to become of these young Army fliers when they run into weather like this. Their little aircraft don't have the proper instruments, and their training has nothing to do with transporting airmail all over the country in all kinds of conditions. Either they're going to fall off the schedules completely, or they're going to crack up their ships just about everywhere. What's needed here are planes big enough to house the best instrumentation and with the carrying capacity to safely transport large loads of mail and passengers. Small planes are dangerous in the civilian arena, no two ways about it."

JACK FRYE   Breech had me give Rickenbacker a call.

"Rick, my friend, we've got to lay down a marker that will make it crystal clear that we're far better qualified to fly the mail than the Army. Sure there may have been a little funny business in the past, but now the papers are trying to say there's something wrong with our pilots and our planes. We both know that's bullshit. Let's show the sunzabitches they've got their collective heads stuck up their asses."

"You're preaching to the choir, Jack. But what in hell are we going to do?"

"Don't worry. We've got something in Santa Monica that's gonna blow their socks off."

In all forms of evolution inevitably there arises a key progenitor, a revolutionary prototype that sets the entire context for further development. Among dinosaurs it was the theconodont, which slunk out of the Mesozoic ooze to dominate the Triassic and Jurassic.

Among airliners it was the Douglas DC-1, the gleaming aluminum bird which first rolled onto the runway of Clover Field, California, in late 1933, destined to rule transport aircraft design until the advent of the Boeing 707. Heretofore commercial planes tended to be lumbering high-winged, three-engined hulks, with fuselages so rickety that a particularly mean downdraft could easily rip them to shreds. Back in those days, instead of bonus miles, frequent flyers got letters from the Rock and the Good Hands People canceling their life insurance. Donald Douglas's wunderplane changed all of that.

Begun at the instigation of Jack Frye, Vice-President for Operations at TWA, the Douglas design team under J.H. Kindelberger quickly realized it was within their grasp to dramatically exceed the airline's already ambitious specifications. Rather than a three-engined loper barely capable of 150 mph, they generated a design calling for two 700-hp fully cowled and supercharged Wright Cyclone motors, either of which could keep the plane aloft in emergencies, and together they were capable of pushing it well past 200 mph.

But the prodigious whirling of the DC-1's Hamilton Standard variable-pitch propellers barely scratched the surface of the plane's design features. A low-winged cantilever monoplane, it had wing spars positioned to pass beneath the passenger compartment, allowing an unobstructed cabin tall enough for passengers in the back to stand erect. Yet the entire structure was remarkably rugged, employing a fully stressed aluminum skin and revolutionary monocoque construction. The wing in particular was an engineering marvel, a multicellular affair so strong that it would eventually allow for engines more than double the horsepower of the originals. Besides accommodating massive fuel tanks in their center sections, the wings incorporated fully retractable landing gear and wing flaps, an industry first that drove the plane's stall speed down below 60 mph.

Together, all of this spelled safety, reliability, and fast, smooth air travel. It was at once the magic carpet that would fly the airlines into the future, and the hammer that would smash Harold Pitcairn's dream of an autogiro for everyman. Altogether over 10,500 DC-1s, 2s, and 3s would be built. But in February 1934 there was only one, and it sat quietly in its hangar waiting to be introduced to the world by Jack Frye and Eddie Rickenbacker.

ELIZABETH   My boy had only a little time to talk to his poor sick mother ven he come to California. But zis time he had a good excuse. "Mother," he told me, "I'm doing the Lord's work."

MAE WEST   The truth can now be told. The Ace of Aces paid court to the Venus of the Great American West. Fields always said he was my kind of man. So when I hooked up with him over at Harry Chandler's—they was writing some kind of speech together—I figured I better not miss my chance. I had a memorable coupling in mind—Mars meets Aphrodite—and that's what I got. But strange, real strange. We were in the very act when he looks up and mutters something about murder bein' legalized. Thought for a minute I had a homicidal maniac on top of me, but no . . . just preoccupied.

After the festivities were over he continues in this vein, ranting on about Roosevelt, airplanes, and mail contracts. "Look," I finally says, "the only mail I care about is spelled M-A-L-E." That kinda brought him down to earth, and in a few minutes he was out the door. Can't say I was sorry to see him go.

Next day I sent Fields a cable in New York—"Rickenbacker: Hydraulics as advertised; screw loose in the Brain Department."

JACK FRYE   The press breakfast the morning of the flight couldn't have gone better. Rickenbacker was in rare form. First, they asked him about meteorological reports that a blizzard was supposed to hit Newark twenty minutes after we were scheduled to arrive, and hadn't we better get out of Burbank a couple of hours early.

"The purpose of this flight is to demonstrate the efficiency of a privately run air transportation system. I want the American people to know that [we've] progressed to the point that we can call our own shots. We'll leave on schedule."

Then, right on cue, one of our guys brings that morning's copy of the *L.A. Times* with the story of the three Army mail fliers being killed plastered all over the front page. Eddie gets all red as if he hadn't seen it and lets loose.

"That's legalized murder."

"Jesus, Eddie, can we quote you?"

"You're damned right you can quote me." Well, that line followed us right across the continent.

• • •

I intended to deliver a parting blast at the airport. NBC had a fifteen-minute slot reserved coast-to-coast. But just as we were about to go on the air, the producer Skeets Miller received strict orders from Washington to cut me off if I said anything that would add fuel to the fire. So I had to rip up the speech Harry Chandler and the boys from the *L.A. Times* had written me, and content myself with a few conciliatory remarks on how that tyrannical bastard Roosevelt was ruining the country.

It was not until we took off that I could sit back and admire the instrument of our retribution, the DC-1. It was hard to believe in just fifteen years we had gone from the powered box kites I flew during the War to this huge sleek silver bird. As we roared off my breast swelled with a mixture of pride and humility that of all possible aviators, including the famed Lindbergh, I had been chosen to show the world what she could do. Our mission was simple: deliver the last bag of contract mail in record time.

We climbed immediately to 14,000 feet to clear the first range of mountains. Up here our supercharged motors drove us through the thin air considerably faster than Don Douglas thought they would, averaging 230 mph on the first leg. The crew waiting in Kansas City filled our tanks in just ten minutes and we took off just before dawn. Soon, from a vantage point of 10,000 feet, we saw the top of the sun rise out of the East. Jack Frye had the stick for much of the trip, but I spelled him enough to be sure I was fully a part of the mission. We stopped for fuel a second time in Columbus, and then caught up with the huge snowstorm about forty miles further. Jack simply climbed to 14,000 feet, his steady hand guiding us safely over it. We got ahead of the storm for good over eastern Pennsylvania, and slipped into Newark under mildly overcast skies. Combined time in the air was thirteen hours and two minutes, almost two hours under the transcontinental record.

As we taxied slowly toward the terminal, our ship's intercom blared out that my scheduled NBC broadcast on arrival had been canceled. So Roosevelt had managed to silence me that day. But he couldn't shut me up forever. And since then, if I've said it once, I've said it a thousand times: Ordering Army pilots to fly the mail was nothing less than legalized murder.

DAMON RUNYON, *New York American, February 19, 1934*
You may have heard that lately Army aviators have been falling from the skies like pine cones. That's because President Roosevelt came upon some questionable deals with the airlines and ordered the Air Corps to fly the mail instead.

It's not been going well. Could be you noticed that your special delivery letters have been landing in your box a day or two late. That's just a minor inconvenience. Those Army fliers have literally been killing themselves trying to deliver your mail through the rain, the sleet, and the snow of the worst winter on record. To date ten have died, piling into mountains and every other obstacle you can think of. Their little planes are without instruments, they fly blind when the weather's bad. That's the reason they die, and there's no hope of fixing it anytime soon.

Unless of course you're impressed by what happened yesterday. At around two in the afternoon a giant airliner roared into Newark after successfully racing a blizzard right across the country. When it taxied to a halt, out of the pilot's compartment stepped Eddie Rickenbacker—you remember him, America's leading war ace—carrying a big bag and looking madder than a bear awake in the middle of winter. He stalked into the terminal and slammed that bag at the feet of the local postal officials.

It contained the last mail the airlines were required to deliver under their now-canceled contracts. It had been brought from Los Angeles in record time—two hours under the old transcontinental mark. Rickenbacker and his copilot were in constant touch with meteorologists. When they ran into bad weather, their ultramodern Douglas DC-1 was able to fly right over it. They were safe and in control at all times. This is the kind of skill and equipment the airlines bring to the table. Maybe it's time President Roosevelt swallowed his pride and let professionals trained to fly the mail do what they do best.

JAMES FARLEY, POSTMASTER GENERAL   The President called me in and admitted the obvious. "We're trapped, Jimmy. Once again my sense of propriety has overcome my better judgment. This can only lead to further embarrassment. If there's any acceptable avenue of retreat, I implore you to find it. Otherwise, I'll simply have to capitulate."

It was an emergency for all concerned. Despite their bravado the four dominant airlines were each known to be losing an average of a quarter million dollars a month, and would soon be out of business. It was in everyone's interest to compromise. The President did not object to the size and efficiency of the major air carriers, only the monopolistic manipulation of the public contracting process.

Therefore, I proposed to reopen competitive bidding subject to certain stipulations. Executives directly involved with the corruption of the process by the previous Administration were barred from further participation. Similarly, the major airlines would be obliged to cast aside their aircraft manufacturing affiliates, and to reorganize under new nomenclature. Consequently, Eastern Air Transport became Eastern Airlines, American Airways was changed to American Airlines, United Aircraft and Transport shifted to United Airlines, and Trans Western Air was now Trans World Airways.

Some have maintained that this was merely cosmetic, that when the new bids were proffered and accepted the map of assigned routes looked much as before. This misses the point entirely. These provisions, formalized in the Air Mail Act of 1934, rendered the process fair and open. This was all the President desired. He never wanted to destroy the airlines. Nor was he vindictive toward their leadership. Quite the contrary . . . uhh . . . well, with one exception. I don't think he ever forgave Captain Rickenbacker for his intemperate remarks about "legalized murder." To be frank, it was wise to avoid even mentioning this gentleman's name in the President's presence.

GOD They never seemed to be able to decide if they were better off in a herd or alone. You'd have thought when they attempted something as foolhardy as flying they'd at least have the prudence to do it in a way that gave them some control over the situation . . . just as that Pitcairn kept insisting. But no, the morons seemed to believe—or at least could be convinced by the likes of Rickenbacker—that there was safety in numbers. Birds do fly around in flocks, but they have the sense to bring their own wings. You don't see them piling into aluminum pipe bombs drenched with hightest. Well, at least now when I was pissed off or bored I could swat them out of the skies by the scores. Economy of motion, one of my best ideas.

ELIZABETH   Grandchildren, not from her. That slut couldn't give him no heirs. Vat ve got vas converted orphans.

ADELAIDE   He was a wonderful father. It's true he was away a great deal. But he was never distant. After the boys could read, or at least be aware of what was in the papers, they would see a picture of him and almost go crazy, running around the house pretending they were airplanes. Once, I remember he came home after a long trip and they both came up shrieking, "Ace Drummond! Ace Drummond!" They wouldn't stop until finally he became very serious and told them, "I'm not Ace Drummond. I never want to be Ace Drummond. All I want to be is your daddy."

That was the part of him the world never saw. In public he was always cocksure . . . insufferable even. But the doubts and insecurities were there, believe me. After the Lindbergh kidnapping he was terrified that David and Billy might be taken also. He spoke of it as some kind of conspiracy to get even with the top aviators. Later, in the midst of the business with the mail contracts, I came out of a deep sleep to find him wide awake in the middle of the night. "Roosevelt hates me, Adelaide. The President of the United States hates me and I don't know what to do about it." I thought for a while, and finally suggested that he simply write a letter apologizing. "I can't do that. We've chosen sides and that's that. You can never show weakness. In the public arena there's no forgiveness. I wish there were, because I have a feeling this may be the end of me."

ERNIE BREECH   Mr. Sloan thought we better hold off for a few months, until things cooled down. But late in December he gave me the okay to call Rickenbacker and ask him if he wanted to run Eastern. I hardly got the words out of my mouth before he said yes—faster than the proverbial pregnant bride at the altar. "Hold your horses, Eddie, there's a few stipulations we need to go over."

"Like what?"

"Like Eastern is going to be the first profitable airline to refuse any government subsidies."

"Are you crazy? There's no way in hell that can be done."

"Sure it can, Eddie. You're just not looking at the larger picture."

"What larger picture? I don't know what you're talking about, Breech."

"Sure you do. You're just forgetting that you have us behind you."

RICKENBACKER NAMED GENERAL MANAGER
OF EASTERN AIRLINES

"This is a real New Deal for the airlines," the angular war ace announced. "The Army's failed attempt to fly the mail has convinced me that the only route to success for this country is through free enterprise, unshackled from the retrogressive forces of government interference. Therefore, my first act as head of Eastern will be to renounce all federal subsidies beyond those that can be honestly earned by carrying the mail. But I have no doubt that Eastern's future is in carrying passengers. We will do this, and we will do it profitably using the superior cost accounting methods of our parent company, General Motors. In light of this my second act is to cancel all free passes granted to various politicians by my predecessors. . . ."

Air Enterprise, January 5, 1935

CHARLIE FROESCH   I got this call—no howdy-do or nothing—just: "Froesch, I want you over at Eastern. Name your price." Of course, when I did name a price he howled. But I had a good bead on him from our time together at Fokker, and I was pretty sure he needed me. "I'm gonna turn the line inside out, and your job is to junk the crap we're flying now, and get me enough DC-2s and Electras to make some money."

When I got over there, he's already pretty much fired the whole first line of managers, and brought in Paul Brattain, who I knew from TWA, and Bev Griffith, who I didn't. I remember the three of us feeling each other out those first weeks, none of us with any idea that this was the beginning of a thirty-year association. Actually, it was a little like getting to know your cellmates on Devil's Island.

BEVERLY GRIFFITH   I knew him from Hollywood days. I'd spent my whole adult life working for the movies. Then out of the blue he's on the phone informing me that I'm Eastern's new director of public relations.

"My God, Captain, I don't know the first thing about public relations."

"That's your problem, fatso. Do you want the job or don't you?" For some reason I took that as a challenge.

PAUL BRATTAIN I'll never forget coming into that office. It was basically just empty desks. He'd absolutely cleaned house. In the corner was Charlie Froesch trying to get through to California, and then screaming at the Douglas people that unless Eastern got priority for DC-2 deliveries there'd be hell to pay with GM—this after TWA had gone to the wall to get that plane out. On the other side of the room sits Bev Griffith, all three hundred pounds of him sweating to map out an ad campaign for Florida, with the Captain circling like a vulture:

"No pictures of broads in bathing suits, I'm warning you, Griffith."

"But . . . but . . . that's what they wear in Florida . . ."

"Not on my planes they won't. We're selling Florida as a family vacation, remember that. Besides, I don't want a bunch of letters from priests and rabbis."

And that wasn't all. He was refusing to hire back the stewardesses who'd been furloughed when the airmail contracts had been canceled.

My position on stewardesses was sound and reasonable. A year was about the maximum extent of their careers. You see, working for the airlines was the best possible way to meet a prospective husband. No sooner was a girl trained, at a cost of nearly a thousand dollars, than she would show up with a ring and be gone. I knew this was true, and when I took over at Eastern I was determined to solve the problem by replacing them with stewards. These young men were not only stronger at handling baggage and better able to deal with emergencies, but, dressed in the trim uniforms we gave them, imparted an aura of professionalism to Eastern cabins that could not be matched by our competitors.

PAUL BRATTAIN The entire industry was scouring the country for pretty young things to decorate their airplanes, and we get rid of ours. It was hard to imagine anything dumber. Finally, we got some customer surveys that showed pretty clearly we were losing business because of it. This was a dollars and cents issue now, the kind of thing that might actually sway Rickenbacker. But he was pretty hard over on this, and there was always his temper to contend with. So, knowing he'd never listen to anybody but a pilot, we decided to have Herman Wilhelm, one of his favorites, bring it up at the next big staff meeting.

Well, when the time came Herman stood up—there must have been at least a hundred in attendance—and carefully began making the case for stewardesses point-by-point. Unfortunately, with each point Rickenbacker's face got redder and redder. Finally, Herman concluded by mildly asking why, in the face of such evidence, would the airline want to avoid bringing the stewardesses back. "Because," the Captain roared, "I pay you bastard pilots enough dough for you to buy your own pussy." That was the end of that until the War forced our hand by drafting all the stewards.

JOHNNY RAY, CHIEF MECHANIC, EASTERN AIRLINES   No doubt he was a cheap son of a bitch; but he got results. First year under him, flying the DC-2s, we doubled our revenue factor and flew three million more passenger miles with twenty-eight less aircraft. Went from a million and a half in losses right into the black, and stayed there so long as he was watchin' the till. For years you had to have his personal okay to spend anything over fifty bucks. But he never cut corners on safety. If the men needed overtime to work on a plane, they got it. He made sure we had the best-equipped shops in the industry. But God help you if he thought you was spending money on gimmicks. Take the autopilot. He hated 'em. For years he made sure they was not just disconnected, but taken out of every new plane we got and sent back to the factory for a refund. "Those goddamned pilots earn enough to pay attention," he says to me once. "If they wanna read magazines, they can do it on their own time." Pilots had it different. "Anything wasn't on a SPAD," they used to say, "we're not gonna get."

BRAD   WALKER, CAMPBELL-EWALD   ADVERTISING   AGENCY Eastern was my account and I worked directly with Bev Griffith. They had all these new planes, but they still looked like shit. Part of it was their logo, a big ugly map that sort of resembled the Eastern Seaboard on an even bigger orange background—the kind of thing you'd put on a freight car. As far as I was concerned, your image in the transportation business began with your equipment. So I had our art department come up with a streamlined peregrine falcon, which I then matched up with the slogan "Great Silver Fleet." It was slick and elegant. But Bev was worried about the Captain, who had the taste of a rhino.

"Look," I told him, "don't talk about wanting to make changes, talk about improvements and the future."

"That sounds good, Brad, but you do the talking. Remember, I've got a job to lose over this." So in we went.

"Captain, we've been working on a few things that will fit right in with your modernization program. I think this falcon will work well as our new emblem." Then before he could say anything, I added: "We chose this particular falcon, the peregrine, because it's the fastest bird in the air." That did it, he was sold. Next, I moved to the sketches of the DC-2s with "Great Silver Fleet" placed just above the window line of the otherwise unadorned aircraft. In thirty seconds he bought that too. We were home free, or so I thought.

I hadn't banked on his modifications. He added little American flags, and names for each plane like "Florida Flyer." Soon enough "Great Silver Fleet" was replaced by "Fly Eastern Airlines," so now the planes looked like billboards. Then, in true Rickenbacker fashion, he took credit for the entire new look, which of course was a blessing in disguise.

SHEPPY He was a difficult employer, this much I will grant. He worked seven days a week and had little sympathy for those not similarly motivated. There were those who went so far as to claim the proctoscope was his favorite management tool. He did seem to take an almost perverse pleasure in upbraiding people in public. On the other hand, he also made it his business to know which employees were suffering from hardships or illnesses. For them his wallet was always open. I've seen him pay large hospital bills out of his own pocket, while simultaneously threatening employees with instant dismissal should they breathe a word of it to anyone. The circumstances of his life seem to have taught him that harshness connoted strength and kindness the opposite. He was never cruel or mean-spirited. But this was only apparent to those who truly knew him. As for the rest, he did his best to make them think he was an ogre.

ADELAIDE   Before the boys reached the age of ten, Edward insisted that they be sent away to school. Given his travel schedule, I've had friends suggest his intent was to allow me more freedom to accompany him. I suppose there were also those who attributed it to some form of social climbing.

Actually, no one missed the boys more than Edward; it was extremely painful for him to send them away. But he was ambivalent about his own childhood. In one way he greatly regretted having had his education cut short; but in another he believed the lessons he learned making his way at such a young age were invaluable. He looked at prep school as a means of combining education with a kind of independent existence for the boys. Life to Edward was a series of hard challenges. No matter how secure you might feel at any one moment, the situation could change overnight, requiring you to rise to the occasion. The faster the boys learned that, he believed, the better off they would be.

ALFRED P. SLOAN   By 1938 it had become apparent that the potential for a crisis had passed. The autogiro had been thwarted, and the fantasy of personal aircraft was fading from the public's mind. Meanwhile, the airlines themselves were attracting increasing numbers of passengers through improved safety and the introduction of the exemplary DC-3. Under the circumstances, there was a growing consensus within GM that our direct involvement with the air transport industry was no longer critical. I voiced this at a Board meeting, but more as a topic for discussion than as a statement of fact. Unfortunately, certain parties took this to indicate that a decision had already been made, and then acted without specific authorization. The result was a chain of events that proved both confusing and embarrassing.

I was sitting at my desk one afternoon in early 1938 when the phone rang. It was my good friend Les Gould, the chief financial reporter for the Hearst papers. "Eddie, the story here is that John Hertz has just been given an option by General Motors to buy Eastern for three million. What have you heard?"

I felt as though somebody had punched me in the stomach. "I don't know what to say, Les. This is news to me." After I hung up it took only a moment's reflection to realize I should have seen it coming. Hertz was already tight with GM. He had built the

Yellow Cab Company, including the Hertz rental car system, and then sold a half-interest to the automaker—part of the deal being to use their cars exclusively in the future.

Hertz also didn't like me, that I knew for certain. One evening a couple of months earlier I got a phone call in Bronxville; on the other end was a voice I knew to be John's.

"Eddie," he said.

"You got him," I answered. With that he began denouncing me in the crudest possible terms: "Rickenbacker this, and Rickenbacker that. I'm going to get that Rickenbacker"—always using my last name. Finally, I realized he thought he was talking to somebody else. "John, this *is* Rickenbacker. What the hell are you talking about?" With that he hung up.

Now sitting at my desk I figured out he hadn't said "Eddie" at all, but "Ernie." At last I smelled the rat, and his name was Breech. He had opposed my acquisition of Wedell-Williams Transport, which brought us into Houston, and he was fighting my efforts to grab New York–Chicago from American. Next, he wanted to see me thrown out on my ass and replaced with somebody who didn't know the business. Well, I wasn't going down without a fight.

ALFRED P. SLOAN   He arrived in a state of high dudgeon, and immediately began a curious recitation. Hadn't he pushed Eastern in the right direction routewise? Hadn't he taken a fleet of flying junkers and turned it into the most modern in the industry? Hadn't he brought in GM cost accounting? Hadn't he moved heaven and earth to increase earnings every year? All of this I readily conceded, still unsure where it was leading.

"Then why, Mr. Sloan, are you selling the airline out from under me?"

"Eddie, I'm not sure to whom you have been talking. But I think you've been led to believe the situation is more urgent than it is." I told him to come back in a few days, and perhaps something could be worked out.

It was obvious my earlier speculations on Eastern's fate had produced unintended consequences. Once we divested ourselves of the airline, it simply would not do to have an individual directly associated with the automotive industry, like John Hertz, running it. On the other hand, he was part of GM's corporate structure and had to be treated carefully. I had to appear completely impartial, but at the same time nudge the participants in the right direction. The solution lay in Rickenbacker's audacity and impudence, both of which I believed I could count on.

"Mr. Sloan, if I can pay you three and half million cash—five hundred thousand more than Hertz—would you sell Eastern to me?"

"Yes, Eddie, I'd have to. The Board would demand it."

He didn't have the money, of course. Nor was there any prospect of him getting it from the bankers. But I was aware that Kuhn, Loeb had successfully underwritten the initial offering for Rickenbacker Motors. Therefore, under the premise that even a blind pig eventually finds an acorn, I went over to see John Schiff and Fred Warburg and quietly arranged the financing. From that point, it was simply a matter of waiting for him to find his way to Kuhn, Loeb and for this little charade to play out.

The final negotiations with GM seemed to be going nowhere, with Breech bringing up every possible objection. Then, for no apparent reason, he shut up and the air cleared completely. Within an hour the final terms were set.

This took place on Friday afternoon. My deadline to buy was 6:00 P.M. Sunday or the door would be open again to Hertz. I started to wonder how in hell Warburg and Schiff would come up with $3.5 million on a weekend. By Saturday night I was close to panic. I phoned Mr. Sloan at his apartment—it must have been nearly eleven—and requested to speak to him in person for a few minutes.

He said yes and answered the door in robe and pajamas. I told him frankly that I was afraid the bankers might not be ready with the money on Sunday. He listened for about fifteen minutes and then stood up with a strange little grin.

"If I were you, I wouldn't lose any sleep over this, Eddie."

Well, I went home and got in bed, but didn't sleep a wink. At 10 the next morning the doorbell rang, and in walked Freddy Warburg with a certified check for the entire amount. That night I thanked God first and then Mr. Sloan. The next morning I had the pleasure of handing him the check in person.

"Congratulations, Eddie, good luck, and never call me past six."

GOD Good advice. Can't stand that late-night praying either. This Diety-on-Demand crap just goes to show how thoughtless they really are. If I didn't value my privacy, why in hell am I invisible?

So Captain Eddie was once again a captain of what counted—an industry. He had returned to the ranks of entrepreneurs, reassumed the mantle of free enterpriser. Of course, it was necessary to turn a blind eye to a few details—GM's continued financial backing and subtle but vital government subsidies such as super-bountiful capital amortizement on taxable income. There was also much that he simply didn't understand—the true machinations of one A.P. Sloan and who in hell really held the mortgage. But as spring brought life to the land of 1938, Rickenbacker could look out over his little empire of flying machines and reasonably conclude he was a prime mover in the most exciting industry on earth.

Exciting it may have been, but profitable it was not. It was the high-tech of yesteryear, the archetypical glamor stock held aloft by Daedalian fantasy, gleaming modernity, humanity's insatiable evolutionary urge to move, and schemes so oblique that even their originators hesitated to put them into words, lest it become obvious how far they dangled from the bottom line. But it was simple really. Planes cost a lot, guzzled fuel like a drunk, and someone was always coming up with a faster one that could carry more passengers, necessitating even more investment. This was the iron law of the airlines, at least until the coming of the jet, and it was written, intermittently in the blood of crashes, but mostly in red ink. Yet this could be hidden by men in eyeshades with garters on their sleeves. And air transport, serving purposes other than those purely economic, could persist even in a business setting. As for Eddie, he may have known, he may not have known. It didn't matter. He would continue as he always had, surfing the wave of success with the instincts and aplomb of a pure survivor.

My Declaration of Independence
April 1938
(1) My job here is to push, push, push for Eastern Airlines.
(2) I will plan for the future and make the future adhere to my plan.
(3) I will stick strictly to a philosophy of "Pitch in and Help." None of us is doing so much that he cannot do more.
(4) Because working for Eastern Airlines will be a pleasure and

a privilege, our labor costs can and will be the lowest in the industry.

(5) I will always compete fairly but firmly, operating under the assumption that foot-draggers inevitably get rolled over. You cannot strengthen the weak by weakening the strong.

ROBERT J. SERLING, *From the Captain to the Colonel: An Informal History of Eastern Airlines*
"His official title was president and general manager. Unofficially he was 'the Captain,' and that title was synonymous with absolute authority; no airline chief executive had more autonomy or greater power. He was a dictator with the saving grace of sentimentality, a corporate potentate with a conscience, an egotistical autocrat with a strange streak of humility, a feudal baron demanding total allegiance, yet not quite capable of suppressing both affection for and a sense of responsibility towards the serfs."

PAUL PETERSON, HOUSTON STATION MANAGER   If he ever got wind of one of us giving a passenger the short end of the stick, there was no help for you. You were gone. But that doesn't mean the customer was always right. I'll never forget him coming down on a regular who had been making our lives miserable. "I've been on the lookout for you, you sorry excuse for an asshole. You've been making trouble for everybody in this airline, and they don't deserve a bit of it. If I ever see you anywhere near an Eastern ticket counter again, I'll personally wring your little pencil neck." Even the passengers cheered. It was all we talked about for weeks. You knew he was on your side.

J.J. MEHL, TREASURER, EASTERN AIRLINES   The pay stunk, no question. He even shortchanged himself. Set his own salary in 1938 and kept it there for twenty-five years. Told the rest of us we were lucky we didn't have his boss, Sheppy, who was really cheap. But as usual he had a gimmick—stock options. That was his carrot. Basically, the original purchase of the company was rigged to give him an option on ten percent of the stock for five years at ten dollars a share. He split that with the employees, working out a formula as to how much you could buy based on salary and seniority. It was very generous, especially for that time and place. But as usual he announced it as gruffly as possible, threatening anyone caught selling stock for anything but emergencies with the wrath of God. Of course, when the stock climbed to the 140s in the early sixties, a number of guys found themselves rich men just because they were afraid to sell.

SID SHANNON, OPERATIONS MANAGER   He loved to fire people. But you could never be sure it would stick. Once he axed Paul Brattain two times in one day for different reasons, and then got in an argument with him over whether you could fire somebody twice. "If you'd left in the first place, you cocksucker, I wouldn't have had to fire you again."

He fired me in a staff meeting. But when I got up to leave he said I had to wait, because the meeting wasn't over. I did, but I was damned if I was going to work in the morning. First thing I know he's calling the house, mad as hell.

"You fired me yesterday, Captain."

"Yeah, well that was yesterday, this is tomorrow, and you better get your ass down here." Lest you think there was some logic to this, consider the poor bastards who got fired, then showed up the following day to find their desk cleaned out and a check for two weeks' pay.

BEV GRIFFITH   Eastern was always a north-south airline, Florida being the key to our profitability. But Captain Rickenbacker never gave up the dream of becoming a transcontinental system, and took every opportunity to expand westward. Because of the animosity of the Roosevelt Administration toward us, this entailed some pretty arcane schemes. Probably the Captain's best was his famous "zero bid."

We already had a foothold in Texas, but late in '38 the Captain saw an opportunity to consolidate our position with the Houston-Brownsville mail contract, which would also give us exclusive rights to carry passengers. Our competition was Braniff, headed by two brothers of the same name, Tom and Paul. They considered themselves a Texas airline and were dead set against outsiders. In addition, they had a number of influential friends in Texas politics. Unfortunately, the Captain had some of the same friends.

Jesse Jones, later Chairman of the Reconstruction Finance Corporation, was a Texas power broker. A few weeks before the drop-dead date for bids on Houston-Brownsville, I happened by his Washington office. He couldn't have been more cordial.

"Eddie, comeonin and set awhile," he said, oozing folksy charm. "Been thinkin' 'bout you." We chatted for a few minutes, going nowhere in particular. Then, without a bit of warning, he sprung it on me. "What'cha bid gonna be on the Houston-Brownsville mail contract?"

The abruptness of the question caught me napping. "We can drop to a penny a mile if we have to." As the words left my mouth, I realized I might as well have been talking to Tom Braniff. They say loose lips sink ships. Well, it looked as if they could also shoot down an airline.

BEV GRIFFITH The postmortem was pretty grim. Nobody had any good ideas. All Braniff had to do was bid less than a cent. It looked like we were losers for sure. Then the Captain got that big, cat-who-ate-the-canary grin.

"Less than less-than-a-cent is zero. That's what we'll bid, boys, zero!"

He had Smythe Gambrell and the lawyers check for precedents, and sure enough they came up with several non-airline-related instances when companies had supplied the government with services for exactly nothing.

Well, the day came for the sealed envelopes to be opened and announced. The process was alphabetical, so Braniff went first with a bid of $0.00001907378. There were a few guffaws and a little backslapping on their side and a hail of boos and catcalls from the other airline reps, who obviously didn't expect anything this low. Then William Howe, the Assistant Postmaster General, ripped open Eastern's folder and blinked in amazement. "Eastern's bid is zero-zero-zero." Tom Braniff jumped up yelling, "That's against the law!" But the Captain roared right back, "The hell it is!" waving the precedents like some kind of sword.

Braniff sued, and waged a publicity campaign all over Texas aimed at convincing the people down there that this would drive the local line out of business. But the Captain shadowed him, maintaining there was plenty of room for both. And whenever he came face-to-face with Tom he would always give him the high sign, his thumb and forefinger curled into a big zero.

We won in the courts, and with our new Texas routes we were now the country's third biggest carrier in terms of mileage. The Captain was also able to swing a three-million-dollar stock issue that allowed us to convert to all DC-3s, forty-six of them. Those planes were pure profit, and in 1940 we made a million and a half bucks. Eastern was booming, and the Captain was the difference.

GOD Rickenbacker was starting to remind Me of Me, something I never like in a minion. He was a fairly good Judas sheep, that much I'll grant. He packed 'em into those flying bombs like a Japanese subway stuffer. But his bleating was getting more grandiose by the day . . . and so were the manifestations of megalomania. The same capricious mix of beneficence and rancor that makes Me so lovable is always unwelcome in a mortal. It's the whole basis for Divine retribution, Greek tragedy, and the inevitable fall of tyrants. Human, know thy place, or get flattened. That's the long and the short of it.

Rickenbacker's sin was twofold. In his addled arrogance, he believed he had maneuvered himself not only into a position of power, but also one of relative safety. Daredevil metamorphosed into businessman. Well, that's why I keep Justice blindfolded. Lets the sword fall where it may. So step aside, scribe; it's time for some Old Testament shit.

Airports were critical to us, and I spoke for their expansion whenever I could. Early in 1941 Birmingham, the center of the South's steel industry and one of its fastest-growing cities, was considering whether to build a multimillion-dollar municipal air terminal. For weeks the Aviation Committee down there—composed of several good friends of mine—had been after me to make the case for the new facility at a Chamber of Commerce luncheon. This affair was set for the afternoon of February 27, and I had a very important Board meeting in Miami at eight the next morning. I just didn't think I could do justice to both, and told them so. But they kept after me, finally suggesting that maybe I was too important for little Birmingham. Well, I couldn't have that coming from friends. So reluctantly I agreed.

JOHN DOS PASSOS, *The Big Money*

"Charley turned her into the wind and let her have the gas. At the first soaring bounce there was a jerk. As he pitched forward, Charley switched off the ignition. . . . 'Hey doc,' he managed to croak, 'can't you get these aluminum splinters out of my side?' The damn ship must have turned turtle on them. Wings couldn't take it, maybe, but it's time they got the motor lifted off me."

SHEPPY The Captain had been restless all afternoon. He kept staring out the window at the bleak, inclement weather, telephoning several times to check on conditions farther south. At one point he instructed me to make railway reservations, only to countermand himself five minutes later. I could hear him pacing. Finally, he packed up his papers and ordered a car to La Guardia. As he left he told me to plan on taking Sunday off, which was odd, since we both worked all week during the winter travel season.

10 Rockefeller Plaza
February 26, 1941

William F. Rickenbacker
The Asheville School
Asheville, North Carolina

My dear Bill,
I am going on a trip and have only a few moments to write. But your last letter upset me so much that I simply had to make the time to get this off my chest.

I won't beat around the bush, I don't like the way you have been treating your brother, and I like even less the tone in which you refer to him. You are a very intelligent young man, but believe me you have overlooked what should be the most basic lesson of boyhood: blood is thicker than water.

I know for a fact that Dave is behind you in everything you do, and that he would stick up for you no matter how rough things got. You should do no less. Dave may not be much of a scholar, but he knows who his friends are and he keeps them.

Believe me, you will too. I am not going to tolerate disloyalty. And if teaching you this simple lesson demands that I remove you from your present pleasant circumstances and place you in a military academy, then so be it. The choice is yours, persuasion or compulsion. But in either case you will come to understand that Rickenbackers stick together.

Love and best wishes.

As always,
Daddy

ROBERT SERLING, *From the Captain to the Colonel*
"His plane left New York at 7:10 that night—Flight 21, the 'Mexico Flyer,' bound for Brownsville with intermediate stops at Washington, Atlanta, Birmingham, New Orleans, and Houston. Rickenbacker was pleased to find that the aircraft was one of EAL's five brand-new DSTs—Douglas Sleeping Transport, the designation for DC-3s equipped with berths. He didn't intend to sleep, but Eastern's DSTs had a small private room just behind the cockpit; called the Sky Lounge, it afforded privacy and a chance for Rickenbacker to read over his notes for the Birmingham speech."

JAMES A. PERRY, PILOT, FLIGHT 21 We were over Spartanburg, South Carolina, and the latest meteorological reports were lousy. I decided to consult the Captain and stepped back into the Lounge.

"The weather over Atlanta doesn't look good. We could have some problems getting in there."

"You're the captain, for Christ sakes," he said, looking up from his papers. "We pay you to make those decisions."

Interim Accident Report, Civil Aeronautics Board, April 1, 1941
At 2341 hours Flight 21 began an instrument approach under low but legal ceiling and visibility conditions. The aircraft followed the range beam over, then past Atlanta Regional Airport, and two minutes later commenced a 180-degree turn back toward assigned runway Number 3. In the course of this maneuver the plane's left wing came into contact with trees lining a ridge five miles north of Jonesboro and ten and one half miles south of the airport. The resulting impact was sufficient to sever the wing, and cause the plane to somersault into the ridge, coming to rest on its tail, the fuselage being ruptured in two places. . . .

. . . In the absence of further evidence, it is the judgment of this Board that the crash resulted from a combination of pilot error and a malfunctioning radio altimeter leading to the final evolution being undertaken at an altitude approximately 1,000 feet below that which is stipulated in Section 11, subparagraph 2. However, the pilot's prompt action in switching off the ship's electrical system before the final collision probably prevented an all-consuming fire, which would have . . .

GOD Pilot error? Radio altimeter? It was a backhand. The topspin made the plane bounce.

CONGRESSMAN HALE BOGGS Ah was on muh way to Loozianah. Just as we was 'bout to set down in Atlantuh, there was a brushin' sound followed bah a terrible crash. Next thing ah knew, we was upside down in the dark, folks groanin' an' screamin'. Pilot and copilot both daid, an' most a' the passengers seemed tu be pinned in the seats. But ah fell free, an' commenced to crawlin' till ah found muh way out through a big hole in the fuselage. Once muh eyes adjusted, ah found Mr. J.S. Rosenfeld of N'Awlins, who also got out pretty much unhurt. It was cold an' rainin' an' Mr. Rosenfeld had just suggested buildin' a fyar, when we hurd a raspy screech from inside the wreck. "For God's sake don't light a match. The gasoline will blow us to kingdom come." That was Captain Rickenbackah, mo daid than alive, as it turned out—but still givin awduhs.

DR. FLOYD W. McRAE, CHIEF SURGEON, PIEDMONT HOSPITAL He was in dreadful condition when they finally brought him in, almost eight hours after the crash. Twelve broken ribs, dislocations of both left knee and left elbow, crushed hip socket, and pelvis broken in two places. In addition, his thrashing after the crash had led to a broken nose and the slicing of the muscle tissue around the eye socket so that when the rescuers found him, the right eyeball was lying on his cheek, attached only by the optic nerve.

I recognized him immediately—since, coincidentally, I'd worked on his mastoid infection during the War. But he appeared extremely weak and basically beyond help. It was only after a priest, about to administer the last rites, asked if he was Catholic and drew the response—"I'm a goddamn Protestant like everybody else"—that it occurred to me that he might survive. Still, there was very little we could do initially, beyond replacing the eyeball and morphine to ease the pain.

I could tell I was dying. I remembered the sensation from almost bleeding to death after my tonsillectomy. The approach of death is sweet and completely deceptive. But the drugs were making it even better, literally impossible to resist. I realized suddenly that if I was going to live, I had to get the doctors to take me off morphine, no matter what the cost in agony.

DR. McRAE   When he regained consciousness, he was obviously hallucinating. He kept demanding to be taken off morphine. This was impossible. The pain alone would have killed him. But I lowered his dosage slightly, and told him we had done what he wanted. He seemed satisfied.

That accomplished, I could go about the business of recovering. My first task was to make my peace with my Maker. I firmly believed that the crash was no accident, and that there was a larger purpose behind it. But I needed to find out why it had happened, and what that purpose was. So I prayed.

"God? . . . God? . . . GAAAAWWWWD!!!!!"

Chapter Six

GOD   For sheer functional merit, nothing beats the old one-two. Take boxing . . . my favorite example. Combinations are what elevate the purely brutal and mundane into something ethereal. Granted, you do have memorable pugs like Joe Louis and Rocky Marciano, even Ingemar Johansson, who took 'em out with one big punch. Sudden, impressive, but where's the science? Where's the beauty? Compare that to the way Sugar Ray Robinson disposed of Bobo Olson, or Muhammad Ali flattened Cleveland Williams— two lightning punches . . . one gets 'em going, the other comes out of nowhere. It simply doesn't get any better than that for airbreathers. Of course, their towering sense of their own significance rebels against the obvious. That's why they keep trying to ban boxing and hype things like the Sistine Chapel.

Talk about kitsch—all those fluffy clouds and rotund bodies. Tell me, how are figures that fat supposed to fly? Blasphemous too . . . reaching out to touch My Finger. What misleading allegorical crap.

Give me Dempsey–Tunney II anytime. Had it all—ups and down, rules changes, numerical foibles, drama, heartbreak, blood, sweat, and above all, some of the sweetest combinations ever thrown.

It's much the same with history. The majestic passage of time clearly demonstrates that the best means of grabbing their attention is to hit them with a good one-two combination. The Peloponnesian War, the first two Punic Wars (the Third was a walkover), and the Thirty Years' War amply illustrate my point.

And this basically is the leitmotif of the first half of the twentieth century. I could have kept Round One going a bit longer. But both sides were basically out on their feet by the fall of '18. So I granted them a respite, let them go back to their corners for a breather. This gave the handlers a chance to close the cuts, apply ice to the swelling, and figure out what went wrong in the ring.

When the bell sounded again the fighters were refreshed and ready to give each other a real pounding. New tactics and strategy, even better weapons . . . Float like a butterfly, sting like a bee. Zoomin' and stompin', butting and goring. Bombs away. No holds barred . . . turning fields to ashes and cities to rubble. Killing everything in sight and finishing with a nuclear knockout . . . Hiroshima and Nagasaki—the old one-two again. Ooooooooo . . . Sweet Science.

Kindest thing I ever did. It was always just a matter of time until they figured out why stars burned and how their little universarium actually worked. And they were easily stupid enough to blow the lid off everything. Their time was growing short, and the cleanup job looked pretty substantial, so I decided to intervene, admonish them the best way I knew how. Two big helpings of mercy. A bit messy, but bountiful, baby, Bount-Ti-Ful. I'm that kind of Diety. Generous to the core.

In 1935 I took a busman's holiday in Europe, traveling aboard the various national airlines and gathering ideas we might apply at Eastern. But I also had been asked by some of the boys in the War Department, who knew I had good connections with the Germans, to take a close look at what they were doing with military aviation. Goering and Udet, the two old fighter aces, gave me a royal reception, as they would Lindbergh a little later. They had both obviously taken a big step upward since the last time I saw them, Goering especially, who was decked out like the Student Prince.

"Herr Eddie, you perhaps recall what I said about our air force's destiny when you last paid us a visit."

"How could I forget, Herr Goering?"

"*Sehr gut*," he said nodding with such energy that his double chin jiggled. "But just to be sure, Ernst Udet will show you everything we have accomplished."

I knew Heinies, and I knew how they think. So I had every confidence he'd do just that. Our first stop was what had been Richthofen's Flying Circus, now fully combat-ready, with virtually every man, even the cooks, flight-rated. I saw aircraft factories, many of them hidden and in some cases partially buried, turning out military and civilian planes on parallel lines. I was given access to every kind of testing device, including their massive wind tunnels. They showed off their latest hardware—motors, instruments, and airframes, even the super-secret Heinkel 112, which looked to me like something out of science fiction. Altogether it was an awesome display, and a frightening one.

As soon as I got home I wrote up a report for Army Intelligence, making it absolutely clear just how potentially dangerous the situation was. A polite thank-you note was all the response I got. Some months after, I was approached by Lindbergh. The so-called "Lone Eagle" was just as impressed as I was by the growth of German air power, but not the least bit concerned about it being in the hands of Nazis. "Here's a government finally doing something about the Jewish problem," he told me. Well, that was a matter for him and Mr. Ford to mull over. As far as I was concerned the real issue was our own unpreparedness.

The fact was that all the skills and technology of our aviation industry were being hamstrung by idiots. We didn't have an air force worth talking about, and until we did, I firmly believed we had better steer clear of the Germans and war in general. That was why I numbered myself among those who were for America First. If the brass hats and the politicians had listened to Billy Mitchell, the prophet of Air Power, we would not have been in such a fix. But instead, he was court-martialed and drummed out of the service. That was the thanks he got from his country, and it broke his heart.

GENERAL CARL "TOOEY" SPATZ We considered ourselves Billy's boys—Hap Arnold, Jimmy Doolittle, and myself. But when the Old Man took sick it was Rick who carried the ball. The General was in Doctors Hospital near Gracie Square. We got up from Washington whenever we could, but Rickenbacker was in his room practically every day. Always the same routine—"What the hell's the matter with you? Finally caught the clap, huh? Get outta bed, you lazy fuck, I got two hot numbers down in the lobby." His liver was shot and he was pretty weak, but Rickenbacker never failed to cheer him up.

When the General passed away, Rick was out of town. But he caught the first available plane and was back in New York within a matter of hours. There were about five of us, plus Mitchell's sister. We escorted the coffin through the bowels of Grand Central Station to the mail car that would take him back to Milwaukee for burial. It was dark and you could hear our footsteps echoing off the stone walls. Afterward we all went to the Commodore Bar. Nobody said much. We just drank ourselves stupid.

SHEPPY The months before Pearl Harbor were not happy ones for the Captain. He was discharged from the hospital in Atlanta by the early summer, and spent the remainder of his convalescence in a bungalow on Candlewood Lake. He enjoyed the time with the boys, but the crash had resulted in a great deal of muscle damage which was very slow to heal. A masseur worked on him every day. But he was in continual pain, and his drinking increased noticeably. When he found he had trouble operating the clutch of an automobile, he simply gave up driving—not an entirely unwelcome occurrence, since he had never bothered to take out a license. But he also seemed to be losing interest in the airline. Although we knew he was ambulatory, he kept putting off coming into the office.

Finally, I began making weekly jaunts out to Connecticut in an effort to get him reengaged. I brought along papers for his signature, took notes, and relayed messages; but we were simply going through the motions. It was the first and only time I saw him truly depressed. It was not so much his injuries as his general situation. He talked a good deal about General Mitchell and being put out to pasture. He was involved with the America First movement. But I think he knew war was inevitable, and worried that we were not doing enough to prepare for it. He wanted to make some sort of contribution, but was convinced that President Roosevelt hated him and would never let him help. So he sat staring at the ice cubes in his highball.

One day, when I could stand it no longer, I looked him square in the eye and told him exactly what I was feeling. "I'm beginning to think you'll never be the man you once were. You sit out here and mope, but you don't do a damned thing to help yourself. You talk about coming to the aid of your country, but I'm not sure you have it in you. Frankly, I'm ashamed to be working for you."

At first he simply looked hurt, and my heart sank. But then he drew himself up and got that mean Rickenbacker look in his eyes. "You can't talk to me like that. . . . You, you, you . . . hussy!

You're fired! Get out of my house! . . . From now on when we meet, it'll be in my office." On the train back to New York I had a stiff drink and a good cry.

JOHN DOS PASSOS   It was shortly before we entered the War that I got the first of my calls from Rickenbacker. Initially, he was quite cordial, insisting that he admired my work. I was very much on my guard given the existence of the Charley Anderson character and my understanding of his political views. . . . I was a New Dealer at the time. Rickenbacker the person was every bit Charley's equivalent as a blunt instrument, so it didn't take long for his motives to become apparent. He truly believed I knew what was going to happen to him. After the Atlanta crash, I suppose it was not entirely unreasonable on his part to suspect at least some clairvoyance on my part. But it was his blockheaded persistence that really annoyed me. I was under strict orders from my lawyer to admit to nothing. But after Pearl Harbor the calls really became a burden. I had my number changed, but he got hold of the new one. His importuning by this time was truly hysterical—wheedling and abusive at the same time. I remember his words exactly. "You Commie fuck, it's your patriotic duty to tell me what's going to happen to me in the War." There was no cognition, the words simply formed in my mouth. "You'll be marooned in the Pacific on a desert island with Amelia Earhart."

ADELAIDE   Edward was at the office on Sunday when he heard over the radio that Pearl Harbor had been attacked. He arrived home to inform me that we were moving to Miami to live on the Sloans' houseboat in Biscayne Bay. "I need to get into condition, and this will be the quickest way to do it."

He spent the days in bathing trunks and a broad-brimmed planter's hat soaking up the heat of the Florida sun. It was really quite eerie considering what happened later. After a month he was brown as a nut, and the muscle spasms in his back and legs had largely disappeared. He continued to walk with a limp—he would for the rest of his life—but special orthopedic shoes rigged with pieces of shower clog he stuffed in the heel made it almost unnoticeable. One day after lunch he marched up to me and announced, "Adelaide, I'm ready to go to war." Within a week, he received a call from Washington to report immediately.

GENERAL HENRY "HAP" ARNOLD Rickenbacker posed a real problem. We needed the support of the airlines, especially since we were about to requisition most of their planes and crews. He could help smooth that over. Also, he was the last war's Ace of Aces. Everybody knew it. We had to do something with him. But every time Mr. Stimson proposed an assignment, we'd get a two-word reply from the White House. "No Rickenbacker."

Finally we decided to go the Secret Mission route. We'd send him out, but keep it very low profile. The troops would see him; he'd do a little quiet inspecting and might even accomplish something useful. 'Course keeping Rickenbacker under cover was like stashing a water buffalo in a grass hut . . . a temporary solution at best.

I'd known Hap Arnold since the twenties, when he was a young captain. Now he was a lieutenant general running the Army Air Corps. As I walked into his office in the War Department I didn't know what to expect.

"Eddie, I'm hearing some rumors coming out of the combat squadrons we're putting together that I don't like. The story is they don't have the aggressiveness they're going to need when they get down to it. I need you to go out and blow some smoke up their collective asses, inspire the bastards. And also poke around a bit and see if you can't uncover some other problems. Got it?"

It was exactly what I'd been praying for. "Hap, this is perfect. But I need about a week and a half. My boys are coming down to Florida, and we—"

"Eddie, my friend, you're missing the point. There's a war on. Some of these squadrons are gonna be on their way to Europe by then. Unless you're ready to leave tomorrow it's no go."

"Well, why didn't you say so, sir? I'm on my way." I even saluted.

COLONEL HANS CHRISTIAN ADAMSON I was his designated handler, as if anybody could handle the Captain. We also brought along a masseur to keep the old campaigner from stiffening up between stops. Fat chance. Forty-one flight groups in thirty-two days.

In Tallahassee, he came upon a squadron of qualified Negro fighter pilots, who had yet to receive either their wings or their commissions. "Goddammit, Hap," you could hear him booming away on the phone, "if these bastards are going to risk their asses for their country, then they gotta do it as officers like the rest of our fucking pilots." Within a month we had a fresh batch of black second lieutenants. For the Captain there were just two kinds of people—our side and their side.

I'll never forget him haranguing the kids of the 94th, his old squadron. By the time he was through they were frothing at the mouth.

"In my day we called 'em Heinies. You call 'em Krauts. But they're the same fucking Germans they always were. They look a lot like you and me—not like those monkey-faced Jap baby butchers—but they're not the same on the inside. They'll probably put up some kind of fight; but take it from me they'd rather be raping your mother or your sister. And they will if you let 'em. Winston Churchill said the Huns were either at your throat or your feet. You make sure it's the latter.

"Look, I killed about twenty-five of the cocksuckers and never lost a minute's sleep. Best thing I ever did. Twenty-five less reasons for trouble in the future. Now it's your turn. Kill 'em. Kill 'em anywhere you can. Shoot 'em on the ground. Shoot 'em in the air. Shoot 'em in their fucking parachutes.

"I had a 100-horsepower SPAD with twin Vickers peashooters. You have these new P-38s with 2,500 horsepower and eight 50 cals up front. Use them. But remember, the principles of air combat haven't changed. Keep the sun at your back. Hit 'em when they least expect it. Get in close. And give 'em plenty of lead.

"One more thing. I hear some dickless wonder back in Washington wants to take away your Hat in the Ring sign. Over my dead body. That insignia was the last thing a lot of Heinies saw on this earth, and it's gonna be the end of a lot more. It was my calling card, and it'll be yours too."

Considering the President of the United States probably wished he'd turn up underneath a tank tread somewhere, this was not a bad gig. A kind of forties version of Fire Marshall Bill Goes Patriotic. Fast Eddie Rickenbacker's very own bloodthirsty USO show. You could almost hear the chorus of high-steppers belting out: "Let's hear it for Homicide; / Let's widow that Nazi bride. / Don't stop that Crimson Tide; / Not until a million've died."

He could also do meeting. Called the other airline execs to Washington. "Okay, you guys, ditch your chisels; this is about your country, not your airline." They were going to hand over their planes to the government no matter what. But Eddie imparted a sheen of self-sacrifice to the transfer, the proper patina for expropriation.

And if rumors abounded that our combat planes weren't up to the mark, that the Curtis P-40 Warhawk was really an underpowered pig, Captain Eddie Rickenbacker remained available to speak seriously to you about America's fighting machinery. . . . "The P-40F has more firepower—heavier guns—and carries more ammunition than the Zero. The P-40F has protected gasoline tanks. The Zero has none. American incendiary bullets turn it into a flaming coffin." He might have added that the P-40F's Allison engine wheezed pathetically at anything over 30,000 feet. But then again, it was Eddie who bought Allison engineering for GM in the first place, and besides, that was classified.

Everyone agreed. He was doing an excellent job. The War Effort's version of a good utility infielder—a little of this, a little of that. Famous for being outspoken, he knew when to shut up. They sent him to England and he blended in with the scenery, quietly getting behind the P-51 Mustang which the Brits were pushing as the best of the new American fighters. When they tried to make him a general, offered him two stars even, he shrewdly ducked the honor and gathered trust and IOUs instead. He'd been climbing all his life, and he knew how to carve out a foothold and make sure it was solid before moving on.

None of this was lost on Henry Lewis Stimson, the Secretary of War. He signified rectitude without limits. The man about whom there were no doubts. Andover, Yale, Harvard Law, Elihu Root's law partner, government service galore. Republican down to his toenails, he only occasionally stepped out of the Cabinet—Secretary of War under Taft, Secretary of State under Hoover, and then back again to the War Department for FDR, the Democrat's Democrat. He was that trustworthy.

Rickenbacker both attracted and repelled him. Much of his own life was devoted to riding horses in bad weather, shooting large mammals, and swimming in water too cold for seals—the WASP overcompensation thing. He had been a colonel in the Artillery in the First War. His temper was frightful, if hardly profane. His life was a series of challenges overcome. Yet it was all basically abstract; he never really had to get down in the dirt. Stimson's life was the Official Boy Scout Manual of success in America.

Eddie's was the unexpurgated version; you bought it under the table. He fought and clawed his way to prominence. He killed men and had his way with women. When he got mad, his every third word was obscene. But he knew what he was about. And Stimson, no fool, recognized they were both about the same thing . . . competence. Rickenbacker could be trusted. He would get the job done.

And as it happened, there was a job tailor-made for Fast Eddie. Douglas MacArthur was off the farm. Holed up in Port Moresby, he answered to no one . . . not to Chester Nimitz, his immediate superior, nor to the authorities in Washington. The war to him had become a personal vendetta. The Japanese had thrown him out of the Philippines and he would return the favor. He would see them in hell or in Tokyo Bay, whichever came first. Now this may have been good box office, but it was absolutely unacceptable to the White House and everything it stood for.

FRANKLIN DELANO ROOSEVELT   We met in the early evening. There were just three of us in my office—Harry Hopkins, Secretary Stimson, and myself.

"Henry, this simply cannot go on. The man has become a law unto himself. No military officer can be allowed the latitude he is exercising."

"I realize that, Mr. President. But I think you will agree that relieving him at this time will be terribly demoralizing. Like it or not, General MacArthur has become a symbol of our will to win in the Pacific."

"Oh my goodness, you don't have to tell me that. But I also realize this situation is intolerable. What are we going to do with this man?"

"Mr. President, it is my belief he must be told that he is very near the end of his rope. That if he wants to remain out there, he must ease up on the self-serving publicity, stop complaining about the Joint Chiefs, and cease fighting with Admiral Nimitz. If he does not do these things forthwith, he will removed, regardless of the consequences."

"All right then. But I want this message delivered personally and in a way that cannot be misinterpreted. Frankly, I want it said as rudely and directly as possible. Now then, who do you think can do that for us, Henry?"

"Eddie Rickenbacker."

"Impossible! You know how much I dislike that man. Why do you persist in bringing him into the picture?"

"Because, Mr. President, he is literally the most insulting individual I know in Washington."

"Well . . . umm . . . that much I will concede. . . . You know, Henry, every once in a while I am reminded why Harry here's idea of having a Republican as Secretary of War was such a stroke of genius. Now that that's settled, let's play some poker."

GOD   So, the lords of war were not yet finished with Edward. But then, neither was I. The first crash had barely dented his thick skull. By all appearances the only thing he took from it was that silly shoe stuffed with rubber. He remained, as before, besotted with Arrogance, the very soul of Disobedience. Fear, guilt, remorse, existential *cafards* of one sort of another—none of this seemed to apply.

That's what made him such fun. Plucky little cockroach. Stomp him once, he just limps away. So step on him again . . . the old one-two. I wanted to see him absolutely in extremis. This is the territory where he and his ilk become most interesting. What *were* his limits? Who knew? So why not shoot the messenger? . . . or at least hang him out to dry.

I had my instructions, a message too secret to even write down. I was to deliver it in my own words as I thought best. Once again, my aide-de-camp was Colonel Hans Adamson. But before taking off into the Pacific, I took the opportunity to visit with my mother, who had just turned eighty and continued to live with my brother Dewey in Los Angeles.

ELIZABETH   My boy didn't look so good. Ven he had his crash, za smart doctors told me nothing about it for a long time. Zey said it might kill me, vich vas pretty stupid since it vas Edward who vas in za crash und almost died. Ven you get old, people tell you less and less. I asked Edward where he vas going. But he says he vas on a secret mission and couldn't tell me nothing. Vell there are things I didn't tell him either like, "How's za whore und za orphans?"

HANS ADAMSON   We flew civilian, Pan Am, out to Honolulu. It was a smooth fifteen-hour run, and both of us were able to catch some shut-eye. When we landed, Rick, ever the go-getter, went off with General Lynd to inspect Hickam Field and give some pep talks to the lads.

We were scheduled to take off at 2230 hours, and the General himself drove us to the plane, a well-used B-17D. On the way out Rick wanted to know about the crew and was assured that they were all members of the Army Transport Command, some with airline experience. I sat in back, wishing we had had the time to catch some sun at Waikiki. Enough sun was about the only thing I didn't have to worry about.

LIEUTENANT JAMES C. WHITTAKER We had been scheduled to ferry the beat-up Fort to the mainland, when we got word we were going in the other direction with no less than Eddie Rickenbacker as cargo. We were out on the flight line with the engines warmed up and the tanks topped off. Captain Bill Hamilton was in command, I was copilot on the right. In the dark we didn't see the Jeep drive up to us, and just felt the Fort shift a bit as our passengers climbed on board. Next a hand sort of shook me: "I'm Rickenbacker, this is Adamson, who the hell are you?" We didn't say much, just our names. Then Hamilton gave the high sign and the two of them strapped themselves in behind us.

I brought the motors up to max power and we rolled off toward the first of an unbroken string of fuck-ups that would turn the next three weeks into a living hell. About 2,000 feet down the runway, a tube to the left brake burst, locking up the wheel. The Fort veered, and the first thing we knew it was headed toward the hangars. But Hamilton was up to the challenge, ground-looping the plane, and bringing it screeching to a halt but in no shape to continue. "Nice move, but that was one sorry rollout," muttered Rickenbacker over his shoulder. From that point there would be no love lost between him and Hamilton.

HANS ADAMSON General Lynd carted us back to his quarters and around midnight we got word that a second B-17, a much later model, was checked out and ready to go. We took off at 0115 hours without further incident, and the Captain and I turned in on the cots set up for us aft. There were blankets but it was cold and I slept only in snatches. At 0630 daylight broke. I had a Danish, orange juice, and hot coffee from a thermos, then settled in with my paperwork propped up by a mail sack. The Captain seemed restless and went forward.

All was peaceful in the cockpit. The weather was clear and Hamilton, the pilot, had the plane on autopilot, something I never like. Our destination was Canton Island, a four-by-eight-mile speck about one third the distance to Australia, where we would refuel. The E.T.A. at Canton was 9:30 A.M., and about one hour before Hamilton began the slow descent from 9,000 feet down to about 1,000 before leveling off. All that remained was for the island to appear.

We spent the next six hours waiting. It never happened. We raised Canton for a bearing, only to be told the equipment was still in crates. We called Palmyra Island, another tiny base about halfway along our route, but they couldn't bring us in without knowing our position. We tried boxing the compass—flying forty minutes in each direction, asking Canton to begin firing AA set to explode at 5,000 feet. Still we saw nothing. In desperation I consulted the charts. Near Canton and just a bit northwest was Howland Island, the objective of Amelia Earhart when she disappeared in 1937. It sent a cold chill down my spine.

2ND LIEUTENANT JOHN DEANGELIS, NAVIGATOR Rickenbacker came stalking back and settled on me like a vulture. "Young man, tell me how in hell you got us so lost?" As if I was supposed to know. I tried to explain that my octant had taken a pretty good shot in the first crack-up, and maybe we had misjudged the tailwind. He wasn't buying that. "All the training, the best American equipment, perfect weather conditions, and you manage to miss a whole fucking island. How is that possible?"

GOD I moved it. . . . Almost forgot to put it back. Now *that* would have caused a stir with the cartographers.

Hamilton had shut down and feathered the two outboard engines, and was running the others as lean as possible. Our only hope now was to locate a ship. But the sea remained empty. We sent an SOS. There was no acknowledgment. We were down to fifteen minutes' flying time. It was plain we would have to ditch.

I took time to study my comrades. I'd known Adamson for over a decade, long before he became my military aide. Like me he was fifty-three years old. He had once been an explorer and an astronomer, but now, also like me, he was deskbound. The Pacific Ocean was no place for either one of us.

Up front I knew nothing of Hamilton except that he was twenty-seven, had flown for American Airlines, and had a very unmilitary appearance. Well, his cowboy boots and goatee were about to look pretty stupid in the drink. Whittaker, the copilot, seemed to be better material. Probably around forty, confident and well-built, he had that indefinable look of toughness. I was willing to bet he was a survivor.

The rest were mainly kids. DeAngelis was a wiry little Dago in his early twenties, who looked as if he could take some punishment. But Brady, the flight engineer, and Reynolds, the radioman, were both fair, skinny, and looked a lot like fish bait to me. Then there was Sergeant Alex, a poor little Polack with a name too long to pronounce. He had just gotten out of the hospital on Oahu from an appendectomy and a serious bout with jaundice, and was being ferried back to his unit in Australia. He was a chipper little guy, but he seemed far from recovered and I didn't like his chances.

That was the eight of us. Not exactly your ideal crew for open-ocean sailing. And that presumed that Hamilton could set the fuel-starved Fort down in the water without killing us all.

JIM WHITTAKER   At low altitude the ocean's smooth surface was transformed into an endless field of fifteen-foot rollers. If we hit them head on, the crest would probably flip us over and break the fuselage in half. I told Hamilton that maybe we could approach crosswise and set her down between two crests. "Sounds good. But let's do it while we've still got some gas, so we can come in on power."

In the back I could hear Rickenbacker giving orders and getting the crew to lie down and brace against the bulkheads. Looking at Hamilton I held out my hand. "It's been good knowing you, pal."

"Hold on, buddy, you ain't gettin' out that easy. This landing's gonna be smooth as a baby's bottom."

Just then DeAngelis broke in over the intercom. "You guys have any objections to me saying a prayer?"

Something about his tone pissed me off. "If I was you, DeAngelis, I'd be directing my thoughts of salvation up toward Captain Hamilton here."

Seconds later Rickenbacker started his version of a countdown. "Fifty feet! Forty feet!"

Little Johnny Brady was busy removing the wing nuts that secured the escape hatches, causing the lids to rip off almost immediately.

"Twenty feet!"

The wind was howling, roaring into the open ports.

"Five feet! . . . Three feet! . . ."

"Shut it down!" Hamilton yelled.

I jerked the main, cutting the motors and every electrical circuit in the plane. Bill drew back on the stick and the tail caught the water, then the body of the plane thumped down into the trough. I felt like my safety harness was cutting me in two. My eyes went black. I could taste blood. Then it was over. We had gone from ninety miles an hour to zero in probably something like ten yards. Next thing I knew I was out of my seat, yanking on the handle that would free the five-place raft stowed farthest forward.

When Hamilton and me climbed through the hatch, Rickenbacker was on the wing wrestling with the aft five-placer, which was already inflated. DeAngelis and Alex pushed the little three-man inflatable through the port above the bomb bay. Somebody was yelling, "Get in the rafts! Get in the rafts! The plane's sinking!"

I scrambled in with Hamilton and Reynolds, who had a helluva cut across his nose. Rickenbacher's bunch took longer to get clear—Adamson had wrenched his back and couldn't hardly move, and Brady gashed his hand fending off the raft from a jagged piece of metal. Worse off still were DeAngelis and Alex, who turned over in the three-man. Finally they got the thing righted and dragged themselves back in; but Alex sucked in a bunch a' seawater and was puking his guts out. There was more bad news to come.

"Where's the water? . . . I thought you had it. . . . Is it back with you guys? . . . No . . . I . . . uhh . . . Well, that's all we fucking need. We'll have to go back an' get it."

STAFF SERGEANT JAMES REYNOLDS "*No!*" It was Captain Hamilton and Rickenbacker, the both of them. "That plane is goin' down any second. You wanna be dragged down with it?" So we sat watching as the fucking Fort refused to sink—it must have been ten minutes before she went under. When we got around to figuring out what we did have in the way of survival gear, it came down to four little aluminum paddles, a long rope we used to tie the rafts together, two hand pumps for bailing and keepin' the air pressure up, a couple a' canvas buckets, two fish-hooks and some twine, a penknife, a service revolver, a Very pistol with eighteen flares, and a first aid kit. Somebody—probably those scavenger mechanics—filched the rations that were supposed to be stored in the rafts. In their place we had four little oranges that Hamilton fished out of his flight jacket. That was it. Eat hearty, mates.

Unless you have been in the middle of an ocean in a tiny craft, you cannot imagine how it overwhelms you. On this day the swells smacked us around like Ping-Pong balls—knocking us together, then jerking us apart, all the while raising and lowering us so that one minute you were staring over the top of a cliff and the next you were plunged into the deepest valley. Just the movement was exhausting.

Then as we drifted, I thought I saw something dark below the surface. Suddenly a dorsal fin appeared, followed by another and another. Sharks! Big ones. Sea demons, some as long as one of the rafts. And they smelled blood . . . our blood . . . Brady's and Reynolds's blood.

GOD
Old Man River gottin' in my shoes
It's no use sittin' an' singing the blues
So be my guest, you got nothin' to lose
Woncha' let me take you on a Sea Cruise
Oooowe . . . Ooooowee Baayybee . . .
Woncha' let me take you on a . . . Sea Cruise.
Huey P. Smith, "Sea Cruise"

PRIVATE JOHN BRADY That first afternoon weren't so bad. It was already past the hottest time of the day. My hand was aching with all the salt, but the bleeding was down to a steady ooze. We was gripin' and wisecrackin' back an' forth; but I think everybody was feelin' pretty lucky to be alive. Mr. Rickenbacker said he'd give a hundred bucks to the guy who spotted the plane that rescued us, and that cheered us up some.

But then the sun sets and things started to get really miserable. Right away this cold mist come down on top of us. Here we was just about on the equator and we're all freezin'. I tried to sleep. But with the waves and all, every time I closed my eyes I felt seasick. You could hear Alex in the next raft over with the dry heaves, and Adamson was groanin' some. Then something hit the raft from underneath. It scared me half outta my wits, 'specially when I figured out it was one a' them sharks. I didn't think I'd make it till morning. And I don't mind telling you, there was many a time out there I wished I hadn't.

As dawn broke I took stock of our situation. It was not good. The idea of calling these rafts five-man and three-man models was criminal. The two larger ones were 6 feet 9 inches by 2 feet 4 inches, which doesn't sound too bad until you stop to consider that a good deal of the internal space was taken up by the flotation roll. There was barely room for three. And our raft was worse, since Adamson's injuries demanded that he be given room to stretch out. That left Brady and me jackknifed in the corners. I was barely recovered from the Atlanta crash, and my hips and knees throbbed mercilessly. Sitting still in that raft without complaining was the toughest challenge I've ever faced.

But I knew I had to do it. The seven others bobbing with me alone in the Pacific were a typical slice of young American manhood—each had his strengths and weaknesses. I was the one who had faced death over and over, and I knew they were counting on me to pull them through. If I showed any signs of weakness, the starch would go out of them and we would be finished.

JIM WHITTAKER   Breakfast time and Hamilton and Rickenbacker clashed over how and when to divide the oranges. Bill thought we should split them one a day on the grounds that they would dry out anyway, while Rickenbacker was wanting to stretch 'em out as long as possible, so we'd have something to look forward to. Finally, we voted for a compromise. We'd divide the first one right away, and the others on alternate mornings. That way they would last eight days. The boys had me carve. I studied that sucker like a diamond cutter. There wasn't much in the way of liquid. But the pulp stimulated some saliva flow and you didn't feel so thirsty . . . for about five minutes.

It got hot quick. Blazing hot. It felt like you were under a fucking broiler . . . your skin was screamin'. When we got in the rafts it seemed like a good idea to ditch our shoes; Reynolds and Brady even stripped to their shorts. What a mistake. Every inch of exposed flesh was being cooked, then basted by the salt water, which got into your flesh and burned and cracked and dried and burned again. Only Rickenbacker was fully clothed—business suit, fedora, and wing-tips . . . a tie even. He'd looked pretty funny on day one. But now, not a one of us didn't envy the son of a bitch . . . and pay heed to what he said. "Don't move more than you have to, try to cover your heads, and keep the chatter down during the hottest part of the day, it'll dry out your mouth. Above all, don't drink any salt water." Wise words. The difference between life and death, as it turned out.

JIM REYNOLDS   From about four in the morning to about nine and then from three to eight P.M. it was bearable. That's when most of the talking got done. When the sea was down we'd pull the rafts together and try to figure out what the fuck to do. Over the first couple of days it was pretty upbeat. Later, things got more desperate and nasty and religious. . . . Oh yeah, we all got religion out there.

HANS ADAMSON   Rick's role was somewhere between drill sergeant and camp counselor. He'd do anything to keep us occupied. At one point he had us singing cowboy songs at sunset. He'd also invent these ridiculous games. The only one I remember specifically was Rap the Jap. The idea was to begin with an epithet and continue topping it—slant-eyed, buck-toothed, pigeon-toed, slackjawed, pig-nosed, slope-skulled, dwarf-dicked, etc. We played that exactly one time.

Besides Alex, I was probably in the worst shape of anyone. The landing left me racked with muscle spasms, and when the waves were running the pain was unbelievable. But this didn't exempt me. He was after me continually. "You okay, Hans? You're a man of many experiences. Tell us a story, pal." Because I was stretched out and could look straight up without moving, he saddled me with lectures on the stars. "You worked at the Hayden Planetarium for Christ sakes, entertain us, you bastard." It didn't matter that the night mist blotted out much of the sky, or that nobody was much interested. He just wanted to keep me in the ball game. He was that way with all of us. He'd find some angle—a weak point or special talent, anything—and keep probing, picking at it like a scab. Anything to keep you alert. As time passed he got more and more cruel. He didn't care what any of us thought of him . . . only that you didn't give up.

I tried to steer the conversation away from eating and drinking, but it was impossible. Every one of us had a special obsession. Hamilton harped on vanilla ice cream. Whittaker talked about swimming in a giant tub of cold beer. Reynolds went on about how many soft drinks he could down, and then got in an argument with Brady over the relative merits of carbonated beverages versus fruit juice. We went round and round from ice water, to jellied consommé, to cherry frappes, to Eskimo pies, to mandarin oranges, to coconut milk, to pineapple juice, and back to ice water—a thirst-quenching merry-go-round.

I began to feel an unmistakable taste in my mouth. Back in Des Moines thirty years before, when I was with the poverty-struck Duesenberg team, my daily diet was reduced to a steady procession of chocolate malteds, each fortified with a raw egg. Now I felt that smooth, syrupy liquid rolling across my tongue, and I began swallowing involuntarily. The loss of control frightened me. And that wasn't the end of it.

During the night I began to see things, floating forms both sinister and beautiful—shapely females, fantastic animals, all sorts of things. Adamson told me he saw them too, that they were just combinations of clouds and moonlight. But he was wrong. These were much more real . . . too real to talk about with anybody else.

JIM WHITTAKER   There was no sign of help. We divvied up the second orange on the fourth morning. And things were so bad at dawn of the fifth that we broke down and had the next-to-last orange. On both days Hamilton and Rickenbacker baited the fish-hooks with bits of peel and tried to catch the sleek delicious mackerel that we could see swimming just below us. The fish would have none of it.

Without thinking much about it we began talking over what better kinds of bait we might come up with. Brady suggested fingernail clippings.

"Too hard. You couldn't get them on the hooks."

"Well, how about a little more of us?"

"Wha? . . . You mean like a toe, or an earlobe? How 'bout your left nut?"

"I'm serious. You got any better ideas?"

"I don't see any of us volunteering for surgery."

"What are we supposed to do, draw straws?"

"We ain't got no straws."

When we all found ourselves staring over at poor little half-dead Alex, we got off that topic quick . . . at least temporarily.

He was stuffed in the three-man with DeAngelis, packed in so tight that the two of them had to sit face-to-face hanging their legs over each other's shoulders. DeAngelis tanned, but Alex's skin just burned and peeled and burned and peeled until it was a raw mass of sores.

He kept crying out for water. It was getting to the other men, so I pulled over and reamed him good for sniveling. It was only then that I noticed he had what looked like trench mouth and it was eating away his gums so that his front teeth seemed to be at the point of falling out. It took us a few more days to realize he was drinking from the sea at night when we couldn't see him. DeAngelis woke up to find him head down lapping up what amounted to a form of poison. Salt water was tormenting him, literally pickling his insides. No wonder he cried out.

But even this grew faint as he became weaker. During the day he rolled himself into a ball, mouthing the words of the Hail Mary. At night the cold left him shaking so violently that DeAngelis could no longer sleep. There was no helping Alex. He was dying and all we could do was watch.

Meanwhile the sun continued to beat down on the rest of us, slowly draining our hope and energy. On the sixth day we cut up the final orange. The juice had dried up, and it was rotting. Realistically, it made no sense to hold on to it. Still, I tried to tell the others we were fools to finish it off. That shriveled little thing was all we had, our ace in the hole. Now we were left with nothing. Just the empty sky, the blank horizon, and the sharks who were our constant companions. For the first time I began to seriously contemplate that we might all die out there floating in a desert as merciless as any on land.

ADELAIDE When they came to tell me that Edward was lost at sea, I remember saying something like: "Don't worry. He'll find a way out." Perhaps if I'd known his true situation, I would have held my tongue. But I truly believed he was alive and would be back. . . . So did the boys. He'd been through so much and survived. We just came to expect it from him. As they said later—he was the man who always returned.

BEV GRIFFITH When we heard the news, we just went into shock. It was like Eastern headquarters had been taken over by zombies. We were reduced to shuffling around, going through the motions without the slightest idea of what might happen next. He was our reason for being and suddenly he was gone . . . vanished.

It was Sheppy who kept things together. She ran his office as if he would charge in anytime and begin digesting the stack of papers waiting for his signature. Every morning she'd put fresh flowers on his desk, sharpen the pencils, and change the water in his thermos. Then she'd call over to Café Louis and reserve his table for lunch, only to cancel it at noon. "I wouldn't give up on the Captain," she kept telling me. "He will be back. And when he discovers all the work that has gone undone, there will be hell to pay."

FDR The news had both negative and positive implications. On one hand, we appeared to have lost a valuable means of chastising General MacArthur . . . but on the other hand, it seemed as if we had lost Rickenbacker.

RICKENBACKER'S PLANE MISSING

WASHINGTON, Oct. 22 (UP). Captain Eddie Rickenbacker, America's most successful fighter pilot in World War I and special assistant to Secretary of War Stimson, has been reported missing on a flight between Oahu, Hawaii, and another Pacific island.

Although the official announcement that reported his plane overdue was not optimistic, there is plainly hope that Rickenbacker may still be found. The U.S. Navy and Army Air Force have mounted a major rescue operation, throwing every available aircraft into the search.

Should the effort fail, Rickenbacker would join a list of notable aviators—Amelia Earhart, Australian Charles Kingsford-Smith, and Pan American Airways Captain Edwin C. Musick—all lost in the same proximity over the last five years. . . .

Los Angeles Times, October 24, 1942

RICKENBACKER DEAD?

Eddie Rickenbacker, Eastern Airlines President and one of the best-known figures in American aviation, was reported missing this afternoon on a flight from Hawaii to a secret destination somewhere in the Pacific. While the official announcement held out some hope of rescue, sources within the Army indicated that the chances of recovering him alive are slim. . . .
New York World-Telegram, October 23, 1942

DAMON RUNYON, *New York American,* October 29, 1942
The word on the Big Street is that Eddie Rickenbacker is done for. He has been missing for a week on a flight somewhere in the Pacific. The Captain's a big man, but that's a bigger ocean. A few high rollers are still banking on him sitting on some island sharing a coconut with his pals Amelia Earhardt and Fred Noonan. But every day that passes stretches the odds against him a little further. If it's true and he's gone, then we're all going to have to cinch in our belts a little tighter if we expect to win this war. You just can't take a loss like that and not feel it. He was a keeper. Not just one of our best aviators, but one of our best men.

Now to Damon's caffeine-constricted eyes, peering out from his favorite table at Lindy's restaurant with a perfect view of Broadway and not much else, war may have taken on a deceptively utilitarian cast—a kind of input-output model replete with regression equations, one of which was War Hero Wastage. He should have read the *Iliad.* Wars weren't just about winning and losing, they were rabid melodramas fueled by the blood of the valorous. That's why there were priests wielding obsidian knives atop the pyramids of Tenochtitlán. The oblation of the killer angel was the essential sacrament of organized violence. Only by mixing the blood of lions with that of lambs could the otherwise pacific masses be persuaded to rush headlong into the meat grinder. So wartime America was primed to embrace the death of Eddie Rickenbacker, to wallow in it. Of course, from a sheep's-eye view it was all about propitiation—serving up a nice fillet so the Lord of Hosts might overlook the lesser cuts. Fat chance. Which just goes to show how misled everybody was.

For the hero in question was very much alive, a grizzled old buzzard with only limited appetite appeal, except maybe to his new pals the sharks. And the Deity in Charge—had he been willing to shed a measure of his ineffability—might have reminded many of the Joker in the Deck.

JIM WHITTAKER I couldn't get them out of my head. Those verses I had learned as a kid in high school now came back to haunt me.

> *All in a hot and copper sky,*
> *The bloody sun, at noon,*
> *Right up above the mast did stand,*
> *No bigger than the moon.*
>
> *Day after day, day after day*
> *We stuck, nor breath nor motion;*
> *As idle as a painted ship*
> *Upon a painted ocean.*
>
> *Water, water, everywhere*
> *And all the boards did shrink;*
> *Water, water, everywhere,*
> *Nor any drop to drink.*

I don't know how many of the others knew it, probably some. But nobody breathed a word of the thing, even when that fucking poem seemed to be running our lives.

BRADY It was the uncannyiest thing I ever seen. I look up, an' this seagull lands on Mr. Rickenbacker's head, right on top of his hat. Nobody said nothin', but it weren't a second before we was all starin' right at that big delicious gull, just sittin' there. At first he didn't do nothin'. Then slow, reeaaallll slow, he brings his hand up . . . first to his nose, then sneakin' right around the brim. I don't think none of us was breathin' by this time. You could see his hand just creepin' a little closer all the time. . . . Then quick as a wink it shoots up and grabs that feller by both legs, just as he tries to take off. It was an act of God, no question in my mind.

WHITTAKER It took maybe five seconds for Rickenbacker to wring that bird's neck, and no more than five minutes to get rid of the feathers, gut it, and divide it into eight shares. Mine was a

leg. It smelled bad, was hard to chew, and tasted better than anything I can remember . . . bones and all. And it was only the first
course, because we used the guts to catch a twelve-inch mackerel
and a good-lookin' sea bass, both in about ten minutes. It was
hard not to be struck by the difference between fishing with orange
peel and real bait.

The seagull episode began the camp meeting phase of our time
in the rafts. It seemed like the rest of them found the Lord right
then and there. I gotta say, I was a lot more skeptical. All I could
think of was that cursed poem, and that our troubles were far from
over.

> *At length did cross an Albatross,*
> *Through the fog it came:*
> *As if it had been a Christian soul,*
> *We hailed it in God's name . . .*
>
> *God save thee, ancient Mariner!*
> *From the fiends that plague thee thus!*
> *Why look'st thou so?—With my crossbow*
> *I shot the Albatross.*

Uhh . . . no disrespect intended, Lord, but I'm planning to pitch
this to a pretty discriminating audience. You know . . . modern,
well-educated readers . . . sophisticated, good background in the
classics, romantic literature, that sort of thing. I know it happened
this way; but frankly it's beginning to sound . . . uhh . . . pretty de-
rivative. I mean couldn't we maybe . . .

GOD Whaaa? First it was Dos Passos, now this. Is there any end
to your carping? It's what I get for working with a novice. I knew
I should have put somebody with a track record on this . . . a scribe
with an appreciation for time-tested material. If you've got a good
story line, why not use it again? It worked with *Jaws*, didn't it?
Besides, I hadn't touched this stuff since 1798. You think Cole-
ridge minds . . . or if he did, we couldn't shut him up for a couple
vials of laudanum? Just remember, jerk-off, I hold the copyright
on everything.

Brady had a New Testament with a waterproof cover. He was a
simple young fellow. But seeing him study his Bible, and the com-

fort he seemed to derive from it, gave me an idea. I have always believed God was watching over me. And now I thought it was especially important to acknowledge his presence. So we began holding morning and evening prayer meetings. We drew the rafts together in a triangle, and passing the New Testament around, each of us recited a passage. None of us was all that familiar with the Good Book, but by thumbing through it we found more than a few readings that suited our needs. The Twenty-third Psalm was a favorite, of course. But one that never failed to move us was Matthew 6:31–34.

> Therefore take no thought, saying, What shall we eat? or, What shall we drink? or, Wherewithal shall we be clothed? . . . For your heavenly Father knoweth that ye have need of all of these things. But seek ye first the kingdom of God, and his righteousness; and all these things shall be added unto you. . . .

GOD Nice sentiment . . . but considering the circumstances, not the least bit plausible. Dying of thirst, baking in the hot sun, bodies covered with salt-encrusted sores, and they expected Me to take them seriously when they maintained that they'd rather see Me, find Me, believe in Me, than, say, guzzle down about ten pitchers of ice-cold gin and tonics.

This whole prayer thing, I continue to find it troubling. I suppose it makes them feel better. But it's invariably transparent, and when I'm doing earthquakes or volcanoes it can get downright distracting. Christians are particularly annoying. Always making a big deal of the necessity to believe in me. Why should I care if they believe in me? I'm God. I have a good self-image. Do they think I'm going to feel neglected and jump into a black hole? It's them, not Me. If they really believed in Me, they wouldn't always be exhorting each other to believe in Me.

Still, what had been going on in those rafts was pretty interesting. And if I didn't hose them down soon, they'd all be dead. . . . So I suppose you can mark this one in the Answered Prayers column.

WHITTAKER Day nine. Hamilton hadn't said much. He was still technically in command and Rickenbacker continued to consult him. But it was plain they didn't much like each other, and that Rickenbacker's constant scolding and cheerleading got on his nerves. So it really caught me off-guard when I looked up and realized it was Hamilton who was leading us in prayer.

"Lord, I won't beat around the bush; we need some water. We've all done as well as we could in this situation. But the string is about run out, and if You don't decide to help us pretty soon, we'll be at the end. It's Your choice, life or death, whatever You think is best. . . . Amen." That was it. But there was something about his tone and conviction. I just felt like God had to be listening. While we wallowed helplessly from crest to trough, I was thinking that this was God's best chance to make a believer out of me.

Then something told me to look to my left. A cloud that had barely been there just minutes ago had suddenly turned black and was expanding by the second. The next thing I saw was a wall of streaks descending down to the sea. Rain! A downpour sweeping right at us, riddling the waves. Minutes later we were being raked by giant drops of cool sweet water washing the burning salt off our aching skin. Instinctively, each of us cupped our hands to pour as much as possible down our parched gullets.

Slowly, our minds overcame our urge to swallow as fast as we could. We had to think to the future, collect as much water as possible. Each raft had some kind of storage vessel. In our case it was a spare Mae West. But the valves opening into the rubber bladders were designed for pumping, not pouring. A little thought solved that problem. We stripped off our shirts, saturated them with rain, wrung them out into our mouths, then spit the water through the valves. We kept at it for almost an hour and the Mae West was nearly full. Just then, as if to show He taketh as well as giveth, a monster wave rolled out of nowhere and flipped us. The Very pistol and all the flares, a paddle, and the revolver were gone; but Reynolds and Hamilton managed to hold on to the precious Mae West. With the help of the others we were able to right the thing and get back in. As the storm passed we found ourselves with almost two quarts of fresh water, our spirits transformed. Even Alex looked better.

Relief was short-lived. The next morning the blazing sun was back, and the reality sank in that our water supply amounted to only about two jiggers a day per man for each of the next four days. That evening one of the men—I won't say who—prayed aloud for God to end his suffering for good. I jumped down his throat, ordering him to stop bothering the Good Lord with that kind of whining, and offered to do the job myself with Adamson's pen-knife. That shut him up; but I knew we'd soon be faced with the reality of death among us.

Alex's time had come. The poor little fellow was doomed as soon as we hit the water. He never should have been on that plane in the first place. Now, we all could see he was fading fast. As burned as he was, his skin turned gray and clammy to the touch. His throat was rasping as he tried to breathe, and he could barely move. I think it was on the thirteenth night that I asked Brady to switch rafts, so that Alex might be more comfortable in our longer one. As weak as we were, he seemed light as a feather when we transferred him. At first I stretched him on the craft's rubber bottom. But soon his shivering caused me to take him into my arms, hoping the warmth of my body might comfort him. He had been muttering in Polish, but now he looked up at me and smiled.

"Is that you, Snooks?"—the name he used for his girl.

"Yes, Alex, it's me. You're home. We're gonna get married. Everything's fine." Then, without thinking, I kissed him. He relaxed in my arms and stopped shaking. After a while, I could no longer feel him breathing, and I knew he was gone.

I said nothing to the others dozing around me. In the darkness I continued to cradle Alex's body, attempting to pray for his departed soul. But I had an uneasy feeling. The Lord didn't seem to be listening. I felt no contact. Were we alone . . . abandoned? No, I decided. There was something else, something further to be done. I wasn't sure what it was, but I had a strong feeling it would require all of my strength to accomplish it.

ADAMSON   Around dawn I opened my eyes and looked up at the two of them. I didn't have to ask; Alex's mouth was hanging open and his eyes were rolled up. I was in horrible state by this time, and remember feeling jealous. "What are we going to do, Rick?"

"I'll tell you what we're gonna do. We're gonna pull these rafts together. We're going to pray over this boy's body. And then we're going to bury him at sea."

I simply nodded my head—partly because I didn't have the strength to waste words, but also because I knew there would be trouble.

When it was light enough for the others to realize what had happened, the tug of war began. Rick started up true to form.

"Okay. Here's the drill. I want at least two of you to feel for a pulse, make absolutely sure he's dead. Then we'll want to get the rest of it over with as fast as possible . . . before the heat of the day. Hamilton, as commander, I think you should lead us in prayer. Then once we let the body over the side, I think it's best to paddle away so we don't have to see—"

"Wait just a fucking minute!" It was Hamilton. "You're right about one thing, Rickenbacker. I'm in command here, and as far as I'm concerned this body could be the difference between life and death for the rest of us. There are fish down there—lots of them. And they'll take fresh bait. We've seen 'em do it. . . ."

"What are you talking about? That's not a crime . . . it's beyond crime. When a comrade falls, he has every reason to expect—"

"Bullshit! When a comrade falls, he's fuckin' dead . . . gone. His body is disposed of because it's of no further use. Our case is different."

"It's never different . . . you . . . you sacrilegious bastard! Why don't you cut out the fish . . . they're just middlemen. Get down to some real eatin.' You want a leg, Hamilton? How 'bout an arm?"

"If it comes down to that, we may have to—"

"Who's got dibs on Alex's pecker?"

"You self-righteous shit!"

"Cannibal cocksucker!"

DeAngelis They went at it hammer and tongs, both of them croaking like frogs. It's a wonder they could come anywhere near yelling, given how dried out we all were. Nobody else said much more than a word or two, and it was hard to know what the others were thinking. Captain Hamilton kept going on about how many fish we'd have. And Rickenbacker shot right back—logically enough, it seemed to me—that within twenty-four hours in this heat Alex's corpse would be so rank that not even the fish would want it. But mostly he stuck to his guns as far as there being certain things you just couldn't do. "Do you want to be rescued and have to tell the folks back home that we cut up our dead buddy for fish bait?"

Brady and Adamson were nodding their heads, and Hamilton took a new tack. "That's fine for you to say, Rickenbacker, because you need to protect your precious reputation. If and when they ever find us, does anybody think the papers are gonna say 'Reynolds and Whittaker Found!' No, the press is going straight to Captain Eddie, here, and *he's* gonna have to explain what happened to Alex."

That seemed to stop Rickenbacker in his tracks. He didn't say anything for a minute or so, and then he was whispering to Adamson. The next thing we knew the two of them rolled the body into the water. Before we could do anything the sharks moved in. All the commotion seemed to have got them excited. The water was thick with 'em, all circling Alex. There was no way we were gonna get him back.

GOD Well, that settles that. We finally got right down to it, didn't we?

So, this was really about the sanctity of the dead?

GOD Nooooo! Scribes are usually jabbering numskulls, but you seem notably dim-witted. This is Rickenbacker, not Antigone. I wanted to see if there was anything he wouldn't do to stay alive. Capiche?

Okay, then, the situation is pretty much resolved. You know what you wanted to know, and we can put this miserable oceanic locale behind us. . . .

GOD *Oy vey!* There's no helping you, is there? I've seen Dictaphones with more intuitive grasp of the dramatic. This isn't just about choices. It's about living with them. So on with the show, scribe. . . . Let's desiccate these suckers still more!

BRADY It was the worst thing I ever seen. Sharks . . . my God . . . They surely is creatures of the Devil's own making. They just ripped him apart. In a minute the water was all foamy and pink. One of them musta got hold of an arm, 'cause all of a sudden you saw a hand break the surface, racin' away from the rafts like a periscope with fingers. Then a big one flipped the whole body, or what was left of it, out of the water with its tail. One leg was almost chewed through, his guts was bein' pulled out, only thing they hadn't got to was his head—lookin' down at the rest of him, kinda mournful-like. It was bad, real bad. But there weren't no way not to look. Then it was over. Alex was gone. The sharks was gone. Just a couple of pieces of cloth left floatin' in the water.

Nobody said nuthin' for a while. Then Captain Hamilton pipes up an' starts yellin' at Rickenbacker. I think all of us was thinkin' in our minds just about the same thing as he was sayin'.

So there it was, in living color. Fast Eddie, the Top Predator's top predator, had managed to squander his little band's chief fungible asset to a bunch of Mesozoic gourmands with brains the size of golf balls and table manners that would embarrass Godzilla. Was it any wonder his compatriots might question his priorities as a caterer, his credentials as a survivor, and his overall competence as Alpha Ape at Sea? Indeed, it would not be an exaggeration to say that at this point everyone—with the single exception of Hans Adamson—despised him. And soon enough Eddie would be presented with the opportunity to make it unanimous.

We had been out of fresh water for two days, we had nothing to eat, and one by one the men were losing their will to live. I knew I'd be the last to go. With pain came perseverance, and I'd accumulated plenty of both. Whittaker possessed the stamina to hang on almost as long. Hamilton and DeAngelis were about equal to each other as survivors, but I knew they'd go before us. Reynolds and Brady were next down the line. But in the worst shape by far was Hans Adamson.

He was Danish and looked it—never tanned a bit. By this time his face and hands and feet were swollen masses of tortured flesh, and the rest of him was covered with hard little saltwater sores oozing pus. A sort of paralysis from his back injury was spreading to his arms and legs. We didn't realize it at the time, but he already had diabetes and the first stages of lobar pneumonia. Yet his spirit was in worse shape, and that's what worried me.

WHITTAKER Our morale kept sinking, and Colonel Adamson's seemed to be the lowest of the low. I noticed Rickenbacker eyeballing him, and expected he would say something. But he didn't.

It was in the middle of the afternoon, and the heat was unbelievable. The Colonel sat slumped in a kind of gloomy trance, shaking his head. Then he just lifted himself over the flotation roll and slipped into the water. Rickenbacker grabbed him right away, and

Hamilton and me helped pull him back in. It was pretty pathetic. The Colonel tried to grab Rickenbacker's hand, but he pulled it away and growled something like, "I don't shake with cowards."

You could see it in Adamson's face. Now he was being driven by the same thing that was driving us. We all hated him. We wanted to see him suffer. We wanted to see him at the end of *his* rope. That's what was keeping us alive.

I was alone. By this time everything I said drew scowls. Well, that was all right if it gave them something to rally around. I even caught two of them conspiring, and called them on it. "It's nothing, Eddie; we're just planning your funeral." Made me laugh then, and it makes me laugh now.

Still, it wasn't pleasant to be in such a tight fix and have everybody lined up against you. I was just as thirsty as any of them, and in constant pain from my injuries. I remember looking down at my watch. I had risked my life for that little mechanism. Now it was corroded and completely useless. Even if it had been working, time had no meaning out here. Neither, it seemed, did any of my accomplishments. By nightfall I had hit rock bottom. The only thing holding me together was my pride and my stubbornness.

Sleep in the rafts came in fits and starts . . . not much more than dozing inevitably cut short by some stray wave or a shark bumping into us. For me, even this was increasingly given over to visions so real that you couldn't tell if you were asleep or awake. On this night they reached their maximum, a succession of visitors from my earliest days. I felt like Scrooge . . . just as helpless and afraid.

BLANCHE CALHOUN   I loved you, Eddie. Why didn't you marry me? I had such a short life. I wouldn't have been much trouble.

SPENCER WISHART   I thought you were my friend. You killed me. Then you tried to take my wife.

JIMMY HALL   You shot me down. We were wingmen, and you wanted that Albatross. So you flew right through me.

ANNA LEE HUTCHINSON   You couldn't make love with a decent girl, could you?

FLIEGER FRANZ SALZMANN   I was barely sixteen when you shot me. No one should have to die at such an age.

W.C. DURANT I did my best to help you, Eddie. But after I lost my fortune, you just sort of forgot. . . .

CLIFF DURANT She's still mine. I had her first, and I fixed it so she'd never give you a son.

BILLY MITCHELL Why didn't you stick with me? If you'd campaigned for Air Power like you should have, the Nazis and the Japs never would have dared to attack us.

"I'm in the water, Eddie . . . over here."

"Amelia? . . . Is that really you? Come closer so I can see you."

"I haven't got anything on. I swam over from the island. It's beautiful . . . there's a waterfall. I think of you always. Come along. We can ride the dolphins."

"I love you. . . . But I can't . . . can't leave them. . . . They'll die without me."

"Come with me . . . come . . . please . . . I'm going over . . . I'm . . .

"I can't. . . ."

GOD Not too shabby. Remarkable steadfastness of purpose right down to the end. Maybe you were worth the extra attention.

What? . . . Who? . . . Who are you?

GOD Who do you think? You'd prefer, say . . . a Burning Bush? I suppose it could be arranged, but it's liable to wake up the others. This is just between you and me. Some might say you passed the test, although that would amount to a rather stark over-simplification of my intentions. You know I was at the point of slaying your corporeal self on several occasions. But certain questions remained unanswered. In this regard, from your perspective at least, the vicissitudes you have encountered have a certain meaning. Now, it seems, the puzzle is solved—the sole remaining issue being: What do I do with you?

I bring this up because choice—albeit of a limited nature—is about the only reward I offer you air-breathers for exaggerated behavior of one sort or another. So what'll it be, Rickenbacker, life or death? Some more (I won't say how much) of the same, or a chance to open the door at the end of the long hall, which of course you will eventually be dragged through in any case?

• • •

I . . . I don't want to die. . . .

GOD Ahh, they almost never do. . . . Well, enjoy your Golden Years. . . . Now, sleep it off, you've had a rough day. Meeting Me always takes some getting used to.

Scribe, where are we, around day seventeen? Why don't we arrange to have them picked up in about four more, so that . . .

Four days! It's been making me thirsty just to put this down on paper. Drinking and pissing so much my wife thinks I'm diabetic. You know what you wanted to know. Let it go; let these poor bastards off the hook now. Why do they have to suffer more? Give me one good reason.

GOD Discounting the fact that's it's never a good idea to yell at Me (Care for a little cancer? How about a retrovirus?), I would remind you that I have a whole World War to choreograph, keeping tabs on tens of millions of mortals, most of you hellbent on chaos. Remember, I stand for the orderly (relatively speaking) unfolding of events. I can't just have people found in the middle of the ocean for no good reason. These things have to be arranged and scheduled.

But more to the point, what makes you think I care about suffering? How many kids are nice to their toys? And don't even bring up how immature that sounds. What's maturity but coming to terms with your own limitations? Think about it, dolt. I'm God.

Explain the ways of Me to man? Well you could do worse than thinking of a big selfish child with a Cosmic Visa Card. You still wouldn't be that close, but it's about as much as you can comprehend. Now this is beginning to bore Me. Get back to the story.

The next morning it rained hard, not just a squall but an extended downpour. We refilled the Mae West and then directed as much down our gullets as possible. For the first time in over two weeks we had something approaching enough to drink. The worst of it was over. I knew now that God's central purpose in all of this was to test me. But it also meant that the others were here simply because they happened to be with me, and therefore it was my duty to see them through. Just as He planned to save me, I must be the instrument of their salvation.

WHITTAKER It was nearly sundown and we had just finished our water ration. I looked over at Hamilton just as he sat bolt upright.

"It's an engine," he whispered. Then all of us heard it. Rickenbacker spotted a tiny, fast-moving shape outlined just over the horizon. In a minute or two we could see it was a patrol plane and its line of flight would take it within a few miles of us. We screamed and waved, every one of us thinking of those flares now at the bottom of the ocean. When it droned right past, it was like letting the air out of a balloon. We went straight down to our lowest point yet. A few guys were even sobbing.

Rickenbacker put a stop to that quick. What followed was a masterpiece of obscenity. He a choice phrase for each of us, and topped it off with a blast against the whole bunch. Cleaned up, what he said was that one plane meant there would be others. That we must be near an airbase and anybody but a pantywaist would have the courage, the patience, and the faith to wait calmly for help.

A little after sunrise of the nineteenth day the patrol plane flew over again, at around a thousand feet, and then returned that afternoon—this time coming within a mile. Each time we went crazy with excitement, and then sank into the blackest gloom when it ignored us. And each time Rickenbacker was back on the job, cursing us like a lord. I don't know how this went over with the others, but Hamilton was seething.

DEANGELIS I was alone in the little raft half-asleep when Captain Hamilton reeled me in. "You get in with Whittaker, we're trading places." Seemed like a good deal to me—big raft for little raft. Besides, I didn't have any choice.

"Listen up. It's time we give Fate a little goosing. I'm taking the small raft and cuttin' myself loose. If we all split up, we'll triple our chances of being seen."

"You're crazy," Rickenbacker shot back.

"I may be. But one thing's for sure, if we spread out the rest of us won't have to hear you run your mouth."

"I order you to stay!" It was Colonel Adamson, back in Rickenbacker's camp. "I outrank you, and I order you to stay."

"Fuck you, Hans. I'm still commander, and I'm leavin'."

"That's desertion!"

"Desertion is what I decide it is. This is scouting."

With that, Hamilton cut himself loose and started paddling. Nobody said anything for a while. Then Whittaker turned to me. "He was right, you know. We'll have a better chance of being seen. From the air three rafts close together look the same as one." I didn't have any problem with that; Rickenbacker had been riding me hard ever since I missed the island. So off we went too.

That night was cold and lonely, only to be followed by a scorching hot day. Friday the thirteenth of November, our lucky day. I must have dozed off toward the late part of the afternoon. Then I heard Brady. "Planes, Captain, planes!" There were two of them right on the deck, heading straight at us. Brady and Adamson couldn't do much of anything, but I took off my trusty gray fedora and began waving it to show we were alive. They just kept on flying. That worried me, because I was pretty sure that one more night would mean the end of at least one of my companions.

Then they roared back. As they passed I could see one pilot waving. The plane on the left flew off, but the other circled in for a landing. It was a Navy seaplane. God bless America.

The others had been picked up earlier in the day. Reynolds was in serious condition, but Whittaker, DeAngelis, and Hamilton were not in any immediate danger. In my group, Brady and especially Adamson were very sick. We found out later that each of us had lost between forty and fifty pounds.

That night I slept on clean sheets. Brady and Adamson each had intravenous tubes in both arms, but I had a bucket of ice water on the floor next to the bed and strict orders not to drink more than two ounces an hour. I finished off the whole bucket in half that time and bribed the orderly to get me two more. Didn't hurt me one bit.

JAMES C. WHITTAKER, *We Thought We Heard the Angels Sing*

"In the next room lay Eddie Rickenbacker. . . . The world knows him as a daredevil automobile racer who turned aviator and became the nation's greatest ace in the first World War. He is known as a genius at business organization and he is the head of a great airline. . . .

"Out on the trackless Pacific our little band met the Rickenbacker the world doesn't know; the human man, the undoubting leader. I, for one, hope that if ever I have to go through hell like that again, Eddie Rickenbacker or someone like him will be along."

COMMANDER JAMES DURKIN, M.D. We had a very small medical facility on Funafuti, in fact these were our first real patients. I examined each carefully and concluded that, while Sergeant Reynolds and Private Brady were suffering from severe dehydration and exposure, only the case of Colonel Adamson was truly critical. On these grounds I determined to have the remainder of the group, plus Adamson, flown immediately to the much larger base hospital on Samoa—the danger of transport in the latter instance being balanced by the much better care he would receive there.

JOE BELCHER, SCRIPPS-HOWARD NEWSPAPERS Timin's everything. I'd been on Samoa less'n forty-eight hours, an' outta the blue in flies the Rickenbacker party—biggest story in the Pacific plopped right in my lap. The word was that these guys were unanimous in saying they owed their lives to the Good Captain. The first couple of days they didn't let us close to any of 'em. But once they were up and about, I made it my business to corner a couple and do in-depths. Sure enough they said it was Rickenbacker who kept 'em alive. But when I asked why that was, they shot back: "Because we wanted to see the son of a bitch die before us." Good angle, but you had to report the Party Line or find yourself back in Chicago without a job.

RICKENBACKER FOUND ALIVE!

Boston Evening Globe, November 14, 1942

RICKENBACKER PARTY RESCUED; AIR ACE IN GOOD CONDITION

New York Herald Tribune, November 14, 1942

RICKENBACKER CHEATS DEATH AGAIN!

HONOLULU, Nov. 14 (UP). U.S. Pacific Command announced today that its forces had performed a daring rescue of Captain Eddie Rickenbacker, lost at sea for twenty-four days in Japanese-infested waters. Surviving crew members of the ill-fated aircraft on which Rickenbacker flew were unanimous in their praise for this apparently indestructible man of aviation. "He was an inspiration to all of us out there, one that literally kept us alive. . . ."

New York American, November 14, 1942

One of the first things I did on Samoa was to wire Washington that I would soon be ready to complete my mission. General Arnold communicated back almost immediately, promising to dispatch a plane as soon as I was sufficiently recovered. I drank water and fruit juices by the tankload, ate anything that didn't move, and gained fifteen pounds in eleven days. In the meantime, I stayed busy cruising around the island in a Jeep I requisitioned from the Army. My bum knee made it impossible for me to operate the clutch; but my racing skills stood me in good stead, allowing me to synchronize the gears using the throttle alone. It was the last time I can remember driving; but I was enjoying the experience thoroughly, my recent trials at sea practically forgotten. Then it happened.

I had just emerged from a narrow jungle lane into an open area when I came upon a small group of young native women—all naked to the waist. In an instant temptation was upon me in a way I hadn't experienced since I was a very young man. I was confused and embarrassed until I realized this was God's way of checking on me, ensuring that I was worthy of being saved from the sharks. Still, it took every bit of self-control I could muster to turn that Jeep around and race back to the hospital in Pago Pago. When I arrived I must have looked flustered, because two orderlies asked me if I had seen a ghost. "Boys," I told them, "I've just turned my back on the Devil."

FIRST SAMOAN GIRL The cadaverous white man had an extremely large penis. He retained all the ardor and impatience of a boy my age, but with none of the attractiveness. Still, his need seemed so great that I felt I had done the world a favor by accommodating him.

SECOND SAMOAN GIRL It is customary here under the palm trees for a maiden to take an old man as a lover. But this one wanted to pay. I took his picture money to be polite, but what good is such a thing here?

THIRD SAMOAN GIRL Like all the interlopers in tan suits, he was strange and ashamed of what is most natural. I agreed to meet him by the North Beach, and he seemed anxious to see me. But after he would not even give me a ride in his vehicle back to Pago Pago.

HANS ADAMSON I could feel myself slipping away. I had come down with pneumonia and the doctors had given me heavy doses of the new sulfa drugs to counteract it. But my diabetes went undiagnosed, and my body's reaction to the drug was nearly fatal. Only three rapid transfusions, using blood donated by the hospital's staff, kept me alive. But I was poised on a razor's edge. In the midst of the crisis, Eddie came to visit.

"I don't want to leave you, Hans; but I've got to get out and talk to MacArthur. It's vital. But I swear I'll be back. I brought you out here, and I'm bringing you home. I know you've been through a lot. But please . . . please just hold on, so I can get you the kind of care you need."

To this day I'm not exactly sure what happened. But Eddie Rickenbacker—who never begs—was begging me to live. I guess I simply took it as my responsibility to do what he wanted.

GENERAL DOUGLAS MACARTHUR There was a record of acrimony between myself and Captain Rickenbacker. I had been a member of the Mitchell court-martial, and we had clashed publicly during his testimony. Therefore, it was rather easy to deduce that he had been handpicked by the authorities in Washington to deliver to me what would amount to an unpleasant message. Still, the man's dedication to duty after what he had been through tugged at my heartstrings, and I could not help embracing him when he arrived at Port Moresby. At that moment all animosity between the two of us melted, and the visit proceeded with what I believe to be mutual respect and even admiration.

Still, there was the matter of the message. Over dinner that night he brought it up with some reluctance, noting that he was obliged to deliver it in the spirit that was intended. I told him I understood completely, and he proceeded to state his case in the crudest and most personally insulting terms imaginable. Obviously, it was a difficult moment for both of us. But I bore him no ill will then, nor do I now. It was simply his misfortune to act as the agent of elements darker and more perfidious than either of us would have willingly served.

It was time to head home. I flew into Samoa ready to pick up Hans. But he had new problems—this time a lung abscess had demanded an operation. He stayed alive for me, but he was still in pitiful condition. I decided that a kick in the pants was in order. "Hans, I'm pulling out in a week. The doctors are saying that if you show some progress, you'll be able to come along. If not, then you'll be stuck out here for another three months." Then I showed my wild card. I knew how devoted he was to his wife, so I added, "If you can make it to Hawaii, then I think a telephone call to Helen can be arranged when we get there." That did it. Within hours the doctors could see he was improving, and when the time came he was ready to leave. Never underestimate the power of positive thinking, and a little bribery on the side.

ELIZABETH   Dewey vun day comes unto my room and says Edward's been found and zat zis is a miracle. To me it doesn't sound like such a miracle, because he never tells me my boy vas lost in za first place. Besides, Edward vas a good boy and alvays comes home. So, pretty soon ve vas all having a good visit. But zen it's just me und him alone, and he tells me something he von't say to nobody else.

"Mother, I spoke to God out there. He said I had passed his test and gave me the choice between life and death." I told him zat zis vas nice. But inside I vas thinking zat maybe my boy got too much sun, since most a za time God only talks to religious big shots vith beards.

For sure zat whore he married vasn't talking. He's calling her over und over back in New York, and never getting an answer. Zen za building operator comes on an' says no such party lives at zat address. Edward gets real mad und says zis is impossible, but I'm thinkin' that she and za orphans moved out on him.

ADELAIDE   Everything was confusion after the rescue. There had been so many calls that we had to have the number changed. When Edward finally got through, all he seemed to be able to do was apologize for what he had put me through. We weren't actually reunited until the ceremonies in Secretary Simson's office on December 19th. After that, there were endless press conferences and briefings, along with a national radio address. Edward was fine, I could see that; but there didn't seem to be a moment for us to be alone.

Then, when we finally got back to Bronxville, an argument erupted over, of all things, the gifts he had brought back for the boys—a samurai sword for David and a toy called the "Juicy Jap" for Bill. This was what caused the trouble. It was a little soldier with slots in its chest for a bayonet. You could screw off the head and fill the thing with catsup. We warned them only to play with it outside, but soon the sword was caked with red and the rugs were full of stains. To Edward it was funny, but all I could think about was my clean house.

No sooner had this passed than he received a phone call from Walter Reed Hospital at 10 o'clock on the night of Christmas Eve. It was an emergency and I knew he had to leave immediately for Washington, but I just broke down. It seemed so unfair that we couldn't have even this one night of peace and joy together.

HELEN ADAMSON Hans had been recovering, but then went into another tailspin. The doctors seemed helpless. He was dying right before my eyes. I was desperate, I didn't know what else to do. When I called there was never a moment's hesitation.

"I need to phone over to Newark and get a plane on line. I should be there before two. Tell him I'm coming." He made it almost to the minute. He seemed so large as he entered the room and sat down by the bed. I stepped out, but watched him from the hallway, talking constantly—sometimes softly, other times almost yelling. Hans could barely move, but you could see from his eyes he was listening intently. At around four Eddie came out. "I've shot my wad, Helen. There's nothing more for us to do but wait and hope."

I headed back to National and caught an early plane to New York, arriving home in time for Christmas breakfast and presents. Still, I couldn't bring myself to celebrate much. Finally, the phone rang. Hans was alive and a whole lot better. The crisis had passed. He was soon out of the hospital, and went on to live a useful and effective life. So the ordeal was finally over. Thanks to me, seven were saved, and I'm certain Alex is in Good Hands.

BOO HERNDON, THE GHOSTWRITER When Rickenbacker began talking about his time in the raft, he became noticeably uncomfortable. After a few minutes he called out for a pitcher of ice water, and then proceeded to empty it over the next half-hour or so. He tried to laugh it off, but this alone seemed pretty indicative that the episode had made an indelible impression on him. Also, his reporting of other events in his life was characteristically, even transparently biased; but in this case he really seemed to be trying to be fair. He readily admitted that nobody's conduct was above reproach . . . including his own. Also, you got the distinct impression that more went on out there than he was letting on.

SHEPPY   The Captain returned from the Pacific just as he always was . . . only more so. On the positive side, the ill effects of the Atlanta crash seemed completely erased. If anything, his time out in the ocean seemed to energize him . . . toughened him even further.

Unfortunately, there were also deleterious side effects. His self-assurance increased to the point of true intolerance. His judgment—both technical and commercial—remained sound; but from this point he would brook no opposition. It was almost as if he believed the Good Lord Himself was on his side.

The Captain had always been plainspoken, but this too became exaggerated. He seemed to revel in being undiplomatic. This delighted those who agreed with him. But it did have the effect of creating controversy, where none might have existed with more careful phrasing. His remarks about American defense workers—particularly those about letting boys down at the front and forcing them to trade places with those in foxholes—were certainly well-intended, but not necessarily well-received.

Finally, there was that awful incident in Cuba. The Captain was just about to address the Havana Chamber of Commerce, when someone handed him a message stating that President Roosevelt had died. The papers reported that he had opened his remarks by saying he had "wonderful news." That was absolutely untrue. I was there, and what he actually said was, "I have news that some might think of as wonderful." Still, I must admit that his earlier statements about Mr. Roosevelt probably opened him up for this kind of misinterpretation. Yet forcing him to leave the country that very night was completely unwarranted—just the sort of thing a corrupt Latin American dictatorship does to curry favor with the authorities to the North. The Captain always believed Juan Trippe and Pan American were behind the whole thing, and I don't disagree with him.

So the product was complete. His adventures on the high seas put the final touches on both Eddie's reputation and his personality. He was what he would be. The representative American rampant on a field of opportunity . . . a Hawaiian shirt of a man, pulled up so high by his own bootstraps that he confused anoxia with transcendental zoot. It didn't matter. A huckster selling war-weary America tickets to palm trees, soft breezes, and fat creamy beaches couldn't miss. All he had to do was expand Eastern's fleet and milk Miami. Meanwhile, he could talk all manner of trash, and live the life of an industrial statesman—icon, caricature, and gear head— all wrapped in a custom-tailored suit and topped off by the fetid fedora upon which once sat the sainted seagull. Democracy's whelp . . . but doomed, of course.

Eddie would live to see internal combustion shadowed by pollution and petro-dependency, cars and planes grow generic, and business leaders retreating to the gossamer filaments of microcircuitry, learning to shut up in the face of gender and genetic outrage. His time had come, and it would pass.

Yet as we titter at the foibles of Fast Eddie Rickenbacker we might remember that he and his generation strung together success after success until they nearly ruled the world. They were pigheaded, wasteful, and cruel; but they were also self-reliant and tough to a degree that the shambling legions of the sensitive can barely imagine. And there was the certainty that came with having the sanction of higher authority.

GOD   And they wonder why I say so little. The fact is that every time I try to have a conversation with one of them, he or she turns into a bigger asshole than they were in the first place. Hundred percent, death and taxes, you can bank on it. They think because I choose to make a few offhanded comments on their squalid circumstances, this somehow endows them with some cosmic personal significance. Couldn't be further from the truth. They forget I'm both nearsighted and farsighted. Just because I can watch over everything doesn't mean I care about the individual details. What about spreading my semen in strings ten billion galaxies long, what about my quark count, what about turning time inside out? I'm busy. I'm engaged. I don't have a lot of help. You figure it out.

Chapter Seven

The War was over and Eastern was back in business. Unfortunately, so was everybody else, and they were buying new equipment like drunken sailors. The hot item was the DC-4. It was nothing more than a stretched DC-3, with a couple of extra motors. But once the stampede got started, all you heard was "four engines . . . it has four engines." The fact was those two more motors only added about twenty miles an hour to the cruising speed, and you still had to fly through weather rather than above it, because the cabin was unpressurized. But this didn't seem to dawn on the sheep running the other airlines, so we were forced to follow suit. Luckily, I was able to pick up a bunch of war-surplus C-54s (the military designation) for $170,000 each, and had the boys at Martin Aviation bring them up to civilian standards. I was damned if I was going to pay Don Douglas a premium for doing the same work, especially when Lockheed had something much better than the DC-4 already flying. The problem was getting my hands on it.

Just before the War, Howard Hughes had ponied up a million and a half of his own money and ordered Lockheed to build him a true transatlantic airliner. In return, TWA would get exclusive rights to the plane for at least three years. The first flight was in 1943, and by VJ day they were already in production. Hughes and TWA had the jump on all of us. The L-49 Constellation flew 70 mph faster and 1,000 miles farther than the DC-4; it carried sixteen more passengers in a fully pressurized cabin that gave it a service ceiling in excess of 20,000 feet; and to top it off, it had the sexiest shape of anything in the air. The Constellation looked like an angel, flew like an angel, and was just as hard for outsiders to get ahold of. Everybody in the industry was convinced that Howard had a tighter grasp on that airplane than he did on Jane Russell. Everybody except me.

But getting my pitch across was another matter. Howard at this point was not the easiest guy to locate. I tried every means of communication on God's green earth—letters, telefax, telephone, telegraph, we even radioed his plane. Jesus, I would have resorted to skywriting if I thought it could get around that bunch of Mormon yes-men he surrounded himself with. Nothing worked . . . dead silence. Then, out of the blue, I get this postcard from Las Vegas: "Meet me in Leadville alone, Oct. 24—Hughes." That was it, and when we checked the maps there's no Leadville in Nevada. The best we could come up with was an abandoned mine site around a hundred miles off, up in the northwest corner of Arizona. I wanted that plane. So Charlie Froesch and I flew to Vegas, picked up a car, and he drove me out there. Around half a mile short I had him stop, and hoofed it the rest of the way in. A more godforsaken site you could not imagine. Nothing but rocks, dust, and a single tumbledown shack. I would have bet my eyeteeth there was not a soul within twenty miles. But when I pulled open the door, there sat Howard with a bottle of red-eye, madder than hell because I was late.

HOWARD HUGHES   I told him right off, I always considered him an unscrupulous son of a bitch, which I prefer in my business associates, but that I didn't see we had any business to negotiate. He broke out this big snaggletoothed grin, and begins laying on what he must have thought passed for charm. "Look," I said when I couldn't stand any more, "we both know why you're here. You want the L-49 like everybody else. But why should I give it to you? I've got the whole industry by the short hairs. Now if you can give me just one good reason why I shouldn't pull 'em out one at a time, then maybe I'll listen to your proposal."

Well, he starts off with this song and dance about the Rickenbacker car, four-wheel brakes, and the dangers of being first in anything. Then he cut to the chase: "Now we both know the Constellation is a good plane. But it's a new plane, and accidents do happen. If TWA is the only one flying them, then the heat's going to be on you and you alone. But if Eastern also flew Constellations, then the repercussions would be spread out. Share the wealth, Howard, and we'll help you share the risk."

The old goat had a point. But as far as wealth went, he was going to do the sharing. "Two million per plane, Eddie. A million for Lockheed, and a million for me." I saw a man hanged once, but I don't think he turned quite that shade of purple. He must have called me every name in the book. But he never said a word about not buying the airplane. "So we can drink on it, Eddie?"

"The hell we will. I know one thing, Hughes, God is always watching. And you'll rot in Hell for doing this."

GOD Hey, who am I to argue with the Invisible Hand?

ALFRED P. SLOAN In the fall of '46, Eddie paid me a visit. He was very concerned about an impending aircraft purchase. He had agreed to pay forty million dollars for twenty Lockheed Constellations, when the going rate for a top aircraft was less than a million. I told him very frankly that this was a splendid opportunity, a chance to obtain superior equipment at a time of unprecedented mobility. Prosperity was no longer around the corner, it was upon us. A few extra dollars spent on that basis would not be missed. Still, he remained dubious, and I understand he ended up leasing out some of those aircraft to cover his bets.

I found this ironic. Here was a man who had risked his life on countless occasions hesitating simply over a matter of money. It exposed a conservative streak I hadn't previously observed. The day had long passed when the automobile companies served as an incubator for commercial aviation. It was now a significant industry backed by an important manufacturing base. The stakes had risen dramatically. Yet the original players, as daring as they were individually, had trouble adjusting. In the future, success would depend on audacious equipment choice and route expansion. Yet, in the latter instance especially, this would be largely a matter of politics. The government determined who could fly where. Acceptability in both camps, Democrat and Republican, was preferable. Yet the airline magnates—C.R. Smith at American, Howard Hughes, National's Ted Baker, Juan Trippe of Pan Am fame— were all high-profile, outspoken figures whose political views were well-known. And none of these was more loudly partisan in a conservative direction than Eddie—all in a time of Democratic dominance. This was unfortunate, and did not bode well for the future. Yet at this point he was beyond such advice.

JOHN DOS PASSOS I got a call late one night shortly after the war ended. It was him. He wanted to know what I thought of constellations. At the time, I hadn't the slightest idea what he was talking about. So I told him I always liked Orion, but that the Big Dipper was the easiest to find. He got abusive, and for once he was the first to hang up.

CAPTAIN DICK MERRILL, EASTERN AIRLINES We took delivery on the first of the Constellations in May of '47. I was at the controls, flew her into Miami from Burbank in six hours and fifty-four minutes, a new record. When I landed, I don't think I ever saw the Captain happier.

He was nuts about that plane . . . I mean nuts. We had to call 'em Constellations, instead of Connies like everybody else in the country. "It's like calling your wife Trixie or some other floozie name," he told us at one of his big meetings.

So what's he do? Plasters the fuselage with FLY EASTERN AIR LINES, and fixes up the cabins like the inside of a bus—puke green and cream with five-abreast seating instead of TWA's four. So I guess it's okay to dress your wife up in cheap clothes, send her out on the street with a sign that says "Fuck Me," and encourage everybody you can to climb aboard—just so long as you call her by her Christian name.

W.A. PATTERSON, PRESIDENT, UNITED AIRLINES He was never popular among his competitors. I was probably the only airline chief who was on anything better than bare speaking terms with him . . . and at times I found him insufferable.

During Air Transport Association meetings, we used to gather for private executive sessions to kick around larger policy issues. He never failed to harangue us on the subsidies we were receiving from the Government for flying unprofitable routes, not once conceding that Eastern's inherently lucrative route structure was the only reason he could avoid such federal support. After one particularly obnoxious performance he joined us at dinner and realized immediately that he was the subject of our conversation.

"Talking behind my back again, huh?"

"Quite the contrary, Eddie," C.R. Smith of American chimed

in. "Some of us were simply speculating how pleasant it would be if you were back in the raft."

Cover story, *Time*, April 17, 1950

By the rules of fate and chance, that scarred and willful old warbird, Edward Vernon Rickenbacker, should have been back home in Columbus, Ohio, last week with a cane, a bad temper, a book of yellowed clippings, and a half-interest in a suburban gas station. Instead, after 38 years of derring-do, he was one of America's most famous and successful men—not only a kind of Buffalo Bill of the gasoline age, but an intimate of rulers, and a self-made captain of industry. . . . [He remains] one of the shrewdest, toughest, most highly admired and ferociously damned of U.S. businessmen, and the only living human soul who has ever been able to wring consistent profits from that debt-ridden peacock of modern transport, the airline industry.

As such, he is a completely individualistic and often baffling combination of Daddy Warbucks, Captain Midnight, Scrooge, and Salesman Sam. A product of McGuffey's Reader and the International Correspondence Schools, he has a fierce faith in God and in the attitudes and platitudes of the last century. . . .

A Howard Chandler Christy portrait of the young Rickenbacker hangs, bathed in light, in the foyer of his ten-room Manhattan apartment. A British overseas cap is cocked over the young pilot's bold and insolent eyes, a dashing camel's hair greatcoat rests on his shoulders, and spitting aircraft fill the wild blue sky behind his head. At times late at night, Rickenbacker stops before it. Admiringly he says, "I was quite a fellow in those days." Then, grinning: "I'll fight like a wildcat until they nail the lid on my pine box down on me."

ELIZABETH   I vas thinking zat maybe I vould live forever. Eighty-three and nothing much changes . . . except zat Dewey is fussing over me all za time. Vun day he says I may have to go to za nursing home, since I am now so much trouble. "I vouldn't be no trouble," I tell him, "if you vould leave me alone."

Dewey vas a good boy, so after zat he gives me more time to look out za vindow und pray to za Good Lord. Maybe at za end, I'm thinking, he vill come an' talk to me like he did for Edward. But no. Vun day za coughing starts and von't stop. After a while, things go black. . . . Kaput!

ADELAIDE   After Edward got word that his mother had died he asked me if we would go with him to the funeral—the boys and myself. "Of course we'll go," I said without thinking much about it. "We're your family."

That was the last he said of it until we got back to New York. He took me aside that afternoon and told me that of all the things I had done in our marriage, he appreciated this the most. Then he put his head in my lap and wept. In over forty years together, it was the first and only time I saw him shed a tear.

SHEPPY   On the surface, at least, the Captain did not seem greatly affected by the death of his mother. He returned to the office almost immediately, and threw himself into his work, just as he always had. Several weeks later, early one evening after the office had cleared out, he called me back—ostensibly just to chat.

"You know," he said almost offhandedly, "all my life, just about everything I have accomplished was done with the idea of making my mother proud. Now that she's gone—as crazy as this sounds—I'm not sure what to do and what not to do."

With that he pulled out a piece of paper. It was a note Damon Runyon, who had throat cancer and could no longer speak, had passed to him at lunch. "I'm finished, Eddie. The docs say I'm down to my last couple weeks. After I'm gone, fly my ashes over this burg . . . but remember, not before."

"Our legal department tells me this constitutes public dumping and there'll be a big fine if the newspapers get a hold of it . . . which they will. What do you think?"

I told him that Damon Runyon was his friend, and that his mother was still watching over him.

"You're goddamned right she is. And I'll tell you, she never minded a little dust here and there either."

ALICE WHITNEY PAYSON   Through a combination of good fortune and discretion I had not laid eyes on the man for nearly three decades—although a certain awareness of his exploits was hard to suppress. I was up for the weekend at the Atwoods', and we went over to the Sleepy Hollow Club for tea. We had just been seated when an uproar broke out in the bar. Before we knew it this rollicking crowd of golfers had invaded the solarium. The Rockefeller brothers, Laurance and David, and my cousin Jock were among them, so Roy Atwood invited them to join us for champagne—

not realizing what was being celebrated. Well . . . it quickly became evident that the center of attraction was the ever-buoyant Mr. Rickenbacker, who had just managed to strike a hole-in-one on the links.

I watched him closely. He seemed perfectly at ease with this group . . . in fact, a number of them seemed to be fawning over him quite shamelessly. Finally, when I could stand it no more, I collared my cousin and informed him that the barbarian was no longer at the gate, he was in the parlor with his feet on the divan.

"My God, Alice, keep up. Eddie sponsored David Rockefeller's membership in this club."

Other Memberships: Bohemian Club, Links Club, New York Athletic Club, The University Club, 29-Club, Question Club, Skeeters, Piping Rock Club, Congressional Country Club, Cosmos Club, Indianapolis Automobile Club, Detroit Athletic Club, Key Biscayne Club, Confederate Air Force, Ancient Order of the Himalayas, Loyal Order of Moose, and the Royal Order of Ground Hogs.

10 Rockefeller Plaza
December 10, 1947

William F. Rickenbacker
Harvard University
Cambridge, Massachusetts

My dear pal Bill:
After reading your last letter, I have been extremely concerned about your problems with Dean Leighton. First, let me tell you frankly there is nothing necessarily wrong with an occasional off-color story. The question in your mind must always be "Who might be listening?" It goes without saying that you never expected the Dean's wife to be within earshot. But the damage has been done. And if Dean Leighton expects contrition, as I am certain he will, then by God you better serve him up a heaping portion, or risk losing the privileges which come with matriculation in Cambridge. I don't have to remind you of the value of a Harvard education. Throughout your life it will open doors which simply cannot be opened by any other means. I know this from personal ex-

perience. So swallow whatever bitter medicine is necessary, and leave the incident behind you once and for all.

On a more pleasant note, I am happy to inform you as Christmas approaches that I have once more acquired in your name $3,000 of U.S. Savings Bonds. These Bonds, along with the others you have received, are at this very moment earning you money, which if kept intact will provide you a handsome foundation for your future endeavors. Remember, Bill, in America nobody gets something for nothing. However, it is possible through the careful application of resources and plain old hard work to raise yourself above other men, and in doing so provide financial stability for yourself and your family. Finally, Mother sends her love and hopes you will take the advice herein provided completely to heart.

Love and best wishes,

As always,
Daddy

10 Rockefeller Plaza
February 15, 1949

Ben Hogan
El Paso Methodist Hospital
El Paso, Texas

Dear Ben,
I hear your ass is in a sling, and the sawbones are all shaking their heads and looking down at the floor. I know the feeling. After the Atlanta crash I was in pretty much the same fix. Crushed pelvis, busted up knee and elbow, cracked ribs, the whole nine yards. I can just hear them telling you, "*If* you live, Mr. Hogan, you'll never walk much less play competitive golf again." Don't bank on it. They told me the same stuff, and a year and a half later I was out in the middle of the Pacific for twenty-four days without water, keeping a bunch of young fellows alive.

It's going to be the same with you. These doctors don't know what they're dealing with. God watches out for tough bastards like ourselves. Besides, I've hit the little white pill around enough in my day to know it's nerves of steel, not some Charles Atlas physique, that makes a golfing champion. You've still got what it takes. So mark my words, buddy, you're going to be out there winning tournaments faster than even Nelson and Demaret and the rest are dreaming in their worst nightmares. The Hawk's shadow is far from being erased from the game of golf.

> Don't let the bedbugs get you down,
> Rick

WESTERN UNION

6/23/50

BEN HOGAN
MERION COUNTRY CLUB, PA.

TO 1950 U.S. OPEN CHAMPION AND FELLOW GIMP. WHAT'D I TELL YOU?

RICKENBACKER

BOO HERNDON, THE GHOSTWRITER   Rickenbacker was a Curtis LeMay anti-Communist. Although he'd been to Russia during the War and came back thinking bolshevism might collapse of its own accord, he wanted to provide a helping hand with a huge air force and a "bomb them back into the Stone Age" agenda. He was also worried about American Communists, especially their penetration of the labor unions. And although he definitely supported the McCarthyite campaign against Foggy Bottom, he wasn't frantic. As far as Rickenbacker was concerned, the State Department was no nest of Communists, it was a nest of idiots.

> 10 Rockefeller Plaza
> February 8, 1948

Mr. William Rickenbacker
Harvard University
Cambridge, Massachusetts

My dear pal Bill,
Please find a check for $750 which will cover your expenses for a while and allow you to put a little aside for a rainy day, which I know you will. I have also just mailed you and Dave

both copies of Martin Ebon's new book *World Communism Today*. I understand that under ordinary circumstances your studies must come first, but this is an exception. I want you to read this book as soon as possible. Unlike most fuzzy-headed commentators, Ebon makes it crystal clear that communism is the equivalent of cancer, and must be cut out of the body politic wherever we may find it, be that at home or abroad. Like cancer, communism survives and spreads because it carefully hides itself in ways that prevent the social organism from knowing it is there until it is too late. It is vitally important that informed Americans understand this, and Ebon is the best I have found at dissecting this insidious malignancy.

You asked me about Eastern Airlines and the industry in general, which very much gratifies me since I think there is a bright future for you here. Unfortunately, at the moment, business is not simply not up to expectations—it is plain lousy. Miserable weather, crashes, and the attending bad press reports have all cut deeply into industry-wide load factors. While we are no exception, fortunately our steadfast adherence to a strategy of saving as much as possible and scrupulously refusing to spend more than we earn, is allowing us to steer around the worst of the storm. So as long as we continue to be able to exert this kind of control we should emerge, when the skies clear, as one of the very few flying without a crushing burden of debt.

But I must tell you frankly this is very much a matter of luck and the Good Lord's will. Yesterday could have left Eastern the victim of the biggest disaster in the history of the industry. I was in the midst of speaking to a crowd of at least 300 at the University Club, when Hugh Knowlton interrupted to inform me I had an emergency phone call. This had to be serious, but just how serious I couldn't know until I picked up the receiver and heard that one of our Constellations had suffered major engine damage 130 miles out to sea off Jacksonville, Florida.

Apparently, one of the blades of the right-hand inboard engine let loose and went into the forward fuselage near the galley, cutting the flight steward in half and proceeding out the other side. Not only did the plane experience a rapid loss of pressure, but the unbalanced portion of the propeller tore out the motor's reduction gear and started a serious fire perilously close to the fuel tanks. Fortunately, Dick Merrill, probably Eastern's best pilot, was aboard, and was somehow able to wrestle the aircraft down to an emergency strip in Bunnell, Florida, with all sixty-three passengers safe and unhurt.

We will all be eternally grateful to Dick. But I must tell you that I fervently believe that the Good Lord Himself must have had his hand on the stick to avert such a disaster. Danger will always be a part of air travel. And since we cannot always depend on Divine Intervention, our best policy must be eternal vigilance, and the tightest possible management procedures.

Love and best wishes.

> As always,
> Daddy

GOD Well, I've certainly always been a believer in management.

SHEPPY He was always at his best during a crisis—particularly after a major crash, when everyone else was falling to pieces. He remained calm and never attempted to fix blame—"that can wait for the investigators," he would say. Instead, he made it his business to reassure the others, get them to work things through one step at a time. This was when his many brushes with death became most apparent. He was on familiar territory and knew how to cope.

I'll never forget his reaction when we called down to his Texas ranch to inform him that the Port of New York Authority had shut down Newark. This was in 1952 and they had experienced three terrible crashes in less than sixty days. No Eastern planes had been involved, but 65 percent of our operations and all of our New York maintenance was handled there. La Guardia had offered to take 20 percent of our spillover, but no more.

"What are we going to do?" I remember asking him.

"We'll move to Idlewild."

"But it's brand-new. We don't have a terminal or any hangars even."

"We'll use tents. Hell, if they were good enough for the Hat 'n Ring, they'll be good enough for us."

"Tents, but how are we going—"

"Never mind, I'll take care of that."

Two days later, several big trucks from Ringling Brothers arrived, and by nightfall we were ready to resume operations. The tents did make for a somewhat gamy work environment, but they kept us in business.

SID SHANNON, VICE-PRESIDENT FOR OPERATIONS, EASTERN AIRLINES   I know the Captain has been criticized for what some call miserly policies. It's true he could squeeze a buck as hard as any, but he also knew how to spend where it counted. Sure, National hired the best-looking stewardesses, dubbed itself "The Airline of the Stars," and served everybody filet mignon and cheap champagne; but we put the money where it counted—in the planes, the maintenance, and with more flights to Florida than all our competitors combined.

Dependability . . . Confidence . . . Experience. That's what Eastern Airlines was selling. We got you there quickly and safely. You had a good time after you landed. My God, the Captain practically built Miami Beach. He was the one who convinced the hotel owners to stay open year-round and ran those "Visit Florida in the Summer" ads year after year, when everybody else laughed. Well, it worked, and they all profited—the public who got off-season rates, the other airlines, and the city itself. You don't think they named the roadway between Miami and the Biscayne Keys the Rickenbacker Causeway for nothing, do you?

BRAD WALKER   Bev Griffith and I learned through hard experience that if an ad campaign had anything to do with religion, children, or the handicapped, EVR was for it. I remember once we did up a picture of a granny sitting in a window seat reading her Bible, with a little girl asleep against her shoulder. He took one look and grabbed me by both arms: "Now that's advertising! Why the hell can't you guys come up with this kind of stuff on a regular basis?"

Walking back from his office, Bev turned to me and said: "If we could have worked in a Seeing Eye dog, I think he might have come in his pants."

LAURANCE ROCKEFELLER, EASTERN AIRLINES BOARD OF DIRECTORS   He was the epitome of a monolithic leader. He wanted your support and if you didn't give it to him, he'd get it from someone else. It was very difficult not only to organize a group to oppose him but to do it without breaking him. Let's be realistic about it—as long as Eddie was succeeding, no one ever really disagreed with him.

PETER VREELAND The Board of Directors of Eastern Airlines was an oxymoron. It didn't matter how much stock we owned individually or corporately, we had no control. The Captain *was* the captain. And like so many men of great talent and responsibility, he was thin-skinned and prone to act impulsively.

Take, for example, his outlook toward the competition and particularly his fixation on Ted Baker and National Airlines. I don't think I ever saw two individuals hate each other quite so much. But Baker had the advantage since he was smaller and could play picador to the Captain's Toro. This was a man who had once convinced a prominent attorney to forgive a substantial legal fee in return for a cabin cruiser that had sunk the day before. He was nothing more than an amalgam of horsefeathers and belligerence, yet Eddie was constitutionally unable to resist his provocations. If National persisted in providing free drinks to their passengers, Eddie would call a press conference with the Temperance Union trying to ban in-flight alcohol on the Sabbath or some such thing—this from one of the great elbow-benders of the age. Or take the time National scheduled a midnight flight to Miami. Eddie had to follow suit. Jesus, our load factor was next to zero, probably the only passengers were vampires.

All of this would have been amusing, since we had something like ten times more business than National, had it not distracted Eastern's management from the real danger—the rise of Delta Air Lines, which was not only extremely well run, but took care not to antagonize people.

C.E. WOOLMAN, PRESIDENT AND GENERAL MANAGER, DELTA AIR LINES We began as a crop-dusting outfit, and I don't think the industry moguls ever got over it. It was as if they expected us to show up to meetings wearing canvas helmets and DDT-spattered goggles. Well, that was fine by me. Small was good. It meant we were agile and alert. Even after we got big, I wanted us to think small. We never threw money around. When Eastern paid two million a copy for Connies, we waited for the DC-6. It was pressurized, just about as fast, shared a good many parts with our other Douglas equipment, and it cost us under $650,000. That was no fluke. We chose every plane as if our corporate life depended on it. I'm proud to say Delta was the first in the business to do true life-cycle costing—operating expenses, parts availability, capital depreciation, all the chickens that might come home to roost. We missed a few, but over the long haul we were right more than we were wrong.

Also, we were from the South and proud of it. I don't know how many times I told our folks that inviting people into one of our planes was just the same as inviting them into your own home. They were honored guests and deserved every courtesy. Delta was as much about making friends as it was about carrying passengers. And I like to think this philosophy pervaded everything we did. Never had much trouble with the unions. Organized labor thrives on suspicion and distrust and that just never got started here. We told our people the truth and we paid 'em as much as we could— which was more than most. If you were in management, you had better be on a first-name basis with everybody down to the baggage handlers. We may not have been family, but I swear sometimes it felt like it.

Congressman Hale Boggs Mr. C.E. Woolman and Cap'n Rickenbackah, theyuh was a study in contrasts if they evuh was one. Now it's no secret that in the ayline business—as in most entuprizes in this country—you eithuh expand aw you diah. The difference is that 'spansion in thuh ayuh meant gettin' thuh routes, an' that meant Washin'ton.

Well, I don't think Mr. Woolman ever made a trip out heah but that he didn't stop in fo' a friendly chat with me, or Mr. Sam, or Lyndon. An' sure 'nough, if ah expressed an interest in a mess a' crawdads, or Lady Bird wanted some Texas venison for a barbecue, you could count on them bein' theyuh thuh next mohnin'. Nevuh asked fo' nuthin' in return. Just an all-round nice felluh.

Now Cap'n Rickenbackah, who I also admyud, spent most a' his time heah surrounded by lawyuhs over at th' CAB moanin' 'bout who shot John. Well . . . always seemed tuh me that you catch mo' flies with honey 'n vinegar—an' that includes places to fly. So Eastern ended up staying just 'bout thuh same, and Delta took to spreadin' liahk some kind a' big spiduh web.

Maurice "Lefty" Lethridge, VICE-PRESIDENT, EASTERN AIRLINES I remember somebody got hold of a picture of what seemed to be the whole Delta staff doing some kind of line dance to celebrate the opening of their new General Office. We all thought it was hilarious—"allemande left, do-si-do, what a bunch of hicks." But the Captain didn't think it was so funny. He got this look and said, "I wish we had that kind of spirit around here." In a way that's what I think his big meetings were all about, however twisted they may have become.

I've always said: "If you grab 'em by the balls, their minds and hearts will follow." That was the idea behind the big meetings we held twice yearly in Miami. All three echelons of management were present—about 500 in all—and every one had to deliver a verbal report in front of the whole gang on his particular area of responsibility. It was our version of a camp meeting. Questions could be asked and criticisms leveled at any time. Some of 'em were so jittery they could barely talk into the mike. But I'd give'm a good pat on the ass an' nine times outta ten they settled right down.

I wanted my guys to learn to think on their feet, and I wanted them to listen. After a week of reports on every aspect of the business you had to be a moron not to come away with a better understanding of how the whole puzzle fit together. That went for me too. No bastard in that audience ever left thinking he could pull the wool over my eyes for long.

NAJEEB HALABY, FUTURE HEAD OF THE FEDERAL AVIATION AGENCY It was more a cruel fraternity initiation than a business meeting. . . . Captain Eddie dominated the proceedings. He stayed through every session, eight hours a day for four days, asked some very embarrassing questions, and took a number of people to task right in front of their peers. . . . I had never seen a more dictatorial example of centralized management nor such public humiliation of employees, to say nothing of the waste of time.

PAUL BRATTAIN There were actually some pretty funny moments at those staff meetings, but you never would have known it. I remember once the manager of Eastern's smallest station— Columbus, Georgia—got up to give his spiel. The standard stuff . . . passenger boardings, traffic forecasts, revenues. Then he turned to the Captain and said he wanted to get something off his chest. "I think one of our biggest problems is we keep getting mislabeled baggage from Columbus, Ohio."

Rickenbacker jumped up, pounding the rostrum. "You're absolutely right, son. Why, we've got some ignorant cocksuckers working for this airline who don't even know Hartford's in Massachusetts." Well, you could have heard a pin drop. There wasn't so much as a guffaw disguised as a cough.

Then there was the time the Captain himself tried to lighten up the proceedings. At the end of the day he starts reading from what he claimed was a confidential compilation of maintenance reports.

"Just listen to this shit. We're lucky the CAB doesn't padlock our fucking hangars.

"PROBLEM: Left inside tire almost needs replacement
RESOLUTION: Almost replaced left inside tire.

PROBLEM: Something loose in the cockpit.
RESOLUTION: Something tightened in the cockpit.

PROBLEM: Evidence of hydraulic leak in right main landing gear.
RESOLUTION: Evidence removed.

PROBLEM: Dead bugs on windshield.
RESOLUTION: Live bugs on order.

PROBLEM: Number three engine missing.
RESOLUTION: Engine found on right wing after brief search."

At this point he breaks up and starts braying like a mule. But out in the audience, aside from a few brave souls who managed to crack a smile, all you got was stony silence and some very long faces.

Actually, they had every reason to look gloomy—especially the maintenance pukes. Their job was to keep flying what deserved to be in torque wrench intensive care. The fact was that America's air carriers were attempting to cart around Mom and Pop and Sis in planes powered by what amounted to racing engines. For he who flew fastest, flew fullest.

It had begun back in World War II with the development of 18-cylinder double-banked supercharged radials—Pratt & Whitney Wasps and Wright Cyclones—designed to push hot-rod fighters like the Vought Corsair and the P-47 Thunderbolt up over 400 miles per hour. Not unexpectedly the slide-rule and pocket-protector crowd took to stuffing them into bombers, and, of course, Howard Hughes made sure four 2,200-horsepower Cyclones were jammed on the wings of his first Constellations.

The gauntlet was dropped and a horsepower race ensued that made Detroit's Hemi-heads look like Tinker Toys. Compression rations were squeezed ever higher, cylinders multiplied until they edged toward thirty, exotic materials were introduced—magnesium for aluminum, aluminum for steel—so that weight dropped just as power curves soared.

The acme was reached with the turbo-compound Wright 3350 series, which could pump out in excess of 3,500 horses. Rather than superchargers, which drew power to generate more power, compound motors harnessed formerly wasted exhaust gases to drive impellers which packed the engine's many cylinders with even more combustible charges, producing up to a 10 percent gain in power with no loss in efficiency. Wright 3350s soon graced the airfoils of the big new Super G Constellations and the DC-7Bs. In fact, a prototype of the latter model averaged 447 miles per hour on a trial flight between Santa Monica and New York. The problem was that it landed with one engine barely running, and as many as twelve pistons in the other motors warped beyond repair. A total overhaul was required. Now Enzo Ferrari might not have minded; but for traffic managers tied to regular scheduling this spelled disaster. Piston engines were melting like ice cream cones, and it wasn't just the turbo-compound models. The problem had to do with reciprocation itself.

Take, for example, your basic automobile engine, which consists of a bunch of pistons all attached to a central crankshaft, each moving up and down in its own hollow cylinder. On the first upward stroke, air and vaporized fuel in the cylinder are compressed and then ignited to produce an explosion, which then drives the piston in the opposite direction, imparting power to the crankshaft, which in turn reverses the piston's direction to clear out the exhaust gases and then pulls it back down to draw in more air and fuel to start the process all over again. This is known as the Otto cycle. There are some variations in terms of ignition, arrangement of cylinders, and cooling. But all share a central characteristic, a lot of back and forth movement under very violent conditions, so the engines essentially work against themselves. No wonder 28 rebounding pistons, 3,000 horses, and turbochargers meant to pressurize things still further added up to a lot of melted and mangled metal.

Fortunately for folks in a hurry, there was a way around all this rip-roaring reciprocation. Turbines had been around for some time . . . you might say since windmills and waterwheels. More recently, steam turbines had pretty much replaced clunky triple expansion engines at sea, although they still continued to be weighty devices which required separate boilers to generate the necessary vaporized water. Meanwhile, a true gas turbine remained a mirage not only because it had to burn fuel internally, but also since it had to be inherently light if it was expected to power anything much less ponderous than Cleopatra's barge. Still, the concept had its attractions, not the least of which was its inherent smoothness; instead of dealing with power in a rapid series of herky-jerky outbursts, it handled it in an even and continuous flow. The problem was coming up with a device that capitalized on this principle and actually worked.

Then out of the English mist stepped RAF no. 364365, Flag Officer Frank Whittle, with a solution so simple, light, and elegant that even after he built a working model, his critics had trouble believing it wasn't a hoax. Essentially it consisted of three parts—a spinning compressor at the front which drew in and densified the airflow, a combustion chamber where fuel was mixed and ignited to create a rapid blast of hot gases, and just in back a turbine which was kept whirling by the exhaust so as to drive the compressor. Meanwhile, downstream from the turbine the gases were expelled into the atmosphere to create propulsive force . . . a lot of propulsive force, so much that the first prototype caused the test crew to run for their lives. And they weren't necessarily overreacting. When the exhaust gases were properly measured they were found to be exiting at well over a thousand miles an hour. This too was highly significant, because there was also a very basic problem with the propellers on conventionally powered aircraft. In level flight they were unable to push air back much past 470 mph without demonstrating an unfortunate tendency to fly apart, thereby imposing some very inelastic speed limits on all but the most foolhardy or suicidal of air enthusiasts. On the other hand, with turbines smoothly flatulating exhaust gases at unheard of speeds, all bets, even supersonic ones, were off. Certainly there were problems of heat-resistant materials, compressor design, fuel metering, and airflow augmentation to be solved. But if there ever was an aerial power plant of the future, this was it.

C.R. SMITH, PRESIDENT, AMERICAN AIRLINES   You know, it's the craziest thing. I don't think Rickenbacker ever understood why jets worked. Bob Six of Continental told me that Eddie once took him aside and said: "Now look, you've got a background in science. So will you please tell me how something without a propeller is supposed to be able to take off." Well, of course, Bob immediately mentioned Newton's third law of motion and how for every action there's an equal and opposite reaction. This only pissed Rickenbacker off. "Yeah, yeah, that's what all my engineers tell me. But not one of 'em can explain to me why it works . . . except that it's a basic law of the Universe. So we're supposed to risk the whole future of this industry on something nobody can explain."

GOD   That depends on your perspective. From my point of view, Creation was already crazy enough. There had to be some rules, especially after I created humans. Now do you think as a responsible Deity I was going to let those lunatics do anything that wouldn't be immediately and absolutely counteracted? Besides, if we all didn't get behind this Conservation of Energy, what would happen to the whole concept of Eternity, not to mention my job security?

TONY PITISCI, EASTERN MASTER MECHANIC   This is a true story, I swear. We was overhaulin' one of those piece-a-shit Wright engines, an' no matter what we do, it won't run smooth. We must'a tore it down at least three times and couldn't find nothin' wrong.

About then the Captain comes by an' takes a look-see. After a couple minutes he picks up a gear 'bout the size of a saucer. "Tony," he sez, "how many teeth's this thing supposed to have?" I checked the blueprint and it's forty-five. "Well this one's got forty-six, that's your problem." I'll be fucked if it didn't. How's any normal person supposed to see somethin' like that? You got me.

CHARLIE FROESCH   Eastern's problems moving to jets had everything to do with Eddie. First, after his experience with his car company, he never liked to be first with anything. But the ride in the Comet sealed it.

Everybody knew jets were coming, it was just a matter of time. Then in the summer of '52 the first of DeHavilland's new Comets went into service for B.O.A.C. It looked like the Brits had the jump on everybody. The planes were beautiful—four Ghost turbojets buried in the wing roots, a 500-mph cruising speed, and a cabin big enough to carry fifty passengers in comfort. Comets didn't have true transatlantic range, but they would have been perfect for the New York–to–Miami run.

Eddie was interested enough to go over to England with me, Paul Brattain, Lefty, and the other VPs. And on the way he even talked about ordering up to thirty-five, if they lived up to expectations.

The initial talks with the DeHavilland people went well, and we all climbed aboard for a demonstration flight. Acceleration on the runway seemed a bit sluggish, but once we were aloft the ride was amazingly smooth and comfortable. It was hard to believe we were at 40,000 feet flying across England at 525 mph. Eddie went up front and even took the controls. He seemed happy as a lark. Then he walked back into the passenger compartment, and the next thing we know he's screaming like a maniac.

"This thing's a death trap, get me the hell off it! You Limey fucks were dumb enough to think I was a German spy, and now you're still too stupid to design anything sound that flies." He kept on like this until we finally landed. The British were mortified and we were all pretty embarrassed. But that didn't quiet him down. As soon as we got off that plane we were out of there, without so much as a good-bye.

In the car nobody said much. Finally, I turned to him and said: "What the hell set you off?" He looked amazed.

"Charlie, didn't you see the sides of the fuselage vibrating in and out? That plane is a time bomb. Before long that metal is gonna fatigue and crack apart, and at altitude the pressurized cabin will blow to Kingdom Come."

Well, we'd all looked that plane over stem to stern and none of us had seen anything that looked remotely dangerous. So we didn't take him too seriously until Comets started exploding in midair. The inquests showed he was exactly right. The man was sixty years old and he still had the eyes of an eagle. Unfortunately, his view of the future wasn't quite so acute.

SID SHANNON   "Boys," he said, "we're going with the Electra." I thought Bev Griffith, who was in charge of marketing, would cry. "Captain, we've done survey after survey. The public wants jets."

"These *are* jets, goddammit . . . prop jets. . . . Allison turbines hooked to the biggest most efficient propellers you've ever seen. It's gonna be almost a decade before they perfect the pure jets, and in the meantime we'll be flyin' the most cost-effective planes in the air. The operations guys tell me we can fly them at a profit on runs anywhere between 100 and 2,400 miles. They're perfect for our route structure. I still know a good airplane when I see it, and we're gonna bet the farm on this one. I've already cut a deal with Lockheed—forty Electras plus parts for 100 million. It's a steal."

Somebody—I think it might have been Brattain—had the guts to point out that this would just about deplete our war chest for the big jets of the future that Boeing and Douglas were developing. But that didn't stop the Captain. "You're just thinking short-term. These Electras are going to make us so much money that we'll be able to buy anything we want when the time comes."

CHARLIE FROESCH   There was no question, the L-188 was an excellent aircraft. The test pilots and the pre-introduction crews swore it flew like a fighter. And they weren't just blowing smoke, the thing had twice the reserve power of any transport built to date. Once Herman "the Fish" Salmon, Lockheed's chief test pilot, had me and American's Si Bittner up over Burbank and he starts cutting the engines and feathering the props . . . first number one, then number two. Finally, he gives the copilot the order to feather number three. I thought Si would drop dead on the spot. But that plane, flying on one engine, didn't lose a foot of altitude. Also, the Electra was the first passenger aircraft with true "wave off" capability—you could touch down at your normal rollout point, pull back the yoke and go to max power, and you'd be up to 3,000 feet and climbing by the time you flew over the end of the strip.

The L-188s were beautiful, too. The engines were so long that they caught the lines of the fuselage, and made the whole thing look like a big aluminum torpedo. Of course, the Captain insisted on his usual placard . . . this time it was FLY EASTERN'S PROP-JET ELECTRA. The bigger the planes got, the more he had to say.

At least this time he didn't get to screw up the interior. When the guys in Burbank asked him what he wanted on the seats, he came up with the usual: "As many asses as you can get on 'em. . . . But on second thought, how about a nice olive green, since it doesn't show dirt? Then we can go with cream for the rest. Nice and tasteful and it'll match the rest of our planes."

I think the Lockheed guys thought he was kidding. But we knew better. It was time for emergency measures. Fortunately, somebody thought to pay a visit to Harley Earl, GM's design chief and the last word in style as far as Eddie was concerned. Well, Harley put a couple of his young guys on it, and promised us something good. I kept calling, asking what he had up his sleeve.

"I'll tell him myself, Charlie—I know just what he'll go for." When the mockup was ready, he phones Eddie.

"Rick, you're gonna love it. Royal blue Dacron brocade flecked with gold threads. It's exactly what we're putting on next year's Coupe de Villes."

"Cadillacs? . . . Caddies? . . . My God, you're a genius. And to think I pay assholes around here to decorate my planes."

So there it was. The plane of our dreams. Except for one big problem. The wings kept falling off.

LAURANCE ROCKEFELLER   Even though the seeds of failure had been planted, they didn't sprout until some time later. He . . . ordered Electras because down deep he lacked faith in pure jets. In my opinion that huge Electra order really started Eastern downhill.

PETER VREELAND   That plane was jinxed from the outset. Less than a month after it went into service in January 1959, an American Electra hit the East River 5,000 feet short of La Guardia's Runway 22, drowning sixty-five passengers and two of the crew.

And this was simply a prelude. Seven months after, a Braniff Electra cruising at 15,000 feet in absolutely clear weather over Buffalo, Texas, suddenly lost a wing and plunged straight down, killing thirty-four. Then, as if to drive the point home, on March 17, 1960, a Northwest Electra on its way to Miami from Chicago shed one of its wings, and dove 18,000 feet into a cornfield somewhere in Indiana. It was estimated to have impacted at 618 mph, leaving sixty-three more bodies and a fuselage one third its original length.

The drumroll refused to cease. In September, another American Electra hit a dike at La Guardia and flipped over. The plane was a total write-off and there were numerous injuries; but thankfully no one was killed.

We weren't so fortunate. On October 4th, one of Eastern's Electras—Flight 375—taking off from Logan lost power and corkscrewed into Boston Harbor, leaving fifty-nine more bodies to fish out.

There was blood on everyone's hands, and hell to pay. Load factors dropped faster than the planes themselves. One newspaper headline read: "Mourning Becomes Electra," and a joke was circulating that one didn't purchase a ticket on an Electra, one bought a chance.

Gallows humor was one thing, but the FAA was another. Pete Quesada, the agency's administrator and Ike's chum, was livid. He wanted to ground the entire fleet, all ninety-six L-188s. We were fortunate to escape with a thorough inspection of every aircraft and a reduction in operating speed to 259 mph.

After an immense amount of testing, Lockheed finally located the problem—the wide spacing of the engine nacelles set up catastrophic oscillations at certain speeds, which literally tore the wings asunder. To their credit, the company successfully corrected the problem at a cost of twenty-five million, not a penny of which did they attempt to pass on to the airlines.

Nevertheless, the damage was done. Eastern, more than any carrier, was associated with the Electra—now viewed as an aeronautical hearse, and one mandated to fly no faster than a DC-6. Eddie actually thought the problem might be substantially ameliorated by dropping the term "Electra" and substituting "Golden Falcon" in our advertising.

This, of course, was laughable. And to me, at least, it symbolized the steady decline in his judgment. Meanwhile, the vaunted hiatus between piston and jet power amounted to no more than a hiccup. The 707s and the DC-8s, with twice the speed and carrying capacity of anything in the air, were ready for delivery . . . and thanks to Rickenbacker, we found ourselves virtually last in the queue.

Jets sent the debt-strapped airline peacocks soaring into the black. And they weren't just swept-wing cash cows. They amounted to icons a-go-go . . . aesthetic manifestations of the speed, grace, and all-consuming zoom the fifties were certain the sixties would be all about. Who needed a Calder mobile when you could book passage on a dream capsule and end up somewhere else so fast that only jet lag could describe the creepy feeling that parts of you were still trying to catch up.

Back in those days, jets weren't tubby look-alikes and they didn't load them like subways, so the only thing you saw was the door. They marched you out on the tarmac. Maybe you got a little wet or cold, but you got the chance to eyeball all that streamlined metaliferous splendor . . . slim power-packed engines poking arrogantly out from beneath wings swept a full thirty-five degrees, slender fuselages tapered both front and rear as if by giant pencil sharpeners, and topped off by lofty canted vertical stabilizers that made the tail fins of Detroit look positively fetal.

And awaiting male voyagers atop the passenger ramps were supremely bouffanted paragons of young American female pulchritude. Stewardae . . . the *Playboy* bunnies of the air. They smiled a lot, guided you to your seat, served you alcohol and hunks of meat, and then left you to fantasize as to what sort of sexual ecstasy might be possible with such heavenly creatures. If there had been laptops then, many would have been propped at impossible angles.

But jet-passengerhood was not simply elevating to the spirit and the anatomy, it came to constitute a rung on the great national ladder of success. Flying a jet implied you had to be somewhere fast—that somebody needed you pronto. You were *a priori* important. Nobody had to bribe you with frequent-flyer miles, flying jets frequently was its own reward . . . a status-enhancer like no other. James Bond, between acts of mayhem, was practically jet-propelled. And at the absolute pinnacle were the Jet-Setters, proverbial squatters in first class, folk fortunate enough to tease Mach I with utter nonchalance, barely aware of where they were going, but secure in the knowledge that the ride would never end.

And in the background could be heard adding machines ca-chunking the numbers and counting the cash. For jets weren't just popular and stylish, they were hallucinogenically profitable.

Initially there had been some misgivings. After all, turbojets were true gas-guzzlers, burning something like five times the fuel of equivalent piston engines. But instead of 101-octane aviation gasoline, jets belted down kerosene at eight cents a gallon. So who cared?

Meanwhile, whirling turbines proved miraculously more reliable than pounding pistons. Overhaul intervals stretched from hundreds of hours all the way up to ten and even fifteen thousand hours in some cases. Concomitantly, the elimination of propellers proved soothing not only to passengers but also to airframes, cutting maintenance costs still further. And all of this good news was compounded by the ability to fly twice as far, twice as fast. Utilization skyrocketed, and cost per passenger nosedived, roughly quintupling productivity.

Money at last . . . Money at last . . . Thank God Almighty . . . Money at last. And as the lucre flowed in, orders went out to Seattle and Santa Monica. Assembly halls sprang up like mushrooms and triple shifts were the rule; but still, supply couldn't keep up with demand. And somewhere in the background stood Eddie Rickenbacker, with his hands in his pockets and a very perplexed expression on his battered, danger-scarred face.

BOO HERNDON, THE GHOSTWRITER   Something quite surprising took place during the latter stages of the project. His affect changed. He became, if not exactly penitent, then at least somewhat remorseful. Partly, I suppose, it was because virtually everything we spoke of must have reminded him that he was coming to the end of his life. But plainly the focus of his misgivings was his management of the airline during the last part of his tenure. Alternately, he would rail against Eastern's bad luck and then bemoan his own decisions at critical points.

Of course, his anguish became my anguish, since I had to generate some kind of coherent narrative out of this tangle of conflicting emotions. He seemed genuinely torn between defending himself and providing a forthright rendition of how things went downhill.

Nothing I put together even remotely satisfied him. "No! No! No! You've got it all wrong. Don't you listen, Herndon? I was crystal clear on that matter, and now you make it seem like I don't know what I'm talking about. There's not even a trace of a similarity between what I tell you and what you write."

This went on and on. He must have waved aside at least five separate drafts, until finally I cobbled together an abbreviated and self-congratulatory soliloquy filled with statements like "During my twenty-five-year stewardship of Eastern Airlines we were never in red ink, we always showed a profit, we never took a nickel of the taxpayers' money in subsidy. . . ." Technically true . . . but far from the real truth.

I don't think he really wanted it this way. I believe he intended to honestly explain himself and his actions in a time of turmoil. But he simply could not bring himself to do it. So in the end we managed to retain consistency with the central theme of the autobiography—Captain Eddie was never wrong.

LEFTY LETHRIDGE Rick had every bit the business sense of a Woolman or a Patterson. He just never had a feel for the softer side of the operation . . . the service angle. To his friends he was decent, even lovable; but he never showed this side to Eastern employees at large. And it was this tough-guy image that they started to project in their dealings with customers.

JEFFREY LINETSKY AND TOMMY JESSUP We got to talking one night over a few drinks. I was mad as hell because Eastern had lost my luggage for the third time running, and just that week Tommy had been left stranded in Altoona after they rerouted his flight. It wasn't so much the screwups but their attitude. Like they were doin' us a favor letting us ride on their planes. Finally, Tommy got so torqued off he yells out to the whole bar: "How many here hate Eastern Airlines?" Next thing we know we're surrounded by pissed-off passengers. That's how it got started.

ROBERT J. SERLING, *From the Captain to the Colonel*
"It was about this time that WHEAL was formed—the initials standing for We Hate Eastern Air Lines. The originators were a pair of Pittsburgh businessmen and exactly how many members they garnered in response to a few newspaper advertisements is uncertain—'several thousand,' according to one official at Eastern. . . . "

PAUL BRATTAIN Looking back, it should have been obvious we were setting ourselves up for a fall. We had a Plain Jane image at a time when everybody wanted chrome and mink. Competition and customer resistance were building and we were getting by on sheer size and frequency of flights.
Rickenbacker was a fanatic on utilization—keepin' the planes in the air—so to some extent we were flying just for the sake of flying. But if you wanted to get from Jacksonville to Charlotte at 8 P.M. we probably could get you there and the others couldn't. The problem was, flying that route at that time meant a load factor almost never exceeding 50 percent and marginal profits at best. What kept us in the gravy was New York and Philly and Chicago

to Miami. And when the others got jets and we didn't have 'em, there was hell to pay. Our customers deserted us like we were lepers.

TED BAKER, NATIONAL AIRLINES   It was the slickest deal I ever pulled off—two pricks with one stone. Any idiot could see that jets were coming. But for us, getting them would be no easy trick, since we could only afford a couple, and that would put us at the back of everybody's line. Well, I got to thinking about alternative cat-skinning procedures, and I thought of my dear friend Juan Trippe. . . . Now Juan—Mr. Sanctimony himself—had dedicated his life to keeping everybody except Pan Am out of the international arena. At one point, he actually had the gall to try to get his airline officially designated "the chosen instrument of the U.S. Government."

Well, Trippe had nothing but contempt for National. But we did have one thing he wanted—domestic routes. To a Yaley astride the earth, shutting everybody out abroad was only fair, but being shut out at home was a monumental injustice—and one he did everything he could to put right. Meanwhile, Pan Am had something we needed—jets, lots of 'em. On his long routes they couldn't fail, so he was the first of the major carriers to jump in big time.

But in the end he fell for the oldest trick in the book—bait and switch. In return for letting us lease two of his jets during the peak months of '58–'59, I offered him enough options on National stock for him to eventually gain control of the company. He went for it like a tarpon goes for a chumsicle—too greedy to realize the Feds would never approve the deal and by that time I'd have jets of my own. So that took care of prick number one.

Now for the bank shot. This required a little patience. Rickenbacker had let loose a publicity blitz announcing Eastern's Electras and how they would be the quickest way to get down to Miami. Every ad was doing a little more to convince the public what a good thing it was to fly to Florida fast. In the meantime, the deal between us and Pan Am was kept absolutely secret. We had the two planes squirreled away in our hangar out at Idlewild, painting them up with National's colors. Finally, a little more than a week before putting them into service, we let 'em have it—full-page ads in all the Miami and New York papers. "National has jets . . . Real jets." On the first flight we had Ronald Colman, Bob Considine, and Gypsy Rose Lee aboard . . . and God love her, she tells a reporter in Miami, "It's the first plane I've ever seen where the john actually flushes."

We flew those planes night and day at a hundred percent load. John or no john, the public would have flocked to 'em; they were slaphappy to fly jets. Meanwhile, the Electras were falling out of the skies and scaring the shit out of everybody. We had caught Captain Eddie square in his legendary pecker.

C.E. WOOLMAN   I've got to admit, I was as conservative as anybody when it came to pure jets. Delta had made great strides, but it remained small in spirit and resources. Four and a half million a plane at that time seemed like an awful lot of money, particularly when Electras could be had for one point eight. They looked like attractive aircraft, 'specially for short hauls. But when we talked to the folks at Lockheed, American and Eastern had pretty much sewn up production for a year and a half. I felt ourselves being painted into a corner; we had to do something fast or we'd be flying Connies and DC-7s in the face of a whole new generation of equipment. Then, thank the Good Lord, the waters parted. I discovered that Eastern had given up the rights on its first six DC-8s, on the grounds they were underpowered. Donald Douglas assured me the planes were perfectly safe and we grabbed them. It was about the most impulsive decision I made in thirty-odd years as an airline executive, and I spent a good many nights praying I had done the right thing. Well, my prayers were answered. These would prove to be great days for our flight crews as far as competition with our Eastern friends was concerned. It was a thrill for Delta pilots to be able to climb to altitude and cruise right past the fastest thing Eastern had flying, pointing out to our passengers over the PA that we were traveling over 150 mph faster.

GOD   I wish people would stop blaming me. Rickenbacker was stupid enough in this instance to provide his competitors an entirely adequate measure of good fortune.

PAUL BRATTAIN   Rickenbacker kept rolling—and they kept comin' up snake eyes. I don't think any of us will forget the meeting on the DC-8 contract. First thing, Charlie Froesch announces that Don Douglas has informed him that the plane was coming in heavy, and would have to take off wet—meaning the jets would need water injection to boost the thrust. "Basically," the Captain jumps in, "the cocksucker is trying to sell us an underpowered airplane. Now we've got a couple of alternatives: we can just swallow it, and hope the things can cut it; or we can wait for Pratt and Whitney's JT-4, which will have the power to fly dry. But this is gonna hold us up for ten months." (It ended up being fourteen.)

As you might imagine, this provoked a storm of questions and not a lot of support for canceling. Rickenbacker was steamed, but he tried to sound reasonable. "Look, I understand how important this is. And in spite all the bullshit I hear about Eastern being an autocracy, I'm ready to go with the majority. So let's have a secret ballot." He gives everybody a piece of paper, and then counts the votes himself. "It's a landslide, boys, we're going to pass on the first six DC-8s and wait for the JT-4."

Later in the day the VPs kept stopping by my office, asking how I voted. As near as we could figure, none of us had gone for postponement. We decided the score was really 8-2 against, with only Froesch on the Captain's side. Then we find out that Charlie actually voted with us, on the grounds that backing out would simply cost us too much. I'll tell you—you never wanna let a dictator hold an election.

LEFTY LETHRIDGE The times were passing him by and he didn't know it. Rickenbacker's style of micromanagement was okay for a small operation. But by this time we were big—over 18,000 employees working to keep a fleet of nearly a hundred planes flying thousands of passengers a day to something like ninety destinations. Air transportation was becoming mass transit, and he just wasn't ready for it. He wanted to have a hand in every job in the company. He'd happily work sixteen-hour days and expect us to be there with him. But he was incapable of delegating, so what we got was logjams and inefficiency.

Also, he was a guy who never got over his prejudices. Take the issue of stewardesses. He had driven Brattain and Shannon crazy on this in the old days, and even tried briefly to get rid of them after the War. Finally, we had gotten to the point that we had good-looking broads on our planes like everybody else, and suddenly he wants to start hiring stewards again. It was one of the few times he provoked open and vocal opposition. Somebody said he was acting like a relic. And he comes back that it's *us* who were the cavemen. "We're looking at a co-ed future and you guys better get used to it. The days are coming to an end that we can fill our aisles with floozies and think that constitutes service. Woman passengers, for one, are not going to stand for it." It just goes to show he was capable of using any stupid argument in a pinch, if it served his purposes.

IRENE BRADLEY, EASTERN FLIGHT ATTENDANT In spite of all his power, about the only thing he was known for among us was calling all the stewardesses "girlie." One particular night, I was working the Houston-Miami run and the Captain was aboard. We stopped off in New Orleans, and then got grounded by a tremendous thunderstorm. The flight was eventually canceled and some of us wandered back to the hotel bar for a nightcap. Mr. Rickenbacker came in, and before long I found myself drinking with him alone. He looked like my grandfather, but he was a fascinating guy. I was also a little looped, so when he asked me how I liked working for Eastern, I came back with something like: "Well, it'll never take the place of sex."

"It has for me, unfortunately," he said kinda sadly. "You know, getting old reminds me of driving a racing car about to blow. Your every instinct tells you to keep pushing, but you can't, and besides it's okay because the situation is out of your control." I must have looked at him kind of funny, because he said: "When you're my age you'll know exactly what I mean."

I am, and I do.

ADELAIDE During this period, Edward and I argued a good deal. Much of it centered around the boys and their future. He had such plans for them! David was never much of a student, but everybody loved him and we both could see that he would be best off working with people. But Edward's expectations were so high that I don't think David ever felt secure in what he did accomplish. I tried to act as a moderating influence, but Edward didn't seem to be able to temper his criticism and conceal his disappointment.

Bill was different. He was much more intellectual and introverted. Yet Edward saw him as a leader of men, and desperately wanted him to follow in his footsteps at Eastern. Bill did what he could to humor him, even to the point of joining the Air Force and earning his pilot's wings. But as far as spending his life running an airline, this was out of the question. I could see it . . . everybody

could see it. William had a God-given talent for writing and a
wonderful grasp of politics and foreign affairs. This was his true
calling, and he simply would not be deterred by his father. They
were both very strong-willed, and so I suppose was I. We were
never a family that took refuge in stony silences, and this issue led
to some very vocal three-way quarrels, frequently with poor Dave
caught in the middle trying to act as peacemaker. He was a gentle
soul, and I think perhaps he was the one hurt the most.

> 10 Rockefeller Plaza
> October 23, 1955

Mr. William F. Rickenbacker
450 East 63rd Street
New York, New York

My dear Bill:
First I want to make it very clear to you that I am extremely
pleased by what you have been doing over at the *National
Review*. Bill Buckley is a fine young man and has a good head
on his shoulders. Also I realize that journalism does have possibilities for someone with your qualifications and is a natural
stepping-stone, not simply broadening your vision, but allowing you to make contacts with men who are doing things that
are worthwhile. I also understand that you feel strongly about
some of the issues closest to my own heart, creeping socialism,
excessive regulation, the necessity to fight Communists
wherever we might find them. You have always been ready to
man the barricades of freedom, and I applaud that.

But I must tell you frankly that there is a time and a place
for everything. Defending free enterprise with the pen is important, but so is practicing it. In this regard I have to tell
you that Laurance Rockefeller has informed me of your lunch
together, and that when he brought up the possibility of you
becoming Eastern's eventual president, you showed no interest whatsoever. Bill, I know we have been over this many
times before, but you must understand that such a man does
not bring up such subjects lightly. The damage you have done
can still be undone. But your window of opportunity is steadily closing. I cannot maintain control here forever. If you are

to have time to learn this business and be in a position to take control, you must move now. I don't know how to make this any more clear to you.

As always,
Daddy

BRAD WALKER   He was approaching seventy, and everybody in the company sensed a change might be coming. For some reason—probably because I was an outsider—he took me aside: "Brad, the time has come for me to step down. Bill's never coming in, and I still have the chance to engineer a smooth transition. Dick Jackson has drawn up a list of presidential possibilities, but I've talked to Laurance and the Board and we've agreed on Malcolm MacIntyre, the Undersecretary of the Air Force."

"What are the other Eastern guys going to say . . . especially the ones who want the job?"

"I don't care what they say. I can't bring somebody up from the ranks. It would stir up a hornet's nest. They'd all end up fighting among themselves, or quitting. Besides, MacIntyre is a crack lawyer and a first-rate mind, everybody respects him. He is short on experience running an airline, but I'll be around to get him over the initial rough spots."

At that instant my nostrils caught the faint aroma of a well-known rodent. The sly old bastard wasn't presiding over his own abdication, he was elevating a sacrificial lamb.

GOD   Certain traditions do have to be observed. At times a fatted calf is good too.

Eastern Airlines Special Report to Stockholders, October 15, 1958
> . . . In addition to a strong financial performance this quarter, the Board is pleased to announce that as of October 1 Malcolm A. MacIntyre assumed the duties of President and Chief Executive Officer of the company. Mr. MacIntyre brings to Eastern a long and distinguished career in aviation, first as a Colonel in the Air Transport Command, then as General Counsel for American Airlines, and most recently as Undersecretary of the United States Air Force. Thomas A. Armstrong has also been named Executive Vice-President for Finance. Finally, we are pleased to inform you that Edward Vernon Rickenbacker has been elected to the Board of

Directors and will serve as its Chairman. Captain Rickenbacker will also head the Operations Committee, whose membership includes the executive directors of all the airline's departments.

Conversation in the fifth-floor men's room of the Eastern Airlines Building, Miami International Airport

"A fucking lawyer . . . and a drunk to boot."

"A drunk? Who says?"

"All the guys in New York. Rolls into the office after lunch—loose as a goose, raisin' hell . . . every day."

"Shit . . . I personally saw the Captain down ten martinis an' never blink. Now we got a shyster who can't hold his booze. As if we ain't got enough troubles!"

MALCOLM MACINTYRE   Quite frankly, Eastern was not in good condition when I took the helm. Rickenbacker in his calculating manner had managed to paper over the company's many short-comings, propping up profits and stock values. But the airline's true condition was much more akin to that of the *Titanic* moments after its collision with the iceberg—very much afloat, but far more gravely wounded than anyone could imagine. Like the doomed ship's captain, I immediately made it my business to determine the true nature of our condition. The results were not reassuring.

The staff, for example, was made up almost exclusively of old-timers who had come up through the ranks learning as they went. While there is nothing inherently wrong with experience and on-the-job training, it should not be the only standard of competence. Nonetheless, my survey indicated that at the very time we were moving into a period of unprecedented aeronautical sophistication, there were only ten college graduates among Eastern's 20,000-odd employees, excluding the pilots.

Then there was the matter of equipment. There was obviously a severe shortage of jets. By this time the Air Force was almost totally reliant on jet power, and it had proved itself an over-whelming success. But I arrived here to find a sea of whirling pro-pellers and a septuagenarian fighter pilot pontificating about the dangers of putting four-wheel brakes on a car he had built in the twenties. It was a bizarre experience, to put it mildly.

While it is true that I resigned largely out of disgust over govern-ment intervention, which allowed other airlines to duplicate routes we had pioneered, I remained sincerely committed to fostering a new generation of leaders at Eastern from my unique vantage point as Chairman. Unfortunately, MacIntyre had other ideas. He arrived with his head full of so-called "modern management" and very little understanding that it's people that make an airline work. Those people had managed to put together twenty-three straight years of increasing profits, and it only made sense to give them the benefit of the doubt and tread lightly at first. But that was exactly what MacIntyre refused to do.

Instead, he came up with a "Survey of the Eastern Airlines Work Force," filled with Fancy Dan statistics supposed to show that we were all a bunch of dopes. Personnel slipped me an advance copy and I literally begged him not to let it go forward. But he wouldn't listen, and then wondered why the reaction was universally negative. Didn't he think the troops would see a message behind all the mathematical mumbo jumbo? . . . That they weren't smart or well-educated enough to run the airline. The fact is, a man should be allowed to grow into whatever job he is capable of doing. I had suffered from the same sort of prejudice in World War I, when the Army didn't want me to fly because I didn't have a college degree. That mattered very little in the skies against the Germans, and I felt the same way in this case.

Another point of contention between us was his campaign to get rid of unprofitable routes, and turn them over to local carriers. He never understood that those routes acted as feeders to our main lines, and if we gave them away it was only a matter of time before the locals merged and we'd have whole new airlines to compete against. To him it was just a matter of dollars and cents. As a newcomer he didn't seem capable of taking the long view—that in this business sometimes you have to do the hard thing now, in order to position yourself to compete more effectively later.

I'm not saying I was a hundred percent right on every issue. But I had a wealth of experience plus the loyalty of the people at Eastern, and as Chairman I expected he would hear me out. This was not the case. He chose to interpret my efforts to help as back-biting and disloyalty. As a result of this and other factors, black ink turned to red. During his first year as President we lost over eleven million dollars, and for his entire period Eastern's losses totaled over sixty-four million. Nothing in my career is more painful to relate.

MALCOLM MACINTYRE I realized rather quickly that one of my key challenges lay in making our obsolescent fleet as useful as possible until it could be modernized. At the heart of the problem was our lumbering collection of Constellations—ten Super Gs, twelve Super Cs, and eighteen still older 749s—a total of forty aircraft too big for short hauls and too slow for the longer routes. I looked at the problem from a number of perspectives, but nothing showed much promise until one day Bill Morrisett, our VP for Traffic and Sales, paid me a visit with a plan that Rickenbacker had rejected three years before.

The idea was simple in its essence—a shuttle between New York and Washington with guaranteed seating and ultra-low fares. If a plane filled up we would simply put another on line, regardless of the load. We could do this because the Connies were fully amortized and could be configured to carry up to ninety-six passengers. Even at this stage we could see the numbers we would draw were inherently very large. In fact, there was every prospect of once again dominating a traditionally vital Eastern route with a resource that otherwise would go largely unutilized.

I approved the Shuttle immediately only to have it rejected by Rickenbacker's Operations Committee. I was not about to be thwarted. This concept was simply too good. So I raised the issue to the level of the Board for a full vetting. We went through an hour-and-a-half presentation with every conceivable projection, at the end of which Rickenbacker, with a sour look on his face, said simply: "It won't work."

At this point I lost my temper. "We've gone to the mat over this and all you can say is that it won't work. That's not sufficient. Will you give me at least one reason *why* it won't work?"

"You've obviously never heard the old joke about the widget tycoon who planned to lose a little on each item so he could make it up in the volume."

Well, I hadn't heard that one, but we did institute the Shuttle and it did work. True, it didn't bring big profits, but it brought a huge increase in traffic and got Eastern back on people's minds.

CHARLIE FROESCH We needed a new airplane. Not just a jet, but a jet specifically designed for short-to-medium ranges. I wanted something easy to land on small runways and capable of climbing very rapidly to efficient operating altitudes. Boeing had been kicking around a configuration like the French Caravelle, with two engines aft-mounted on the fuselage for cleaner airflow over the wing. They had the right idea, but I wanted a third engine buried below the empennage and fed from an intake at the base of the vertical stabilizer, which would be configured like a T to raise the control surfaces out of the jet stream. After preliminary calculations of weight and balance, Boeing came back and told me the thing would take off like a skyrocket—exactly what I wanted.

As far as landing, the design team in Seattle incorporated what they called their "Wonder Wing"—triple-slotted rear flaps extending in tandem with forward edge flaps to produce a 25 percent increase in surface area for low-speed approaches. Yet everything remained totally retractable to regenerate a slender airfoil with fully thirty-two degrees of sweep for high-speed cruise efficiency.

And it all worked together in the prototype even better than predicted—10 percent more fuel efficiency, 20 mph higher cruise capability, and stability during final approach unmatched since the days of the DC-3. It may not have been the perfect airplane, but it was the perfect airplane for Eastern. Boeing called it the 727.

LEFTY LETHRIDGE   The 727 was obviously the way to go. Charlie and I took it to Mr. Mac, and, if anything, he was even more gung ho. There was just one catch. Boeing wouldn't go into production unless they got at least a hundred orders. American and United were willing to spring for thirty apiece. That left forty for us, plus I wanted to take an option on an additional ten to sweeten the deal. That was all right by Mr. Mac; but when we took it to Rick the 727 hit a brick wall.

"It's an untested aircraft. We'd be crazy to take any more than twenty."

I think this was probably the last straw for MacIntyre, because he let him have it right between the eyes.

"Are you such an old fool that you can't grasp the simplest concept? There won't be a 727 unless we go for forty, you numskull."

"You call me that again and I'll rip your head off. You don't know the first thing about running an airline. You've fucked things up around here from the word go. All you can do is spend money and whine about disloyalty. I built this airline with my two bare fists, and I'm not going to see a dickless wonder like you destroy it."

From this point, their frank exchange of views went straight downhill, until I thought the two of them would end up rolling around on the floor. Finally, I just started gathering up my papers and shoving them in my briefcase.

"Where do you think you're going?"

"It's over, Captain. We've been slaving over this for four months, and I think we've got it about right. But you've made up your mind, and, as far as I'm concerned, that's it."

"Gimme those papers, Lefty." Mr. Mac nodded okay, so I did. He went through them for about five minutes. I doubt he saw a thing, since he wasn't wearing his glasses, which he hated. Then, without even looking at MacIntyre, he turned to me.

"I'm okay with the first forty, Lefty. As far as those ten options—let's hold off and see what happens."

Later Mr. Mac called me into his office. "From now on, Lefty, it's him or me. Understand?"

I understood. But I couldn't help thinking we'd be better off without the both of them.

CHARLIE FROESCH It was pointless to present Eddie with reasoned technical analysis. Everything had now to be related to something in the past. I was careful, and I told my people to be careful, to refer to the 727 as our new Tri-motor.

Also, when Boeing wanted to replace the pure jets with turbofans, I had to explain it to him in a way that made me sound like Mr. Wizard on the television.

"You see the jets can swallow a lot more air than they can burn. So why not run a big fan—basically just a propeller—off the main shaft and shoot the extra out the back?"

"Exactly why I liked the Electras, Charlie. You can talk all you want about that action-reaction shit; when it comes right down to it you're gonna be hard put to replace the good old propeller."

PETER VREELAND There was a mounting sense of depression on the Board, as Eastern lurched toward what some feared might be oblivion. And this was only exacerbated by an awareness that the controls were in the hands of two sworn enemies, each of whom was more intent on destroying the other than pulling the airline out of its very steep dive.

While he did have certain successes, MacIntyre's stewardship was cratered with a string of disasters frequently made worse by his own intercessions. Too often, there was no sense of continuity to his actions; he simply reacted to the crisis at hand. And they came like a drumroll—two disastrous flight engineers' strikes in less than two years; the loss of our key bid for expansion—the southern transcontinental route—and defeat after defeat before the Kennedy-dominated FAA; the botched merger with American and the harebrained scheme to align ourselves with Northwestern, to say nothing of his inability to join in the liquidation of Capital when it went under. He even managed to turn success into failure by extending the shuttle to Miami over everybody's objections that we needed a hundred percent load factor to break even.

All the while, of course, we were hemorrhaging money, MacIntyre's only solution being to slash scheduling so rapidly that our loss of competitive status obliterated any operational savings we might have accrued. From flying too much to flying too little, the pattern was typical as the airline reeled like a drunk through the early sixties.

Here too MacIntyre set the tone. He may not have been quite the alcoholic his enemies made him out to be, but too often at lunch I saw him down that extra Bloody Mary that effectively rendered him useless for the rest of the afternoon. And soon enough the staff took his cue, drowning their own sorrows at midday, until we began to be known as "the Airline of the Sots."

Of course, who would not have been driven to drink by the increasingly malign and nonsensical presence of Edward Vernon Rickenbacker? There was a time when I found Eddie refreshingly contrarian—a tonic against will-o'-the-wisp thinking. Now he was simply obdurate. His technical judgment, once one of his major strengths, grew abysmal. Meanwhile, he delighted in making not only MacIntyre but everyone around him miserable. And to make matters worse, as his political views became more reactionary, he seemed compelled to broadcast them ever more loudly and indiscriminately. The liberals were in charge, and this was simply killing us.

Others certainly were sensitive to this. Laurance approached his friend Harper Woodward and explained: "These route decisions going against us are all political—if I'm there as a Rockefeller, I'm sort of a negative influence, so why don't you go on the Board as my replacement?"

Hoping, I suppose, the Captain would take a hint, they met him for lunch at Louis XIV.

"That's the greatest idea I've ever heard. Laurance, you're a real handicap to me—in the wrong politics and everything else. Now Harper will be wonderful—nobody has ever heard of him."

Three weeks later, in the midst of the search for MacIntyre's replacement, Rickenbacker announced he had secretly sold all 100,000 shares of his Eastern stock.

"I had all my eggs in one basket, and the goddamned basket is full of holes."

That was the last straw. Floyd Hall, the new president, made getting rid of him a condition of his coming on board. But the issue had already been decided. Rickenbacker was finished.

SHEPPY   His retirement dinner was held at "21." I was the only woman invited. Lefty, Charlie Froesch, and Dick Merrill were there, but the guest list consisted primarily of outsiders—Board members, financiers, the people with whom the Captain socialized. None of them had any idea who I was, or why I was there. A few introduced themselves, thinking I was Adelaide; one even asked me to get him a drink. Most simply ignored me. So I sat and I watched.

The rathskeller decor and false joviality reminded me of the collegiate smokers my brothers had described, except that this one was populated with old men. As the pace of the alcohol and cigar consumption increased, the noise level in the room built to the point of discomfort. I remember looking up at the bar lined with beer mugs and pictures of young women in their underwear. There stood the Captain with his arm around Floyd Hall, the new president, both of them smiling ear-to-ear for the camera. Next to him was little David with a perfect replica of his father's cocky grin, his only bona fide legacy. Only tight-lipped George Champion of Chase Manhattan Bank could afford to betray any hint of what was behind this gala charade.

The Captain left early, still laughing and clapping the assembled shoulder blades. But as he went through the door he turned and stared with a most peculiar look on his face. His eyes, usually so tightly focused, seemed miles away. It was as if . . . as if—oh, I don't know.

At that moment, Fast Eddie Rickenbacker was amazed to see the oak-paneled walls of this most exclusive Gotham watering hole melt into transparency. As his eyes ventured beyond, he found himself back at Radio City, firmly in control of Eastern Airlines; then in the raft; still further on gathering advice from Mr. Sloan in his office; test-driving a Rickenbacker; obliterating a Fokker with twin Maxims; forcing a slender red racer into the wall at Ascot Park; sweeping up at Frayer-Miller; breathing Old Man Zenker's marble dust.

On his way back through the decades he was greeted by friend and enemy alike, long made invisible by death's sleight of hand. Now they were rematerialized, crowding around him whispering the same message.

"What is it? Speak up, for Christ's sake. . . . What?"

"The world, Eddie . . . the world no longer needs you. The things you championed, risked everything for, are taken for granted. Cars, planes, boisterous gasoline motors. They're no longer objects of wonder. They're in the background. And so are you. Defunct like Buffalo Bill, an impediment to progress. Something to be moved out and forgotten . . . no longer of any use."

GOD Well, maybe to you faddish air-breathers. As for myself, I still found him a serviceable villain.

Chapter Eight

GOD The cat was out of the bag, the scorpion crawled out of the bottle, the nukes were lining up to level the landscape. I had to do something. Stupid dinosaurs never amounted to much, but at least they had staying power. These damned anthros were about to walk off the edge after only 300,000 years . . . too smart for their own good, but too dumb to know it.

I suppose it was partly my fault. This particular universe was an early model, threw it together in less than a week. That's what you get for building with marbles and fire. Admittedly, $E=MC^2$ was a little dicey. But what were my choices? $E=M^2C$ just left me with a bunch of goop. $E=M^2/C$ was worse—a perfect cube, twelve gazillion light years on each side, made out of the same stuff as bowling balls. Where was the fun in that? I got more sophisticated later, but back then I was young and in a hurry to make my mark. Fusion worked pretty well, safe and hard to get started unless you had really strong hands. It was those damned heavy elements that caused problems. Giant nuclei, all packed in like a jack-in-the-box, ready to fly apart at the slightest provocation.

Well, it didn't take those swellheaded apes long to figure out that if you put a little of that shit together—like, say, plutonium (a bad element if there ever was one)—you could start a chain reaction and then . . . KABLOOWEY! And that wasn't the worst of it. All that heat you generated meant you could move right into the thermonuclear arena, which if you were them meant building bombs and using them against each other.

From an emotional perspective this was not a problem—even if they did bear a certain resemblance to the Basic Avatar. But it did raise a fairly important theoretical issue. How was I supposed to make any creature smart and aggressive enough to be amusing, if that meant they inevitably would find the keys to the kitchen and blow themselves off the face of creation? Entertainment-wise, things looked grim. Had I painted Myself into a corner? Was I doomed to a future of adorable dunces—Bambis, bunnies, and harp seals? I found the whole prospect nauseating. No, it was better to try to figure out a way to save the humans.

I was certainly under no illusions as to their basic inclination to play nicely. They liked to fight, especially the Alpha males who usually ran things. And those females who occasionally got some power—Cleopatra, Catherine de' Medici, Goldie Myerson—turned out to be just about as feisty and even dirtier fighters. Nope, I had to go with the aggressive flow . . . turn it into a positive. Now, if two 500-pound gorillas are determined to beat each other to death with sticks, you give them a bigger stick, and a bigger stick after that, and still a bigger stick, until it finally dawns on them that their respective skull-crushing potential has grown far beyond the point of useful and enjoyable violence and entered the realm of the truly suicidal. And so was born the concept of Mutually Assured Destruction (MAD), one of My proudest achievements from a humanitarian perspective.

But that was theory; I had to make it work on the ground. Crank up a Cold War and keep it rolling with just the right amount of fear and loathing—too much and it goes critical, too little and they slink back to Complacent Acres or wherever they go at night. And all the while, mind you, I was working with the worst raw material you can imagine, the biological equivalent of those damned heavy elements. Big heads, big nuclei, it's all trouble.

At least the Soviets were marginally predictable. You could trust atheists to do the right thing. No moralizing and hand-wringing, no hypocritical speculation as to what I really might want them to do. Just suspicion, class hatred, and lots of bombers and missiles and warheads. Nothing subtle, they simply turned the Evil Empire into a mechanism for fabricating weapons. There were a few whiners like that Sakharov and Academician Korolev, but for the most part they were a solid bunch filled with useful idiots like V.I. Smirnov and Dmitry Ustinov, the eternal Defense Minister. And, of course, you had Communists in charge. It always pays to have stupid politicians when you're trying to get things done.

The Americans, though, were a real pain in the ass. Basically they were working off the same sheet of music, but you never heard such weeping and wailing between stanzas. What could you expect from a tribe conceived in hypocrisy and dedicated to the proposition that My memory was as selective as theirs? Take Oppenheimer and his crowd, stalwarts at Los Alamos, then refusing to work on the H-bomb—all the while mouthing the most moralistic poppycock. These people had not the slightest concept of a blessing in disguise.

And then there was Eisenhower. I, for one, Never Liked Ike. But he did do some good work—he and his pals the Dulles brothers and that Beetle Smith just about built the Stateside version of the Cold War. Wouldn't even contradict Kennedy when he said there was a missile gap. I loved that.

But at night, tucked away in the Lincoln bedroom where even Mamie couldn't hear him, there he was, down on his knees, begging My forgiveness for everything from Kay Summersby to the U-2. It was embarrassing. And then he goes public with that "Beware the Military-Industrial Complex" jeremiad. Sent all the wrong signals, got even more of them feeling guilty and conflicted.

This nuclear deterrence was tricky; humanity balanced on the slippery curve of a hair trigger. You couldn't have people jumping on and jumping off like it was a trampoline. I needed steadfastness of purpose in my warmongers . . . adrenaline and testosterone, not serotonin.

And despite what those revisionist historians want you to believe, such specimens were hard to find at the top. Just because they knew what they wanted, they tended to scare the hell out of the vacillators and get demoted, pushed aside, and otherwise emasculated. They did have a few good ones though—Ed Teller, Admiral Radford, and Curtis LeMay (you know, he once tried to have himself kidnapped, so he could crack down on Strategic Air Command security). Exactly the kind of rabid true believers I needed to force the others to take nuclear war seriously, and not sweep it under the carpet as if it were some improbable abstraction—the most dangerous thing they could have done.

This was where Rickenbacker fit in. Who said it was all downhill after the raft? In fact, in the air-breather community few spoke with less caution and more sheer belligerent consistency. And because Rickenbacker was a so-called private citizen, he could say things even the most sanguinary of apparatchiks didn't dare repeat in public. He carried the ball when nobody else would.

Cold Warrior from First to Last

ADELAIDE After the war we were almost always on the move. Frequently, it had to do with business. But many times it was out of a sense of responsibility. Edward felt that the dangers of communism and the requirements of national defense were being traitorously neglected by the liberals in charge of our government. No matter how small the group or how far away, he was always ready to set the record straight. "If you've got an airport within a hundred miles," he used to say, "I'll be there. Remember, I am Eastern Airlines."

Radio broadcast, June 7, 1949

SLATER: This is Bill Slater, bringing you another program in the outspoken and hard-hitting series we call "Speak Up, America!" In this series you're going to hear from a wide variety of Americans—a great champion like Gene Tunney, movie stars like Ginger Rogers and Robert Montgomery—you'll hear from businessmen, professional men, and clergymen—and even from housewives like your own next-door neighbor.

Now, the man who has his own special place in the affections of his fellow Americans—hero in two world wars, the President and General Manager of Eastern Airlines—Captain Eddie Rickenbacker.

THE CAPTAIN: Thanks, Bill! Fellow Americans, I'm going to speak my mind on the subject of security—world security and home security. That is the number-one subject on all our minds today. . . . Is there any hope at all for America and the world?

Let me give you my personal answer right now! There is *every* hope—IF we can be realistic and face the facts as they exist in this atomic year 1949.

SLATER: Well, Captain Rickenbacker, I know everybody is eager to hear how you see the conditions for that IF.

THE CAPTAIN: Russia has a weapon we don't have. That weapon is The Lie! Honor and morality have no part in the Communist character, and they admit it and brag about it.

SLATER: So what are the facts, Captain Rickenbacker?

THE CAPTAIN: Fact number one: There's not a country in Western Europe today that can offer one-half the military resistance it threw against Hitler ten years ago. Fact number two: There is a strong Communist Fifth Column in every country—including these United States—and these traitors have publicly announced that in the event of war they will fight for Russia. Fact number three: The men who control Russia understand only one thing—FORCE. The men who control Russia fear only one thing—POWER.

SLATER: Well, those facts certainly add up to a program of positive action for us—what should that program be, Captain Rickenbacker?

THE CAPTAIN: We must make America strong and safe. . . . We must build the most powerful war machine possible—with the main emphasis on Air Power—FORCE! POWER! That is what the Russians understand. That is what they fear!

SLATER: You don't think these men in the Kremlin are particularly impressed by the North Atlantic Pact?

THE CAPTAIN: I think [they] are impressed a great deal more by the performance of one Air Force bomber . . . flying nonstop around the world and another bomber flying 10,000 miles nonstop with a full load of blockbusting bombs. I maintain that is the only guarantee we can give Western Europe, a strong America. . . . That is the only guarantee—Force and Power—that Russia understands.

SLATER: Well, Captain, unless I very much miss my guess, I think that's a guarantee we can all line up behind.

RICHARD NIXON I always liked Eddie. Christ, we grew up on him. Read "Ace Drummond" when I was a kid. My brothers and I used to play dogfight out back, when we got a chance to play, which was not a lot. Work . . . always work . . . not like today. All of us wanted to be the Red Baron or Eddie Ricketyback. Boy, I can remember those days. You know, kids back then admired tough guys. Rickenbacker worked his way up from nothing—abject poverty. The only support he ever had was his mother. . . . When I used to meet with him we always talked about our mothers . . . saints, the both of them.

He had no education—self-taught. That's why the liberals hated him . . . that and the fact that he put his life on the line for his country. Squat-to-piss Ivy League assholes, Eddie used to drive 'em crazy. Had a drawer full of honorary degrees, you know . . .

good schools—Lehigh, Ohio State. . . . But still they looked down their noses.

After a while, you had to be careful what kind of audience you put him in front of. Goldwater once told me: "He's a national asset, but so is uranium." He'd always speak his mind, long after it was fashionable. Never backed off. Called a fucking spade a fucking spade. Of course, there was a backlash . . . there always is. Got so you couldn't appear on the same stage with him. That was too bad. I missed Eddie. Brave guy, patriotic guy, loved his mother. . . . That's why they hated him.

Speech to the Leadership Council of the Loyal Order of Moose, Dade County, Florida, December 10, 1962

It's a pleasure to be once again among my Brother Moose. First I want to thank my two good friends Bill Creyton and Sam Jacobs for extending me an invitation to address you at this very important annual meeting. I don't have to tell you that, if there's such a thing as Mooses' Mooses, these are two of them. Also I'm certain they understand what's at stake in these troubled times, and I think that's why they invited me here tonight.

I know I'm among friends. So let me get right to the point and speak to you very frankly about the sad state of our nation. Wherever we turn our heads the cause of freedom is in retreat . . . not only abroad, but in the very bosom of this country. . . .

Why have we, as a nation, fallen into this disgraceful, craven state? The answer is simple. We have been stung by the Communist serpent. The venom of International Marxism has entered the arteries of our leaders, and poisoned the once-pure blood of Americanism. . . .

What this country needs today is a Teddy Roosevelt, or men with convictions and confidence in our way of life. . . .

Certainly, we don't need the type of left-sided individuals who call themselves Americans. We had a man once in our United States Senate who believed in the American Way of Life, who despised left-wingers, one-worlders, do-gooders, fair-dealers, socialists, and Communists. He had the courage to expose Communists, Communist sympathizers, and left-wingers within our government and within the borders of our great land. Someday the American people will erect a monument to the memory of the late Senator Joe McCarthy.

Why is it that we hear of *peace* at any price, but not, as in the days of old, of *freedom* at any price? . . . Regarding *neutral* nations, we need to remind ourselves that it is immoral to be neutral between right and wrong. . . .

Why are we so insistent upon a nuclear ban, when it is only nuclear weapons which give us any chance at all against the hordes of Red manpower in Russia and China? . . . *From all indications we are heading toward an ultimate surrender.* For honor and our undying souls, let's fight and die before the final enslavement.

There is no greater Valhalla than that to which an honorable fighting man goes. . . .

As other generations of honorable Americans have done, let's carry the fight to the enemy. . . . "But," you say, "that would be aggression. . . ." The Communists have been clever enough to make "aggression" a nasty word. . . . *What's wrong about aggression?* We went to war in Europe in 1917 . . . that was defensive aggression. We went to war in 1941 to save the world . . . that was defensive aggression. . . .

Then, are we not prepared for defensive aggression? . . . Are we afraid to fight this plague with all the powers at our disposal? . . .

Let's sever relations with the U.S.S.R. and all other so-called neutrals. . . . Let's finally recognize a war of total enmity to which our enemies are irrevocably committed.

Look at Cuba. The enemy landed there, made it an armed camp, and brazenly declared a fight to the death against us. And what did we do? Nothing. Does even one of you believe that there aren't still Russian missiles poised and ready to be launched from Cuban shores? This idea that we stood up to them down there is just the sort of hoax left-wingers always perpetrate, so as to make their next conquest even easier.

Fortunately, I believe the day of reckoning is almost upon us. Americans everywhere will join the battle lines of freedom, firmly anchored by the divinely inspired concepts of our forefathers. And that line will hold, buttressed at many points by brave Moose from all the corners of this nation. And when International Communism finally realizes what they are up against, it will collapse of its own accord. Of this I have no doubt. It is God's will. . . .

GOD "Bully!"

LOOSE TALK

Captain Eddie Rickenbacker once again finds himself at the center of controversy, as a result of a speech he delivered here last Tuesday on the dangers of world communism. He is a familiar, even beloved figure in South Florida. The names Captain Eddie and Eastern Airlines are practically synonymous with the postwar boom in this region. In addition, more than practically any other portion of the United States, the citizens of Dade County are familiar with the dangers and consequences of communism. Cuba is our problem as much as it is a problem of our nation and the world.

Nevertheless, the kinds of unproven assertions and reckless prescriptions uttered by Rickenbacker have little place in a sane discourse on the future of this country. Times have changed since Captain Eddie fought valiantly over the Western Front. We live in a world poised on the edge of nuclear disaster, and have just been through a very dangerous period. Yet, as the White House reiterated yesterday, "unimpeachable intelligence sources give us every reason to believe all the Russian missiles have been removed." Our objectives have been met. This is not a time for loose talk, even if it comes from those we like and admire.

Editorial, *Miami Record,* December 15, 1962

Samuel P. Attenborough
Director of Scouting Activities
Greater San Antonio Council
Boy Scouts of America
August 21, 1968

Colonel Alfred J. Moyers, USA (retired)
Chief Scout Executive
Schiff Scout Reservation
Boy Scouts of America
Mendeham, New Jersey

Dear sir:
It is my duty to report to you on the circumstances surrounding an event which has, frankly speaking, given Scouting something of a black eye in the San Antonio area. Approximately one week ago, on the evening of August 13, Captain

Edward Vernon Rickenbacker delivered an address to com-
memorate the fifteenth anniversary of his generous gift of the
2,700-acre Rickenbacker Ranch in Kerr County to the BSA.
Captain Rickenbacker arrived at his former ranch, now known
as Camp Smedley D. Butler, on time and seemingly in good
spirits. After a short ceremony, presided over by myself, he
was asked to make a few remarks.

His address proved most unfortunate, given the nature of
the audience, made up almost exclusively of local Scouts and
several of their family members. Captain Rickenbacker began
by telling a rather off-color joke, which, although amusing,
must be considered inappropriate considering the age and im-
pressionable nature of those listening. He then launched into
a somewhat incoherent monologue on the threat of communism and the needs of our national defense. At one point
during this very strident talk, he indicated to the Scouts in
the audience that eventually it would be their "sacred duty
to lay their lives on the line for their country," and that this
was what Scouting was all about—training them for that day.

This, of course, is far from the truth. Fortunately, there
were no reporters in attendance, so there has been no press
coverage. Nonetheless, the incident did have an impact. A
number of parents called the Council to complain, and some
reported their children had trouble sleeping that night. All
local Scout Leaders have been instructed to state clearly to
their troops that Scouting has nothing to do with war or military training. And I think the situation is now well in hand.

However, I believe it is only prudent to inform you of these
circumstances, and respectfully suggest that steps be taken to
ensure that any speech delivered by Captain Rickenbacker to
Boy Scouts in the future be carefully screened.

Sincerely,
Sam

Remarks of Captain E.V. Rickenbacker to the American Legion
Chapter of Goose Creek, South Carolina, March 31, 1971

When your Commander, Lieutenant Colonel Lem Hardy, invited
me to speak to you tonight, I hesitated. Frankly, I have curtailed
my speaking engagements of late, because when you reach the ripe
young age of eighty, people say it's time to slow down a little. But

then I turned on my television receiver that night and saw the lies they are still broadcasting about our military—that so-called My Lai massacre, for instance—and it got me madder than a wet hen. By God, I thought, while I still have some strength left, I'm going to do what I can. So here I am.

War is ugly. I don't have to tell you, because you've seen it firsthand. But Communism has declared war, and we have no choice but to fight back. That's something that these peacenik fellow-travelers will never understand. There's no such thing as negotiating with them. If Hanoi signed an agreement, would they keep it? Don't make me laugh. Look at the Middle East. One act of Soviet chicanery so monumental and brazen that our government couldn't first believe photographic proof that it was happening, was the Russian-aided installation of anti-aircraft missile batteries inside the Suez Canal stand-still zone. Mark my words, in a year or two those Egyptian Communists will come across the canal and attack Israel by surprise. That's the way they work.

Meanwhile . . . Russia for months has been reported to be building—or preparing to build—a naval base on the south shore of Cuba to serve its nuclear submarines. The do-gooders in Washington thought that issue had passed nine years ago, naively assuming that Communists ever give up on something they want. . . .

We let Russia get ahead in space, because we were afraid of racketeers, who held up production of rockets by strikes and featherbedding. We didn't have the courage to risk being tough. . . .

Nothing worth having is ever won by weakly pecking at it, by being afraid of it. . . . Once, when I was a boy and a young man, we lived and worked in a country we all could be proud of, a country where the Constitution and the Golden Rule were supreme. Then, the worm entered the apple, or figuratively speaking, a serpent slithered its way into what was a Garden of Eden of human freedom on this benighted planet. The name of that snake was Communism, and we must drive it from the face of the earth. I say give us back our Garden, no matter what the cost!

I firmly believe the American people will back our President and Government in risking everything to preserve freedom—the *American* brand of freedom, not some watered-down foreign version of it. Even if such a stand means the atomic bomb, it is earnestly believed that all decent, all real Americans would say once more— Give me Liberty—or give me death!

REED CHAMBERS I hadn't seen him for years. Then in '61 we got together for a reunion of the 94th out in Colorado Springs at the Air Force Academy. We had a hell of a time, up till two in the morning drinking bourbon and reminiscing. I hadn't had so much fun in decades; we ran the pants off those two young lieutenants they sent over to keep an eye on us.

About six months later I had some business in New York and called Eddie at the Regency, where he and Adelaide were living, suggesting we do the town.

It turned out to be quite a toot. Dinner, drinks, more drinks, and still more drinks. Around midnight we got a cab and Eddie told the driver to take us to some jazz club in Harlem.

"I ain' takin' you up deah. It ain' safe. Besides, that place been outta business fuh maybe twenny yeahs. . . . Look . . . you wanna hear some blues; I know a place you ain' gonna get kilt."

We found ourselves over in Brooklyn in what looked to be a converted warehouse. It was filled—Negroes, whites, some Puerto Ricans. Everyone was drinking beer and seemed to be in a good mood. They were also passing around marijuana cigarettes. Some girl handed Eddie one as a joke.

The band finally came on stage. There were sidemen. But the spotlight centered your attention on this extraordinary Negro, playing an electric guitar . . . Muddy Waters. He was surprisingly well dressed—white shirt, tie with a stickpin, neatly tailored gray suit. As he played, his face remained completely impassive, like the mask of a Buddha. Yet the music couldn't have been more blatant, slower than jazz, thumping, carnal, utterly unrepentant. I looked over at Eddie. He was transfixed. It may have been my imagination, but I think his mouth was hanging open. The marijuana smoke was everywhere . . . like a fog.

The experience sobered the both of us. But on our way back across the river not much was said. Then, as he got out of the cab, Eddie looked at me: "There's going to be trouble, Reed, and not just with the colored."

"What kind of trouble?"

"I'm not sure. But it's going to have something to do with that music."

JOHN LENNON Was during the '64 visit to the States—Sullivan show 'n' all—just before we took off. Crowds had the terminal surrounded, gettin' a bit rowdy. We wanted t'say hello—'specially Ringo. But Security was dodgy 'n' stashed us in some muckety-muck lounge. As we was walkin' in I heard one of the birds there call 'im Mr. Rickenbacker. I couldn't believe me ears. Introduced meself right off. Weren't a bit friendly though. Musta been the hair.

"Couldn't be more serious. Me 'n' the lads owe ya everything."

"You know about me?" Broke into this unattractive grin, 'n' shook me hand two-fisted like a recording Mogul.

"Not a bloke in the business doesn't know you."

"Really? Sometimes I think . . . well . . . you know . . . It's been a while since I retired."

"Hell, we'd still be in Hamburg playin' for the whores without yer Model 14. Tone unmatched in the civilized world. Aincha heard 'You Can't Do That'?"

Stared at me like I was a bloody lunatic. Then he gets this look a' disgoost 'n' walks away. Turned out t'be some old-time militry man, the American Red Baron. When I finally met up with the real Adolph Rickenbacker we had a bit of a giggle.

SHEPPY   It was not a good situation. He had an office at 45 Rockefeller Plaza, a virtual duplicate of the old one at Eastern, just across the street. He arrived every morning promptly at eight. But when I looked in on him around nine, he was usually asleep. One day he came out to my desk: "I know you see me dozing in there, but you must never tell a soul. Do you understand?" I knew enough to simply nod.

The ostensible purpose of his daily sojourns was the organization of his papers for a contemplated memoir. I did my best to get things cataloged. But in fact he was simply going over the invoices, letters, and clippings as a means of transporting himself back to his days of glory. There was no purpose in it. It was sheerly vicarious. Then the lights went out . . . literally.

November 9, 1965. I'll never forget. It was eventually traced to some transformer problem upstate, which resulted in a blackout of the entire Northeast. The Manhattan skyline was a dark shadow, just as it had been during the War. The only lights were the cars in the street. It was around six and I was alone in the office. "Well," I thought, "here I am and here I shall stay." I was a bit concerned about getting down to the bathroom, but other than that I was fine. Then I heard the rattling of a key and some cursing. I would have been terrified, but I recognized the voice.

"Come along, Sheppy, I have the chauffeur. We'll go to dinner." He had climbed eighteen floors to fetch me. We made our way down in the dark and he found a cozy Italian place with checked tablecloths and candles burning in Chianti bottles. After a very satisfactory meal cooked on a gas stove, he dropped me off at my building on West Fifty-fifth and insisted on accompanying me up six flights to my door. He then went back to the Regency and marched up another twenty-one flights. Adelaide called me in the morning and announced he had arrived fit as a fiddle. I pondered the episode for some time, and then did the only thing I could do.

"I'm leaving. You're wasting my time and you're wasting your own."

"What in the world are you talking about? We have work to do, important work."

"This is a charade and you know it. You come here every day and slide back into a world that no longer exists. I thought it was because you were old and tired. But last night put an end to that. You're simply beaten down!"

"That's a lie! How dare you. Why . . . why . . . I ought to—"

"Fire me? Ha! I just quit."

"You can't. . . . Please, I . . . I can't do this alone."

"Do what? That's just the point. You're not doing anything."

"I will . . . I will . . . If you'll stay . . . I promise."

"Well then, you better get started. You know you can't fool me."

"I know . . . I'll get going. I promise."

ADELAIDE His favorite show was *Bonanza*. I don't think he ever missed an episode. Well . . . one day he came in literally beaming. "Mother, who do you think I just saw in the elevator? . . . Lorne Green. Knew who I was right off. We had a drink in the bar, talked for maybe an hour. He asked me all about the raft; even said it might be a good subject for a special." Nothing ever came of that, but I swear that meeting cheered him up for a month. He told everybody we knew.

It was why they tied Odysseus to the mast. The irresistible wail of the siren: "I'll make you famous, you big adorable Achaean." A factor to be reckoned with, even back in those days. Just not the main factor. That came later, maybe with Napoleon. Sure he conquered most of Europe, but that's not why Raskolnikov killed the hag and thought he could get away with it. It was because of the "little dead dude"—if you were famous enough you could do practically anything. The problem was that Raskolnikov wasn't famous at all, and Jennifer Capriati wasn't famous enough. But they had the right idea.

Eddie was badly misled. He thought fame to be primarily a matter of accomplishments . . . the Smith-Barney slant. But fame wasn't really rooted in anything—its essence was lighter than a cloud. True enough, accomplishments could haul you up there into the ether of celebrity. But so could a public misunderstanding of those accomplishments, or an accident of birth, or plain dumb luck. This is how people managed to be famous simply for being famous. It was that ineffable, frequently just a quirk that excited large numbers at the same time. But folks get bored, so fame is fleeting. And the process was accelerating, an obvious fact to sophisticates like Warhol, but something that only infuriated Eddie. He had run guys off the road, shot them out of the skies, named a car after himself, owned a famous (that word again) racetrack, nurtured an entire airline, survived multiple plane crashes, mastered the art of rubber boat navigation, denounced Communists in the most uncertain terms—and now found himself deep in the process of being forgotten. To the rational Eddie, nothing could be more unfair. But the unconscious Eddie—the Eddie who had always pursued fame like a moth chases headlights—knew Miss Shepherd was right. There was just one thing to do—get back into print before it was too late; tease John Q with warmed-over tales of what it was like, and then push the sucker for all it was worth.

BOO HERNDON, THE GHOSTWRITER   One day in the spring of '66 I got a phone call.

"Herndon? This is Rickenbacker. You know who I am?"

"Of course I do. . . . Everybody does."

"Not everybody. But it's a good thing you do. . . . You want to write my autobiography?"

You could have knocked me over with a feather. Here I was, arch-liberal Booton Herndon, being courted by a personage so far right as to be virtually off the scale.

"Well, that sounds interesting. But you're going to have to talk to my agent, Max Wilkinson. I work everything through him."

"You think you're some kind of fucking movie star? Look! I've got five published authors champing at the bit to write this thing. The only reason I called you was because I liked your book on General Tunner. . . . If you want to play coy you can go fuck yourself."

At the risk of an anatomic impossibility, I stuck to my guns. Which was a good thing because I'm sure he had every intention of screwing me himself. In the end I'm not sure the contract we managed to squeeze out of him—$15,000 advance and 20 percent of his royalties—was worth the pain that man inflicted on me.

He saw me strictly as a hired hand. I was to conduct no interviews. He supplied all the records and information—his own version of the truth. At times I'd locate some inconsistency or a less-than-flattering nugget, but it only prompted one of his tirades if I brought it up. I might as well have been working for Stalin. In fact, I remembered reading somewhere how the airplane designer Yakovlev dreaded his Tuesday meetings with Uncle Joe. I felt much the same about my weekly sessions with Rickenbacker.

The pattern of abuse never changed. I would have sent over a chapter for his initial review. Miss Shepherd would usher me into the office, where he was waiting behind his big glass-topped desk, like a vulture.

"Ah . . . the playboy of the Western world. One-chapter-a-week Herndon, fresh from painting the town red, no doubt. It wouldn't be so bad if this stuff you give me was any good. But, unfortunately, that's not the case."

It was summer, and I was living at the New York Athletic Club working absolutely as fast as possible so I could get back to Bonnie and the kids in Charlottesville. But soon enough I gave up trying to defend my work habits. If I had done two chapters, he would have wanted three; three, then it would have been four. The man was a congenital slave driver . . . and a bully to boot.

"I've fixed this crap so at least it's accurate and grammatical."

What he would have done amounted to an overlay of self-congratulatory chicken scratch. I learned not to ask too many questions, since as often as not he couldn't decipher his own handwriting. I simply changed what I could make out, assuming he wouldn't know the difference. And for the most part he didn't.

But a deal was never a deal with Rickenbacker. He kept insisting that I amend what we already had agreed to. It was like water torture, only worse, because it was accompanied by a monologue of moralizing and advice, usually prefaced by phrases like: "If you'd ever done anything with your life, Herndon, you'd know that . . ."

I began trying to think like a whore—"You can do what you want to me, but I've got your money once this is finished." But it didn't work. I was too degraded. Finally, I settled on the fantasy of going after him with hedge clippers. One weekend in Charlottesville I even went over to Gleason's and picked out a pair. Bonnie saw right through me, and took them out of my suitcase before I went back. Still, I felt better for having made the purchase.

SHEPPY   I could overhear everything that was said, and I found myself taking a certain malicious pleasure in the way the Captain was treating him. It was only then that I realized how bitter I was over the whole arrangement. I had edited or rewritten virtually everything he had composed for nearly forty years. No one had a more thorough knowledge of his life. It seemed only right and proper that I should have been delegated this task. Finally, after a particularly violent dressing-down, I confronted him.

"You are spending a great deal of money on someone you're unhappy with, when I could have easily written your life story."

"No you couldn't. You're too close to it. I needed an outsider."

"That is unfair and demeaning."

"No it isn't. It's just the simple truth. This book is my last dance. It's got to be done right. Herndon is a hired gun. . . . I can tell him exactly what I think. I couldn't do that with you. You're a woman; you couldn't take it. Besides, you're my friend. Outside of Adelaide and the boys, you're the only one I've got."

Well, as if to drive his point home, I burst into tears. At least he didn't gloat. He simply put his arm around me, escorted me to the outer office, and left for the day.

PETER CAPPSHAW, TRADE DIVISION, PRENTICE-HALL, INC.   We were excited about the Rickenbacker book. A number of houses were interested, including Doubleday, which had reissued *Fighting the Flying Circus.* But he chose us, solely, he claimed, on the basis of our textbook marketing—he wanted as many copies as possible in public school libraries. Actually, we worked out a complicated and advantageous arrangement designed to lower royalties, while compensating through payments to his children. We assumed this was for tax purposes, but I later heard it had to do with Booton Herndon, who held a percentage on the book.

In the end, all parties made out quite well. Sales were more than satisfactory—four substantial printings and ten weeks on the *Times* bestseller list. This was due in part to Rickenbacker himself. From a commercial standpoint he was a model author—a kind of prototype for future celebrity memoirs. The man was nearly eighty, but if it helped sales he would do it. He personally bought something on the order of 2,000 copies and gave them to his acquaintances at Eastern Airlines. He set up a fund and tithed his friends to defray the costs of distributing copies to the libraries of all the schools we dealt with. Then there were the publicity tours, most of which he financed himself. Considering what eventually transpired, this was probably fortunate.

ADELAIDE   Before it was over, he autographed more than 10,000 books. . . . David computed that figure. He also observed that Edward spent a full thirty seconds on each signature—even in his later years he took great care in signing his name. Yet the trips themselves were probably more arduous. By then I was having increasing trouble with my eyesight, and all that autographing aggravated the arthritis in his hand, making it all but impossible for him to get a full night's rest. But he carried on, as, I suppose, did I. It seemed we went everywhere—South Florida, along with most of the cities in Georgia and the Carolinas with Eastern links; Southern California, Oregon, and then Seattle, where Boeing was located, Denver—even Phoenix. . . . We stayed with the Goldwaters there. . . . Then, of course, there were the multiple trips to the Midwest. It was during the last of these that he finally came to grief.

Actually, the trip began very well. First, we went to St. Louis, where we toured the McDonnell plant. In a giant hangar they had set up a desk between a SPAD like the one Edward flew in the First War and a Phantom jet, which was our finest plane in Vietnam. Here, he autographed books for what seemed to be hundreds and hundreds of employees. Then it was on to Ohio—our third visit in as many months—first to Columbus and afterward to Cincinnati. There, the signing was at Shillito's department store, in the central court, which was quite beautiful. I remember watching him from several floors above, bent over the books. It reminded me of working on an assembly line. I think he signed something like 400; it took him all day. He was absolutely exhausted and got almost no sleep. In the morning he was in a very bad mood and in obvious pain. It was in this condition that he arrived at the Indianapolis 500.

ANGELO SANSEVERO, MANAGER, STP RACING TEAM   When the Granatellis brought the turbine to Indy in '67, it was pretty much of a joke. We'd been working on it in secret for over three years. STP was sellin' so we had plenty of developmental cash. It was a sophisticated piece, not just the jet, but four-wheel drive, and a lot of advanced materials. It looked funny though. We showed it to Parnelli Jones in January. He said he'd be laughed right off the fuckin' track. When we told him the turbine put out the equivalent of a thousand horses, he changed his tune pretty quick. He was desperate to win the 500 one more time, and just then he saw his chariot.

Like I said, when we got there, they was all yukkin' it up. But when we did a few test laps an' the thing went like a bat outta hell, they changed their tune too. Hulman and USAC wanted to ban it right off—just what you'd expect. Well, Andy Granatelli was nobody's fool. So we got the thing off the track an' laid low. No more practice. Just had Parnelli qualify the thing late and slow . . . sixth row at 166. Then on race day . . . fagetaboutit.

GEORGE BATTEN, STP PIT CREW   Parnelli was nervous as shit. In other cars you never knew, but this should have been like a sure thing. The weather was shaky from the beginning, but with 200,000 people in the stands they was gonna start the race no matter what. With four-wheel drive and that kinda power we could go way deeper in the corners and accelerate out a hell of a lot faster. So in turn three Parnelli just drove around the field. It was like a Sunday drive—smooth, quiet. . . . We was sittin' pretty, when the fuckin' heavens open up. You couldn't see nothin'. So in they come after only eighteen laps.

We're all sittin' in the pits chain-smokin' and hopin' against hope for the rain to stop, when up comes this geezer. Nobody had any idea who this guy was or how he got in. But he's yellin' about what a piece of shit the turbine is and how it's gonna ruin racing just like it ruined airplanes. There wasn't even time to get mad before they hustle him out. But it was weird, like some kinda omen.

TONY HULMAN, OWNER, INDIANAPOLIS MOTOR SPEEDWAY The show must go on. But I don't think anybody except the Granatellis was looking forward to it. The skies were clear the next day and we restarted at noon. Exactly the same thing happened. The STP car just drove away from the field. A lot of the owners were madder than hell. We'd just been through replacing the Offy roadsters with rear-engine jobs, like they race in Europe. Now we were lookin' at another entirely new generation of equipment. Nobody was more adamant than Eddie Rickenbacker, who sold me the track in '47 and was sitting in my box. "Tony, the thing barely makes a sound. Tell me, what fan is going to come out to watch a bunch of race cars go whoosh?" I had to admit he had a point.

The laps kept piling up and the turbine car was running like a top. Early on they had a problem in the pits; the crew spilled kerosene all over themselves and the car. I heard Rickenbacker saying something about a cigarette, but they got it back on the track. Toward the end Granatelli kept waving at Parnelli to slow down, since only A.J. Foyt in the Coyote and Dan Gurney were even on the same lap. It looked like curtains for sure. Then with no warning the STP car just stops—three laps from the finish—and A.J. goes on to win the race. It turned out to be a twenty-five-cent bearing holder in the transmission. Saved the day for us. But just as things were settling down, there was this crazy altercation in the STP pit.

Rickenbacker had gotten back down there and was taunting Jones—apparently called him and the Granatellis about every name in the book. Well, a couple of the pit crew went after him. Rickenbacker, the crazy old coot, wasn't about to back down. Nothing much happened, just a lot of pushing. Luckily, the reporters and TV cameramen had already left for the trophy presentation. But then Rickenbacker collapsed and had to be taken to the hospital. Everybody was worried, but nothing about the fight made the news.

ADELAIDE It all happened so quickly. At first the doctors told me it was simply exhaustion and required a few days' rest. Then it was pneumonia. Then a collapsed lung and he was moved into intensive care. They told me his condition was grave, and perhaps

I should call the boys. Still I hesitated. I knew him, and I knew he wasn't going to go that easily.

GOD I tried being reasonable. I pointed out that the timing was perfect. The book had put him back in the spotlight. "It's good to go out on a high. Leave now, while some of your old friends are still around to eulogize you. You don't want to be mulled over by a bunch of strangers, do you?"

But the stubborn bastard would have none of it. As usual he had a million excuses for putting it off. Finally, I got sick of listening to him. "All right, but the next time I come around, I'm not going to be so gentle."

DAVID RICKENBACKER After the book my father really did retire. They moved from the Regency to a smaller place in the Dorset on Fifty-fourth between Fifth and the Avenue of the Americas. But Mom was spending more and more time at the house in Coral Gables. I think Daddy was pretty lonely. One by one his pals were passing away. He told me once he was afraid to read the newspapers. Laurance Rockefeller wanted him to spend time working with the Boy Scouts, but they always seemed a little standoffish. Maybe it was his politics.

One night Patty and I were supposed to eat supper with him at the University Club, but we got caught in traffic coming down from Westchester, and got there about an hour late. He got sick of waiting and went upstairs to be seated. We found him up there in this great marble dining room that was just about deserted. You could see him across the room, alone at this little table bent over his food. As we walked over to join him, I thought . . . this is what it's like to be old.

ADELAIDE Edward finally gave up on New York. Besides the children, who preferred to visit us down here, there was really nothing for him. We sold the place in Coral Gables and moved across the Rickenbacker Causeway—he always called it "My Causeway" and I called it "Your Causeway"—onto the grounds of the Key Biscayne Hotel. It was secluded and really very nice. We had a two-story house along the seawall, with a good view of the ocean. There was a nine-hole golf course and a putting green he liked to practice on. He also liked to sit in the sun and watch the boats.

• • •

Actually, he liked to watch the girls in their little tennis outfits with their deep luxurious tans. They always waved and said: "Hi, Captain Eddie." And he always imagined them walking over to his chair with that same youthful insouciance, slipping off their panties, and straddling him . . . rocking back and forth . . . making those excited little yelping sounds in their throats, rubbing themselves harder and harder against him. And as he thought these thoughts and became increasingly excited, he was surprised that his genitals were not in the least affected. It was as if the two, his mind and his body, were no longer connected. More and more, he felt he was becoming two separate people.

GOD   I take my replacement schedule seriously. There can be some give-and-take, but overall I demand a steady turnover. It really boils down to a matter of politeness . . . knowing when to leave. The Alpha types always give me trouble. It's just like them to fight over crumbs. Now Rickenbacker had definitely overstayed his welcome. Nobody but Adelaide and a few fanatics still listened to him on the Cold War. Besides, it was getting closer to Endgame Time, and I needed more subtle types. There was simply nothing more for him to do. So, I gave him a good shot in the head.

DR. TIMOTHY RODRIGUEZ, MERCY HOSPITAL, MIAMI   The CVA was massive. We had to operate immediately to relieve pressure caused by subarachnoid hemorrhaging. He came through that well enough. But we were still faced with some intracerebral bleeding and a significant thrombosis in the left hemisphere. The patient was no longer comatose, and he did appear to be responding to Mammitol. Then, unfortunately, he was beset by a series of complications. Aphasia set in and then, in rapid succession, he suffered pulmonary and then renal failure. At this point the prognosis was almost certain mortality. Through it all, however, his heart functions remained strong, and remarkably he began to get better. The aphasia proved temporary and there was no paralysis. Within six months he had basically regained all functions. Besides the recuperative powers of the individual patient, there is simply no medical explanation for this sort of recovery.

GOD   I hit him hard enough to kill a horse. After that, he simply slipped my mind. Then one day I realized he hadn't checked in.

Well, I looked down and there's that stubborn son of a bitch, alive and out by the seawall. Ordinarily, I would have finished him quick . . . a big wave full of sharks or something. But this was Rickenbacker, survival was basically all he knew. Just as you can't blame a squirrel for eating acorns, I really couldn't hold him accountable. So I told him that considering his suffering a short respite was probably in order, but that the next time there would be absolutely no excuses. He swore up and down that this was more than fair, and that his stalling was at an end. He even believed it himself.

ADELAIDE   For some reason, Edward decided that he wanted to go to Switzerland, to see the village where his parents had been born. He begged me to come with him. Basically, I was in no condition to go anywhere and neither was he. But I thought even if one or both of us were to die there, what did it really matter? He was nearly eighty-three and I was eighty-six . . . a total of almost 170 years. Then Sheppy said she would join us, and that settled the matter.

We flew up to New York from Miami, and as soon as we got to our room I realized I had lost my passport. It was the first time I can remember that he didn't seem angry that I had misplaced something. But when I suggested he call a senator or someone to get it back, he smiled: "Adelaide, the days when I could do that are long gone." Bill and David helped us, though. They got the hotel to put in bright bulbs so I could see, and they badgered Eastern until they came up with the missing passport.

So the next morning we left for Zurich. The flight seemed to take forever, and we were all uncomfortable. Even though it was summer, the city was cold and damp. Almost as soon as I got off the plane I could feel a bout of pleurisy coming on. At the hotel there was a Swiss doctor who came up and examined me. He wrote out a prescription, but didn't seem overly concerned. He didn't like the look of Edward, though. He took his pulse and listened to his heart; then he came into my room and told Sheppy and myself that if would be best if Edward went along to the hospital for some tests. We were both concerned about telling him, but he surprised us by saying it might be a good idea.

Later that evening I was feeling much better, and we went over to join him. He seemed very relaxed and comfortable, propped up against a starched white pillow. He didn't say a great deal, but we stayed until the close of visiting hours. As we walked out he smiled and said: "I love you both."

"It's time."

"I know. . . . But still, I've come a long ways. This trip hasn't been easy. . . . Couldn't I maybe just see my parents' birthplace?"

"No. . . . Besides, why do you want to see some cutesy Swiss village where they'll overcharge you for everything, when you can come up and talk to them in person?"

"I can?"

"Absolutely. . . . Although I don't think you're going to like your father."

"Well, he did take some getting used to."

"You ready?"

"Uhh . . . well . . . okay, you win."

"Of course I win. I always win."

Edward Vernon Rickenbacker died at 4:17 on the morning of July 23, 1973. He is buried in Columbus.

POSTSCRIPT   After a prolonged series of financial crises, Eastern Airlines ceased operations in 1991.

Grateful acknowledgment is made to the following for permission to reprint previously published material:

John Dos Passos, *The 42nd Parallel* and *The Big Money.* Copyright 1930, 1932, 1934, 1935, 1936, 1937 by John Dos Passos. Reprinted by permission of Lucy Dos Passos Coggin, Executor, Estate of Elizabeth H. Dos Passos.

Grider quotes reprinted from *War Birds: Diary of an Unknown Aviator* by John McGavock Grider, by permission of the Texas A&M University Press. Copyright © Texas A&M University Press, 1988. All rights reserved.

Time Warner Communications Inc.: excerpt from cover story ("Durable Man"), April 17, 1950, *Time.* Used by permission. All rights reserved.

"Sea Cruise" by Huey Smith, © 1966 (renewed) Cotillion Music, Inc. All rights administered by Warner-Tamberlane Publishing Corp. All rights reserved. Used by permission. Warner Bros. Publications U.S., Miami, FL 33014.

Other Sources:

Dial Press: *From the Captain to the Colonel: An Informal History of Eastern Airlines* by Robert J. Serling, copyright © 1980.

Dutton: *We Thought We Heard the Angels Sing* by James C. Whittaker, copyright 1943.

Houghton-Mifflin Company: *Rickenbacker's Luck: An American Life* by Finis Farr, copyright © 1979.

Prentice-Hall: *Rickenbacker* by Edward V. Rickenbacker, copyright © 1967.

Richthofen quotes from *Mein Kriegstagebuch* by K. von Richthofen; *Der Rote Kampfflieger* by M. von Richthofen, 1917; *Als Gast beim Rittmeister* by G. Lampel, 1923.

Time-Life Books: *Knights of the Air* by Ezra Bowen, copyright © 1980.

"Juicy Jap" is a trademark of Thomas Pynchon Enterprises.